Advance Praise for *The Wedding Dress*

The Wedding Dress will capture you from page one with a story only Rachel Hauck could weave.

—JENNY B. JONES, award-winning author of
Save the Date and *There You'll Find Me*

The Wedding Dress is a seamless tale of enduring love that weaves the past and present in an intricate, wedding dress mystery. Hauck again manages to mesmerize for well over 300 pages with quirky characters, a compelling plot, and a satisfying happily-ever-after. Highly recommended!

—DENISE HUNTER, best-selling author of
Surrender Bay and *The Accidental Bride*

The talented Rachel Hauck has given us a contemporary love story enmeshed in a fast-paced mystery. Juggle your reading list, y'all. Brimming with the twin themes of redemption and grace, *The Wedding Dress* deserves a spot at the top!

—SHELLIE RUSHING TOMLINSON,
Belle of All Things Southern and best-selling author of
Sue Ellen's Girl Ain't Fat, She Just Weighs Heavy!

Rachel Hauck's writing is full of wisdom and heart, and *The Wedding Dress*, as artfully and intricately designed as the most exquisite of bridal gowns, is no exception. This novel tells the story of four loveable women, miraculously bound by one gown, whose lives span a century. Their mutual search for truth and love—against the odds—will most certainly take your breath away.

—BETH WEBB HART, best-selling author of
Sunrise on the Battery and *Love, Charleston*

From the moment I heard about this story, I couldn't wait to get my hands on it. A wedding dress worn by four different women over 100 years? Yes, please! I loved the story of these women . . . and their one important dress. For anyone who's ever lingered over a bridal magazine, watched a bridal reality show, or daydreamed about being a bride, Rachel Hauck has created a unique story that will captivate your heart!

—MARYBETH WHALEN, author of *The Mailbox, She Makes It Look Easy,* and *The Guest Book.* Founder of www.shereads.org

A tender tale that spans generations of women, each a product of her time and ahead of her time. A beautiful story laced together with love, faith, mystery, and one amazing dress. Rachel Hauck has another winner in *The Wedding Dress*!

LISA WINGATE, national best-selling and Carol award-winning author of *Dandelion Summer* and *Blue Moon Bay*

The WEDDING DRESS

The WEDDING DRESS

RACHEL HAUCK

THOMAS NELSON
Since 1798

NASHVILLE DALLAS MEXICO CITY RIO DE JANEIRO

Published in Nashville, Tennessee, by Thomas Nelson. Thomas Nelson is a registered trademark of Thomas Nelson, Inc.

Thomas Nelson, Inc., titles may be purchased in bulk for educational, business, fund-raising, or sales promotional use. For information, please e-mail SpecialMarkets@ThomasNelson.com.

Scripture quotations are taken from the NEW AMERICAN STANDARD BIBLE®. © 1960, 1962, 1963, 1968, 1971, 1972, 1973, 1975, 1977, 1995 by The Lockman Foundation. Used by permission.

This novel is a work of fiction. Any references to real events, businesses, organizations, and locales are intended only to give the fiction a sense of reality and authenticity. Any resemblance to actual persons, living or dead, is entirely coincidental.

Library of Congress Cataloging-in-Publication Data

Hauck, Rachel, 1960–
    The wedding dress / Rachel Hauck.
      p. cm.
    Summary: "One dress. Four women. An amazing destiny. Charlotte Malone is getting married. Yet all is not settled in the heart of Birmingham's chic bridal boutique owner. Charlotte can dress any bride to perfection-except herself. When she discovers a vintage mint-condition wedding gown in a battered old trunk, Charlotte embarks on a passionate journey to discover the women who wore the gown before her. Emily in 1912. Mary in 1939. And Hillary in 1968. Each woman teaches Charlotte something about love in her own unique way. Woven within the threads of the beautiful hundred-year-old gown is the truth about Charlotte's heritage, the power of faith, and the beauty of finding true love"—Provided by publisher.
    ISBN 978-1-59554-963-1 (pbk.)
    1. Brides—Fiction. 2. Wedding costume—Fiction. I. Title.
    PS3608.A866W43 2012
    813'.6—dc23

                                   2011051933

Printed in the United States of America

12 13 14 15 16 17 QGF 6 5 4 3 2 1

To Jesus, the glorious bridegroom

Chapter One

Charlotte

April 14

*I*t was the breeze, a change in the texture of the unseen that made her look up and walk around a stand of shading beech trees. Charlotte paused on the manicured green of the Ludlow Estate for a pure, deep breath, observing the elements of the day—blue sky, spring trees, sunlight bouncing off the parked-car windshields.

She'd woken up this morning with the need to think, to pray, to get closer to heaven. She'd tugged on her favorite pair of shorts and driven up to the ridge.

But instead of solitude, Charlotte found her piece of Red Mountain busy and burdened with shoppers, seekers, and bargain hunters. The annual Ludlow antiques auction to raise money for the poor was in full force on the estate's luscious grounds.

Charlotte raised her sunglasses to the top of her head, resenting the intrusion. This was her personal sanctuary, even if the rest of the world didn't know it. Mama used to bring her here for picnics, parking on a gravel service road and sneaking Charlotte along the Ludlows' perimeter, laughing and whispering, "Shh," as if they were getting away with something fun and juicy.

She'd find a spot on the back side of a knoll, spread a blanket, open a bucket of chicken or a McDonald's bag, and exhale as she looked out over the valley toward the Magic City. "Isn't it beautiful?"

"Yep," Charlotte always said, but her eyes were on Mama, not

Birmingham's lights. She was the most beautiful woman Charlotte had ever seen. And almost eighteen years after her death, she still was the most beautiful woman Charlotte had ever seen. Mama had a way of just *being*, but she died before she imparted that gift to Charlotte.

Shouts invaded Charlotte's memorial moment with Mama. Bidders and buyers moved in and out from under the auction tent spread across the side lawn.

Shading her eyes from the angled sunlight, Charlotte stood in the breeze, watching, deciding what to do. Go back home or walk the grounds? She didn't need or want anything that might be under that tent. Didn't have the money to buy even if she did.

What she needed was to think through—pray about—her recent tensions with Tim's family. His sister-in-law Katherine specifically. The whole mess challenged her to reconsider the leap she was about to make.

As Charlotte turned toward her car, the wind bumped her again and she glanced back. Through the trees and beyond the tent, the second-floor windows of the Ludlow stone-and-glass mansion shone with the golden morning light and appeared to be watching over the proceedings on the ground.

Then the wind shifted the light, a shadow passed over the window, and the house seemed to wink at her. *Come and see . . .*

"Hey there." A lofty woman's voice caused Charlotte to turn around. "You're not leaving already, are you?" She lugged up the slope of the lawn with a box in her hands.

Charlotte recognized her. Not by name or face, but by aura. One of the classic Southern women that populated Birmingham. Ones with dewy skin, pressed slacks, cotton tops, and a modest string of pearls. She stopped by Charlotte, breathless.

"You've not even gone up to the auction tent. I saw you pull in, sweetie. Now, come on, we've beautiful items for auction. Is this your first time here?" She dipped into the box and pulled out a catalog. "Had to run to my car to get more. We're busy, busy this year. Well, you can see that by the cars. Remember now, all the proceeds go to the Ludlow Foundation. We give millions in grants and scholarships around the city."

"I've admired the foundation for quite a while." Charlotte flipped through the catalog.

"I'm Cleo Favorite, president of the Ludlow Foundation." She offered Charlotte her hand. "You're Charlotte Malone."

Charlotte regarded Cleo for a moment, slowly shaking the woman's hand. "Should I be impressed you know me or run screaming back to my car?"

Cleo smiled. Her teeth matched her pearls. "My niece was married last year."

"I see. She bought her dress from my shop?"

"She did, and for a while, I believed she was more excited about working with you than marrying her fiancé. Quite a business you have there."

"I've been very fortunate." More than any poor, orphaned girl dreamed. "Who is your niece?"

"Elizabeth Gunter. She married Dylan Huntington." Cleo started toward the tent. Charlotte followed so as not to be rude.

"Of course, I remember Elizabeth. She was a beautiful bride."

"And she wanted the whole wide world to know it." Cleo laughed with a pop of her hand against the breeze. "She darn near sent my brother to the poorhouse. But you only get married once, right?"

"I hear that's the idea." Charlotte touched her thumb to the shank of her engagement ring—the reason she'd driven up here today. She paused at the edge of the tent.

"So, Charlotte, are you looking for any particular item? Something for your shop?" Cleo dropped the box of catalogs on a table and started down the main aisle as if she expected Charlotte would follow. "We have some beautiful wardrobes for sale. The catalog tells you the lot number, when and where to bid. The auctioneer just moves to the piece. We found that to be easier than—well, what does any of that matter? It's a great auction and it runs smoothly. Tell me, what are you looking for?" Cleo tipped her head to one side and clasped her hands together at her waist.

Charlotte stepped under the tent's shade. "Actually, Cleo,"—*I came up here to think*—"my bridal shop is strictly contemporary." Charlotte rolled the catalog in her hand. "But I guess browsing is always fun." She could walk the aisles to think and pray, right?

"Why sure it is. You're bound to find something you like as you . . . browse." Cleo winked. "It works best if you go ahead and give yourself permission to spend some of your hard-earned money."

"I'll keep that in mind."

Cleo trotted off and Charlotte picked a side aisle to wander, examining the pieces as if the answer she longed for might be lurking among the ancients and the antiques.

Maybe she'd hear, *He's the one*, as she passed a twentieth-century breakfront or a nineteenth-century wardrobe.

But probably not. Answers didn't often just appear to her out of the ethereal realm. Or drop on her suddenly. She worked for her life answers. Just rolled up her sleeves, evaluated the situation, calculated costs, and decided. She'd have never opened Malone & Co. otherwise.

Charlotte paused in front of a dark wood foyer table and traced her fingers over the surface. Gert had one like this in her foyer. Wonder what ever happened to it? Charlotte bent to see if the underside had been marked with a red magic marker.

It hadn't. Charlotte moved on. That table wasn't Gert's. Oh, she'd been so mad when she discovered her niece had run amuck with that red pen.

At the end of the aisle, Charlotte halted with a sigh. She should head back down to the city. Her hair appointment was in a few hours anyway.

Instead, she started down the next aisle, let her thoughts wander to Tim and the struggle in her heart.

Four months ago she'd been perfectly ensconced in her steady, predictable, comfortable day-to-day life. Then the contractor who remodeled her shop harangued her into accepting his Christmas dinner invitation. He seated her next to Tim Rose and changed Charlotte's life.

A dull, tired rolltop desk caught her eye. Charlotte stopped in front of it and smoothed her hand along the surface. If the grain could talk, what stories would it tell?

Of a husband figuring the family finances? Or of a child working through a homework problem? Of a mama writing a letter to the folks back home?

How many men and women sat at this desk? One or hundreds? What were their hopes and dreams?

One piece of furniture surviving time. Was *that* what she wanted? To survive, to be a part of something important?

She wanted to *feel* like she belonged to the Rose family. Katherine certainly didn't make Charlotte feel like a part of the gregarious collection of siblings, aunts, uncles, cousins, and lifelong friends.

On their first date when Tim told Charlotte he had four brothers, she couldn't even imagine what that felt like. It sounded thrilling. She drilled him with question after question. Charlotte only had Mama. Then old Gert when Mama died.

She'd never lived with a sibling, let alone four of them. Let alone a boy.

Was that why she accepted Tim Rose's proposal after two months? Fascination? At the moment, she wasn't sure her reason was love. She wasn't even sure it was to be part of a big family.

Charlotte glanced down at the one-carat diamond filigree and platinum engagement ring that had belonged to Tim's grandmother.

But the ring had no answers. *She* had no answers.

"Charlotte Malone?" A round, pleasant-looking woman approached her from the other side of a dining table. "I read about you in *Southern Weddings*. You look like your picture."

"I hope that's a good thing." Charlotte smiled.

"Oh, it is. Your shop sounds magical. Made me wish I was getting married again."

"We hit a lucky break with that piece." When the editor called last fall, it was the last in a wash of fortunate waves breaking Charlotte's way.

"I've been married thirty-two years and I read *Southern Weddings* about as religiously as the Good Book. I just love weddings, don't you?"

"I certainly love wedding dresses," Charlotte said.

"I suppose you do." The woman's laugh lingered in the air as she said good-bye and moved on, touching Charlotte's arm gently as she passed.

She *did* love wedding dresses. Since she was a girl, the satin and sheen of white gowns practically made her giddy. She loved the way a bride's face changed when she slipped on the perfect gown, the way her hopes and dreams swam in her eyes.

In fact, she was on the verge of her own transformation—slipping on the perfect gown, hopes and dreams swimming in her eyes.

So what was the problem? Why the holdout? She'd considered

fifteen dresses, tried on none. June 23 would be here before she knew it.

A year ago February, she was barely getting by, investing all her capital in inventory while duct-taping her shop—a 1920s Mountain Brook cottage—together.

Then an anonymous bank check to the tune of a hundred thousand dollars landed in her account. After weeks of panicked elation trying to find out who would give her so much money, Charlotte redeemed her gift and finally, finally remodeled her shop. And everything changed.

Tawny Boswell, Miss Alabama, became a client and put her on the map. *Southern Weddings* called. Then, as if to put a bow on the year, Charlotte attended the Christmas dinner and sat next to a handsome man who charmed everyone in the room. By the time she'd finished her first course of oyster soup, Tim Rose had captured her heart too.

The feathery kiss of destiny sent a shiver over her soul as the breeze rushing over the mountaintop tapped her legs. Did she smell rain? Dipping her head to see beyond the lip of the tent, Charlotte saw nothing but the glorious sun possessing a crystal blue sky. Not one vanilla cloud in sight.

She started down the next aisle and her phone buzzed from her jeans pocket. Dixie.

"Hey, Dix, everything okay at the shop?"

"Quiet. But Tawny called. She wants to meet with you tomorrow at three."

Sunday? "Is everything all right? Did she sound okay? Like she was still happy with us?" Charlotte had spent months trying to find the perfect gown for Miss Alabama, lying awake at night, whispering to the God of love to help her fulfill Tawny's dreams.

Then she discovered a new, small designer out of Paris and

Charlotte knew she'd found her own brand of white-silk gold. "Call her back and tell her tomorrow is fine. Do we have crackers and cheese in the refreshment bar? Coffee, tea, water, and soda?"

"We're all stocked. Tawny seemed enthusiastic, so I don't think she's going to tell you she's going with another shop."

"How long have we been working in the bridal gown business together, Dix?"

"Five years, ever since you opened this place." Dix, forever pragmatic and calm.

"And how many times have we lost a customer at the last minute?" Even after countless hours of scouring designers to find the perfect gown.

"We didn't know what we were doing then. We're the experts now," Dixie said.

"You know very well it has nothing to do with us. Listen, I'll call Tawny and tell her we'd be happy to see her tomorrow."

"Already told her. Didn't think you'd want to turn her down." Dixie's voice always carried the weight of confidence. She was a godsend. Support beams for Charlotte's dream. "So, where are you anyway, Char?"

"Up on Red Mountain. At the Ludlow estate. I came up here to think but ran into the annual auction crowd. I'm wandering among the antiques as we speak."

"People or things?"

Charlotte grinned, scanning the gray heads among the aisles. "A little of both." She paused in front of a locked glass of jewels. Unique pieces were the perfect accent for her brides. Charlotte maintained an inventory of one-of-a-kind necklaces, earrings, bracelets, and tiaras. It was the small things that helped seal her success.

"Speaking of weddings," Dixie said low and slow.

"Were we?"

"Aren't we always? *Your* wedding invitations are still on the storeroom desk, Charlotte. Do you want me to bring them home tonight?" Dix and her husband, Jared, Dr. Hotstuff as she called him, lived in the Homewood loft next door to Charlotte.

"Wait . . . really? They're still on the storeroom desk? I thought I took them home."

"If you did, they walked back."

"Ha, ha, funny girl you are, Dixie. Yeah, sure, bring them home. I can work on them tomorrow after church. I need to see if Mrs. Rose has a guest list for Tim's side—"

"You're meeting with Tawny at three."

"Right, okay, after I meet with her. Or I can work on them Monday night. I don't think I have anything Monday night."

"Charlotte, can I ask you something?"

"No—"

"You're getting married in two months and—"

"I've just been busy, Dixie, that's all." Charlotte knew where her friend was going with her inquiry. Charlotte had been asking herself the same questions for weeks now, and the need for answers drove her up the mountain today. "I've got time."

"But it's running out."

She knew. She knew. "We should've picked a fall wedding date. Fast engagement, fast wedding . . . it has me spinning."

"Tim is an amazing man, Charlotte."

She knew. She *knew*. But was he amazing for her? "Listen, I'd better go. I need to get back down the mountain in a few minutes so I can get my hair done. Call you later."

"Have fun tonight, Charlotte. Don't let Katherine get to you. Tell her to bug off. Just *be* there with Tim. Remember why you fell in love in the first place."

"I'll try." Charlotte hung up, Dixie's advice settling in her thoughts. *Remember why you fell in love in the first place.*

It'd all been heart pounding and romantic. She wasn't sure she could identify a real, solid reason out of the whirlwind. As Charlotte made her way down the aisle to leave the tent, she found herself herded to one side by a gathering crowd.

She smiled at the man beside her and tried to step around him. "Excuse me." He didn't budge, but remained planted, staring pointedly at the item about to be auctioned.

"Pardon me, but if you could let me through, I'll be out of your way. Are you bidding on that—" Charlotte looked over her shoulder. "Trunk?" *That ugly trunk?*

"Gather around, everybody." The auctioneer jumped onto the riser next to the trunk. The crowd of fifteen or twenty surged forward, taking Charlotte with them. She stumbled back, losing her clog in the process. "We're about to start bidding."

Fishing around for her shoe, Charlotte decided to wait it out. The bidders on this item seemed determined. How long could the auction be? Ten minutes? Might be kind of fun to see the whole process up close.

Twenty bucks. The trunk didn't look like it was worth more than that. Charlotte peeked around to see who she thought might be willing to shell out money for a dull, battered, and scarred box of wood with frayed and cracked leather straps.

The auctioneer was a man with nothing distinguishable about him. Average height and weight. Hair that might have once been brown but was now . . . gray? Ash?

Yet he wore a brilliant purple shirt tucked into charcoal gray trousers that he held up with leather suspenders. He bounced on the risers with his very clean and white Nike runners.

Charlotte grinned. She liked him, though when he looked at her, the blue blaze of his eyes made her spirit churn. She took a step back but remained hemmed in on all sides.

"This is lot number zero," the auctioneer said, and his bass voice sank through Charlotte like a warm pearl.

Lot number zero? She fanned the pages of her catalog. There wasn't a lot number zero. She cross-referenced with the itemized listing in the back. But no trunk, or chest, or luggage, or steamer was listed.

"This item was rescued from a house just minutes before it was torn down. The trunk was made in 1912." He leaned over the crowd. "It was made for a bride."

His gaze landed on Charlotte and she jerked back with a gasp. Why was he looking at her? She tucked her ring hand behind her back.

"It's one hundred years old. A century. The hardware and leather are original and the entire piece is in good but thirsty condition."

"What happened to the lock?" The man on Charlotte's left pointed with his rolled-up catalog at the gnarled brass locking the lid in place.

"Well, that's a tale in and of itself. It got welded shut, you see." The auctioneer leaned farther toward his audience. Again, his roaming, fiery blue eyes stopped on Charlotte. He wiggled his bushy gray eyebrows. "By a gal with a broken heart."

The women in the group "Ooh'd" and angled for a better look at the trunk while Charlotte took another step back. Why was he directing his attention toward her? She pressed her hand against the heat crackling between her ribs.

"But to the one willing, there's great treasure inside."

He scanned the crowd that seemed to grow thicker and winked. Laughter peppered the air and the auctioneer seemed satisfied he'd drawn everyone in.

Okay, Charlotte got it. There wasn't *really* a great treasure inside. He just wanted them to believe there could be. He was quite the salesman. Kudos.

"Let's start the bidding at five," he said.

Several from the crowd peeled away, releasing the pressure Charlotte felt to stay penned in. The swirl of cool air around her legs felt good.

"Do I have five?" he said again.

Charlotte checked the faces of those who remained. Come on, someone, bid five dollars. Now that the trunk had a price and had endured laughter, her sympathies were aroused. Hearing a bit of its story changed its dismal appearance.

Everyone, *everything*, needed love.

Another few seconds ticked by. Bid someone, please. "I'll bid five." Charlotte raised her rolled catalog. She could donate the trunk to the children's ministry at church. They were always looking for items to store toys or to pack with mission trip necessities.

"I have five hundred." The auctioneer held up his hand, wiggling his fingers. "Do I have five-fifty?"

"Five hundred?" She balked. "No, no, I bid five dollars."

"But the price was five hundred." The auctioneer nodded at her. "Always consider the cost, little lady. Now you know the price. Do I have five-fifty?"

Please, someone, bid five-fifty. How could she have been so stupid? The innocent-old-man routine fooled her.

The man next to Charlotte raised his catalog. "I'll go five-fifty."

Charlotte exhaled, pressing her hand to her chest. Thank you, kind sir. She flipped through the catalog pages again, searching for a description, some information, anything on the trunk. But it was flat not listed.

"Five-fifty, do I have six? Six hundred dollars." The auctioneer's eyes were animated, speaking, and his cheeks glistened red even though the mountain air under the tent was cool for April.

The woman next to Charlotte raised her hand. "Six."

Three more bidders peeled away. Charlotte regarded the trunk through narrow slits, thinking she should just take this time to be on her way too. She'd experienced enough of the bidding process.

Besides, she wanted to grab a bite of lunch before her appointment. By the time she left the salon, she'd have just time enough to go home and change before Tim picked her up at six.

"Six, do I have six-fifty?" The auctioneer's voice bobbed with each syllable.

"Six-fifty." The man on her left. "I can use it for replacement parts on a steamer I'm restoring."

"Seven hundred," Charlotte said, the words bursting from her lips. She cleared her throat and faced the auctioneer. Used for parts? Never. Something inside her rebelled at the thought of tearing the trunk apart. "This trunk deserves its own tender, loving care."

"That it does, young lady. I rescued it myself. And what I rescue is never destroyed." The auctioneer's eyes radiated blue with each word and sent a burning chill through Charlotte. "Do I have seven-fifty?"

The woman next to her lifted her hand.

"Eight." Charlotte didn't even wait for him to up the bid. "Hundred. Eight hundred."

Run! Get out of here! Charlotte tried to turn, but her legs refused to move and her feet remained planted on the Ludlow lawn. A blunt brush of the April breeze cooled the flash of perspiration on her forehead.

She didn't want this trunk. She didn't need this trunk. Her loft was contemporary, small, and so far, clutter-free. The way she liked it.

Malone & Co. was an upscale, classy, exquisitely contemporary boutique. Where would she put a beat-up old trunk? Never mind that she'd spent her windfall money on the remodel. Every last dime. And her personal bank account had just enough to foot the expense of a small wedding. Eight hundred dollars for a trunk was not in the budget. If she was going to blow that much cash, she'd buy a pair of Christian Louboutin shoes.

"It calls to you, doesn't it?" The man in purple leaned toward Charlotte with a swoosh up of his bushy brows.

"Unfortunately, yes." Tim would have a fit if she brought that thing home.

Charlotte regarded the trunk. Who was the man or woman who owned the trunk in days gone by? What about the bride the auctioneer spoke of from 1912—wouldn't she want a home for this battered old piece?

"Eight-fifty." The second man on Charlotte's left made a bid.

"One thousand dollars." Charlotte clapped her hand over her mouth. But it was too late. She'd made the bid.

Oh, she'd have to explain this to Tim.

"Sold." The auctioneer smacked his palms together and pulled a slip of paper out of his pocket. "This trunk belongs to you."

Charlotte read the preprinted slip. *Redeemed. $1,000.* She whirled around. "Wait, sir, excuse me, but how did you know . . ."

But he was gone. Along with the crowd and the hum of voices. Charlotte stood completely alone except for the battered trunk and the glittering swirl in the air.

Chapter Two

Charlotte leaned into Tim as they watched his parents' anniversary party from their table. A bluish amber hue fell over their dinner plates as the party lights chased around the ballroom.

"Dinner was good, wasn't it?" she said. *Come on, Tim. It's only money.*

"It was great."

Charlotte looked over at him. He was picture-perfect to her. If she could use such a word. His straight nose aligned over full lips and an even, square chin. His long, sandy hair fell in a soft sheen against his sculpted cheek.

But at the moment his normally vibrant, charming countenance was brooding.

Oh, why didn't she wait to tell him until the ride home? Now the family—Katherine—would blame Charlotte for Tim's lack of participation.

"Do you want to dance? Look, Jack keeps waving at us."

Jack was Tim's younger brother, the one right after him in the line of five boys. David, Tim, Jack, Chase, and Rudy.

"In a minute." Tim gestured for Jack to hold on.

Every guest at this fortieth wedding anniversary celebration was on the floor jukin' and jivin', singing "celebrate good times, come on" at the top of their lungs.

Everyone except Tim and Charlotte.

"Come on, Tim, it's not that big of a deal. Let's dance." Charlotte stood, smoothing her hands over her skirt. She'd determined to have a good time tonight, forget her Red Mountain mission that went bust and let her inner extrovert rule the night. She had a long talk with *that girl* this afternoon while sitting in the chair getting her hair and nails done.

She'd worn a new party dress, a navy number with a fitted bodice and short, flared skirt. And a matching pair of Jimmy Choo Mary Janes she'd bought on sale.

The night was going so well. Tim couldn't keep his eyes off of her and for the first time, Charlotte actually felt like she was a part of the inner-Rose circle.

Then, fifteen minutes ago, Charlotte leaned into her man and said, "Oh, Tim, I forgot to tell you, but I ended up at an auction today up on Red Mountain and bought a trunk. For a thousand dollars." There now, that wasn't so bad.

Then she noticed the light dimming in his eyes. "A thousand dollars?" Tim kept the wedding budget and had every penny accounted for until June 23.

After that, they whispered harshly to each other over dinner about why and how she could've spent that much money without talking to him. The muffled debate concluded as dessert arrived.

"I hope you didn't buy that five-thousand-dollar dress you wanted because we can't afford that now."

"No, I haven't," Charlotte said with a bit of sass. "I haven't bought my dress yet."

The confession hung between them and dimmed the last bit of merry light from Tim's eyes. "We're getting married in two months, Charlotte. You own a bridal shop."

"I know, I know." When would she learn to keep her mouth shut? Her timing missed by a country mile.

They ate their carrot cake in relative silence.

"Sure you don't want to dance?" Charlotte tugged on his elbow.

Tim shoved away from the table, standing. "I'm going for some air."

"O-okay." Charlotte watched him go through watery eyes. "Tim?"

He turned, gazing down at her.

"Sorry about the money."

"I know, Char." He brushed his fingers lightly over her neck and relieved her fears. "It's okay. Promise. I'll be back in a minute."

In the four months she'd known Tim, she'd learned that he needed time to process. He rarely made snap decisions. Which was another reason to contemplate this whole wedding ordeal.

He never did anything impulsively—so why the marriage proposal so quickly? Was it a moment of romantic weakness? She wasn't sure he even *wanted* to marry her. What made him drop to one knee two months after they'd met and slip a ring on her finger?

Did she want to marry *him*? Charlotte might have to drive back up to Red Mountain in the morning.

But oh, his proposal was perfect and romantic. Charlotte blurted yes without thinking. She led with her heart. At least that's what Gert always told her.

The band brought down the music and the dance-floor lights dimmed. Couples stepped together and swayed in time to "I Only Have Eyes for You."

Charlotte grabbed her clutch and headed for the ladies' room. If she sat there any longer, someone would inquire about Tim.

Shoving through the door, Charlotte was grateful to be alone. She leaned against the vanity counter and studied her reflection in the mirror, ducking under the glare of the unkind lights.

The strands of hair that had slipped from her updo curled around her neck. Pressing her finger under her eye, she dabbed away a spot of mascara. As she opened her clutch for her lipstick, a voice crawled over her shoulder.

"You look beautiful tonight, Charlotte."

Charlotte glanced in the mirror. Katherine, older brother David's wife, stood behind her. "As do you. I love your dress."

Katherine moved to the vanity and leaned toward the mirror, checking her hair and makeup. She was the first and only daughter-in-law in Marshall and Blanch Rose's family. A distinction she took seriously and guarded jealously.

"Are you having a good time?" Katherine's smile was stiff and forced as she fished a tube of lipstick from her clutch. "You and Tim have a fight? You were whispering to each other all through dinner. It's a good thing Blanch couldn't see you directly." She smoothed red color over her lips. "Tim's usually the first on the floor and he's not been out there yet. He never misses 'Celebrate.'"

"I'm having a lovely time, Katherine, thank you." Charlotte side-stepped the woman's hunt for information. Her conversation with Tim wasn't any of his sister-in-law's business. "Forty years of marriage is quite a milestone."

"You know, Charlotte"—Katherine tore a tissue from the box—"if you're going to be a Rose, you should start trying to act like a Rose. You keep dragging Tim to dark corners and holding personal conversations like he's not allowed to associate with his own family. It's not going to sit well with everyone if this keeps up." She dabbed the corners of her red lips with the white tissue.

"That shade works well with your complexion," Charlotte said, unwilling to go on the defensive and debate the Rose family with Katherine. It would be futile. She'd rather stay on her turf. Home field advantage. "My assistant Dixie does makeup for our brides and she's using soft pinks on the brides with fair complexions."

Katherine tossed her lipstick back into her clutch. "Well, it was recommended by the girl at the Saks sales counter. But don't change the subject, Charlotte."

"Is there a subject?" It felt more like an inquisition. Charlotte clicked her clutch closed and reached for a tissue. She needed a distraction. Bolting for the door would only incite the bee in Katherine's bonnet.

"Let me tell you a story, Charlotte. I lived next door to the Roses from the time I was three until my freshman year in high school." Katherine wadded the tissue and tossed it in the trash bin. "David walked me to first grade. Yep, he did. He was the older man, a second grader. Then the summer before seventh grade, my dad moved us across town to a mansion in an exclusive, gated community. We had a pool, tennis courts." Katherine folded her arms and leaned against the vanity. "But my parents had to work eighty-hour weeks to keep us in the life of luxury, and it tore the family apart. My parents settled their divorce the day after I got my driver's license." She stared at her hands. "I felt pretty lost so I drove over to the old neighborhood. To the last place we were happy. Dave and Tim were raking the fall leaves into piles for Jack, Chase, and Rudy to jump in. It was like time stood still at the Rose place except David had turned into this tall, filled-out, gorgeous boy. He saw me and waved. I pulled into the driveway, in so many ways, and never left."

Charlotte regarded her in the mirror for a moment, their eyes clashing. "I'm not very good at reading between the lines, Katherine." She held her voice low and steady. "What is it you're trying to say?" Charlotte walked to the sink to wash her hands, to break the laser line of Katherine's gaze.

"I'm just going to let out the clutch and speak my mind."

"Please do." Charlotte turned off the water and reached for the hand towels, and with an inhale, tightened her ribs around her heart.

"I don't think you two belong together, Charlotte. You don't fit in with the family. It's not that you can't, but you won't. What's going to happen once you're married? It'd kill Dad and Mom Rose if Tim drifted away from us."

"Why . . . why would he drift away from the family? Katherine, you're making up stuff that isn't there. When has Tim missed a family event, or Sunday dinner, or birthday party since we've been together? Not one."

"Charlotte, Tim proposed to you with his grandmother's ring after knowing you for two months." Katherine flashed her fingers at Charlotte. Two. "It took him that long to ask out his last girl-friend for the first time. He prayed, talked to her after church, got to know her a bit, talked to people who knew her to see what she was like. They dated for six months and we thought she might be the one because Tim didn't waste time dating a woman if he didn't think it was going anywhere. Then, out of the blue, he meets you at a Christmas dinner and we didn't see him for almost two weeks. We thought he'd lost his mind. Mom Rose feared he'd miss Christmas day with us."

"The relationship took us both by surprise," Charlotte said, prop-ping her shoulder against the opposite wall. By the door. "But he is right for me. I'm right for him." Isn't he?

Charlotte had never met anyone like Tim. Never felt the way he made her feel. Never been this far in love. And despite the terror of free-falling and her drive up to the ridge this morning to shut out the city's noise and hear God, Charlotte desperately wanted Tim to be her forty-year man. The love of her life.

Katherine squinted at her. "David tells me he and Tim haven't picked out their tuxes yet."

"There's still time." Charlotte tried to read Katherine. Where was she taking this inquisition?

"I've not seen an invitation or save-the-date card."

"Invitations are at my house. Katherine, is any of this your business? Tim and I are getting married." If only the conviction in her voice would boomerang around to her heart. "And we'll do it our way. Rest assured, we have no plans to break away from his parents or his brothers." Charlotte started for the door.

But Katherine smacked it shut with her hand. "Oh, it *is* my business. This family is my business. Tim is closer to me than my own brother. I won't see him hurt or this family torn apart. I'm raising three children as Roses and I want them raised like their dad, not the mess I had to endure with my parents."

Charlotte grabbed the door handle and jerked hard. As she did, Lauren, Rudy's date for the evening, burst into the ladies' room. "Charlotte, there you are. Tim's looking all over for you. Hey, Katherine."

"Lauren."

Charlotte left without a final glance back. Tim stood in the hall, against the wall, his hands tucked in his pockets.

"Hey," he said.

"Hey." Charlotte fell against him, letting his presence warm away Katherine's cold confrontation. "I'm really sorry about the trunk money, Tim."

"Forget it. I just had to cool down." He hooked his finger under her chin. "I'm sorry for what I said about your dress. You can buy whatever you want. We'll find a way."

Charlotte kissed him, and Tim slipped his hands around her back and held her close.

"Want to dance?" she said.

"I thought you'd never ask."

On the dance floor, Tim curled Charlotte into him and peered into her eyes as the singer crooned about "the house that built me."

"What happened in there?"

"Nothing." Charlotte swayed side to side, round and round with him. "Ladies' room privilege."

"But you're upset. Nothing is that sacred." Tim craned his neck in an obvious effort to see who exited the restroom alcove. "It was Katherine."

"You should've warned me she was a pit bull."

"Didn't think she'd go after you." Tim gently held Charlotte's head between his hands. "Her bark is worse than her bite."

"Have you ever been bitten by her?" Charlotte made a face, almost smiling, the tension of her exchange with Katherine thinning. "She seems to think she has dibs on you. On the whole family. If we lived in biblical times and something happened to David—"

Tim's kiss landed on Charlotte's lips, clipping her thought, and they moved to the rhythm of the melancholy music.

"The most beautiful girl in the room is in my arms," Tim whispered in her ear, "so if it's all the same to you, I'd rather not talk about my brother's wife."

When he kissed her again, Charlotte slipped her arms around his neck and let her burden go.

A little after eleven, Tim drove Charlotte home and walked her up the four flights to her loft, slipping his hand into hers, loosening his tie, and unbuttoning the top of his shirt.

"We're thinking of taking the bikes out tomorrow, going to the dirt track." Tim leaned against the wall as Charlotte unlocked the heavy steel loft door. Tim was a passionate, amateur motocross racer. "Paul and Artie haven't been racing since they moved to Texas." Tonight Charlotte learned Paul and Artie were cousins on his mother's Buchanan side. "Come with us. I've even talked Dave and Jack into coming."

"I have an appointment with Tawny." Charlotte flipped on the entryway light and leaned against the doorjamb.

"You have an appointment on Sunday?" Tim slipped his hand around her and pulled her close to him.

"You're racing? *On Sunday?*" She arched her brow, grinning, mimicking his inflection.

"We're not racing, we're *riding*."

"It'll be a race the moment you start the engines." She reached up to lace her fingers through his hair. "Want to come in?"

"You think you know me so well?" His quick kiss was playful as he stepped past her into the loft.

Did she? His competitive nature and passion for all things extreme weren't hard to see. Tim carried those on the surface. But she didn't have long to contemplate. Tim hooked her away from the door, letting it slam behind him, and drew her tight.

As he did, her heels crashed into something hard and she stumbled backward, falling out of his embrace.

Tim snatched her hand before she hit the floor. "Char, are you okay?"

"I'm fine . . . What's this box?" Charlotte bent down to fold back the flaps and peer inside. "Oh—our wedding invitations."

"What are they doing in the hall?" Tim carried the box to the polished tamburil wood slab coffee table. Charlotte had saved for a year to buy the piece—her first real furniture purchase.

"Dixie brought them home from the shop."

Tim squinted at her. "Do we need to have a wedding meeting? Figure out where we are?"

Charlotte exhaled. "Yes. This week, Tim. It's already the middle of April." She worked her way past him to the dining table where she'd left her iPad.

"Monday night?" Tim tapped his phone's screen. "No, I've got a city council meeting." He peered at Charlotte. "Looks like Dave and I are going to get the downtown refurbishing job."

"Tim, really? That's great. Tuesday I have a consult with the mayor's daughter."

"Mayor's daughter?" He arched his brow. "That's my girl. I'm impressed."

"She read about Tawny in the paper and figured if we could make Miss Alabama happy, maybe we could do the same for her."

"By all means, let's give the mayor's daughter the Charlotte Malone treatment. How about Wednesday?" Tim walked around the sofa toward the dining table. "I'm free. Dinner, then wedding business?"

"Perfect."

Tim tapped on his phone's screen, then gathered Charlotte for a long, slow kiss. "I'd better go because I don't *want* to go."

"See you in the morning." Charlotte exhaled, eyes closed, breathing in the scent of his skin. Then she watched him leave, bracing for the door to click closed behind him. That sound always stirred the phantom fear of being alone. All alone.

Ever since Mama died, Charlotte kept uneasy company with aloneness. She was one of one. Gert used to play an old record, something about one being the loneliest number. Charlotte hated the song and left the house when Gert put it on.

Charlotte Malone ended up being her own island, formed from the landscape of her family—by birth and by death.

Kicking off her shoes, she wandered into the kitchen for a water. Twisting off the cap, she paused by her window and gazed toward the distant orange glow of Birmingham, examining her thoughts and separating her emotions.

She jumped when someone pounded on the door. "Tim?"

"I have a delivery from the Ludlow Estate for Charlotte Malone. A trunk."

Charlotte pressed her nose to the door and eyeballed the man on the other side of the peephole. "It's kind of late," she said. When she paid for the trunk to be delivered, she expected it to be next week. Not at a quarter 'til midnight.

"You're telling me. Just need you to sign and I'm gone."

Charlotte unlocked the door and a skinny man in dirty jeans sporting a Fu Manchu hoisted the trunk into the loft. "It don't weigh nothin'. Hope you got your money's worth." He held out the clipboard. "Sign here."

When he'd gone, Charlotte shoved the trunk to the center of the loft and knelt in front of the welded lock. "Well now, my new friend. Do you know what trouble you caused me today?"

Chapter Three

Emily

August 1912
Birmingham

*S*he was late. Again. Emily took the corner toward Highland, cutting across Mrs. Schell's yard, walking fast, reining in her desire to run, shoving her hair into place by securing the loose pins. She willed the hot August air to stir, to breathe. Perspiration trickled across her neck, beneath her high collar and down her back.

Mother would be irritated. Father, amused. But the suffrage meeting ran long. So many opinions and voices. It made her head ache.

Emily sprinted up the walk and around the house to the servants' kitchen entrance, her skirt flapping against her ankles, her heels *clip-clomp*ing on the pavement.

Well, if Mother scolded her for being tardy, Emily could blame Phillip. He'd intercepted her as she was leaving the meeting. Just the very memory of his kisses in the back of his carriage made Emily's temperature rise.

If only he'd intercepted her before the meeting. They'd have had more time and she could have escaped Mrs. Daily's deplorable speech. Her voice rose up, then down, up, then down.

Mrs. Daily was certainly entertaining. Emily laughed softly, then just as she passed the large evergreen, a hand reached around, gripped her arm, and jerked her behind the tree.

With a shout, Emily whirled around with her fist drawn back, ready to strike. Earl Donaldson, her neighbor and childhood friend, knew the power of her punch. He'd jumped out from behind a tree one too many times, and eventually she belted him.

"Emily, simmer down, it's me. It's me."

She lowered her fists and gazed into the eyes of Daniel Ludlow. Her knees went limp. "Daniel, what are you doing here?" She threw herself against him, the thump beneath his chest loud and clear. It'd been so long, months, since she'd heard from him.

"Looking for you, that's what I'm doing, silly girl. Where have you *been*?"

"Where have I been? Right here, where you found me. Where have *you* been?"

"You know where I've been. Don't tease me." He grinned, shoving his ball cap back on his head, and her resolve to be angry with him jellied. "I looked for you when we were in town. How come you never came to any of our games?"

"I had more pressing engagements." Emily turned away from him, but only by a half step or so. Did he expect her to drop everything and run down to Rickwood Field just to watch him bat a ball?

"What's more important than baseball?" He scooped her up and twirled her around. "I missed you." He pressed his cheek against hers, and Emily locked her arms around his neck.

"Plenty of things are more important than baseball. Art, theater, education, suffrage, learning how to run a household from Mother." Emily pushed away from him when he set her down, leaving his puckered lips to kiss the air. "If you missed me, why didn't you write me? And there is such a thing as a telephone. You've heard of that invention, haven't you?"

"Come on, Em. I'm a poor ballplayer. I can't afford phone calls." Daniel fingered a strand of loose hair curling about her neck. She held her breath, tingling as his fingers brushed her skin. "And I did write you. Every week. The question here, young lady, is why didn't you write me back?"

Emily stepped away from his hand. He was confusing her, plying her with his charm. "Did you come up to Highlands to examine me? How come I didn't attend your ball games? How come I didn't write? You're the one who boarded that jitney and drove off with fourteen smelly men to play a silly game. Imagine grown men running round all day in the dirt, chasing a small white ball."

"Em, it's baseball. America's pastime." Daniel raised his arms, his expression foretelling his passion. "It's the greatest game in the world. And it's getting better, Em." He stripped his cap from his head, combed his fingers through his thick bangs, then settled the hat in place again. It had a big *B* on it for his team. The Barons. "We're getting new rules and more leagues. A good hitter or sacker can make a decent wage these days. Stars are being born. Cy Young, Nap Lajoie, Ty Cobb. Word is he's making a pretty penny up there with the Tigers. Five thousand dollars."

Five or six thousand dollars a year? Father made that, or more, in a month. Phillip Saltonstall and his father, even more. They traveled in Oldsmobiles, not jitney buses, and lived in fine houses, not roadside motels.

"I'm not concerned about Cy Young or Ty Cobb. I'm concerned, *was* concerned, about Daniel Ludlow. Did you come here to tell me you're signing a professional contract worth thousands?"

Emily stood back, folded her arms, and waited. She was definitely late for dinner now, but it was Daniel standing in front of her. Daniel.

"No, as a matter of fact." Daniel turned away, slipping his hands into his pockets. The chain of his gold watch glinted in the sun. "I'm not making thousands of dollars playing baseball. That's why I quit. I love the game, and one day it would be swell if I could purchase my own team, but for now"—a soft smolder beneath his brilliant blue eyes burned away every ounce of Emily's ire—"I've secured a position at Pollock Stephens Institute."

"My alma mater? Doing what? Teaching?" Daniel was coming home. "When did this transpire? I can't believe you're quitting the game you love. I declare it almost makes me not respect you. What would possess you to do such a thing?"

"Don't you know, Emily? You."

"Me?" She was helpless against his advances, and when he pulled her into his arms, she let her heart go. "But I heard nothing from you for five months. Not one letter. Not even a postal card." He smelled of soap and warm, washed cotton.

"I wrote you every day, I promise. Mailed them all myself too." He caressed her shoulder and kissed her temple. Romantic flutters burst open in Emily's belly. "What does it matter, sugar, I'm home now."

"I've missed you so much. I don't have anyone to play croquet with me." Emily snuggled against him. "Or try the new dances. Father and Phillip—?" She pressed her lips together. Phillip. Daniel didn't know about him.

"Phillip?" Daniel touched her chin, dipping his face to see into her eyes, but Emily moved away.

"So tell me, what made you decide to give up baseball?" She crossed her arms and closed her heart. She belonged to another man now.

"Well," Daniel began, slow and deliberate, his eyes on her face. "We lost to the Memphis Turtles in a doubleheader and the boys were pretty riled about it. They were smoking and swearing, drinking, and the jitney smelled like a sewer after a hot, rainless summer, and I had to ask myself, 'Why do I prefer these lugheads over my favorite girl?' Who's Phillip, Emily?"

"But you love baseball, Daniel. What about your chance at the plate, to swing the bat at whatever fancy pitch you choose, to 'feel the thrill of wood cracking' . . . Isn't that what you told me you loved about the game?" Emily popped the air with a pretend bat, smiling, trying to sell Daniel on his own dream, trying to move him away from querying her further about Phillip. She'd not planned for this interaction today. Or tomorrow. Or ever, if she were honest. *Oh, Daniel.*

"I didn't think you were listening to me all those nights we walked the quad at school."

"I heard every word. I loved our evening walks."

"If I'd had money, I'd have taken you to a picture show or fancy dinner." He turned his pockets inside out. "What's a poor college boy to do with a beautiful girl like you? Baseball was all I had to make me sound important."

"You need not sound important to me. Walking the quad was a fine date, Daniel Ludlow. I still think of those times."

"So do I and that's why I quit baseball, Emily. Playing didn't make sense anymore when I thought of you. Which was all the time." His breath thinned as his voice became thick. His eyes searched hers. "I don't love baseball. I love you."

"Love me? How can you love me? I've not seen or heard from you since April."

"I mailed five or six letters every Saturday asking you to wait for me." He regarded her from under the bill of his cap. "You really didn't receive them?"

"Would I say I didn't if I did?" Emily walked around him, toward the swing hanging from the elm. Her stomach rumbled, reminding her Mother would be serving supper soon, but she couldn't leave Daniel yet. She pushed her toes against the grass, setting the swing into motion. Daniel leaned against the trunk of the tree.

"Would I say I wrote to you if I didn't, Emily?" Daniel removed his cap, and his tangled mop of thick brown hair curled over his forehead and around his temples. Emily used to pull his curls free to tease him after he'd worked so hard to slick his hair into place. "I'd like to come calling later this evening if it's all right with you."

Emily kicked her feet and raised the swing higher. The August evening hosted an array of colors—pink, purple, orange, and blue—and gave her no ideas on how to tell Daniel, dear Daniel, the news.

Daniel watched her, smiling, but inquiring of her each time their eyes met. *May I come calling?* Finally he caught the swing and lowered his face to hers.

"What are you not telling me?"

"I didn't receive your letters, Daniel." Panic swirled in Emily's chest and around her thoughts. She slid off the wide wooden seat, trying to press around Daniel into the open yard, but he trapped her in his arms.

"But I'm home now. Letters or not, I feel the same. I've secured a job and a large apartment in the Ridley house . . . Emily, I want to speak to your father."

"Father?" Emily unlocked his arms from around her. "The Ridley?" Did he intend to propose marriage and bring her to live in the Ridley?

"The Ridley is a fine apartment. Not a mansion like your father's . . ." He waved the cap in his hand toward the large stone house where a cut of the blue day seemed to rest on the dark roof. "But it's a good, fine place for couples in love to start out. I don't plan to be a teacher forever, Emily. I have plans to—"

"Phillip—there's the matter of Phillip, Daniel."

"W-what do you mean? Phillip who? I thought we had an understanding, Emily." A sad confusion weighted his expression and his inquiry.

"But you left." Emily spun away from him. Oh blast, how could she tell him?

"I've been gone five months, not five years." Daniel touched Emily's shoulder and gentled her around to face him. "You gave up on me so quickly?"

"Daniel, we took a few turns around the campus quad, attended dances and fraternity socials, but . . . it was hardly an understanding." Emily pressed her hands together. Did her words sound convincing? She'd spent the last five months telling herself what she had with Daniel was infatuation, not love. "Phillip and I became reacquainted at the Black and White Ball. In May."

"I see." Daniel averted his gaze as he pressed his cap onto his head.

Stinging tears washed Emily's eyes when she saw the red tinge on the tip of Daniel's nose. She covered her exhale and quivering lips with her hand.

"Daniel, listen to me, be serious for a moment. Did you really believe we'd marry?" She stretched her hand to him but pulled back without touching him. "We were and always will be college friends. Nothing more." *Please agree, Daniel. Please agree.*

"No, we were much more. I believed we'd marry. That's why I quit the Barons and returned home."

"But we made no *real* declarations. No promises." *No*, she did not betray him.

"How could I ask you to marry me when I was riding off in a jitney? But it was understood, Em. Wasn't it? That we loved each other and wanted to be together?"

"Phillip and I . . . we're right for each other. Our families have been friends for years. We have the same—"

"Social connections? The same opulent wealth?" Daniel's tender pleading about-faced to sour and snarly.

"You knew when we met who I was, where I came from, and what expectations might be upon me."

"Yes, but I thought I met a girl with a mind and will of her own. One who would choose a life and husband she loved."

With mustered courage, Emily stepped into him. "That's exactly what I'm doing. There's more to marriage than college memories. More than rib-splitting laughter and juvenile affection." Surely he knew a girl like Emily had to consider social standing, her privilege, wealth, and education. Her family.

"Is that all we were? A good time? Tell me, are you in love with him?" Daniel's voice wavered ever so slightly as he backed toward a tan and black mustang tied to Father's hitching post. Father's bay had poked her head out the stable window, curling her lip at Daniel's pony, flirting.

"Daniel, I—" Emotion rose from some hidden room of her heart. "Yes, I love him, whatever that means. Love is a subjective sort of thing, wouldn't you agree?"

"No, I would not. It's an action verb." Daniel jerked forward, reaching up to slip his fingers along the curve of Emily's face. "One I'm willing to do. Love you for the rest of your life. I'm willing to speak to your father right now, Emily. I'm a man he can trust with his daughter. I'll prove myself more worthy than Saltonstall."

She stepped away from him, a cool ire mingling with her hot tears. "I can't do that to him."

"But you can do it to me?" Daniel's feelings displayed on his high cheeks and square jaw. Even a few paces away, she could see the rise of his chest, sense the beating of his heart.

"You left me. I had no other choice but to move on or go crazy loving you." Emily gritted her jaw and confessed, "It was the hardest thing I ever had to do."

"I'm here now."

"No, Daniel. We are over. Phillip is a wonderful man, kind and considerate, well-spoken and well-read, educated and respected in this city."

"Respected? Saltonstall?" He laughed, low and cold. "I tell you what he really is, Em. Phillip Saltonstall is a—" Daniel halted, pressing his lips into a taut line. "He has many . . . he is quite the—"

"He's quite the what?" Emily crossed her arms, the breeze cooling her skin but not her heart. "Say what you have to say, Daniel. You seem to know so much."

"I have nothing to say." He backed away, one step, two steps, slowly at first, then faster. "Good-bye, Emily."

But instead of racing across the lawn, he surged forward, gripped her shoulders, and kissed her, passionate and tender.

Hot emotion brewed on Emily's lips and in her heart as she watched him sprint toward his mount and ride off. The *clip-clop* of hooves echoed in the hollow chambers of Emily's heart . . . the places where she'd once believed love for Daniel Ludlow bloomed.

She reached for the fir tree branches, bracing herself, not caring if the needles bit into her palm. "I'm sorry, Daniel," she whispered, praying the wind would carry her words and comfort him. But he was too late. Emily had committed her affections, her mind, to marrying Phillip Saltonstall. It was all for the best, really.

Daniel Ludlow was simply too late. Too late.

Chapter Four

$\mathcal{E}$mily stood at the kitchen sink, pumping cool water over her fingers, the last of her tears dripping from the edge of her jaw into the sink and swirling down the drain.

The five o'clock sun draped reddish-gold ribbons through the trees and left thin, dark shadows on the ground. A warm honeysuckle breeze blowing through the open window did a jig with the curtains.

Splashing water on her face, Emily rubbed her eyes, washing away the heat of tears and the image of Daniel. How dare he come back and interrupt her life? Phillip was expected for dinner soon and she must compose herself.

She snapped a towel from the bar below the sink and dabbed her face dry. If Daniel sent her letters, what happened to them? Where did they go?

"Here ye are, miss." Molly entered the kitchen from the outside, her apron loaded with tomatoes. "I've been searching for ye. Where'd you get off to after the meeting? What'd ye think? Are ye ready to march for the vote?"

"I don't know, Molly. It all seems rather . . . Has Mother been looking for me?" Emily kept her back to the kitchen maid and cook, composing herself. "It's warm today, isn't it?"

"A broiler. Yes ma'am, a bee-roil-er. *Umm hmmm.*" Molly's sing-song words alerted Emily. The woman had a secret. "Yer mother's not been looking for you."

35

"Molly, did you see me just now?" Emily folded the hand towel and draped it over the dowel rod.

"Oh, I don't know." Molly dumped the tomatoes into the sink. "Do ye think I have time to stare out the window so's I can catch you kissing a young man that ain't Mr. Saltonstall?"

"Oh, Molly, you *did* see." Emily came around the worktable to face Molly. "He kissed me. I did not kiss him."

"Sure looked like you were kissing him to me."

"I wasn't kissing him. He just . . . grabbed me." Emily slapped her palm against the thick board where Molly worked. The woman was five years older, and at twenty-seven, she was more like a sister than a servant.

Mother had hired Molly when she was sixteen, fresh from Ireland, with nothing more than a change of clothes in her valise. While shopping downtown one afternoon, Mother overheard Molly inquiring for a job and stood aghast as a transported Bostonian, who had no use for the Irish, mocked and cruelly rejected Molly. Mother hired her on the spot.

That evening at dinner, Mother told Father, "A pretty girl like that would find herself in the dance halls. What would the good Lord charge against me if I let such a travesty happen when it was in my power to do good?"

"Daniel kissed me, you hear." Emily angled forward to grip the burnished-haired maid by the shoulders.

"Saints and all the angels." Molly pulled away from Emily, her hazel eyes snapping. "That was Daniel? Where's he been keeping himself for these past five months, leaving you to wonder and weep in your pillow?"

"I didn't weep, Molly. Where do you get such ideas?"

"I got ears, don't I? And Big Mike can hear a bird chewing on a worm, don't you know." Molly took her knife to the first tomato, cutting it into quarters and tossing the slices into a bowl.

Molly's room was just below Emily's. And Big Mike, Father's liveryman, came into the stable one afternoon when she'd gone up to the loft to hide her tears in the hay.

"He said he wrote letters," Emily said, sinking slowly down to the kitchen stool. "He came here today to tell me he'd quit baseball and had secured a job and an apartment."

"Letters, you say? Ah, look at me mess." Molly motioned to the soupy tomato juice on the cutting board as she added the slices to a bowl. "This knife must be dull as—"

"There's nothing wrong with that knife, Molly." Emily put her hand on the woman's arm. "Don't you get the mail every day?"

"Miss, if you want a rundown of my household chores, speak to yer mother. I must be getting to this supper." Molly averted her gaze, twisting her arm out from Emily's hand. "What your father won't say to me if his summer salad and tomato pie isn't on the table."

"Molly, spill it."

She sliced another tomato with quick motion, her lips tight and pale.

"What happened to Daniel's letters?"

Slice, slice, slice. "Ain't nothing like a lovely salad on a hot summer evening. I ordered ice cream from the iceman for tonight. Mr. Saltonstall is coming to dinner, you know. In fact, I believe he—"

"Where are they, Molly?"

Molly whacked the next poor innocent tomato.

"Oh—" Emily pressed her hand to her chest. "Father. Did he— tell me he didn't toss them into the incinerator?"

Now Molly gazed at her, a bit of spit-and-vinegar in her eye. "Think of your father, Emily. Would he do such a thing?"

"I'd think not, but then why did he take them in the first place? Or was it Mother?"

"Blessed saints, no. Not your mother. She'll be a saint one day for saving me."

Emily fussed with her slipping pompadour, removing the long hairpins, letting her hair fall free, controlling her ire at Father for hiding her personal property. It wasn't like him. "Molly, the letters."

The kitchen door swung open and Father's man, Jefferson, entered. "Miss Emily, there you are." Jefferson wore a light-colored suit with a string tie. Perspiration dotted his limp white shirt and bled through his vest. "Your father is asking for you. He's in his library."

Emily slid off the stool. "All right. What kind of mood is Father in, Jefferson?" She pinched a slice of tomato off the salad, eyeing Molly.

"Quite jolly, Miss Emily. Has a spark in his eye."

"Good. I'll be right there." Emily turned to Molly as Jefferson backed out of the room with a bow. "I'm not done with you."

"Let it go, miss." Molly clutched her arm. "It's spilt milk. Think of Mr. Saltonstall." Her tone waxed soft and dreamy. "He's a fine, handsome man who is suited to you and your station. He adores you, clings to your every word. Mr. Ludlow is also fine, I'm sure, but your father worked hard to give you this life, the very best of everything. Why marry a common man like Daniel Ludlow when Phillip Saltonstall is after your affections? Love only lasts so long when there's no food on the table or money in the bank and the children are crying. Trust me, I know."

Emily considered Molly's words, reaching for the door. "It is better to marry Phillip, isn't it? He's kind and charming . . . educated." As was Daniel, on all counts.

"Educated at a fancy northern university too. Yale."

"Phillip is handsome and witty." As was Daniel. But it helped to list Phillip's wonderful attributes. What a short memory she had. "He'll make an excellent father." But Daniel, too, would be a strong, loving father. "Our parents adore one another." Emily built her argument. "We'll have his parents' house up on Red Mountain."

"I think ye know what to do, miss."

Yes, yes, she did.

Daniel's mother had died when he was fifteen. His father was a police officer in Birmingham and often left Daniel and his brother to fend for themselves. But he'd done well. Gone to college, played baseball, secured a teaching position at the city's most prestigious school, and now rented an apartment at the very reputable Ridley House.

But Phillip was heir to the Saltonstall fortune. He'd be a captain of industry, a leader in Birmingham. Emily would be involved with the women's league or whatever charity or cause she chose. She'd have her heart's desire, including an estate up on Red Mountain the size of four or five Ridley house apartments.

"Yes," she said out loud. "Phillip is the logical choice. The best choice for overall harmony."

"Good, glad we cleared that up. Now, go see what your father be a-wanting and get out of my kitchen. You're distracting me, and your mother will want to know why dinner is not ready." Hazel tears glistened in Molly's eyes. "I'm happy for you, miss."

At the hall mirror, Emily paused to smooth her hair over her shoulders and clip the stray hairpins to her waistband. She tucked in her shirtwaist and dusted her hands over her skirt, satisfied that the evidence of her tears was gone. After she visited Father, she'd wash and change for dinner.

Molly's weepy smile boomeranged in her mind. *I'm happy for you, miss.* But so much emotion over Emily deciding Phillip was the better choice? She had no time to ponder. She was at Father's library door.

"Afternoon, Father." Emily entered the grand, cool room without knocking. Father spent his mornings at his exchange office, returning home in the afternoons to work in the comfort of his library. Beyond the large windows, a stand of cottonwoods shielded the windows from the sun's setting summer rays.

"Emily, my dear." Father rose from his chair, but he was not alone in the room. Phillip also rose as Emily entered.

"Phillip, you're here." She gathered her hair at the nape of her neck. She must look a sight. After seeing him in the city, she rode the dusty trolley home. "I didn't expect you so soon." She glared at Father. "Why didn't you have Jefferson tell me?"

"I arrived early to speak with your father." Phillip was handsome and fragrant, poised and confident with a constant glint of merriment in his eyes. He crossed over to her and kissed her cheek in a gentlemanly fashion—one he did not observe when they were in his carriage alone.

Emily leaned into him, though Daniel's soapy scent and brawny strength flashed across her mind. She lifted her head as her fingers squeezed Phillip's narrow arms and cleared her throat. "You smell like the fancy perfume shops."

"A fragrance I bought when I was in Paris last year. Do you like it?"

"It's you, Phillip. Very rich." Though she preferred the single clean scent of Daniel's lye soap.

"Well"—Father cleared his throat and came from around his desk—"I need to place a call to the office. Excuse me."

Emily watched Father leave, a sinking sensation dragging her heart through her stomach. Once the library door clapped closed, Phillip hooked Emily to him, tilting her chin up and kissing her lips. When he lifted his head, he nodded toward Father's desk. "Shall we tell him the telephone is in here?"

Emily squeezed his hand. "I think he knows." What was going on? Father leaving her alone with Phillip. His ardent kiss . . .

Leading her to the window seat, Phillip brushed his fingers lightly along Emily's jaw. "You are so beautiful."

"I'm a sight. I planned to change my dress and redo my hair before you arrived." She leaned away from his hand, which sent waves of shivers coursing through her. It was as if he knew, *knew*, how to touch her.

"I like your hair down. You must wear it like that for me." Phillip trailed his finger over her chin and down her neck, stoking the small flame he ignited. "I never asked you, how was the suffrage meeting?"

"It was—" Emily swallowed, scooting an inch away from his fingertip. What if Father returned to find her flushed and panting? Besides, all Phillip's touching . . . kissing her nose . . . and the side of her lips. His movements were calculated and cunning.

"The meeting was . . . splendid. Yes, splendid." She jumped up, shoving the perspiration on her forehead into her hair. "It's . . . it's warm today, is it not?" If he continued touching her that way, she'd melt into a passion puddle on the floor.

Mother had raised her to be a controlled, reserved gentlewoman. What would Phillip think of her if she surrendered so easily to his advances?

"I'm sorry, I'm making you nervous."

"You're terrifying me, Phillip. I'm trying to be a lady, but even a cultured Christian woman can only stand so much."

"And a man can only stand so much. 'Tis why I've come." He reached for her and drew her back down to the bench seat, cupping her face, searching her eyes. "I've asked your father for your hand." He bent down to one knee.

"Oh, Phillip." Emily pressed her hands to her chest, anticipation surging through her veins. "I'm wearing an ordinary day gown and—"

"I found this in a Paris shop last fall. The moment I laid eyes on it, I knew it would be for my intended. But I didn't know who yet." Phillip retrieved a small wooden box from his jacket pocket. "Then I escorted you to the Black and White Ball. By evening's end, I knew I'd marry you."

Nestled in the silk bed was a square-cut solitaire surrounded by smaller diamonds. The setting was an intricate, sparkling lattice weave.

"Platinum, my dear. The diamond is an Edwardian cut surrounded by solitaires." Phillip held up the ring. The extravagant stones soaked up the light and splashed a rainbow against the wall. And over Emily's heart.

"I can barely breathe."

"Emily Canton, will you marry me?" Phillip slipped his ring of promise onto her finger.

"Yes, oh yes, Phillip." She fell against him, and when he lifted her up in his arms, all the doubts, all the memories of Daniel, escaped through her heart's open door.

The grandfather clock in the foyer chimed the last moments of midnight. Emily leaned against the front door as it clicked closed, a bit of stardust in her eyes.

She was engaged. To Phillip Saltonstall. He was so sweet and charming tonight, never leaving her side, sneaking kisses while Mother played the piano and sang, while Father glanced the other way.

Then he danced with her on the front porch as the moon lit the sublime night, and when the clock chimed midnight, he held her face in his hands and kissed her good night. Could there be anything as grand?

Emily raised her ring hand into the glow of the gaslight. It was exquisite. More than she ever imagined. My, wasn't Father merry all evening? Mother, so gay and lighthearted.

When the Saltonstalls arrived for a family celebration and dessert, Emily thought she might explode with happiness. This evening paled even her favorite Christmas when her brother, Howard Jr., returned home from his first year at Harvard.

The Saltonstalls appeared content and proud. "Phillip chose well," Mr. Saltonstall had boasted. "Very well."

An engagement party was already in the planning.

But Father's rolling laughter was Emily's favorite sound of the evening. He showed his pleasure in the whole arrangement. Especially after he and Mr. Saltonstall vanished into the library, only to come out shaking hands. "Good to do business with family, Howard."

Father's exchange company would benefit from a man like Cameron Saltonstall.

Emily moseyed up the stairs just as a door creaked at the end of the hall. She leaned to see Molly tiptoeing out of the kitchen.

"Molly, what are you doing up?" Emily laughed when the maid jumped, clutching her robe together at her throat. Her thick hair was tied up in rags that stuck out of her head every which way.

"Checking on you, miss. I couldn't sleep until he left." Molly whispered her way toward Emily and the stairs. "Tell me, did he give you a beautiful ring?"

"See for yourself." Emily descended the stairs, holding our her hand. "He said he bought the ring when he was in Paris. After the Black and White Ball he knew the ring belonged to me."

"Saints and all the angels. I could buy a village back home with such a thing." Molly peered at the ring, then Emily. "Perhaps he'll take you to Paris for your honeymoon, miss."

"Yes, perhaps." Emily drew her hand back, examining her diamond. "We'll stay for a month." She shifted her attention back to Molly. Their eyes locked for a long moment. "What? Tell me."

"The week of the Black and White you wept in your room over Daniel Ludlow." Molly turned slowly for the kitchen.

"I still loved him. But that's changed." Emily scurried after her. "What are you trying to say, you wicked maid?"

"Just that I heard you weeping. Care for some milk, miss?" Molly popped open the icebox.

"Milk? Why would I want milk?" Molly acted so strangely at times.

"Are you sure you don't care for milk?" Molly set the milk bottle on the worktable, then went to the cupboard for glasses.

"If I wanted milk I'd get it myself. What are you up to, Molly? You don't like milk. I've heard you say it a hundred times."

"But you like milk."

In the dark kitchen Emily could only perceive Molly's expression in the pale light of the moon. "It's Daniel's letters. Where are they? In Father's den?"

"You certainly don't think he'd hide them in here, do you?" Molly snickered into her glass but never took a drink.

"Then where?"

"He's me boss, miss. Butters me bread, and I'm kinda likin' the taste by now." Molly held up the half-full glass of milk. "Sure you won't be wanting a glass of milk? Milk is very good. I miss fresh milk from the cows. Remember when we had a cow, miss? Bessy. She'd moo at all hours of the day and night. Now we have a man delivering our milk on the ice cart. I tell you I don't miss milking the old girl meself. Ah, she was a stubborn old broad, like me Grammy Killian."

"Molly, stop talking about—" Emily jutted around the table, laying her hand on Molly's arm so the milk in her glass sloshed up the sides. "The stable. Father hid the letters in the stable?"

Molly eyed her over the rim of her glass. "I wouldn't know what you're talking about, letters and cows and nonsense. Nothing in that stable but smelly horses and a musty ole hayloft."

"The loft." Emily darted to a drawer where Molly kept the matches. The lantern already waited by the door.

"You're not going now are you, miss?"

"Why wait until the morning when Father might get it in his head to move them?" Emily lit the lamp, pausing at the door.

"Careful, miss, the hay is dry. It'll catch afire."

"Molly." Emily raised the lamp. "How do you know the hay is dry?"

"You're not the only lass with a love in her heart, Emily. I had me an evening with the delivery man, Mr. Dawson." She whistled her way back to her room.

"Molly."

The maid's door closed and Emily ran smiling across the lawn, striding against the narrow hem of her gown, the flame of the lamp swaying through the darkness. So, Molly and Mr. Dawson . . . they made a fine pair. Yes, sir. At the stable Emily unlatched the lock and slid open the door.

Father's stable was immaculate. Five stalls on the right, five stalls on the left, separated by a wide stone aisle. The horses raised their heads as Emily marched toward the loft ladder.

"Hide my letters from me. What right has he?" At the ladder's top, Emily cleared a place away for the oil lamp and surveyed the mound of yellow straw. Where would Father hide letters? She inspected the walls for a cupboard or hidden door. If she were hiding letters, she'd put them in a box or sack, then stash them in a corner and cover them with hay.

Emily kicked her way to the back corner, then dropped to her knees, searching the hay. When her hands hit a wooden box, her breath caught. She'd not considered what she'd do if she actually found them.

Carrying the box to the lamp, she sat dangling her legs over the loft's edge. The hay clinging to her skirt shook free and drifted down into the stall below.

The simple box was square, made of cedar, with a small brass lock. When she tried the lock, it wouldn't spring. She'd have to take it inside. She tucked the box under her arm and, grabbing the lantern, hurried back to the house.

She knew where to find the key. Father kept dozens of them in the middle drawer of his desk. She'd stay up all night to find the right one if need be.

In the kitchen Emily set the lantern on the sideboard and prepared to blow out the flame when a small glint caught her eye. A key. A small lockbox key.

Bless you, Molly, bless you.

Emily unlocked the box, set the key on the table, snuffed out the lamp, and snuck along the back staircase to her room.

Chapter Five

Charlotte

*K*ristin, I can tell by the light in your eyes you're excited for your wedding day. You want it to be special. To be about you and Oliver."

Charlotte sat on the sofa next to her client, the pinkish white walls casting a soft mauve hue across the plush mocha-colored carpet and the Logan Stone couch. In her lap she cradled her secret weapon. A photo album.

"Well, we met in high school—"

Charlotte placed the book on the coffee table.

"—and dated all through college." Kristin sighed and smiled. "We only broke up once."

"You two are meant to be, it's obvious. How did you know he was *the* one?" Charlotte opened to the first page of the photo album— a collection of Birmingham brides over the last six months. Every woman wore the exact same style of dress Kristin claimed was *the one* for her. The gown she'd been "dreaming of since she was a girl."

"Oliver?" The blush on Kristin's cheeks outshone her smile. "Like you said, we were meant to be. We belong together. We fit. We're best friends. We love all the same things. Even in high school we completed each other's sentences."

"He makes you feel special, doesn't he?"

"Even after dating for seven years, yes, he does."

Charlotte regarded Kristin for a moment. Did she feel *that* way about Tim? Special? Like they belonged together? When they first met, he consumed her daytime thoughts and nighttime dreams, but lately, since the engagement . . . Charlotte exhaled. What she needed at the moment was to concentrate on turning this fiancée into a beautiful, unique bride.

"Is this the gown you've selected?" Charlotte produced a bridal magazine clipping of the dress Kristin wanted. "It makes you feel special like Oliver makes you feel special?"

"Yes, yes, it does." Kristin's eyes glistened. "I went to a friend's wedding a few years ago and just loved her gown. I looked everywhere to find one just like it. It'll be perfect for me."

What Charlotte didn't get about brides was why they all wanted to look alike. How could a dress just like the one Kristin's friend wore make her feel special?

She considered it her mission, her calling even, to dress her brides as uniquely as possible. When a bride slipped on a truly perfect gown, Charlotte's soul rested in pure satisfaction.

"It is a lovely dress, Kristin." Charlotte held up the picture as if to study it. "White satin strapless gown with an A-line skirt and a chapel train."

"I get weepy every time I see it." Kristin pressed her hand to her chest. Her engagement ring glinted in the afternoon haze that fell through the southern window.

Charlotte scooted forward, inhaling, calculating her next words. Kristin was a reluctant Malone & Co. client, only coming in this afternoon because her mother insisted.

"Well, if you want this dress, really want this dress, then buy it from the shop where you found it." Charlotte peered at Kristin with a gracious, kind smile and tucked her photo album under her arm with exaggeration. Kristin's lit eyes dimmed and followed Charlotte's every move.

"Why can't *you* order this gown? I've seen it in several shops. Surely you could—"

"Kristin, I don't order gowns that are in every other shop. I *dress* brides from the inside out. I'm not a bridal gown mill." She tapped the photo album. "Do you want to see what's in here?" Charlotte scooted closer to her client, opened the album on Kristin's lap, and turned the pages. "Do you see what I see?"

Page after page, the same gown, just a different bride. A blonde, a brunette, young, old, skinny, chubby . . .

Kristin took over turning the pages, the excitement in her countenance fading. "Where'd you get these?"

"The newspaper, websites, all around Birmingham. These are from the last six months."

"I never realized." Kristin's shoulders slumped forward. "Oh my . . . now what am I going to do? I thought I'd found the perfect gown. Just perfect."

Charlotte gently removed the photo album and closed it, placing it on the floor by the sofa. She intended to wake Kristin up. Not crush her.

"We're going to find the perfect dress. Trust me. When we attend one wedding at a time, we don't realize how many of the dresses are exactly alike. But at Malone & Co. our job, our delight, is to find a gown that fits your figure as well as your heart. Kristin, finding gowns for brides that expresses them completely is my one talent in life." Charlotte tipped her head to see Kristin's face and laughed softly. "Don't deny me my one, *widdle* talent." Kristin broke into a smile. "Tell you what, if you don't like the gowns I bring to you, then I'll personally recommend you to a friend of mine who sells the gown you have here." She tapped the magazine cutout Kristin brought in with her.

"My mother insisted I talk to you because she said I could do better than this." Kristin ran her finger over the image of the model wearing her once-perfect gown.

Charlotte sat back, reading Kristin's countenance. "I understand how you feel about that dress. All your friends looked beautiful in the same style and you want to be beautiful too. But I can find you something unique *and* beautiful. Will you take the leap with me?"

"I will. Charlotte, I will." Kristin gripped her arm. "I'm willing to try another dress. Really. Do you think you can find a dress that's just for me?" Tears collected in the corner of her eyes, but she was smiling. "Just don't get me on some kind of ugliest bridal gown list."

Charlotte laughed. "No bride of mine will ever be on an ugly gown list." As she stood, Kristin snatched up Charlotte's ring hand.

"You're engaged too?"

"Yes . . . yes, I am." Charlotte twisted the ring around her finger. The clear and sparkling diamond created a multicolored swirl of light. The switch of attention to her from Kristin made her want to turtle her emotions. Tuck away and hide.

"It's beautiful. I've never seen a ring like it." Kristin smiled at the smirking Dixie standing by the refreshment bar. "Are you helping her choose her dress?"

"Gee, I don't know. Charlotte, am I helping you choose your dress?" Dixie folded her arms and let her sarcasm drip.

"This session isn't about me. It's about Kristin." She stooped for the photo album. "The ring belonged to my fiancé's grandmother."

Charlotte shot Dixie a hard glare. She'd been fussing at her all week about choosing a gown. Charlotte promised she'd get around to it. She would. Then this morning Dixie showed her the new Bray-Lindsay that just arrived from Paris, and Charlotte nearly buckled. "It's too expensive, even with my dealer discount," she said the moment she caught her breath.

At eight thousand dollars the dress better make her feel like

Cinderella, Princess Diana, and Kate Middleton all rolled into one. Charlotte had to *feel* it. Dixie insisted she try the gown on, but she had yet to slip into the handcrafted silk.

How could she explain an eight-thousand-dollar dress to Tim? He nearly froze her out over a thousand-dollar trunk purchase.

"Kristin"—Charlotte locked her gaze on Dixie—"you know, I think we have a gown in the shop that would be perfect for you. It just arrived this morning from Paris."

"Charlotte?" Dixie's arms fell to her side and her smirk became a pinched-brow frown.

"Dix, why don't you prep the Bray-Lindsay of Paris for Kristin and let's show her what it feels like to be a real princess bride."

Dixie regarded Charlotte through a narrowed gaze. "It's quite expensive, Kristin."

"Price is no problem." Kristin jumped up, an eagerness in her tone. "My parents will buy whatever I want. I'd love to see this Bray-Lindsay." She clasped her hands together. "A gown from Paris. Wonderful."

"All right then, let me get it ready for you. Charlotte, can you give me a hand?" Dixie hooked her hand around Charlotte's elbow as she headed out the door, dragging her along. "Kristin, there're refreshments on the bar. Please help yourself."

"Do I see steam coming out of your ears?" Charlotte asked, tripping along with Dixie as she thudded down the stairs to the reveal salon.

Dixie's auburn hair was slicked back into a perfect ponytail and her Malone & Co. suit clung to her curves in all the right places. Charlotte could hate her—raw, honest truth—if Dixie wasn't so smart and sweet. And fun. Dixie Pryor was an amazing friend and an excellent bridal consultant.

"Enough steam to curl your hair." In the salon Dixie flung open the storage closet doors and took the Bray-Lindsay from the rack. "This was your dress, Char. We ordered it for you."

"*You* ordered it for me. I never said I wanted it. It's perfect for Kristin. Think about it, Dix—the gown is too frilly for me."

"Too frilly? You said the Maggie Sottero was too plain. The Bray is the perfect blend of simple and intricate." Dixie carefully prepped the dress to be draped over the dress form on the gleaming, dark-wood center platform. Sofas and lounge chairs circled the mini stage.

"The blend is perfect for Kristin. Really, Dix, how can you doubt me after five years of watching from the shadow of my genius?" Charlotte laughed, easing down to the nearest sofa, watching Dixie work. The silky, luxurious fabric of the gown cascaded over the dress form. The skirt swished and swirled toward the stage floor, a pure milky river. The scene made Charlotte's heart palpitate. But her joy faded when Dix didn't even crack a smile.

"Want to know what surprises me?"

"If I say no, will you tell me anyway?"

"What surprises me is that you're getting married in two months, you haven't selected a dress or tuxes, and you're acting as if that's normal."

"Oh, speaking of, Tim said he'd be by one day this week with Dave to pick out tuxes. How's that for normal?"

"One day this week? Really? That's the third time he's promised to be by 'this week.' It's already Wednesday afternoon. He'd better hurry it up if he plans to make it this time."

Charlotte shifted her magic photo album from one arm to the next. "If you have something to say, go for it."

Dixie billowed the skirt as if to inflate her lungs with boldness. Then she stepped around to Charlotte. "You two just don't act like a couple getting married."

"Is there a book, a guideline on how to act? I'd like to read it so I know."

Dixie cut Charlotte a sharp glance and moved to the riser steps. "Please dim the lights for me, will you?" she said, adjusting the gown's bodice and sleeves.

"Dixie, come on, you know ordering clothes doesn't prove a couple's devotion." Charlotte stepped back to the lighting panel and maneuvered the middle switches. The perimeter lights dimmed as the tracks along the center of the ceiling lit up. A glittery light showered down on the gown and dripped off the thick hem, creating sparkling pools on the polished platform that spilled over onto the plush, burgundy carpet.

The salon was a wedding gown fairyland.

Charlotte had seen this room in a dream. For over a year she considered it an impossible dream until the anonymous check dropped into her account.

Once she knew the gift was legit, she wasted not one moment getting the room designed and built.

The reveal salon was the focus of the *Southern Weddings* article. But with such a magnificent salon, the rest of the shop needed an upgrade. Bye-bye to what remained of the hundred-thousand-dollar gift. Charlotte gutted and remodeled the upstairs, broke down walls, discovered river-rock fireplaces under 1920s plaster, and uncovered thirsty cherry hardwood beneath the worn, matted carpet.

One unmerited gift and her whole world changed.

"Forget I said anything." Dixie stepped off the riser, angling back, taking in the lighted gown. "You'd better have Kristin call her mom and whoever else she wants with her when she tries this on." Dixie billowed the train again so it fell like a snowy waterfall over the platform. "She won't want to be alone when she discovers this is the one."

"I love you for being so honest with me, Dix." Charlotte smiled and started for the door. "And that you agree this is the dress for Kristin."

"It just burns me to no end that you're always right. How do you know?" Dixie huffed, hands on her hips.

"It's in my gut, my spirit, I guess. I just know." Charlotte paused in the doorway. "I think God speaks to me when I'm working, helping the brides." The confession reverberated in her chest, then sank through her, awakening a sublime peace.

"Then ask Him to speak to you about your own dress," Dixie said, walking around the mini stage, an assessing expression on her angular face.

"Dix, I'll know it when I find my dress. I will."

"Are you even looking? You have two months . . ."

"I promise, I'll look this month. Every day, okay? Now, play Michael Bublé's 'Stardust.' Kristin seems like a 'Stardust' kind of girl."

"Already had it queued in my mind." Dixie walked to the back of the salon for the stereo remote. "Great minds and all that, you know?"

"You're a good friend, Dixie."

"I want you to be happy, Char." The strains of "Stardust" drifted down from the mounted speakers. The track lights were programmed to dance and twinkle with the music's rhythm. The Swarovski crystals on the gown's intricate lace bodice caught and fanned out the dripping light. "If any girl in the world deserves happiness and love, it's you."

The melody of Dixie's heart in her confession drew emotion from Charlotte. "I know you do and I have a lot of things that make me happy, a lot of things I love. But right now, I want to sell that Bray-Lindsay to Kristin and make *her* happy. That will be the joy of my day."

It was after seven when Charlotte let herself into her loft, flipping on the entry light, balancing her bring-home work and the mail as her black satchel slipped off her shoulder.

Junk mail fluttered from her fingers to the floor. Crossing the living room through the coming night shadows, Charlotte banged into the antique trunk she'd left sitting in the middle of the room. She moaned and caught the sour word forming on the edge of her tongue.

"Stupid thing." She kicked at it before stooping to pick up the dropped mail. What was she going to do with it? The lock was still welded shut and the pale, parched wood needed a long drink of polish. Both required an effort she wasn't willing to expend at the moment.

But never mind the trunk. She'd had a great day. Kristin Gillaspy walked out of the shop with a Bray-Lindsay of Paris purchase and an appointment next week for her first fitting and to talk about brides-maids' dresses.

Dixie had popped Charlotte a low five as their latest satisfied client exited the shop. "I never tire of watching you work."

"Mama always told me to use my powers for good."

Laughter went well at the end of a sale. However, not so much after cracking her toe against a junky ole trunk. Charlotte dropped her bag on the dining table along with her pile of catalogs and print-outs from the shop to review, then bent to rub her toe. Kicking sharp wooden corners smarted.

She'd left the trunk in the living room for Tim to see. Maybe he could do something with it. After all, he loved restoring the downtown buildings and old neighborhoods of Birmingham. The trunk seemed like a small, simple project in comparison. Maybe the dry leather and thirsty wood would tug at Tim's heartstrings. They certainly didn't tug at Charlotte's.

Pulling her phone from her purse, she checked to see if her man had responded to her two voice messages and three texts.

But her screen was blank. Tim's office assistant said he'd left midmorning and not returned. Said he was "out."

Charlotte stared out her fourth-floor window toward the amber hue rising over the city and the stream of white, bright, after-work headlights. In the quiet, she could hear her heartbeat, hear her own questions about Tim and their wedding.

Something about his afternoon silence fed her doubts. Or maybe her uneasiness was just Dixie's probing and poking about why she hadn't picked her own gown yet. It just didn't seem as fun as fitting brides-to-be like Kristin.

Okay, tell the truth. Was she dragging her feet? Why *didn't* she gush with excitement like her clients? Why didn't she have her own unique set of wedding dreams?

Charlotte's heart ached with the collision of her thoughts and feelings. Maybe Tim wasn't truly *the* one? She loved him, more than she had loved anyone besides Mama—but did she gush and blush like Kristin Gillaspy did when she spoke of her Oliver?

Charlotte gazed down at Tim's grandmother's ring. A piece of vast Rose family history gripped her finger. Her next breath shallowed as if she'd been running for miles.

The girl with no branches on her family tree was marrying into the deep-rooted Rose clan. Charlotte's family tree consisted of Mama as the trunk and Charlotte as the one and only sprig. No father, no siblings. No grandparents. No aunts and uncles.

"Okay, you're depressing yourself, Charlotte." She roused herself, unbuttoning her suit jacket and heading back to her bedroom to change into comfy jeans, her 'Bama t-shirt, and thick socks.

As she rounded the corner, she spotted her wedding invitations under the coffee table. Ah, there they were. She'd had Tim put them there to get them out of the hallway.

But tonight, Tim was coming over to address the invitations to their guests.

The ancient beams of the old-warehouse-turned-loft creaked as Charlotte moved the box out from under the table, as she changed her clothes, washed her face, and gathered her hair into a ponytail. The sounds of the loft comforted her, blanketing her heart.

Pizza sounded good for dinner. She pulled a DiGiorno's from the freezer. Then texted Tim.

Pizza for dinner. You want salad?

Waiting for his response, Charlotte picked up the Blu-ray player remote and surfed to the Pandora station labeled "Oldies."

She took her iPad from her satchel, swung by the fridge for a Diet Coke, and curled up on the sofa to go through e-mail. A new designer had contacted her, requesting a meeting. But her designs were vintage and Charlotte knew without looking they wouldn't fit the Malone & Co. contemporary brand.

As the aroma of baking pizza filled the loft, her stomach rumbled, reminding her she'd skipped lunch. Reminding her Tim had yet to contact her.

Eight o'clock. *Anytime now, Tim.* She peeked at her phone sitting on the sofa next to her. Sometimes the signal didn't reach the loft and she missed a call or text. But Tim's silence was not from a cyberspace hiccup. She *knew* it.

In the four months she'd known him, Charlotte had learned that Tim's afternoons took on a life of their own—client calls, city planning meetings, and consultation opportunities filled the cracks in his schedule. But he always managed a quick text or fast e-mail.

Running late.

Pandora played John Waite's "Missing You." Charlotte eyed the screen. A shiver crept over her scalp. *I ain't missing . . .*

The oven timer buzzed and Charlotte shot off the couch, breaking away from the split moment of rising fear. She snatched up her phone on the way to the kitchen.

T, where are you? I'm eating pizza. Don't promise to save you a piece. She hit Send. Tim loved pizza. The boy lit up at the very word. He'd say the word over and over, teasing and buzzing Charlotte's ear with a snaky "z" hiss.

She took the pizza from the oven, listening for Tim's instant, protesting reply.

But two hours later Charlotte had eaten her pizza, put the leftovers in the fridge, cleaned the kitchen, stacked the wedding invitations on the dining table, scribbled her own guest list on a magnet pad—forty names—put the invitations back in the box, and slipped it under the table.

Where was he and what was he doing? She considered getting angry, but if he was hurt then she'd feel guilty. So she'd just wait and see what he said when he called.

But being delinquent wasn't Tim. He planned and calculated just like Katherine had said. He scheduled his day in fifteen-minute increments. Even the spontaneous meetings that filled his schedule were organized.

At five 'til ten Charlotte surfed her contact list to David and Katherine's number. She took a deep breath before hitting Call and rehearsed what to say. *Hey, I was wondering if Tim was—*

"Charlotte?" The front door eased open.

Thank goodness. Charlotte exhaled and tossed her phone to the table. "Where have you been? I was just about to call David and Katherine. I made pizza—"

From the kitchen, she gazed down the short hall toward the

door. Standing just inside the loft, Tim looked sheepish in his mud-covered racing gear. Giving Charlotte a conciliatory glance, he bent to remove his boots.

"Paul and Artie came over last night after my meeting and—"

"Last night? When I called you said you were tired, wanted to go to bed."

"I was in bed when they showed up with Chase and Rudy." Tim's youngest two brothers were bigger daredevils and fun-lovers than Tim. "Next thing I knew we'd talked Dave into playing hooky and planned a racing road trip."

"Why didn't you call?" Something about his tone, his demeanor, formed a cold rock in her belly.

"I meant to, Char. But it was midnight by the time they left my house. I went into the office at six to get some work done. We left around eleven to drive over to Albertville." He pulled off his racing jersey. Dried mud rained on Charlotte's clean floor. His white t-shirt strained across his chest and his cut, sculpted arms stretched the hem of his sleeves. He motioned to his dirt. "I'll clean it up."

"Shop Vac is in the closet." She motioned to the door beside the fridge. "I still don't understand why you didn't call or text."

Tim motored the hand-vacuum over his mess. "I kept thinking I'd call you, but I never did. You said you had appointments all afternoon so I figured you'd be busy." He shut off the vacuum and returned it to the closet, then stood against the wall, peering mostly at his stocking feet. "I thought we'd be back before dinner."

"It's ten o'clock, Tim. And you do know if I'm busy you can still text me or leave a message."

"Yeah, I know." He angled to see the stove through the dim kitchen light. "Any pizza left?" Tim smiled—slow, shy. Handsome. Winning.

"In the fridge. There's salad in the blue bowl." Charlotte backed away, letting him fend for himself, her own pizza dinner churning in her stomach. It was his way. To win her over so simply. So easily. But not tonight. He had yet to explain himself. "Did you bring the guest list? Maybe we can address some of the invitations. We have an hour or so. Unless you're too tired and need to go to bed." There, got in one barb. Did he know how he hurt her with his silence? Charlotte retreated to her seat at the dining table and stared absently at her iPad.

"No, I'm not too tired." Tim dropped the leftover cold pizza on the plate he took from the cupboard. He took a bite without heating the slices first. "I don't have the list. I'm sorry, Char. I didn't get by Mom's this week."

"Okay, but we have five hundred invitations to address in the next few weeks."

"Can I ask why we're not paying someone to do it?" Tim opened the fridge for a Diet Coke.

"I can't afford it."

"You spent a thousand on a beat-up old trunk, but you can't afford someone to do our invitations? Ever think maybe *I* can afford it? Or *we* can afford it?"

"I'd rather use the money to upgrade the reception food or buy those platinum chains I wanted for the bridesmaids." Since their engagement, Tim spoke in the plural. Us. We. *They* could afford whatever kind of wedding *they* wanted.

But Charlotte struggled, fighting the idea that Tim and the Roses would pay for all of the wedding. *Her* family must pay what they could. Right? Even if *her* family was . . . Charlotte alone.

Now the conversation stalled. Tim walked to the dining table, sitting with a glance at the invitations, then toward the living room.

"Is that it? Your thousand-dollar trunk?"

"That's it." Charlotte reached for his Diet Coke and took a sip. "Think you can do something with it?"

"Maybe." Tim stared at his uneaten pizza. Sitting back with a sigh, he ran his hands through his matted but thick hair. "Charlotte, I forgot about tonight."

"Just . . . forgot? Forgot the invitations? Forgot me? What did you forget, Tim?"

"I didn't forget you." He got up and tore away a paper towel to use as a napkin. "I forgot we wanted to go over the guest list and address the invitations."

"And plan the reception. Figure out the rehearsal dinner, the flowers, the cake, the tuxes. You were planning to do that this week too. Pick out your tuxes. But tomorrow's Thursday already."

"Yeah, I had tuxes on my calendar, but it kept getting pushed to the next day."

In that moment Charlotte *knew*. The ping of revelation resonated and swelled in her chest, drawing her mind and soul to its light. "Tim, what's going on?"

The sound of her own doubt sprang tears from the bottle that Charlotte kept stored in her soul.

"I don't know." He shoved his pizza plate away from him, and Charlotte realized that since he came into the loft, he'd barely looked at her face. Reaching down, he took out one of the invitations from the box. "These are pretty, Char."

"But they're not going anywhere, are they?" When did she really know? Saturday up on the ridge, when the shift in the wind made her look up and stirred her heart with questions?

Tim scooted his chair over to hers. "It's not that I don't love you."

"But you don't want to get married?" She tucked her hands close to her middle and gentled his ring from her finger. When she set it on the table, those darn tears trickled to the corner of her eyes. Tim stared past her shoulder toward the dark window.

"I thought I did." He tried to hold her hand but Charlotte withdrew. "Some of the guys from our local motocross club went up with us today. We were talking about the big race in Florida, making plans to go, when one of the guys looked at me and said, 'Tim, you realize we're talking about the week after June 23. Aren't you getting married that day? Won't you be on your honeymoon?'"

"You forgot your own wedding." Charlotte ran her hand over the cold chill creeping down her arms. Her gaze landed on the trunk and at the moment, she felt an odd kinship to the battered, rejected box. It felt like her only ally in the loft.

"Charlotte, I'm sorry. I don't want to hurt you."

"Katherine was all worried I'd hurt *you*."

"Yeah, Katherine needs to mind her own business." Tim at last peered at her face. "I love you, I do, Charlotte. I'm just not sure I'm ready to get married. Our relationship kind of knocked me off my feet. We moved so fast."

"*We* didn't move fast, Tim, *you* moved fast. Like I was one of your racetracks to conquer."

"That's not fair. I moved fast because I fell in love with you."

"Then what's changed?"

Tim stood and paced toward the living room. "I'm not sure. I wonder if either of us really wants to get married. We haven't done anything to get this wedding together. You don't have a dress. I didn't put the deposit down on Avondale."

Charlotte stared at the ring waiting on the table. "So what now?"

"Postpone? Wait." He gazed at the ring. "Put that back on. We're still engaged."

"Is there someone else?" Charlotte swallowed the fresh rise of tears, staring at her folded fingers in her lap. She made no movement for the ring.

"If there was, would I ask you to put the ring back on? There's no one else except maybe me. My own selfishness. I thought I was ready, but—"

"You're thirty-two, Tim. You're a successful Birmingham architect. If you're not ready, then maybe I'm not the right woman." The sharp accuracy of her own words pierced her heart.

"Am I the right man? Why have you been dragging your feet? Don't brides rush out to buy a gown the moment they get the ring? You own a bridal shop. You have access to the newest, best gowns in the world. But—" He paused to assess her with a tender glance. "Tell me you don't feel like something is out of step with us."

"I guess . . . yeah, maybe." A rebel tear slid down her cheek. "I just thought we were busy, but we'd get around to our wedding. I guess if you were really into me, and marrying me, there'd be no way you'd forget our wedding and honeymoon for a chance to go racing with the boys." Sniffing, she caught a second tear with the back of her hand. "I don't know much about your gender, being raised by Mama and Gert, but I do know this from working at wedding shops since high school: a man will do anything for the woman he loves and is going to marry. Shop on Super Bowl Sunday. Try on ten tuxes even though the first one was just fine. Desert his friends and hobbies, even move across the country. All for love." Charlotte picked up the ring and met Tim in the living room. She pressed it into his palm. "If we're not getting married on June 23, then what's the point of pretending?"

"Charlotte, we're not pretending, we're waiting."

"For what, Tim? For it to feel right? Suddenly? It felt right when you proposed the first time. You can't cancel a wedding but keep the engagement." She'd learned that, too, from working with brides and grooms over the past twelve years. First in the bridal shops of others, then her own. Once the wedding is postponed . . . "If we're not getting married, then we're not engaged."

"I don't want to lose you." Tim regarded the ring, slipping it over his pinky to the first knuckle, then reached for Charlotte, pulling her to him. "You swept me off my feet when we first met."

"Sometimes we don't know what we want until we get it. Then"—Charlotte jerked with the first sob—"it becomes complicated and . . . the brides . . . the dresses . . . the details . . ." Charlotte gave up, tucked her elbows into her ribs and, still leaning against Tim's firm form and sweat-soaked t-shirt, she wept.

She'd sensed this coming, a shift, a change. *This* was what drove her to the ridge Saturday morning. The feeling of *is this really what I want?* It had been coming—if not from Tim, then from herself. But oh, how she hated endings. How she hated good-byes.

Tim stroked her hair, not saying a word, clearing his throat, throttling the rumble in his chest.

"I'm sorry, Char." He cradled and caressed her, rocking slowly side to side, his own tears catching on his whispers. "Shh, it'll be all right."

She wrapped her arms around him and molded against him, his tenderness throttling her sorrow. He might be breaking up with her, but at the moment, he was her best friend, her quiet strength.

When she stepped out of his arms, wiping her face, she kept her shoulder toward him and faced the hall toward her room. "It's easier if you just go, Tim."

Thank goodness they'd held to their convictions and not slept together. How much more difficult this would've been. How cold his side of the bed would've been tonight. "You won't mind seeing yourself out."

"Charlotte?"

"Bye, Tim." In her room Charlotte shut the door and dove onto her bed, burying her head under the pillows, her chest swelling with a ravenous storm of sobs. She'd survived Mama's death. She'd survived being raised by grumpy, yet kind ole Gert. She'd survived celebrating Christmases and birthdays alone. How could she not survive this petty little thing? A broken engagement? Oh, she'd survive tonight, all right. Surely she would. As long as she didn't hear the *click* of the door closing behind Tim as he left.

Chapter Six

Emily

*I*n the flickering gaslight Emily poured the letters from the cedar box onto her bed. There were dozens of them, all addressed in Daniel's smooth, even script.

Why would Father hide them from her? It was so unlike him. Emily sorted the letters by postmark, from April to August, counting forty in all.

Her engagement ring caught on her bedcover as she crawled to the center and propped against her pillows.

Phillip's ring on her left hand, so rich and exquisite, paled for a moment in comparison to the pile of letters in her right. Words and thoughts from Daniel's heart, written in his own hand, seemed more rare than any stone carved from coal.

Emily batted the sleep from her eyes and the weariness from her heart. Such a day. The suffragette meeting, then seeing Phillip in the city, sitting his carriage, warmed by his amorous kisses.

Then running home and into Daniel. Oh, dear Daniel. The memory of his touch made Emily's pulse throb in her veins.

And Phillip's proposal. Tonight of all nights. She'd expected it soon, maybe at the Woodward end-of-summer lawn party on Labor Day weekend.

Emily sank into her pillows and closed her eyes. She had half a mind to march down the hall to Father and Mother's door and demand Father's reason for keeping Daniel from her.

But she knew better. Father never responded to temper tantrums, especially at one thirty in the morning. He'd only tell her to behave herself, go to bed, and be ready to apologize in the morning, and if he felt the need, he might discuss the issue.

Why concern herself with Father now? She had Daniel's letters. Emily roused herself and took the first letter from the pile. She filed the remainder in the box.

April 16, 1912

Dearest Emily,

It's late and I need to get some shut-eye, but I couldn't go to sleep without writing you.

I said prayers for you, and me, tonight. I've only been gone a few days, but I've been thinking a lot about you and any future we may have together should the good Lord so smile on me.

Believe me when I say I have you on my mind every day, even though I'm playing ball and seeming to have a good time with the fellas. I miss you terribly, Em.

Playing ball is a lot of work for a few bucks, if you can imagine. Ole Moley works us hard. If we're not playing, we're practicing. He's called for an early practice in the morning before we travel.

Guess I can't blame the guy. Scully pitched a no-hitter against the Atlanta Crackers tonight. Moley said we must keep the winning fires stoked.

We sleep in run-down motels and even on the ball fields. It rained a week straight and we had to sleep in the jitney. Moley found a nice lady to rent us a room for a hot bath after we'd only washed in a pail for ten days. Don't have to tell you how ripe we all smelt.

What other news can I share? Sure wish I could hear from you so I could talk about your world a bit. Milton's girlfriend wrote that she was engaged to another man. Poor worm. He moped around pretty good until we got to the ballpark and several pretties were waiting at the ticket booth. He forgot his old gal right quick.

But don't worry, Emily, my eyes are only for you. Say, when you write me, can you send along a new photograph? The one I had of you was destroyed when the jitney sank in a mud hole up to the chassis and we had to dig the old girl out. The roads in Tennessee aren't as good as the slag roads in Birmingham.

But you already know that, since your father financed the limestone mine that makes the slag.

My birthday was yesterday. Did you remember? I hope you sent me a birthday greeting on the wind. I craved my mama's cake. I remember the last one she made for my sixteenth birthday, right before she died.

I'd say more if I knew what you were doing these days. Say hello to the folks there for me.

Remember the first night we met in the campus library? My buddies were cutting up, not paying any mind to the rules, talking mischief. You shot fire at us with your dark eyes. I said to my roommate as we walked back to our dorm, "I'm going to marry that girl." I meant it. I'll spend all my life making you happy. If you want me.

One final note, some of the boys and I attended church on Sunday. The preacher was a bit heavy on the hellfire and brimstone, but it got to Scully. He ran down to the altar when the call was made. For me, I just remembered why I love Him. And you.

All my love and affection,

Daniel

Emily folded the letter back into the envelope, not sure what or how to feel. Schoolboy folderol, most of it. Spend his life making her happy. Goodness. What a childish declaration. Daniel should know better since he's a grown man.

Stuffing the letter back in the box, Emily slammed the lid shut, her engagement ring pinging against the wood, and shoved the box under her bed, way back, against the wall.

She was engaged. Why, she was practically stepping out on her intended, reading another man's love letters. How could she be so untrue to Phillip mere hours after accepting his ring?

Emily readied for bed, then sank to her knees, where she said her prayers every night. But instead of closing her eyes, she reached under the mattress for the leather diary where she poured out her heart to Daniel when he first left with the Barons.

April 30, 1912

Dear Daniel,

I think of you, wondering where you are, praying you are well and safe. I wish you'd write to me. I miss you terribly. Who can make me laugh when I'm feeling blue? Father tries, but I'm immune to his old stories now. They only tickle Mother's funny bone.

Yesterday, Mother and I shopped downtown, then came home to work the garden with Molly. It was a glorious day and brought to mind our walks on the campus quad.

Emily slammed the diary closed. The rest of the entry was merely pouring out her heart to herself, trying to make sense of her feelings. When Daniel left she knew she loved him, but in the passing weeks, she'd started to doubt.

Perhaps it was divine that he departed, choosing baseball over her. Phillip called on her a few weeks later and invited her to attend the Black and White Ball.

The invitation seemed more than fortuitous. It appeared divine, indeed.

Shoving her book back to its hiding place, Emily burrowed under her coverlet and sank deep into the feathery mattress, stretching her legs against the clean sheets.

A spark of ire toward Father made her bolt up in bed. Emily shoved her hair away from her face and hammered the quilt with her fist. How different this night might be if she *had* received Daniel's letters. She plopped back down into her pillows and reached for the bedside lamp. Darkness rose in the room as the light faded.

She was engaged. And she'd be true to Phillip with her word *and* her heart.

Charlotte

Charlotte balanced Starbucks lattes in her hand along with a bag of pastries as she unlocked the shop's back door, crossing through the old utility room to the kitchen. She set breakfast on the kitchenette table, shook her arm awake, and went back to her blue Cabrio for the box of unused invitations.

"Dix?" It was five minutes 'til opening, and the lights were on and the music played. Bach this morning and his sweet tones fitting for violins. "Dixie? I brought coffee. And food."

Charlotte angled into the shop, listening for the thunder of her friend's footsteps. But silence answered. *Hmm*, she must be upstairs.

Back in the kitchen, Charlotte dropped the invitations to the kitchen floor and reached for her latte. She had plans for those invites. Dumpster plans. But first, her breakfast.

She had a new lease on life. Yes, she did. Starting over could be good, a chance to shake things up, get focused. Maybe attend a bridal show in New York or L.A. Even better? Paris. She'd planned on a Paris trip this year until Tim swept her off her feet.

Bray-Lindsay had extended her a standing invitation and she had yet to accept.

After Tim left and Charlotte wept her soul raw, she'd managed a midnight call to Dixie, begging her to open the shop in the morning even though it was her day to come in late. "I'm not feeling well. I think I'll sleep in."

But Charlotte didn't sleep much.

"Dixie, hey, where are you?" Charlotte walked toward the sales counter, checking the stairs and second-floor landing. The cash register was up and ready. But locked. Good. "Are you upstairs?" Charlotte stooped by the main display gown to perfect the flow of the chapel train.

"Charlotte, you're here." Dixie came around the corner, from the direction of the reveal salon. She grabbed Charlotte's hand and pulled her along. "Close your eyes."

"And run into the wall? No thanks. What's going on? I brought lattes and pastries."

"Okay, great, but first, close your eyes."

Charlotte skidded along with Dixie, her knees trembling. The high-octane adrenaline of "taking her life back" that fueled her morning shower and Starbucks drive-through was evaporating. And the depleting fumes of hope, of tomorrow being another day, ran thin. She'd fooled herself into believing this was a fresh new day. Forget Tim Rose. Tim who?

No, today gripped her heart with a hard, sad fist. *It's over. Love done gone.* "Dix, really, I'm not in the mood." She paused at the reveal salon door. "Whatever you're up to, I'm not doing it."

Though Charlotte crawled out of bed early, turned on a low lamp, filled a tumbler with Diet Coke, and read John 15.

Apart from me, you can do nothing.

She could do anything if she believed.

"You're going to love this," Dixie said. "You know how you introduced Kristin to her dress. Well, after five years of standing under your genius shadow, your fairy dust fell on me, and I've found *the* perfect gown for you."

"No, Dix, really, I can't."

"You promised me. This week. And I put a call into that man of yours and left a message I'd be there at his office around three with a half-dozen tuxes for him and David to try. Ha! You have to get up pretty early to keep ole Dixie down. Hey, was that a song? Anyway, there's more than one way to tux a groom and I found it." Dixie backed through the salon door, shoving it open, pulling Charlotte with her. "Keep those baby blues closed, Charlotte."

No, no, no. "Dixie, wait, listen to me—"

"Stop protesting. Hold on, let me get you into position." Dixie shifted Charlotte a little to the right, squaring her shoulders. "Open your eyes." Dixie swooped in front of her, arms high and wide. "Ta-da."

On the reveal stage was a simple satin gown with an Italian-lace band at the waist, trimmed in pearls. The elbow-length sleeves touched the top of long white gloves. Tulle and crinoline held out the Cinderella skirt that swept into a shimmering cathedral train.

"Oh, Dixie, it is beautiful." Charlotte battled tears for a second, then gave up. The lights danced over the pristine satin and caught the incandescence of the pearls. If she were getting married, indeed Dixie had found Charlotte's dress.

"I know June isn't a month for gloves, but I thought they completed the look. Do you like it, really? Cap sleeves aren't *in* style, per se, but this dress just speaks to me. Does it you? I tell you, I don't know how you reach into a woman's heart and pull out the perfect gown for her. But you do. I know you better than I know anyone other than Dr. Hotstuff, but I struggled to project your essence into this gown. Well?" Dixie exhaled, eyes wide.

"I told you, my gift is from God." Charlotte's voice broke, but she recovered as Dixie stepped toward her.

"Do you love it? I do. Come on, boss, tell me, how'd I do?"

"Excellent, you did excellent. It's . . . perfect. But please put it back on the rack. I won't be wearing it." Charlotte turned to leave.

"What? Charlotte, come on, this dress has your name on it. See, right there in the pearly light . . . *Charlotte Malone*. Give me one good reason why you can't get married in this dress."

"Because, Dix, I'm not getting married." She held up her bare ring hand. "Please, put it away."

"Charlotte, good grief, what happened?" Dixie trailed Charlotte out of the room. "You're not getting married? Did you break up with him?"

"No, actually, he broke up with me." Charlotte rounded the shop's flared staircase, heading for the kitchen and the comfort of her latte and coffee cake. "He said he wanted to postpone the wedding for a while. I said we get married or we break up." She shrugged. "So, yeah, I guess I did. But he didn't fight me . . ."

"Oh, dear friend, I'm . . . I'm so sorry. I can't believe it. Did he say why he wanted to wait?" Dixie's soft tone sympathized with Charlotte's feelings. "This makes no sense, no sense at all. He just doesn't feel ready? Everyone gets cold feet. I had icicles for toes before Hotstuff and I got married. So what? Tim fell head over heels in love and kept falling until he tumbled right on out? I don't get it." Dixie waved off the pastry Charlotte offered.

Spoken in those terms, it didn't make sense. But, in the deep dark of her heart, something felt right about this. And that, in and of itself, felt wrong. Charlotte sat at the kitchenette and took a small bite of her coffee cake, weary from her boomerang emotions. The pastry looked so good when she was in Starbucks. But at the moment, the sweet bread tasted like cardboard.

"Are you okay, Charlotte?" Dixie pressed Charlotte's arm and pulled a chair up beside her. "I'm so sorry this is happening."

"I didn't sleep well." Charlotte tossed her breakfast to the napkin on the table. "I woke up and read my Bible, but Jesus doesn't say much on how to tell if a guy is the right one. I wanted Tim to be the one, Dix. Maybe for all the wrong reasons." Since it was Dixie, Charlotte let her tears fall. "He's gorgeous, at least to me. He's fun and smart, he makes me laugh. From the moment I met him, I forgot myself and I'd talk without censoring every word, then later wonder if I made a fool of myself. When he called the first time to ask me to dinner, I believed there was something divine about the whole thing because I'm not that pretty and I'm definitely not that good of a flirt."

"Are you kidding me? You're stunning. And charming. Who needs to flirt when they're as smart as you? Tim's darn lucky you gave him the time of day." Dixie sat back. "Snob. That's what he is, a snob."

"I was the lucky one. He's not a snob, Dixie. He's honest. Would you have wanted Jared to marry you if he had any reservations?"

"No, I guess not." Dixie sighed, sitting back, sleeking her hand down the length of her ponytail. "This makes me sad."

"Yeah, but maybe Tim's right." Charlotte's weak smile trembled. "We moved too fast."

"Well, he can blame himself for that, Charlotte. Don't you take that on. Do you think that's why you never picked a dress? You knew, somehow?"

"Who knows." Charlotte rested her head against the wall,

swallowing the swell of emotion in her throat, wanting this day to be years behind her. The harsh overhead light of the kitchen made her feel cold and exposed. "It's just that when it was my turn to be the bride, I didn't know how to make myself ready. In the back of my mind, I thought the dress, the day, the pieces of the wedding would just fall into place. That I'd *know* it was right."

"But you didn't know, did you?"

"I used to have this recurring dream about my wedding. It started right after high school and my 'one true love'"—Charlotte air-quoted the phrase—"broke up with me. In the dream, I'm walking down the aisle toward my groom. I'm alone because I don't have anyone to walk me down the aisle. No father, brother, uncles."

"The Roses are nothing but men."

"Yeah, I know." Charlotte sat forward, rubbing her fingers over her eyes. She'd not bothered with makeup today. Just a swipe of concealer and a brush of powder. "When Tim told me he had four brothers, I literally laid awake that night begging God, 'Teach me about men.'" She laughed low. "I was so afraid I'd regard them like caged lions at the zoo. But I wanted to do the guy's-girl thing and play kickball—"

"Football."

"Whatever."

"Back to the dream. What happened as you walked down the aisle?"

"I'd spin around and run out of the church." Charlotte gazed at the wall, picturing Tim and his brothers. A man's man each and every one, but men who accepted her like a sister. "Usually somewhere between the sanctuary doors and the altar, I'd run out, yelling, 'Nooooo!'" Charlotte tore at the edge of her napkin. "I woke up from that dream two or three times a year. Until—"

"Maybe it's a sign you're not supposed to marry Tim."

"—I met Tim." Charlotte sighed, her gaze on the latte, then on Dixie.

"Oh."

"Yeah, 'Oh.'" Charlotte stood, wrapping up the coffee cake. "Now what? How will I know Mr. Right?"

Dixie dropped to her knees and drew Charlotte into her embrace. "Faith, girl, faith. At the end of the day, that's all we have."

Charlotte rested her cheek against her friend's firm shoulder, releasing the last of her morning tears. Then she sat back, reached for a napkin, and wiped her face. "Let's get to work, Dixie." Charlotte stood, straightening her suit, brushing her hair away from her face. "Today is the first day of the rest of my life."

Chapter Seven

Emily

In all of Birmingham, Mrs. Caruthers was the most renowned dressmaker. Mother made an appointment with her the morning after Phillip proposed. And now, eight days later, Emily walked into her rich quarters in the Loveman's of Alabama downtown department store.

A green gilded wallpaper covered the fitting-room walls and a Persian rug brightened the dull, scarred hardwood. A midmorning light fell over the shiny horsehair settee and sounds from the street below bounced off the closed windowpanes.

A clanging trolley drew Emily to the window. Down on 19th Street, downtown Birmingham hustled and bustled past the broad stone department store. Emily loved the city and came down from Highland whenever she could. Once, she suggested taking a position at Father's exchange, but he promptly rebuked her.

"You're a lady of society," Mother had chimed in. "You employ others. You, yourself, are not employed."

"Then why send me to college only to have me squander my time at home? I'm not too much of a lady to kneel in the dirt and plant a garden." She'd shot an eyeful at Mother, who insisted Emily learn to garden.

"You garden for your family," Father had said with a soft smack of his palm against the table. "You will not go to the city and punch a time clock, working for wages beneath your training and station."

So Emily sat at home, college educated but trained for nothing, and waited. With Daniel gone and her friends either married or touring Europe, boredom drove her to the brink.

When Molly invited Emily to a suffrage meeting, she jumped at the offer. Something to do. Then Phillip called on her and her desperate heart yielded.

Emily's engagement ring tapped against the glass as she angled against the window to see farther down the bustling avenue. Now she was getting married and she'd have a home of her own and be able to determine her own mind as Mrs. Phillip Saltonstall.

She'd most likely have an allowance at her disposal to give to whatever projects she deemed worthy. To shop whenever and wherever she wanted, the mistress of her own manor.

"Mercy, it's warm in here." Mother fanned herself with her gloves, then removed the pins from her hat.

Emily set her reticule and parasol on the table just inside the door. "I'll see if I can open the window, Mother."

"Mercy, no. There are people walking the streets. Do you want them to see you?"

"If it means I won't faint from heat, then yes." Emily shoved open the window and a broad gust filled the room. Thick and muggy, the outside air was pungent with city fragrances, tinted with the gray exhaust of the mills and mines. But Charlotte preferred it to the hot, stale air of Mrs. Caruthers's workroom.

"Mercy." Mother pinched her nose. "We either faint of heat in here or inhale the stench of mines."

"It's the smell of life, Mother." Emily drew deep. "Gasoline, horses, the sweat of men, the perfume of women." She glanced toward the narrow door through which the dressmaker had disappeared, turned to the window, and—careful of the dust—leaned over the sill.

A Model T driver spirited his rig ahead of a slow-moving, horse-drawn delivery cart. "Mother, let's go to Newman's for lunch."

"Not today, I had Molly slice the roast beef—" Mother paused when Emily sighed. Much too loud, but it was too late to retrieve. "Well, all right, it is your wedding dress day." She gripped Emily's arm. "Don't hang out the window like a dance hall girl. Emily dear, just so you know." Mother's voice warbled and her eyes watered. "Father and I are very proud of you. He was practically bursting his buttons the day after Phillip asked for your hand. He ordered fresh cigars to pass out at the club. You've grown into one of the most beautiful girls in Birmingham. You're smart and talented, edu-cated—which I insisted on—and you have a solid, sensible head on your shoulders. You will make Phillip an outstanding man in the community. He's done well to choose you."

Emily came away from the window. Maybe now was the time to ask Mother the question brewing in her heart ever since Phillip proposed. "Mother, did you love Father when you married him?"

"Oh my, I believed your father made the cotton grow in the spring, I did. He was so handsome and smart, told the best stories that made us all laugh, and was the idol of all the girls in our class."

"Grandmother and Grandfather were happy with him?"

"Your grandfather thought him a fool." Mother made a face mimicking Grandfather's expression and affected a deep voice. "'The boy's full of nonsense, Maggie. He's all talk. What's this about start-ing an exchange? He'll lose his shirt, I tell you, lose it for sure.'" Mother laughed with an arch of her brow. "Papa is singing a different tune now."

"No doubt he is, especially after Father bought him a touring car for his birthday." Emily gazed out the window again, watching the life on the street, letting her thoughts drift.

She loved Phillip. Certainly she did or why would she let him caress and kiss her the way he did?

"Where is that Mrs. Caruthers?" Mother paced past the narrow, interior door. "Did she set sail to Paris for the fabric?"

Mother had tried in recent years to book Mrs. Caruthers for special gowns but was always denied. Only since the Saltonstall engagement did Mother *rate* an audience with the queen of seams. It didn't sit well with Emily, but if having Mrs. Caruthers design her trousseau and wedding attire made Mother happy, then it made Emily happy.

"Sit, Mother, don't worry. She'll be along." She needed Mother to settle down so she could process the nagging feeling caught in her chest.

Unlike Mother, Emily knew Phillip didn't make cotton grow. Nor did he make her laugh with his zany stories—at least not often. Not even when they were in grammar school together. However, he did make her shiver right down to her bones when he stroked his hand down the length of her neck.

Emily peeked over her shoulder at Mother, who'd taken a rest on the settee. Did Father make Mother's skin quiver with desire? Oh mercy . . . Emily shut her eyes and shook the very idea from her head. Even if she had the courage and brashness to ask Mother, she did not want to hear the answer.

Angling out the window, Emily drew in a deep, cleansing breath. Yes, she loved Phillip. She must.

On the corner of 3rd Avenue, Emily caught sight of a familiar figure. Tall, lean, wearing a telltale burgundy waistcoat and spats. Phillip. Her heart hopscotched. Like Father, Phillip was handsome and smart, well respected in the city, and most assuredly the desire of all the girls in their circle.

She stretched farther out the window and waved. "Phillip. Phillip

Saltonstall. Man in the spats. Phillip! You're the only man who wears them in the day."

A hand yanked Emily back inside. "Emily Lee Canton, stop that yelling at once. Now you *are* behaving like a dance hall girl. Stars above, a proper gentlewoman does not lean out fourth-floor windows and yell like an uncouth at proper gentlemen. Especially a man of Phillip's reputation and one who is her fiancé. What on earth?" Mother fidgeted with her cotton gloves, drawing them through her hand over and over.

"Mother, it's Phillip, the man I'm going to marry. Why can't I yell out the window to him?" After all, hadn't she just discovered her true affections? Why not tell the world? Emily shoved the window higher still. "My dear, Phillip, I'm up here—"

But Emily's words lighted on her tongue and slipped back down her throat, nearly choking her as her eyes beheld the scene below.

A slender reed of a woman with pale skin and pale hair, wearing a royal-blue dress and carrying a matching parasol, leaned into Phillip as he wrapped his arms about her, bending his lips to her . . . neck.

Emily gasped, moving back inside with a quick jerk, banging her head against the window frame. She cried out, smacking her hand against the wound, squeezing her eyes shut, but seeing the woman's hair glinting in the sun.

"Are you all right?" Mother asked, her attention on the narrow, closed door. "I've a mind to go in there and see what's taking Mrs. Caruthers so long. This is unthinkable."

What was Phillip doing down there? A woman in his embrace, laughing so gay and carefree? In public no less. The blood filling Emily's cheeks burned. Had he no decency? No respect? Too late, a moan escaped her chest.

"Emily, what is it?" Mother angled to see out the window.

"Nothing, Mother, a horse threw a shoe is all. You've seen it a dozen times."

"But you moaned."

"The gelding tripped, I thought—" What? What did she think? Surely she must be imagining things, so far above the ground. She couldn't be seeing correctly. Other men wore burgundy waistcoats and spats. On a week day. Surely Phillip was not the only one.

With another sly glance, Emily captured the end of the embrace. The woman pulled away, laughing, popping Phillip's arm with her umbrella. Phillip reached for her as she headed to the corner, stepping off 19th to cross 3rd.

Emily watched Phillip watching *her* until she vanished in the shadows.

"Here we are, Mrs. Canton. Pardon me for the delay, honey pie, but my assistant failed to unpack all of this lovely fabric. I ordered it from Paris six months ago, quite sure I'd have a special wedding coming up soon. And sure enough, here I do. The lovely Emily Canton. Come away from that window, deary, you'll spoil your beautiful skin." Mrs. Caruthers's arms were laden with bolts of rich, shimmering satin. "I have silk, too, but I do think satin makes such a fine wedding gown. Have you chosen your wedding date?"

"We're considering March," Mother said with a proud smile. Emily's stomach turned. She'd never seen Mother pander to anyone and here she was doing it to Mrs. Caruthers. "Emily, look at this lace. What do you think, darling?"

"I think—" *I think I just saw another woman in my fiancé's arms.* With another look out the window, Emily caught Phillip striding up 19th in the direction of the Saltonstall building. He raised his hat at a trio of gentlemen and paused to converse, bending backward with laughter.

How jovial the man was after holding that twig of a woman with a ghostly complexion.

"March is a lovely time for weddings. Not too warm, not too cold." Mrs. Caruthers and Mother conversed as if everything were right and wonderful in the world. "Gives me plenty of time for dressmaking. How many bridesmaids? Of course, your dress as well, Mrs. Canton, and your mother's, perhaps? And the trousseau."

"Emily," Mother called, "what is so interesting out that window? Please do tear yourself away from your curiosities and tell Mrs. Caruthers what you think of this fabric. Have you thought of bridesmaids? Mrs. Caruthers, this satin is buttery soft."

Emily turned to see Mother smoothing her fingers over a creamy material. "It's beautiful," she said with a glance. "So pure and white."

She went back to the window. The afternoon sat on its celestial perch unaware that a sliver of Emily's heart had chipped away. She was pure. But was Phillip? Her heart beat at the memory of his skilled touch.

"I do believe this shade is perfect for your skin. Please, dear, over here." Mrs. Caruthers guided Emily to the stool in the middle of the room and had her step up. Then she held a corner of the satin to Emily's cheek. "Yes, quite lovely. Shall we decide on a design? I have Goody's books over here."

Mother held up pages while Emily stood for Mrs. Caruthers's measurements.

"You're a full-figured one, aren't you, Emily?" Mrs. Caruthers draped the measuring tape around her neck. "Start drawing your corset tighter, dear, and we might be able to have your waist at a perfect eighteen by your wedding."

"Twenty-two is fine with me. I prefer eating. And breathing."

"Eating?" Mrs. Caruthers arched her brow. "It's quite evident."

Emily shot her mother a look.

"We'll discuss it, Mrs. Caruthers. Thank you for your concern."

Concern? Mother could be too kind. Emily refused to cut off her air or her stomach, for the sake her figure. Northern girls might want to eat like birds, but Southern girls were robust and hearty. Emily glanced wistfully at the window. The woman she'd seen with Phillip was slender, her petite figure molded by her corset.

"The style is for a thin bride." Mrs. Caruthers surveyed Charlotte over her glasses. "I'd think you'd take my opinion on that considering whom you are marrying, Miss Canton."

"I'd prefer you keep your opinions to yourself." Emily stepped off her stool, feeling as if she might faint. "Mother, please—"

"Emily Canton, you know full well Mrs. Caruthers is merely advising you. It's why we've retained her excellent services." Mother pandered quite well. "She's designed gowns for Birmingham's most noted families. Now, please, find your good humor and see what design suits you." Mother tapped a picture in the book. "This style would be lovely on you."

Emily leaned to see. The gown was ostentatious. And the folds and pleats in the back looked a bit too much like the gown the willowy woman in the street was wearing.

"It's too ghastly and heavy. I'll suffocate wearing that much material. Please, keep my gown simple, Mrs. Caruthers." Emily just wanted to go home, hop on one of Father's mares, and race up to Red Mountain to clear her head, think, lift her heart to God's.

Then, perhaps when Phillip came to dinner, she'd find the courage to speak to him about what she'd witnessed today. Though, so far since their engagement, little communication had passed between them using words. Mostly he spoke with impassioned kisses and intimate intonations.

Well, tonight she'd sit on the other side of the parlor, away from his reach. Perhaps suggest a game of cribbage or dominoes.

In the light of day, Emily blushed at what certainly must be the main issue on Phillip's mind. Their wedding night. But if she'd learned anything from meeting up with Daniel last week, it was to get her feelings out in the open.

"What shall we do to secure your services, Mrs. Caruthers?" Mother faced the dressmaker with her chin high, her shoulders square.

"I'll write up a work order, Mrs. Canton. You pay half as the deposit. I'll need Emily to decide on a gown pattern and how many bridesmaids as soon as possible. Of course, she'll need to choose a pattern for their dresses as well. We'll also need to start sewing on her trousseau right away. I have a standard offering of gowns and lingerie that I think Miss Canton will find suitable."

"Certainly. How generous. Do you have a brochure in case Mr. Canton and I want to add to Emily's trousseau?"

"I do indeed. Take the Goody's book for the evening and make your choices. I'll expect your deposit by the end of the week. As you know, I'm quite in demand."

Emily didn't care for Mrs. Caruthers speaking down to Mother. After all, Father with his exchange company was fast becoming one of the most prominent men in Birmingham, perhaps even all of Alabama.

"Only one dressmaker in this city compares to me, but I'll never have to worry about her infringing on my business. She's quite at the disadvantage."

"How so?" Emily stepped between Mother and Mrs. Caruthers. "Tell us her name and we'll decide for ourselves."

"Emily, don't insult Mrs. Caruthers. I'm so sorry, I don't know what's gotten into her today." Mother shot Emily a dark glance. The one that sent her running in terror as a girl.

"I'll tell you her name. No sweat off my nose if you choose her.

But I can tell you she's not for you." Mrs. Caruthers sat at her desk, her broad hips spilling over the side of the chair, her skirt hem piling on the carpet. "Taffy Hayes is her name. A colored woman over on 5th Avenue. Rents a workroom from Mr. Gaston's hotel. I've used her from time to time for piecework. But you won't be wanting a colored woman handling your pretty white wedding dress."

"What difference does it make if she's colored?" Emily picked up her reticule and parasol from the table. "I'm famished, Mother. Let's dine. Fatten me up a bit more."

"Emily, please—"

"Mrs. Caruthers, I'll not be needing a wedding dress or anything from you." Emily stabbed the air with her parasol.

"Now see here, Miss Canton. Did you hear what I said? Taffy is colored."

"I heard you. Come, Mother." Emily's heels clattered against the thick wooden stairs. As she descended, Mother's crisp whispers with Mrs. Caruthers echoed in the stairwell.

She might not be able to do anything about Phillip and *her* at the moment, but she could do something about Mrs. Caruthers.

Outside on the street, in the sunshine, Emily gulped in free, unprejudiced air. Since she was a girl, she never understood the division of black and white. She heard the rules, the reasons, and the whys, but when she opened her Bible and talked to God, none of man's wisdom made sense.

"You shouldn't be so forthcoming with your thoughts, Emily. I'll have to smooth things over with Mrs. Caruthers, but I don't think real damage has been done." Mother sighed, a sure sign of disapproval. Emily looked sideways at her.

"My thoughts. Did you hear what she said about the other dressmaker? The damage has been done by Mrs. Caruthers, not me, Mother. I'm twenty-two, a college graduate, and engaged. In six months I'll have a home of my own. I am of age to make my own decisions."

"Lower your voice." Mother focused on fitting her gloves properly on her fingers. "Newman's for lunch, then?" When it was clear to cross the lane, exactly where Phillip's *friend* had crossed, Mother looped her arm through Emily's.

"Now you listen to me." Mother spoke low in Emily's ear as they walked. "I understand and appreciate your passion for wanting to make your own way. I understand your heart for the underprivileged and the needy. Your father and I make large contributions to causes all over the city. But you'll not insult Mrs. Caruthers and ruin our reputation. Your father has worked too hard. Until another white seamstress of her caliber comes to town, you'll be doing a good bit of business with her, as you'll be a Saltonstall. And frankly, I'd like to keep her affections for me also. I, too, want to use her services. That won't happen if you reject her for *any* reason. Don't you know the woman has the mouth of a steam locomotive? Why, half of Loveman's salesgirls probably know of your exchange with her just now. What if she tells folks you prefer coloreds?"

"She's arrogant and rude. I don't care to do business with her." Emily turned Mother toward Newman's. "I didn't say one word that would disgrace you or Father. Or the Saltonstalls."

"Your implications, along with the hammer of your footsteps down the stairs, spoke louder than any words, Emily. What have I taught you about wooden swearing?"

"Then I apologize to you, Mother. But that woman is not making my wedding dress."

Mother stopped, pulling Emily to a halt with her. The flow of pedestrians parted around them. "You draw your lines in the sand after you're married, my girl. That will be between you and Phillip, God help him, but as long as your father is paying for this wedding, you will wear a gown designed and sewn by Mrs. Caruthers."

"Designed? She's copying Goody's patterns. She's a fraud."

"Your gown maker will be in all the papers and society columns from here to Atlanta and clear down to New Orleans and Miami. No doubt up to Philadelphia where the Saltonstalls hail from." Mother jerked her hand to her head. "Mercy me, I forgot my hat, Emily. How could you let me forget my hat? You run on, I'll meet you at Newman's. Order me a corned beef sandwich with a cold glass of milk if you get seated right away."

"What if they only have warm milk, Mother?" Emily teased with a sigh, forcing a smile at Mother. She didn't like arguing with her. Mother could be her best advocate.

"There, dear girl. See, smiling takes away anger." Mother placed her gloved hand against Emily's cheek before turning back to Loveman's. "Everything will be all right, Emily. You'll see."

Daniel

Daniel saw Emily go into Newman's as he exited the barbershop, settling his new brown trilby with the silk band—quite nice for a former ballplayer—on his newly cut and slicked-back hair. The glint of the sun on Emily's dark head as she passed between downtown Birmingham buildings reminded him of the coal coming out of Red Mountain—rich and sparkling.

At the street corner of 19th he hesitated, wondering how long she'd been in town. Wondering if she'd seen Phillip—if by chance she'd witnessed what he'd witnessed an hour ago. Pray God she did not.

Suddenly the street cleared. The trolley passed. The motorcars and horse-drawn buggies were out of sight. The air turned strangely silent. Daniel inhaled, stepped off the curb, and scurried to the other side of the wide thoroughfare.

Emily. She had a way of drawing him off course. Making him switch up his destiny when he had in mind where he was going and what he was doing.

First, baseball. Now the men's department at Loveman's. Devil may care. New trousers would have to wait.

He ducked into Newman's, hanging back, hiding in the baritone hum of men lunching at the counter. The booths along one wall were stuffed with womenfolk, vibrant with their plume-trimmed hats and high voices.

Daniel eased down the center aisle, eyes darting over the hats, trying to gain glimpses of their faces. Emily came in alone, or so he believed. Ah, there, in the back, with her head bent over the menu. A harried waiter made a quick stop at her table. She looked up, smiled, and uttered a few words. The waiter nodded and marched toward the kitchen doors, a tub of dirty dishes in his hands.

"Good afternoon." Daniel slid into the booth across from Emily.

Her brown eyes rested on his face. "Daniel."

"You were expecting someone else?" He smiled, but not relaxed or at ease, not charming as he intended. His voice even wavered a smidge.

"Mother forgot her hat at Loveman's. She will be here momentarily."

"How are you?" Daniel scooted his hands across the table toward hers, wanting to take hold, but the cool light in her eyes forced him back. Instead, he twirled his trilby between his hands.

"I'm well. And you?" Emily lifted her menu, reading, and if he didn't know better, hiding. "Have you been to the barber?"

"How'd you know?"

"You smell of flower water. Father and Phillip smell the same when they return from there." She set her menu on the side of the table, then tucked her hands in her lap. "I see you've tamed your curls."

"I don't have a gal to mess them up." He removed his hat, as he should've done when he entered. "I read in the paper you're engaged to Saltonstall."

"You sound surprised. I told you I would be."

"Then I'm happy if you're happy." Was she? By her composure, he couldn't tell. He attempted to read her eyes, but she wouldn't give him one of her clear, direct gazes. Blazes, he hated the wall between them.

From the moment he said hello to her in the college library, there'd been a camaraderie between them. As if the marching music in their souls tapped out the same rhythm. But during his five-month absence, she'd changed her tune.

"I'm quite delirious." She dusted her hands over the table, acting like a prim prude. "With happiness that is."

"I don't believe you." There, straight and to the point. Then her ring caught his eye. Daniel sat back with a whistle. "He dropped a fancy penny on that thing."

"He purchased it in Paris last fall."

"Did he now? Certainly he didn't have you in mind, because last fall you were strolling the quad with me."

"What a mean, selfish thing to say, Daniel Ludlow. He bought the ring for his intended. He found one he adored and knew that sooner or later, he'd find the woman to match it." The waiter set a lemonade on the table. "Isn't it time for you to be moving on?" Emily peered toward the bright front of the diner. "Mother will be along."

Daniel halted the waiter and motioned to Emily's glass. "I'll have what she's having."

"So." She sighed as if resigned to keep his company. "You'll be starting your teaching position soon."

"Yes, as a matter of fact. Please keep your alma mater in mind, Em. Education needs benefactors."

"I'm sure Phillip will be most generous to the institute."

"Phillip? Or you?" He grinned. *Come on, Em, give it up. Show me your gorgeous smile.* "You know what they say, men earn it, women spend it. That's the beef with some of my friends and the women's suffrage. Why give women the right to vote, to have a say in the taxes and politics, when the men are the ones out there doing all the work?"

"Such a small, manlike notion. Women work plenty." Emily came to life, squaring her shoulders, lifting her chin, charging up the familiar spark in her eyes. Daniel used to love to bait and debate her. "For no wage at all. Cooking, cleaning, and ironing a man's clothes, bearing his children. The men in the Sloss or Saltonstall furnaces would fall to their knees whimpering at the first labor pain. What price shall we put on labor and birth, *hmm*? What of the unmarried woman? The widow? Should they not have a say in the use of their taxed wages?"

"Good, you made your case. You sat there so stiff, I thought Saltonstall had drained all the spit and fire out of you."

"He's not like that, Daniel. You don't know him."

"Tell me." Daniel angled over the table. "Do *you* know him?" The waiter swung by with another lemonade and asked if they were ready to order. Emily declined, saying she would wait for her mother.

"Yes, I know him. That's twice you've insinuated I don't. I've known Phillip most of my life, as have Father and Mother and Howard Jr."

Daniel reclined against the booth, raising his lemonade for a long, cooling drink. More for his soul than his throat. The sweet and sour blend reminded him that he had options here. Would he tear

Emily down with what he knew or give her his support, be the friend he claimed to be?

Yet, by gum, there was no mistaking what he'd witnessed on the corner of 19th and 3rd Avenue North. He'd know Saltonstall anywhere. He was the only buster in town who wore spats in the day.

"I'm happy for you, Em." Daniel set his glass down and rested his gaze on her face. "Truly, I am."

"Thank you. Your words mean a lot."

"Did you ever find my letters?"

"What does it matter, Daniel? We've moved on. We're different people."

I'm the same man, Emily. The one hopelessly in love with you.

"I'll have my words with the United States Postal Service. I had quite a few good tales in those letters. The time we won thirty to zero. When Broderick and Stonewalter got in a fistfight and I stitched both of them up with needle and thread. The time we went swimming in the Ohio. And the night I heard a banjo player singing about his true love and I couldn't stop thinking of you. I wanted to hold you, dance with you, kiss—"

"Don't, Daniel." She tipped her head to one side. "It's no use now." She lowered her gaze. "Perhaps providence intervened when we weren't wise enough to know better."

"Oh, but I think we did know better." Daniel ran his hand over his hair, springing a few curls over his forehead. "But if you're sure, then I'm sure. I'll be going. Good luck to you, Em."

Daniel reached for his hat as he slid out of the booth. But Emily snatched at his hand. "Danny, wait. When you came to Highlands, to see me, you said something about Phillip. Something about—oh, I can't remember, but you cast a shadow on his character. And just now you asked if I really knew him. What did you mean?"

"It's time for me to go." He lifted her hand from his. But Emily took hold again.

"If you care about me at all, you'll tell me."

"I don't think you know what you're asking, Emily." He regarded her for a moment. "And you are wearing his ring."

Emily glanced down, a ruby blush on her high cheeks. "I trust you, Daniel. Heaven help me, but I do. I saw him on the street corner today." Daniel perched on the edge of the seat. So she did see what he'd seen. "I was on the fourth floor of Loveman's, looking out the window when I spotted him. He's the only man in town who wears spats every day, you know. A thin woman approached him, and before I could bat an eye, he swept her into his arms."

When her voice broke, Daniel slid into the booth beside her, running his arm along the top of the seat and around her shoulders. "Perhaps she was a friend, a cousin, the daughter of an associate."

"Do you think so?" Her tone, her innocent expression . . . it was all Daniel could do not to sweep her into his arms and pledge to protect her heart.

"Ah, it's nothing, I'm sure. Phillip gave his ring to you, not another girl."

So Emily had seen Phillip's intimate kiss on the woman's neck. Daniel burned with embarrassment as he recalled the scene. In the middle of city commerce, Saltonstall carried on with another woman like one would do with his wife in private.

Now Daniel found he had to defend his rival in order to comfort the woman he loved. He refused to wound her further.

"But you know something, Daniel Ludlow, don't you dare lie to me. Otherwise you'd have not intimated as much. I won't be trifled with, hear me?" Emily slapped the table with her palm. The other Newman's patrons lifted their heads, looking their way. "You know people. Your father is a police captain. Your chum is a reporter on the paper. Why, you know the old man Woodward yourself. He recruited you for his mighty Birmingham Barons."

"So I might know a thing or two." Daniel adjusted his hat, the scent of Emily's skin seeping into him, stirring his affections. "You shouldn't ask questions you don't really want answered, Emily."

"I asked because I want to know. Daniel—"

"Fine, then ask me a specific question. What is it you want to know?"

"Does Phillip keep a . . ." Her question faltered.

"A mistress?"

She nodded. Fast. Short.

"Emily, listen to me—"

"There you are, my dear, I thought you'd left the diner." Mrs. Canton slid into the booth across from Daniel and Emily. "I'm sorry it took me so long, but Mrs. Caruthers cornered me and went on and on about her dressmaking qualifications. Daniel Ludlow, good afternoon." Mrs. Canton tugged off her gloves. "What are you doing here?"

"Ma'am, it's good to see you. I saw Emily enter the diner and thought I'd offer my congratulations on becoming engaged." Daniel slid out of the booth, tipping his hat. "You and Miss Canton are two of the loveliest women in Birmingham."

"Thank you. You are most kind." Mrs. Canton set her hat on the table and tucked her gloves under the wide brim with a sigh. "Did you order my cold milk? It's so warm out today."

"I was waiting for you, Mother." Emily peeked at Daniel. "I didn't want your milk to get warm."

"Well, there's a good girl. Excuse me—waiter."

"Have a good day, ladies." Daniel backed toward the door. "Emily, best of everything." Their staccato conversation left him uneasy.

"Excuse me, Mother." Emily slid out of the booth, stepped around the waiter, and followed Daniel to the front of the diner. "Tell me," she whispered. "Does he?"

"Have a mistress?"

She gazed into his eyes. He couldn't . . . it would crush her. Her fingernails dug into his arm.

"Daniel."

"Yes. So goes the word around town. But you should find out the truth yourself, Emily. You know how gossip gets all twisted and maligned."

"No, no." She jutted backward, shaking her head, her dark eyes narrowing. "You're a liar, Daniel Ludlow. I don't believe you." Her accusation stung and Daniel regretted yielding to her desire for the truth. But he couldn't change his path now. She snarled at him. "You're just jealous, spiteful, and petty."

"If only it were true. I'd be a liar ten times over if it meant Saltonstall didn't cheat on you. I warned you not to ask if you didn't want to know, Emily." Daniel eyed her, hard, then jerked open Newman's door so the bells rang out.

Emily stepped after him. "What did you hope to gain by lying to me?"

"What did you hope to gain by asking me if your fiancé had a mistress? You've made me hurt you, and I don't like it."

He stepped outside without looking back and stormed toward Loveman's, heat rising in his chest. So this was it. His last encounter with Emily.

But then Daniel turned on his heel. He refused to let her last memory of him be when he cast shadows on the man she planned to marry. At Newman's, he reached for the door but let his fingers slip from the handle.

Standing in front of the pane glass window, right beside the

"Apple Pie 25¢" sign, he watched her speaking with her mother, no doubt telling her what a cad Daniel Ludlow was.

Look up, Emily. His heart quickened when she reached for her lemonade. She caught him staring, so he raised his hand in greeting, mustering his best sympathetic expression. *Are you okay?*

Emily's weak and slight head tip relieved his heart. She sipped her lemonade, peering at him over the rim of her glass. Should he go inside? Speak with her? Demand a private audience and explain how he knew such a thing about her fiancé?

No, best to leave well enough alone. He'd done enough damage. Two women approached Emily and Mrs. Canton from another table. Daniel watched their exclamations, hands to their cheeks, bending to gaze at Emily's ring.

Saltonstall was a louse. He'd bought that ring for another woman. Daniel knew it. He just couldn't prove it. But whatever the price, it wasn't enough to win a woman like Emily Canton.

Chapter Eight

Charlotte

Charlotte crossed her living room, phone pressed to her ear, when a knock on the door beckoned.

"Thank you, Tawny. I'll see you then." Charlotte motioned Dixie into the loft, crossing back across the living room to her dining room table desk. "Lunch on Thursday, one thirty, at Bellini's." She hung up and tapped on her iPad, entering lunch on her calendar.

"Tawny?" Dix said.

"She's invited me to a luncheon with her bridesmaids. She wants them to meet 'the great Charlotte Malone,' her words not mine." Charlotte grinned. "Only one of them is already married and three others are in serious relationships . . . Bless Tawny for helping my business. Marketing is really all about word of—Dix, why do you have a hammer and screwdriver?"

Dixie clapped the tools together. "Never know when they might come in handy. I might see a protruding nail in your loft." Dix mimed hammering a wall. "Or a find a loose screw somewhere."

"Besides the one in your own head, you mean?" Charlotte finished adding lunch with Tawny to her schedule.

"Or we could use these to open the trunk."

"Open the trunk?" Charlotte met her gaze, exhaling a small laugh. "It's welded shut, Dix. A hammer and screwdriver can't undo welded metal. If they can, I'm never driving over a bridge again."

"Well, it's all I had." Dixie dropped the tools on the table. "Dr. Hotstuff deals in scalpels and scissors. His toolbox is pathetic. All it has in it is a fork, a hammer, and this rusty screwdriver."

"A fork?"

"Yeah, left over from the piece of pie he ate while hanging the pictures in our loft. So, where's this thousand-dollar trunk?" Dixie scanned the loft living area, around to the kitchen.

"In my room." Charlotte gestured toward the short hallway.

"Char, how can you stand not opening it?"

"It reminds me . . . I can't help but think that ugly thing was the catalyst that ended Tim and me." Charlotte took a brief scan of e-mail, glad to have a focus besides Dixie and her tools. Though her friend had a way of barging past emotional welded locks with her tools of boldness.

"You know, you can't avoid things because they're difficult or welded shut."

"I'm not avoiding anything. Just that trunk."

"Char, really, are you okay?" Dixie dropped onto a chair, hammer and screwdriver in her lap.

"You asked me that a hundred times this afternoon. I'm fine."

"If Jared had broken off with me two months before our wedding, I'd still be in bed hugging a box of tissues."

"You hole up in bed with tissues, I work. Move forward. Forget the past." Charlotte set down her iPad. "When Mama died and I had to move in with Gert, I cried for a while, told Gert I was too sick to go to school. But after a month of crying every night, I stopped. Tears weren't going to raise Mama from the dead. They weren't going to bring me a father or grandparents. So I mourned Mama by doing something. I got up, went to school, conquered fractions, grasped grammar, became the first one picked for volleyball in gym class. I was going to make Mama proud." Charlotte stared toward the dark-paned windows, the lights of Homewood beaming up from the ground. "Tears aren't going to bring Tim back either. So I work. I make Mama proud."

The silence between the friends gave Charlotte a moment to exhale and think, digest her own thoughts, put a picture to her feelings. She loved Tim, but something had made her second-guess.

Dixie reached across and squeezed her hand. "Are you hungry?"

"I could eat."

"How's Homewood Gourmet sound?"

"Let's go." Charlotte slung her bag over her shoulder. "I've been thinking about taking a Paris trip in the fall. A visit to Bray-Lindsay and our other designers. You game?"

"Game? I'm the whole party. Absolutely, I want to go to Paris. If you go without me I'll burn the shop down." Dixie sliced the air with the hammer and screwdriver.

"We don't need tools tonight, Dix." Charlotte started down the hall toward the elevator.

"I don't know, we might." Dixie examined the hammer as Charlotte pushed the first-floor button. "One thing we do know, it'll be winter in hades before Jared notices they're gone."

Charlotte ordered pesto chicken with soup and salad, then took a swig of tea, waiting for Dixie to order. She loved the we-welcome-you atmosphere of Homewood Gourmet, the small hum of voices, the clatter of dishes, the anticipation of unique food.

She pulled out her iPad to look at the fall calendar, block off time for Paris. She'd need to contact her designers, determine a good visiting time, hire someone to watch the shop, so she'd best formulate a time frame.

Charlotte gazed up when Dixie finished ordering, ready to ask about her schedule. But as she took in the view of the front door, the words stuck in her throat and her weak heart tumbled to its knees.

Tim. With a beautiful woman.

"Char, what is it?" Dixie whipped around to see over her shoulder. "Oh wow, I don't believe it."

"Let's just go." Charlotte closed up her iPad and jammed it into her satchel. "Once they're seated"—she ducked low to the table, hiding behind Dixie—"we can sneak out."

"Sit up. You're not going to hide, ashamed. He's the one that ought to be ashamed."

"Sure, but he's with a gorgeous date and I'm sitting here with you."

"I'll take that like you intended, not like it sounded, Charlotte."

"You know what I mean." Charlotte made a face, sniffing back the sting of tears.

Tim surveyed the restaurant with his head high as a lovely, golden-haired woman—with a darn near perfect profile—linked her arm through his. He bent to whisper something in her ear and she smiled at him with an utterly flawless smile.

Charlotte felt the heat from the woman's dreamy gaze across the room. She had to get out of here. Calculating how many steps to the front door, she figured ten giant steps would get her out the door fast.

"Dixie, you can stay and be brave if you want, hold your head high and all of that, but I'm leaving." Charlotte yanked her wallet from her bag and left a twenty on the table. "That should cover my food."

Dixie clamped down on her arm. "You're not leaving. We came here to eat, get out, have fun. We came here to forget about him. And talk business."

"How can I forget about him if I have to look at him. If every laugh makes me look around to see if it's her? Wondering what he's saying to *her*. Or why he's here with *her* in the first place."

"Charlotte, she's probably a client, a colleague, something to do with architecture."

"Why are you defending him? She's a date, I can tell. No client gives him the dreamy-eye. Either way, I'm leaving and I don't want him to see me."

The server passed and Charlotte dropped two more twenties on the table. "Excuse me, miss, but we're going to have to go. This should cover our bill."

"What bill?" Dixie waved her hand over the empty table. "We didn't even eat."

"But we've ordered. Uneaten food still costs money." Charlotte stood, hunching forward, eyes on Tim. He sat with *her* on the other side of the door. Charlotte could make a clean escape. Stooping down, hiding behind servers and patrons, she worked through a people maze to the door and burst into the cool April night with an exhale.

Dixie trailed behind Charlotte with an *I'm mad-I'm sympathetic-I'm mad-I'm sympathetic clip-clop* ring to her heels as they pounded the pavement. "This is ridiculous. He broke up with you and you let him drive you out of the restaurant?" Dixie aimed her remote key at the car. The horn beeped. The lights flashed.

Charlotte scrambled into the passenger seat, white-knuckled the door handle, and hugged her satchel to her chest. "I lied, Dix. I'm not so fine. I'm sad and this whole thing hurts." Tears watered her words. "I can't believe he has someone else. She must be the reason he has doubts." Charlotte peered out her window, then turned toward Dixie. "She was pretty, wasn't she? Yeah, she was gorgeous."

"If you like skinny girls with too much makeup, sure. Charlotte, this doesn't seem like Tim."

"You're *still* defending him? Dix, what do we know about him, *really*?"

"We know he's standing outside your window right now."

"Charlotte—" Tim stood by her door, hands on his belt, head cocked to one side, peering down at her. "Can I talk to you?"

She angled toward Dixie, hand cupped around her eyes. "Do you think he's seen me?"

"He's two feet from you. Yes, he's seen you." Dixie laughed, gently pushing Charlotte's hand from her face. "But say the word and I'll back out of here. I don't promise to miss his toes."

"So I should talk to him?" Charlotte peeked over her shoulder. Tim still stood outside her window, peering in at her.

"Do you want to hear what he has to say? He did leave *her* and come out here to talk to you."

Charlotte eased her grip on the handbag she cradled in her lap. She'd always known Tim to be a man of honor and he didn't like to leave things undone.

She climbed out of the car, closing the door behind her. Leaning against it, she folded her arms. "What's up?"

"How are you?" Tim stood a few feet from her. The fragrance of spice with a bass note of something floral settled between them.

"Great. Perfect. Enjoying a night out with my girl, Dix. Jared's working at the hospital."

"She's a friend, Charlotte." He gestured toward the restaurant.

"Who?" Charlotte leaned toward him, then gazed at the restaurant as if she didn't see *her* earlier.

"Kim."

"You were here with Kim? Your ex?"

"Yeah, that'd be Kim." He made a face. "I know you saw us, Charlotte. I saw you sneaking out."

"Tim, what do you want? Why'd you come out here?"

"To explain. I didn't know Kim was in town until she called today. Wanted to talk." He cleared his throat, glancing toward the dark pockets of the parking lot. "Are you okay?"

"Do I look okay?" Her hard retort didn't reflect the softening happening in her heart.

"I couldn't sleep last night," Tim said, low and intimate. "Do you have any—"

"What's done is done, Tim. We can't be engaged if you don't want to get married." She felt like a bit of a coward hiding her own wedding jitters behind his.

He nodded, biting on his bottom lip. "Yeah, I suppose."

"Hey, it's good, Tim, all good." She shifted her stance, uncrossed her arms, and made a smoothing motion with her hands. "It's for the best, you know? At least we didn't send the invitations. Can you imagine returning all those gifts? What a nightmare."

"There's always a silver lining, I suppose. A thin one, but . . ." Tim gave her the same look that beguiled her heart the first night they met. "Can we talk? Maybe sometime this week?"

"About what, Tim? How it didn't work? How you didn't want to marry me? I think we've said all we can say, and I'm doing all I can to move on."

"I miss you." The wind picked up the ends of his hair, blowing them across his eyes.

Charlotte pressed her fingers into her palms, tucking her arms tighter, resisting the automatic urge to reach up and smooth his hair from his face, gently trailing her fingers over his forehead and down his strong, high cheeks.

"It's only been a day, Tim."

He laughed, low. "Longest day of my life. I kept reaching for the phone to call you."

"Don't you find that odd? Yesterday, you couldn't *make* yourself call me. Went racing and forgot all about our plans."

"I've been trying to figure that out all day. The only thing I can come up with is I miss Charlotte, my friend."

"But not the fiancée?"

"That arrangement had me feeling boxed in, like a coon up a tree, but my friend Charlotte—I really miss her."

"What are you afraid of? Marriage in general or marriage to me?"

"Marriage in general. You, I kind of like. A lot. Maybe I didn't know how much."

Charlotte shivered in the breeze. "I was kind of a package deal. Friend and fiancée. Can't have one without the other."

"Yeah, that's what I figured." He gazed toward the restaurant. "Guess I'd better go."

"Guess so." *Fight for me, Tim. Fight your own fears.* Charlotte popped open the car door. "Have a nice dinner."

"I don't suppose coffee or lunch sometime would be possible."

"No, Tim, it's not. I'm sorry you miss your *friend* and the convenience of having me there for you without the sensation of being a treed coon, but you proposed to me. I trusted you. I loved you. And Charlotte the fiancée is kind of smarting now that you're having dinner with another woman twenty-four hours after we called things off."

"She's just a friend."

"Like me? Another member of the Tim Rose ex-fiancée brigade."

He sighed. "She broke up with me."

"Well, there you go." Charlotte hopped in the car. "Now's your chance to get her back."

"Charlotte, come on, it's not like that and you know it."

Dixie was out of the parking lot and heading down the street before the first sob escaped Charlotte's clenched jaw and pressed lips. Shoulders rolling forward, she bent her face to her knees and wept the rest of the way home.

Chapter Nine

Emily

Outside Father's library door, Emily paused a moment before twisting the knob, letting herself in. Since she'd been a girl, Father had encouraged her to come to him anytime she needed, never demanding a knock or voice of permission before she entered. Just come as she willed.

"Emily, come, come." Father set down his pen and rose to greet her. "I'm just writing your brother. Telling him about your engagement party this evening."

"Tell him I wish he was here. He owes me a long, newsy letter." Howard Jr., three years younger, had been one of Emily's best friends—a confidant and champion—until he left for Harvard. She missed his wisdom and teasing "Aw, sis" at the moment.

"I shall, I shall." Father tugged his trousers loose from his knees as he returned to his chair. "Are you looking forward to this evening? All of Birmingham society will be there." Father clapped his hands against his chest, rocking back, looking proud. "My little girl is getting married."

"Yes, she is, Father. Getting . . . married. And tonight . . . tonight is . . . well, a big night for us all." *Just speak it out, Emily. Father will know what to do.*

"Is something on your mind, daughter?"

Yes! Father always could see through her. She came in here with no small thing on her mind. Emily paced over to the window, seeing

105

a phantom image of Daniel's fine, even features in the shadows of clapping tree limbs.

"Remember how Howard Jr. didn't want to go to Harvard? He wanted to attend the University of Alabama as I did, but you insisted. He argued Harvard was too far away, a Yankee school, in a cold Yankee town."

"He's learning his father knows best."

"That is why I'm here, Father." Emily came to the chair by his desk. "I need your best advice."

"What is it, Emily? You sound troubled." Father removed one of his precious Cuban cigars from the humidor.

Despite the fact that Father hid Daniel's letters from her, he was her rock, her support, the one who more times than she wanted to admit had chosen rightly for her. Her education. On occasion, her friends. Even suggesting Phillip as a proper suitor when Daniel left to play for the Barons.

"Is this about Loveman's? Your mother told me what happened with Mrs. Caruthers. Don't take it to heart, dear girl. She's merely a dressmaker and all we need from her is her best work. Your mother will see to that, never fear."

"I do take it to heart, Father. I don't like her, nor her attitude about coloreds." But in light of Daniel's insinuation about Phillip, Mrs. Caruthers's prejudices paled for the moment.

"Careful, Emily, there are laws."

"I'm aware of the laws." *The very unfair laws.* But at the moment, she craved Father's comfort concerning Phillip. "Father, I'm not here about Mrs. Caruthers. I'm here about Daniel Ludlow."

Father averted his gaze to his cigar as he took several deep puffs and relaxed in his winged chair. "I'd heard he'd returned."

"You hid his letters from me." The sentence warranted no quarrel. Just pure, simple truth.

"That's a rather grand accusation, Emily." Father continued to puff on his cigar. Emily went to the window and opened it. The dewy evening breeze, scented with the sunbaked earth, dissipated the tobacco smoke.

"Is it? I found them in the stable."

"What were you doing in the stable?" Father tapped ashes into the ashtray stand by his desk and peered at her. "Molly gave me up, didn't she?"

"She did not. You have a loyal confidante in her. Daniel came to see me. He told me about the letters." Emily held steady with courage—that was the way to converse with Father, head on and confident. "Why did you take them? I believe they belong to me, Father. It's not like you."

"Letters that arrive at my home are my property. To do with as I see fit."

"Not when they are addressed to me. I am not your property. You raised me to be my own person."

"I did. Yet in matters of the heart, fathers know best. Daniel Ludlow is a fine boy, Emily, but he is not for you."

"How can you say such a thing?" Emily leaned over his desk, hands gripping the thick edge. "You barely know him."

"I know him enough, his family and lineage. I watched you two over the last year, and what I hoped was a schoolgirl crush turned into something you considered love." Father pointed at her with his cigar. "I was glad when he left to play ball."

"It's my decision whom I love, Father."

"Do you not love Phillip?"

"We are not talking about Phillip. We're talking about Daniel. You didn't give me a chance to decide for myself between Phillip and Daniel. You manipulated my heart your way by hiding Daniel's letters."

"What do you want me to do? Let you return Phillip Saltonstall's ring? Whether you appreciate it or not, a Saltonstall match is good for you and the whole family, Emily. Your mother is invited to the women's clubs that formerly snubbed her. I've taken a higher position at my own club. Cameron Saltonstall intends to bring some of his banking business to Canton Exchange, as well as give recommendations to his friends. Much more is on the line now than your heart, dear girl. Besides, I didn't raise you to marry a man with no money, no connections, and no future."

"You had no money, no connections, and no future when you started out. But you made connections, you made money, and thus your own future, Father. You didn't fear hard work, and it molded you into a great man of character." She went around the desk and knelt by his chair, pressing her hands on the smooth wooden arms. "That's what I saw in Daniel. Those pieces of you that made you great. But you never gave him a chance."

"Emily dear, years ago, an investor came my way while I was breaking my back to build my company. He offered me a leg up, his financial backing. Do you think I was wise to take it?"

"Certainly"—she brushed ashes from his sleeve—"you're not a fool."

"And neither are you." He regarded her through the swirl of smoke. "Phillip is your offering of a better life, Emily. A leg up in society, a way for your children to have even more than you've had."

"All right, fair enough, but what if . . ." Emily stood, staring down at her hands, a chilly nervousness in her veins. Was this fair to Phillip, to bring up his indiscretion when she'd not confronted him? When she'd not inquired about his side of the story? For all she knew, Daniel lied to her. Though she'd never known him to lie. Not even a little white one. Certainly her own eyes never lied to her. She saw what she saw that day at Loveman's. So had Daniel.

"Emily? You were asking 'What if?'"

She glanced at her father. "Nothing, I suppose." What would Father think if she accused Phillip with such a thing? He'd think she was speculating and foolish, collaborating with her jilted lover. "I just wondered about the letters."

"So Molly is my trusted confidante?"

"She's no fool either, Father."

"Emily, why are you not dressing?" Mother swooped into the library. "Your party begins in an hour. Howard, why are you keeping her?" Mother wore a fitted gown of pale pink chiffon and lace. Her rich brown hair with amber highlights was swept into a thick, full pompadour. Diamond earrings shimmered from the tips of her ears. "Molly has taken your dress upstairs, Emily. Hurry, get changed." Father stood as she approached and leaned to kiss her. "Your tuxedo awaits you in your quarters, Howard."

"Are you finished speaking with me, Emily?" Father began to put away his ledger and pen.

"Yes, Father." She started for the door. "Thank you."

"Emily," Father called. "All brides get nervous. Rest assured, I didn't steer your brother wrong by sending him to Harvard. I've not steered you wrong either."

From atop Red Mountain, overlooking Jones Valley and the flickering lights of the Magic City, Emily was a princess for the night. A hundred guests dined on roasted quail and creamed potatoes, with chocolate mousse for dessert. All in her and Phillip's honor.

Phillip looped his arm through hers as they gathered on the perimeter of the Saltonstall's grand ballroom. The butler shoved open the terrace doors and a cool breeze swept up from the valley. On the far side of the room, a small orchestra tuned, drawing bows over strings, creating a dissonant melody.

"It was a fine dinner, Saltonstall." Powell Jamison, one of Phillip's oldest friends, joined Phillip and Emily in the center of the room and turned in a slow circle, facing the guests. "Ladies and gentleman, as my good friend Phillip's best man, may I offer a toast." He raised a glass of golden champagne. Around the room servants distributed bubbling crystal flutes to the guests. "To Phillip and his lovely bride-to-be, Emily." The guests raised their glasses. "Best wishes for a long and happy marriage. Emily, later you can tell me what the lousy cad did to persuade you to marry him."

Laughter flowed about the room. Phillip anchored his arm around Emily's waist just as she caught Father's eye. He nodded to her with a wink. *Did I not tell you . . .*

Emily raised her glass to him. *To you, wise Father.*

"Thank you all for coming and celebrating with Emily and me." Phillip held her closer as he addressed the ballroom. "How did I win this fine creature as my bride, Powell? Naturally, I wooed her with my charms." Phillip bowed to the room, which rippled with applause and laughter.

"I daresay it's the large ring you gave her." Cornelia Weinberg took a bold step forward, distinguishing herself from the other guests. At thirty-four, she was a widow already, her husband passing three years ago from heart failure at sixty-five. "I tell you it would've wooed my affections."

"Ah, but I believe I'm too young for you, Cornie," Phillip teased. "You like your men more . . . shall we say . . . seasoned?"

Emily leaned against her man, letting all her doubts fade away with the lively banter of friends and the elation of being cele-brated for the night. Cornie was becoming a dear friend and Emily admired her resilience.

Mostly Emily relished moments like these when friendship and camaraderie extinguished all social decorum and folks felt free to laugh.

"If I'd set my sights on you, Phillip Saltonstall, I'd not have missed." Cornie squared off with him in the middle of the floor. Phillip kept Emily tucked in close.

"You're not that good of a shot, Cornie." He lowered his chin but raised his brow.

"I suppose now you'll never know." No other Birmingham belle could jest like Cornie. She had a way of making it all seem so innocent.

"All right, you two." Powell stepped in between them. "The orchestra is ready. Cornie, you can take the first dance with me." He was a confirmed bachelor, and Cornie's husband-hunting tactics didn't scare him.

The guests gathered in small pockets, waiting for the dance to begin. Women chatted about the upcoming debutante season. The men discussed the Barons and Alabama football.

"Phillip, lovely party." Herschel Wainscot shook his hand. "Emily, lovely as always. Do you mind if your intended and I talk business, just for a moment?"

"Only a moment, Mr. Wainscot. This is my engagement party and I won't have it spoiled." Emily gave him a scolding look, but only a quick one. She was too happy.

"I promise not to keep him long, but for some reason I can't seem to track Phillip down during business hours. He's very busy."

"I'm always available to you, Hersh."

"Then stay in the office once in a while. I'll telephone you."

A willowy woman appeared next to Mr. Wainscot. Emily straightened when a flutter zipped between her ribs. The woman from the street . . . outside Loveman's. Her legs trembled beneath her full, taffeta skirt.

"Introduce me, Herschel."

"Emmeline Graves, this is Mr. Phillip Saltonstall and his bride-to-be, Miss Emily Canton."

"Lovely to meet you, Mr. Saltonstall." She offered her hand to Phillip but kept her eyes averted. "Miss Canton, your gown is quite lovely."

"Thank you." Emily braced as she peered up at Phillip. Would he be drinking in the sight of this slender woman? The one Emily saw laughing with him on 19th Street? She had the same thin frame and thick golden hair.

But Phillip barely shook her hand and instead fixed his attention on the bandstand and the orchestra. "How long does it take them to tune, for Pete's sake?" he said. "I'm ready to twirl around the floor with this gorgeous creature in my arms." He peered down at Emily, lifting her chin with a slight touch of his finger.

Mr. Wainscot chuckled. "Well, while we're waiting, let me have a word with you. Phillip, how's the convict-leasing program working for you and Saltonstall mines? We've been thinking of using them to work on the city roads. Save some money on labor. Slag is a bit more expensive than concrete."

"We have no complaints from our overseers."

"But you do from the citizens, Phillip." Emily stepped into the conversation. "The convicts live in deplorable conditions and they're treated brutally. Father has horses and hounds that fare better."

"Emily—" Phillip's glare demanded her quiet submission.

"They're men, not animals."

"They're convicts, Miss Canton." Mr. Wainscot's tone was devoid of his previous charm. "They're paying their debts to society."

"Leg irons, hard labor for a misdemeanor? Half starving,

whippings for the smallest infraction. It's barbaric and beneath a Southern gentleman's ways." She leaned close to Wainscot. "And they're all colored."

"I didn't know you cared, Emily. They've received due process."

"From a white jury and white judges, who give cruel and unusual punishment they'd not hand down to white men. Not for the same offense. I don't see white convicts assigned to this leasing program. The men are cheated, made to work longer than their sentence, to pay for what? Living in squalor? Lining the pockets of the mine owners and crooks who run the city?"

"Miss Canton." Mr. Wainscot squinted at her. She braced for his shallow rebuttal. He burst out laughing and clapped Phillip on the shoulder. "Phillip, you have a spitfire here. Intelligent. Speaks her mind with eloquence. Even better than most men. Perhaps she'll study to be admitted into the bar. Or take up management in the Saltonstall offices."

Phillip chuckled as if Wainscot surely had to be joking. "Emily has no such aspirations."

"How do you know, Phillip?" Emily said. "Have you asked me? It's men like you two that make women want the vote, so we can bring some civility and humanity to politics."

"My dear." Phillip wrapped his hand about her waist and pressed her to him. "You sound like pamphlet rhetoric. I thought you didn't care for the suffrage meetings. Hear now, it's our party. Why don't we"—the orchestra began a waltz—"dance?"

"Yes, of course." Emily dabbed the moisture from her forehead with the handkerchief tucked against her palm. "I'm sorry, Phillip, I didn't realize all of that was inside me."

"Then you surprised us both." He held her face in his hands and stroked his thumbs over her lips, sending a buzz through her. "But you're beautiful when you're fiery. It makes me want—" His lips covered hers and Emily clung to him, and his passion. When Phillip released her, she fell against his chest.

"I didn't mean to embarrass you."

"You didn't embarrass me, love, but make no mistake, I am a man like Herschel Wainscot. A businessman in this city, working to make it better for all of us. Hersh is a bit arrogant, but he's a reasonable, solid character." Phillip brushed his hand over her cheek as he started to waltz her about the room. Step, turn, step, turn. "I never tire of looking at you, Emily. You're so very, very lovely." His low, romantic tone wooed her. His eyes gripped hers and she felt locked into him.

"You are most dear, handsome Phillip. I don't mean to cause you any trouble."

"I look forward to our wedding night. Perhaps you'll reserve some of your fire and passion for me there."

"Phillip," she whispered, burning with embarrassment, though his intentions awakened her desires.

"Don't worry, darling, I'll teach you." His lips caressed the soft flesh at the base of her ear with no regard for the room full of friends and family who might be watching.

Emily shifted her head away from him. It was not their wedding night yet. Though, obviously, he'd like it to be so.

"Phillip, may I ask you something?"

"Anything." He spun Emily about the floor with grace and ease.

"Do you know Mr. Wainscot's friend, Emmeline? Where is she from?"

"I know what you know, dear Emily. Just met her tonight."

Wainscot appeared through the dancing couples, the willowy woman in his arms. "Phillip, do your ole pal a favor. For the grand ole frat, Phi Delt. Dance with Emmeline, and let me take a turn around the floor with this vision of a woman you call your fiancée." He lifted Emily's hand from Phillip's and twirled Emmeline into

Phillip's arms. Wainscot settled his hand on Emily's back, her palm in his, and danced them away.

"Thank you, dear Emily, you rid me of that silly dame." Herschel stepped her around the floor, light on his feet. Emily's skirt swished against her legs. "You're the most beautiful woman here tonight, and I've never been so jealous of my best pal."

Emily darted her gaze to the floor as they turned, heat creeping along her neck. How did he expect her to respond?

"Mr. Wainscot." Emily raised her chin, keeping her voice light and airy, boasting a smile. "If the dame is silly, why'd you force her onto my Phillip?" She coyly peered around his shoulder to see Phillip dancing with Emmeline as if her form was familiar to him. As if her curves belonged beneath his palm.

"Because I wanted to dance with you." He exhaled, his port-tainted breath brushing over Emily's hair. "Phillip's always had the luck with the ladies. I remember our first day on campus, he had the girls fawning all over him. I decided then he'd be my best friend."

"And does he still? Have luck with the ladies?"

Herschel looked in her eyes and exhaled, his breath warm on her face. "He has you, hasn't he? I'd fight him for you if I thought you'd take me after I won."

"Mr. Wainscot." Emily moved out of his arms.

"Call me Herschel, please."

"You seem to be in no short supply of beautiful escorts, Herschel. Emmeline is quite beautiful." Emily knew most every woman in their social circle, even the nieces, granddaughters, and relatives who came to Birmingham for long visits now and then. "How do you know her?"

"She's the daughter of a friend." Herschel offered Emily his arm, motioning to the refreshment table. He handed her a glass of punch, then took one for himself.

The drink was sweet and minty, but the air between Emily and Herschel was hot and sticky. Wanting to escape his company, she scanned the guests for a sign of Mother and Father. Or Phillip. But she couldn't find them among the dancers.

"Emily," Hershel said after a moment, "I hope I didn't offend you earlier. I think your position is admirable."

"You didn't offend me, Herschel." She strained to see where Phillip had gone, wrestling with guilt for suspecting him. Blast that Daniel Ludlow for sowing seeds of doubt in her heart. "I only hope I didn't offend you."

Herschel laughed. "It'd take more than pushing out of my arms to offend me."

She sipped the last of her punch, and as she set her cup on the table, Herschel offered her his hand. "Shall we?"

Emily hesitated, then slowly gave him her hand. "We must find Phillip soon."

"Perhaps it is upon him to find us." Herschel swept Emily around in the dance, the sheen of his blond hair catching the sparkle of the chandelier, his magnificent smile attempting to work his charms.

"You think highly of yourself, don't you, Herschel?"

"No more than any other man thinks of himself."

Emily laughed, moving with him among the other guests. "Perhaps Phillip is right, you're not a bad sort after all."

"You pay me a high compliment."

"We shall have to have you to dinner once we are married."

"At your earliest convenience, please do."

"I'll speak to Phillip at the end of this dance." It was then Emily caught sight of her fiancé's broad back disappearing into the dark, secret shadows of the terrace, dancing with Emmeline Graves in his arms.

Chapter Ten

Charlotte

Charlotte carried the Herrera gown up to the sewing salon, walking under a waterfall of sunlight spilling into the shop from the skylights. The cherry hardwood gleamed beneath her feet.

Her heart still lacked light, but she felt better today, nearly a week after seeing Tim at Homewood Gourmet with his ex-fiancée. She'd slept well the last two nights, after pleading with God for some kind of peace.

Slipping the dress over the dress form, Charlotte smoothed her hand over the ivory satin bodice with handcrafted embroidery set above a full tulle skirt, one of her favorite designs.

A new client had chosen the Herrera—which was perfect for her—and had scheduled her first fitting for Saturday. Malone & Co.'s seamstress, Bethany, always inspected the gown before working with the bride.

Heading back downstairs, Charlotte pictured the bride's face when she slipped on the Herrera, then phoned her fiancé in tears. *I found my dress, baby.*

Why hadn't she ever found a nickname for Tim? A term of endearment? He was just Tim. To her recollection, he'd never called her anything but Charlotte or Char. Not babe or baby. No sweetie or honey.

And if she was honest with herself, which she had the courage to be now, Charlotte held back from him, not really willing to give up her identity as orphan girl made good.

She, Charlotte Malone, could soar high and wide all on her own. She didn't need a man, a family, or her own Cinderella wedding to validate her. She'd proven she could make it on her own and created a good, safe, dependable life she loved.

At the bottom of the stairs, Charlotte paused when the front door opened and the bells chimed. The fragrance of roses swept into the shop. "Welcome to Malone & Co. May I help you?"

The man wandered toward her through the display of Heidi Elnora and Bray-Lindsay gowns. She tried to estimate if he was the father of a bride. Perhaps of a groom? "Are you here about a wedding?"

"As a matter of fact, I am." He paused in front of her. She'd noticed his purple shirt immediately, and his blue eyes pinged Charlotte with something familiar, creating a fiery, stirring feeling in her belly. She stepped back with a gasp. Where had she seen him before?

"Did you open the trunk?" he said.

"Excuse me?" Charlotte slipped behind the sales desk and into a silky cool stream of air that hit her in the chest and swirled down to her feet.

"The trunk. From the auction. Did you open it?"

"You're the one who sold me the trunk?" She laughed low, pressing her hand over her middle. How could she forget such an odd little man? "No, no, I, um . . ." She shrugged. "It's welded shut."

"Yes, but it's good to work at redeeming a treasure."

"Treasure? That trunk is hardly treasure." Charlotte brushed her hands over the chill building on her arms. When he said "redeeming" she *felt* it. "Can I ask your interest in the trunk? Was it yours? Someone in your family?"

"In a manner of speaking." The man walked the perimeter of the shop, hands locked behind his back, inspecting the gowns along the wall. "Very unique gowns. Lovely."

"Do you have a daughter getting married?" Charlotte crossed over to him with her business card. He glanced at it politely, then moved on without taking it. Charlotte tapped the card's edge against her fingertips.

"I have a daughter getting married." He peered over his shoulder at her. "It's the season of the bride."

"Season of the bride?" Charlotte laughed low. Such an unusual expression. "I certainly hope so. I could use the business. Tell your daughter I'd be happy to . . . what's your name again?"

"My daughter knows about your shop. She's quite familiar with it."

Chills crept down her legs when he spoke. It was as if she knew him. As if he knew her. But it was impossible. "What's your daughter's name? Perhaps I have her on file?"

"Charlotte." He walked toward her, hand extended. "I was just inquiring about the trunk. It was good to see you."

His grip fit into hers as if they'd clasped hands a hundred times. The chills multiplied over Charlotte's body while a warm splash hit her spirit. She felt . . .

Encountered.

The back door slammed and Dixie's honey-I'm-home footsteps resonated against the hardwood. She stopped near Charlotte, who faced the windows, watching the man leave.

"Wow, can you say blinding purple?" Dixie rapped on the window. "Dude, the '70s disco era is over." She turned back to the shop, rustling up a flutter of sunbeams. "Who was that?"

"I'm not sure, except he was the man who sold me the trunk

119

at the auction. But, Dix . . ." Charlotte pressed her hand over her quivering middle. "I think I may have just met my father."

In her room, in the glow of lamplight, with music playing, Charlotte aligned her tools. The hammer and screwdriver from Dix. A saw, because Dixie insisted she might need it, and a drill.

"Dix, I don't know how to use a drill."

"What's to know? You aim this rod-thingy at the welded metal and *vwip, vwip*, you got a hole." Dixie mimed her instruction in a *see, simple as pie* manner.

"But a hole gets me nothing. I still have welded metal." Charlotte picked up the drill and leaned to inspect the trunk's lock.

"Well, you might have to drill a hole to get it open."

"Jared." Charlotte looked to the doctor sitting on the edge of her bed. "Do I need a drill?" She held up the tool to Dixie's Dr. Hotstuff, still wearing his blue scrubs, looking like he was ready for a long winter nap.

"Char is right, Dix, she doesn't need a drill. Sorry I can't be more help, but I need to get back to the hospital in a few hours, and I was hoping my Dixie-babe would fix some grub while I snatch some z's."

Charlotte looked around at Jared. *Dixie-babe.* See, lovers had names of affection. She and Tim did not.

"Sure, darling." Dixie got up off the floor. "Did I tell you Charlotte thought her father came into the shop?"

"Really?"

"I don't know, Jared." Charlotte rearranged the tools, large to small, small to large. "I've never met my father. But this old guy, the same one who sold me the trunk, came into the shop and asked if I'd opened it yet. He said he had a daughter getting married. I asked her name, and he said my name at the exact same time, so it sounded like his daughter's name was Charlotte. But he was just saying good-bye to me. I think." She eyed her doctor friend. *What do you think?*

"Wouldn't he tell you if he was your father?"

"Would you, if you'd been out of her life for thirty years?"

"No, I guess I not. Do you think there's a clue in the trunk?"

"I don't know, but he piqued my curiosity. I might as well open it and find out."

After Dixie and Jared left, Charlotte sat on the floor in front of the trunk, picturing the man in the purple shirt and the white Nikes. Was he her father? Did she even want a father?

To what end? To what benefit? Her life functioned fine, just fine, without him. Drama-free and simple. She didn't need him now. When Mama died, she'd needed him. Where was he then?

Charlotte exhaled and took up the hammer, tapping the welded metal lightly with the blunt end.

The answer she'd invented as a girl explaining her father's absence was the same answer she clung to as a woman.

Her daddy was a great adventurer with a wanderlust that spurred him to sail roaring seas and traverse sun-soaked terrains. His call in life demanded he break the boundaries of Birmingham, go beyond the doldrums of everyday life like marriage and raising kids.

Even his deep affection for his daughter—her, Charlotte—couldn't contain his destiny. He must yield to the passions of his heart.

Yes, that was *her* father. One incredible wandering man. A regular Indiana Jones.

Charlotte lowered the hammer. Why did she care about opening this dented and dinged, scarred and rutted trunk? What exactly was she redeeming?

"This trunk belongs to you," the auctioneer, the purple man, had declared.

Charlotte ran her palm over the lid, the wood and leather smoother than she expected. She picked up the screwdriver and tried to find a soft spot in the melted metal that had once been a lock.

She hammered against the head of the screwdriver, trying to create a wedge where there wasn't one. The weld refused to give, and Charlotte was relieved. Like she told Dix before, if she could break a weld with a hammer and screwdriver, then what was she doing driving over a bridge?

She picked up the saw. Ridiculous. How was she going to *saw* metal? But she aimed, settling the saw teeth beneath the lock. After a couple of times back and forth, Charlotte gave up. At least she'd tried.

Whoever wanted this trunk sealed forever was serious about it. Charlotte rocked back, arms around her raised knees. Maybe this trunk shouldn't be opened. Maybe Purple Man didn't know what he was talking about. Maybe she should haul this thing out to the Dumpster before whatever lived inside came alive and crawled into her bed one night.

Or worse, her heart.

Charlotte jumped to her feet. Craziness. The trunk was probably empty. What she needed was to get the thing open and prove to herself all was well. No evidence of her father. No evidence of anything to be redeemed.

What cut through metal? Charlotte glanced around the room. Some kind of power tool. None of which she had in her room or in her loft.

But Charlotte knew who did have the right tools. She dove onto the bed, reaching for her phone on the nightstand, and dialed Tim.

Then hung up, sat forward on her bed, legs crossed. After the exchange in the parking lot last Thursday, she couldn't very well call him for help. Could she?

Friend Tim? Yes. Not fiancé Tim. But she'd told him there was no separation between friend and fiancée. Okay, well, maybe she changed her mind.

Charlotte dialed Tim again, bracing to hear his voice, her heart drumming. As soon as he answered, Charlotte began talking, avoiding conversation and weighty seconds of silence.

"Friend Tim? This is friend Charlotte. I want to open the trunk but I need some kind of power tool. This man came into the shop today and well, it's a long, weird story, but he sparked my curiosity. I thought I'd end up just chucking it, you know, but sometimes old ugly things get to you and you can't bear to get rid of them. Like a security blanket. If you're busy or have a date—do you have a date? I'm sorry. Is Kim there? Don't worry, we can, you know"—Charlotte picked at her quilt, losing her breath and nerve—"do this another time or I can wait for Jared to come home. But he only has a hammer, screwdriver, and a fork in his toolbox. And a drill, but that's only good for making holes. I'd bring the trunk to you, but it won't fit in my car, small convertible and all—"

"Charlotte. Breathe."

She exhaled. "Thank you."

"I'm in the truck. I'll be there in ten."

"So, the man who sold you the trunk showed up at the shop?" Tim snapped a saw blade into place and studied the hasp, pressing on the metal, finding a place to start.

"Yeah, it was creepy, but cool at the same time." Charlotte sat on the floor next to him. "He'd say certain things and chills would run over me. When he left, I got this odd sense he might have been my father."

Tim stopped working. "What do you mean? Like your dad

came into the shop? After mysteriously selling you this trunk at the Ludlow auction?"

"When you put it like that, it sounds completely weird. There was just this odd moment . . . So, do you think you can get this open?"

"I can, but, Charlotte, what made you think he might have been your dad?"

"I don't know." She told him about their conversation clash— when he answered her question with her name. "It just made me wonder. Crazy? Yeah, crazy. He was only saying good-bye."

"Charlotte." Tim set the tool down, facing her. "If your father walked up to you right now, are you saying you wouldn't recognize him?"

"No, I wouldn't. I've never met him, Tim."

"Not even a picture?"

Even on the verge of marriage, Charlotte had never had this conversation with Tim. More proof she held back from him.

"Not one." She picked at a piece of pile rising from the area rug. "Mom met him when she was at FSU, fell in love, got pregnant with me, and when she told him, he bolted. I don't even know his name." Charlotte pressed her fingers to her eyes, then raked them through her hair. "Hey, I didn't drag you all the way over here to talk about my daddy or lack thereof. Fire up that saw, Tim." Charlotte patted the top of the trunk. "Open this baby."

"Not even his name?" Tim insisted on sawing open her closed emotions instead of the closed trunk.

"Well, a few slang names not fit for Christian company. I asked Mama about him once, when I was ten. But she said if he didn't want to give me his name or love, she wasn't going to tell me about him. On my birth certificate, 'father's name' is a big fat *ba-lank*." Charlotte swiped the air with her hand.

"I feel sorry for him." Tim swiveled around to the trunk, picking up the power saw. "He gave up something pretty incredible."

"Maybe he felt like a treed coon."

Tim revved the saw without another word, without a sideways glance at her, but their conversation reverberated in her heart.

"Excuse me." Charlotte disappeared into the bathroom and closing the door, she sat on the lowered toilet seat, unrolling toilet tissue until she could bury her face in a white cloud and cry. Beyond the door, the saw zipped and buzzed.

Emotions surfaced. Longings stirred. The walls around her heart trembled. Tim, her friend, was here, talking to her about her daddy, about the trunk.

But she wanted to talk to Tim, her friend, about Tim, her fiancé. How it hurt. How she missed him. How she didn't blame him for not being ready for marriage when she held back big pieces of herself from him.

When her tears ebbed, Charlotte blew her nose, washed her face, and combed her hair. By the time she opened the bathroom door, the saw had done its job.

Tim held the hasp in his hand. "Sorry, I didn't mean to upset you."

"I upset myself." Charlotte knelt before the trunk. "Let's see what's inside."

Tim gathered his tools. "I'll be out of here in a second."

Charlotte hooked her hand over his arm. "Please, stay. Someone has to witness this grand opening with me."

"Are you sure? I mean, yeah, if you're . . ."

Charlotte looked at him eye to eye for a moment. "I like having friend Tim here."

He nodded, a warm smile on his lips. "Friend Tim likes being here."

"It's just that my friend Tim looks an awful lot like my fiancé Tim."

"Maybe friend Tim will have a little chat with him." He set the drill and bits back into the case.

"Yeah, and what's he going to say?"

"You're a darn fool."

Charlotte grinned. "Okay, friend Tim, but take it easy on fiancé Tim."

"We'll see." He tapped the trunk's lid. "Come on, open this up."

Charlotte raised the lid with a ping of expectation. The fragrance of cedar escaped and surrounded them. Peering inside, she started digging through layers of tissue paper. "I think it's empty. Why would Purple Man want me to open an empty trunk?"

Tim shoved his arm inside and pushed the paper around. "There's got to be something in here."

"Like what, lost treasure?" Charlotte ran her hand along the bottom of the trunk. "Gold? Rubies?"

"Sure, why not? Whoa, Nellie, I think I found something." Tim raised a soft linen bag from the tissue paper. The top was pinched closed with a drawstring.

"What? Let me see." Charlotte moved with Tim as he carried the large bag to the bed.

"Here, you open it. It's your treasure." Tim passed Charlotte the off-white linen sack as if he were handling a newborn.

Gently Charlotte untied the strings and slid a satin bundle free. It appeared to be a gown, a perfectly preserved gown. Stepping back, she held it up, and a lovely A-line skirt with a chapel train fell to the floor.

"Is that what I think it is?" Tim said.

Charlotte swallowed with a quick glance at him. "Yeah, it is."

A wedding dress.

Tim stood, squinting at the gown. "This is really weird, Charlotte. You bought a trunk with a wedding dress in it? Right before we broke up?"

"Hey, friend Tim, tell feeling-trapped fiancé Tim I didn't know this dress was in here."

"I didn't say you did. But somebody knew."

"That's crazy. What makes you say—"

"The auctioneer. The man in purple. I mean, Charlotte, come on, what are the chances of you ending up on the ridge at an auction where you had no intention of buying anything, and you buy a trunk with a wedding dress in it? And what was it the man said to you when he came into the shop today? He had a daughter getting married?"

"What are you trying to say, Tim?" He was killing the glorious moment of discovering this amazing gown. "I'm sorry if this makes you feel *trapped*."

"Stop putting words in my mouth. But come on, Charlotte, you don't find this just a bit freaky?"

"I find it a lot freaky, but get a grip. Your former fiancée Charlotte isn't going to start crying and declare we were meant to be. Or that we should get back together."

"I wasn't anywhere near that assumption."

Yeah? Then why did he looked so relieved?

Charlotte shoved open her closet door and manhandled out an old dress form she'd stored in there. "Don't just stand there, help me."

Tim moved to help, lifting the form over the corner of her bed.

"Put it right here." Charlotte motioned to a bare section of her room where she'd intended to put a dressing table but never did. "Raise it up to its full height."

Tim adjusted the height and stepped aside as Charlotte slipped the gown over the form. The soft, swirling, layered swags of the skirt swished down to the floor as if it were glad to come to life.

Charlotte wanted to melt into the gown. The satin-silk blend shimmered in the low, gold light of her lamps. The threads seemed to glow, if she could use such a bold word. A shell of tulle and crinoline held the A-line in perfect shape. Charlotte billowed and fanned the chapel train.

"It's exquisite." The front of the skirt swooped up into a center V, just enough for a pair of stylish shoes to peep out.

"Where do you think it came from?" Tim said from his retreat to the other side of the room.

"I have no idea." Charlotte turned over the hem to examine the stitching and the seams. The ivory satin was hand sewn, not machine stitched. She'd seen enough to know the difference.

The incandescent pearls of the empire waistline were also sewn on by hand. The simple bodice appeared to be tailored and fitted for the bride. Charlotte wondered how she could find a bride to fit it without damaging the perfect craftsmanship with alterations.

Changing this gown would be like modifying a Rembrandt or adding a face to Michelangelo's Sistine Chapel.

No, she'd have to find, must find, the perfect bride for this gown. She'd know her when she saw her. God entrusted this gift to *her*.

"Tim, maybe this gown is why we broke up." She whirled around to him. It made sense to her now. "I'm a bridal shop owner. This is a wedding gown. There's a woman out there who is to wear this and *I'm* the one to give it to her."

"Excuse me?" He cocked his brow.

"Maybe God . . . wait, you know what the weird man in purple said to me? It's the season of the bride." Charlotte pressed her fingers to her forehead. "I'm not sure what that means, but maybe it means this dress was 'sent' to me?" She air-quoted the word. "To find the perfect bride to wear it."

"All right." He was dubious. Naturally. He was practical and rooted deeper than ancient live oaks. "So . . . I had cold feet because this dress belongs to some *other* bride?"

"Yes." Charlotte grabbed his shoulders, squeezed, then let go. "Maybe. I don't know. But there's something here. More to the story. Look, is there anything else in the bag?"

Charlotte moved across the room for a long view of the gown while Tim searched the linen pouch. She'd seen styles similar to this one in bridal magazines and online, but nothing exactly like this dress.

It wasn't contemporary. But neither was it vintage. She went back to the hem to look for a dressmaker or designer mark. It would be impossible for a gown of this caliber, preserved so perfectly, to be original to the trunk once belonging to a bride from 1912 as the auctioneer claimed. A hundred years old? No way.

If the gown was more than twenty years old, the fabric would have yellowed a bit, the tulle would have decayed. This gown looked like it was made . . . yesterday.

Charlotte's fingers ran over a bit of raised stitching on the back of the skirt, halfway up the seam. She lifted the hem for a better look.

TH

She sat back. TH? The initials didn't spark any recognition. Charlotte couldn't think of one wedding gown designer in the past fifty years with those initials. She'd studied them all when she thought she wanted to design instead of sell.

"Did you find something? There was nothing in the bag, but maybe"—Tim knelt beside the trunk—"there's more in the trunk." He felt around the cedar panels, knocking, cocking his head to the sound. "Sometimes trunks have secret panels."

He lifted away the last of the tissue paper and came up with a sachet. He examined it with his fingers.

"Nothing." He tossed it to the bed.

"Oh no, Tim. Not nothing. This is something. Something incredible. This gown is supposedly a hundred years old and it looks as if it's never been worn." Charlotte lowered the hem and smoothed her hand over the skirt, an electric sensation gliding up her arm and settling in her heart.

Chapter Eleven

Emily

*M*y dear, it's simply beautiful. Even better than I imagined. Mrs. Caruthers, this gown is divine." Mother walked around Emily, hands pressed to her flushed cheeks, eyes glistening.

"I added a bit more material to the skirt than was called for in the Goody's pattern." Mrs. Caruthers puffed out her chest, seemingly pleased with herself. "I always add a bit of my own style and design to each dress."

Standing on the stool in the middle of the room, muted October daylight falling across the floor from the window, Emily wanted to scream at her reflection. She looked puffy and round, nothing like herself.

The tight bodice required an even tighter corset. She couldn't draw a thimble's worth of air into her lungs. The high choke collar squeezed her throat. Her neck seemed to bear the entire weight of the heavy, winter-white satin skirt and cathedral train.

This was enough gown for two brides. Perhaps three.

The top puff of the sleeves almost reached her cheeks, and the elbows were so gripping Emily found it impossible to bend her arms. She looked like one of Howard Jr.'s tin soldiers.

She closed her eyes, pressing down a roiling scream and the urge to run from the room, ripping the dress away from her.

She stepped off the stool and went to the window. Shoving it open, she leaned out as far as she could into the Birmingham day, taking in the cool fall air in short, gasping breaths.

"Emily, do come in from there. Do you want the city to see you hanging out the window in your wedding gown?" Mother touched Emily's arm. "What do you think, dear? Isn't it lovely?"

"It's hideous," she whispered to Mother, one eye on the door, anticipating Mrs. Caruthers returning with a proper pair of matching shoes.

"Emily, what's gotten into you? It is not hideous. It's beautiful. Now you watch your words or you'll insult Mrs. Caruthers and we have a whole trousseau for her to sew."

"She needs to be insulted, Mother." Emily slipped her finger between her throat and the choking, lacy collar. "I cannot wear this gown. How she thinks it's suitable and proper for a spring wedding is beyond me. It's so restricting, I can't move. I can't breathe."

"I shall ask her to modify the neckline, loosen the waistline a bit, but otherwise, the gown is stunning, Emily. Simply stunning."

"The neckline, the waist, and the sleeves, Mother." Emily demonstrated her stiff arms. "The sleeves."

If she didn't fear fainting from lack of air, Emily might have continued arguing with her mother. But she was smothered in lace and satin, smothered in the memory of her conversation with Phillip last night. She'd finally worked up the courage to speak to him about Emmeline. The whole ordeal left her feeling like one of Father's hobbled horses.

"Is she or is she not your mistress?"

"I can't believe what I'm hearing. You're accusing me of an affair before we're even married? At least give me the courtesy of being a married man first."

"Here we are." Mrs. Caruthers set a pair of white leather high heels at Emily's feet.

Emily sat in the chair but was unable to bend over to remove her shoes. Mother had to unlace them for her. She'd not enjoy one moment of her wedding in . . . in this straitjacket.

Mrs. Caruthers finagled Emily's feet into the shoes, the sides gripping her stockings and pinching her toes. When Emily stood, she wobbled.

"I do believe they're too small, Mrs. Caruthers," she said.

"A half size, yes. But you'll get used to it. A bride needs dainty, delicate feet."

Emily scowled at Mother, dropping back down to her chair, her ribs crushing her lungs.

"You're answering my question with a question, Phillip. A simple yes or no will do. Is she your mistress?"

"Emily, there's no simple answer for a man accused of infidelity."

"No seems simple enough. I'm puzzled as to why you can't find that word on your tongue."

"Because I'm trying to fathom your accusation, my dear. I'm stunned by your inquiry."

Oh, the man drove her mad already.

"The gown is quite right for a Saltonstall wedding." Mrs. Caruthers seemed pleased with herself. "I believe it will meet with Mrs. Saltonstall's approval."

"It certainly meets with Mrs. Canton's approval," Mother said with a bit of vim and vigor. *Good for you, Mother.*

"I shall faint if I don't step out of this gown." Emily tried to stand, but she tumbled back to the chair. She flicked the shoes from her feet. "I'll take a pair in my proper size." She eyed Mrs. Caruthers, then raised her arms—rather, tried to raise her arms—to unfasten the eye hook at her neck.

"Careful, you'll rip your sleeves." Mrs. Caruthers batted Emily's hand down and began to work the eye hook, then the buttons.

"Mrs. Caruthers," Mother began in her diplomatic voice. "Please let out the waist a half inch and provide ample room in the sleeves. For pity's sake, the girl will have a bouquet in her hand as she walks down the aisle. And a reception dinner to eat. She'll barely be able to raise her toasting glass."

"I'll give room in the sleeves, but I'm only letting out the waist a quarter inch and no more."

"I daresay we're paying you to do as we ask, Mrs. Caruthers," Mother countered.

"I daresay you're paying me for my expertise." Mrs. Caruthers unhooked the last button. Emily closed her eyes as the air hit her skin. Heaven. "And my reputation."

Stepping out of the gown, Emily begged Mother to loosen her corset strings. She needed air. Freedom. When Mother relieved her from her tight corset, Emily dressed in her black-and-white shepherd's check suit, bid Mrs. Caruthers a good day, and hammered down the stairs, out Loveman's front doors, and into the skirting October breeze.

Hand to her chest, nose tipped toward the sun, Emily inhaled the cool air, finally extinguishing the fire in her lungs.

"Goodness, Emily." Mother stopped beside her gasping, pulling on her gloves. "Be upset if you will, but I'll not have you being rude and insolent."

"She's the one who is rude and insolent." Emily fitted her sailor hat on over her pinned-up hair. The wind tugged at the straight brim. "How Mr. Loveman sees fit to keep her in his employ is beyond me."

"We've been over this a hundred times, Em. Mrs. Caruthers is the best dressmaker in the city and the women of Birmingham trust her." Mother tapped the tip of her parasol on the sidewalk and raised her chin at the passing shoppers.

"I, for one, do not. Mother, please, can't we go to Newman's for an ice cream? I need something cool on my stomach." Emily pressed her hand to her middle, swallowing the bile building in her throat, breathing deep so her lungs could expand.

"It's too chilly for ice cream, Emily. How about some hot cocoa?"

"It's never too chilly for ice cream, Mother."

"Well, you must eat a hot lunch. A lunch of sweets will do you no good."

"I'll ask for hot caramel sauce. How does that sound?"

"I suppose I cannot change your mind." Mother squeezed Emily's hand. "You go on. I want to speak with your father. I noticed the bolts of velvet at Loveman's, and I realized you don't have enough velvet gowns in your trousseau. Mercy, and I've not ordered your trunk. I do wish you'd learn to placate Mrs. Caruthers, Emily. She is doing you a service, whether you believe it or not." Mother stepped off the curb and onto the trolley with the river of Thursday shoppers.

Emily watched her mother go, moving to the curb, waiting for the flow of traffic to allow her to cross. She wrestled with her frustrations. Mrs. Caruthers served no one but herself, and Mother was too determined to fit into Mrs. Saltonstall's society to see otherwise.

But now that Emily was free and making her way toward Newman's, her thoughts roamed freely through the *other* disturbance in her soul. Phillip.

Last night they argued quietly in the shadows of Father and Mother's porch, away from the parlor windows. When they'd exhausted all words, Phillip tried to sooth her with kisses and caresses.

"Whose ring is on your finger? Whose lips are you kissing?"

"Yours." She could barely hear him over her pulse raging in her ears.

"Whose heart do you possess one hundred percent?"

"Yours." He'd kissed her in a sensual, intimate manner, the touch of his hand along the top of her bodice causing her desires to flame at just the memory. Phillip certainly knew how to ignite her passions.

"I do believe I'm flattered. I made the great Emily Canton jealous."

"Don't get used to it, Phillip, it's disturbing. And I'm not the great Emily Canton. I'm just a girl getting married."

"You are the great Emily Canton. And your jealousy is intoxicating. You love me that much."

"Do you love me that much?"

"Let me show you."

He'd backed her against the house and moved his hand over her shoulders, lowering the top of her sleeves, kissing and caressing his way along her neck.

It wasn't the first time he'd answered her inquiries about his love with touches, kisses, and hot-breath murmurs of sharing his bed.

Emily halted her journey toward Newman's and pulled a card from her handbag, the gusting wind tugging at her skirt. She'd asked Big Mike to bring her the card of the colored seamstress.

Taffy Hayes.

Gaston Hotel. 5th Avenue.

"It's a fanciful day."

Emily glanced up and into the broad face and blazing blue eyes of a man perhaps Father's age. There was nothing exceptional about him. His hair was gray, and his tweed suit and vest were not the fashion of last year, but of the last century.

Yet the brilliant purple silk ascot at his throat spoke of something bold and regal about him. Emily felt at once a bit weak in the knees.

"Have I made your acquaintance, Mr.—?"

"Shall I escort you, miss?" The gentleman offered his arm as a courier sped past them on his bicycle.

"And how do you know where I'm going, sir?" Emily pressed

Taffy's card against her waist in case the man was sly and tried to read the address.

"For your wedding gown." He offered his arm. "If I escort you, you'll be safe wherever you go."

"But I do not know you. And you do not know where I'm going." Emily's fingers trembled slightly as she slipped the card back into her bag. Her heart churned. She wanted to run. Yet her legs refused to carry her away.

Again, he offered his arm. "Go on, take it. I'll not harm you. I'm safe."

Emily hesitated, then cuffed her hand around his elbow. He hailed a cab, which pulled over for them immediately, and instructed the driver to A. G. Gaston's hotel.

Gooseflesh pickled along her arms and down her back. "How did you know?" He must have read her card before she protected it.

"Is it where you're going?"

"But I didn't tell you." She held her hands in her lap, swaying with the cab, tuning her ears to the rhythm of the horse's *clip-clop*. The driver smacked the reins and chirruped the gelding into moving around a braking motorcar.

At 4th Avenue, the cab slowed with the flow of traffic. "Have you seen the new picture at the Princess Theater?" The man rested his hands atop his cane.

"I've been rather busy."

"Planning a wedding takes time. I know." The man nodded, gazing ahead, smiling wide. "And patience."

"Indeed, it does." Emily ran her hand over the multiplying gooseflesh on her arms. The gentleman seemed the sort who read the society section of the news. "You're more than a little acquainted with my business, yet we are strangers."

"Might I inquire of you? What is it you're searching for, Emily?"

"If you must know, a wedding gown." She cocked her head to one side, regarding him, trying to figure his angle. If she could, she'd keep him from electrocuting her heart with his blue gaze every time he spoke.

"What about in life?"

The cab *clopped* and rocked past a chain gang of convict lease workers. The white guards talked and joked while the men of color swung axes and hammers against the hard concrete of the city. Emily lowered her gaze. It must be back-breaking, near impossible, to break up what had been set and hardened with time in this city.

"Freedom." Her answer escaped her heart all on its own. As the cab passed the line of glistening black men in the October sun, Emily turned to watch.

The cab turned onto 5th Avenue North and pulled up to the hotel. Dark eyes stared at them from the street corner.

The driver held open her door. "I'll wait for you, miss."

"Thank you. I won't be long." Mr. Oddfellow offered her his arm again. Emily hesitated, then wove her hand through as she stepped down. His arm was taut and warm.

"Cakewalk Rag" played from an opened window across the avenue. Boys on bicycles raced down the sidewalk. A shop owner stepped out of his store to scold them for nearly running over his vegetable tables. The atmosphere buzzed with music and popped with laughter.

"Not what you expected?"

Heat singed Emily's cheeks. She stole a glance at her escort. "I'm not sure what I expected." But the gay atmosphere felt safe and homey.

"Don't you know?" he said, a rise in his voice. "If once you've been bound, your freedom is much, much sweeter."

"But they're not entirely free."

"Ah, in body no, but in spirit, yes." He shifted his blue eyes from the street scene to her face. Emily's heart churned.

"See here," she said. "How do you know so much?"

Instead of answering, Mr. Oddfellow walked Emily into the hotel, asked for Miss Taffy Hayes, then made polite conversation with the young clerk behind the hotel desk.

After a few minutes, a tall, slender colored woman wearing a tailored, vibrant skirt and blouse appeared in the lobby. "May I help you?"

"Miss Hayes?" Emily offered her hand. "My name is Emily Canton."

"I know who you are. The Saltonstall fiancée." Emily took in Taffy's lean, dark features. Her intense brown eyes observed her with a hawklike regard. "I've seen you in the papers."

"I hear you're a dressmaker. One of the best."

"One of the best?" She smiled. "I don't know about that, but I do take pride in my work. The Lord has gifted me."

"I'd like you to make my wedding gown." Emily stepped toward her, focused, the heat churning in her soul, rising. A thin, clammy sheen moistened her forehead and neck. "Name the price."

"I knew you'd come."

Emily glanced around at Mr. Oddfellow. He'd escorted her here. Led her into something surreal. Bewitched her. But he was gone. Instead, a round-faced, brown-eyed man stood in his place.

"Welcome to my establishment, Miss Canton. I'm A. G. Gaston."

"Yes, of course, Mr. Gaston. It's a pleasure."

"Please, make yourself at home."

Taffy waited and when Emily turned around, she was pierced by her steady gaze. She watched Emily as if trying to gauge her fortitude.

"I'll make a gown for you, but there'll be trouble."

"For you or me?"

"Both, I imagine. But I'm used to trouble. Are you?"

The exchange seeped into Emily, through her skin and into her sinews and bones, swirling hot around her heart.

"I don't know, Miss Hayes. I just have a sense you are to make my dress."

"Do you have courage?" Taffy started down the hall. "Come, I have an idea for you."

"For me?" Emily couldn't lift her foot to follow. She felt nailed in place. "How?"

"Like I said, I knew you'd come." Finally, Taffy smiled. A beautiful, perfect, white smile. "Do you have courage?"

"I'm here, aren't I? I want courage. I admire courage." Emily jerked forward, ripping her foot from its invisible anchor on the hardwood.

"All right then." Taffy embraced Emily with one arm as they moved down the hall.

Taffy had expected her. Emily shivered at the notion. She had little experience with God intercepting her path or the path of anyone she knew. Most of her family and friends lived simple, quiet Christian lives of doing good and filling church pews for an hour or two on Sunday. But this? God coming to her in the middle of the week?

But as her footfalls tapped the floor in unison with Taffy's, Emily had the holy sensation of being touched by the Divine.

"Ay, Emily, where have you been?" Molly met her at the kitchen door as a friend, not a servant.

"Meeting frightfully interesting people, Molly." Emily removed her hat, still carrying the glorious glow of her afternoon with Taffy. "I found a dressmaker for my wedding gown."

"I thought the high and mighty Mrs. Caruthers made your gown."

"It was ghastly. Where are Father and Mother?" Emily tucked her hat under her arm and bent to see her reflection in the shadowed part of the window, palming her hair into place, repinning loose ends.

"In the library. Your mother arrived home hours ago. She's been fretting, wondering what happened to you."

"I went to 5th Avenue to see Taffy Hayes." Emily squeezed Molly's hand.

"You don't say, miss. By yourself?"

"Yes . . . well, no." Emily opened the icebox for the bottle of milk. "This odd gentleman with a purple ascot escorted me."

"You went into the colored district with a strange man?" Molly set a glass on the cutting table for Emily, then took the bottle of milk and poured for her.

"I suppose I did." Emily pictured Mr. Oddfellow as she raised her glass. "He seemed harmless. Safe. Like I'd known him my whole life." Or he'd known her. Emily took a long cool drink. "I'd best go speak to Mother and Father."

Pushing through the kitchen door, she took the long hall to the library. She'd intended to meet with Taffy briefly, but once she'd shown Emily the sketches she'd drawn with her in mind, minutes turned into hours.

She was grateful the cabbie waited for her. Father had a large payment to settle with him.

Outside the library door, Emily inhaled, once for courage and again for confidence. "Mother, Father, good afternoon."

Mother stood, setting aside her book. "Good afternoon? It's nearly supper. Where have you been, Emily? When I left you on the corner, you were heading to Newman's for ice cream."

"You worried us, daughter." Father shoved away from his desk and walked around, taking his timepiece from his vest pocket. He supported Mother in her inquiry but winked at Emily when Mother wasn't looking.

"I went on an errand."

"Where? What sort of errand?" Mother said with a look at Father.

"If you must know—" Emily lifted her chin but not so high she gazed at Father and Mother down her nose.

"Sir." Jefferson knocked as he entered. "Mr. Phillip Saltonstall to see you."

Phillip barged in without waiting for an invitation. "What's this I hear, Emily? You went to Gaston Hotel? You were inside for hours. What in heaven's name were you doing there?"

Mother gasped, reaching back for the cloth-covered arm of her chair as she melted into the seat. "Phillip, how on earth?"

"Emily, is this true? Did you go to the colored business district?" Father reached over and patted Mother's hand. "There, there, dear. Emily must have a sound reason."

"You went to see *that* dressmaker, didn't you?" Mother pulled away from Father, her jaw set, ire forming in her eyes.

Emily stepped back, into Phillip. The confidence and courage she'd inhaled before entering the library evaporated. "I did, yes. Miss Taffy Hayes. She is going to make my gown."

"You have a gown." Mother's taut tone belied the decorum of a Southern lady. "We've paid Mrs. Caruthers, Emily. Her gown cost your father seven hundred dollars."

"Taffy's gown, along with dresses for all the bridesmaids, will only cost five hundred."

"Five hundred dollars. For all those dresses?" Mother grabbed Emily by the arms. "I'll not have you walk down the aisle in a shoddy dress with the seams coming undone."

"Mother's right. You get what you pay for, Emily." Father didn't wink at her this time.

"Father, Miss Hayes will not deliver shoddy work. You should've seen the designs she sketched for my gown. Before I even arrived." Emily absently rubbed the tingle from her arm.

"Excuse me." Phillip interjected his presence in the room. "To devil with the price of wedding dresses. Your daughter, my fiancée, spent three hours this afternoon with a Negro woman, in her establishment, in their business district. The news is all over the Highlands and Red Mountain by now. What were you thinking, Emily? You could've been raped or kidnapped."

"Raped or kidnapped? By whom? Good men, fathers and sons, trying to earn a decent living? I found the people kind and cordial, good folks just like us. Are you telling me Birmingham society is whispering a sigh of relief for my safety? Or because they are disappointed I wasn't maimed?"

"They're whispering over your utter stupidity."

"Phillip," Father said. "Let's calm down, get our wits about us."

"My wits are fine, Howard." Phillip paced in short circles, his hands on his waist, holding back his blazer. "I'm not so certain about your daughter."

"Insult me again, Phillip, and I shall leave the room."

"What were you thinking, going to the colored district? Convicts work there, right downtown where you were."

"Chained together, overseen by men with guns and whips. I could've walked down that street naked and been safer with those colored convicts than with those white guards, I tell you. And dare I say half the smarmy businessmen of Birmingham."

"Emily." Mother looked as if she might faint.

"Phillip's the one who brought up rape, Mother."

"You mock me." Phillip faced Emily, his expression stern and set. "I'll not have you going about the city, into the colored district, because you get a wild idea about a new frock. We are the Saltonstalls."

Emily sank slowly into the horsehair parlor chair. "I meant no disrespect to the Saltonstall name, Phillip." She fidgeted, wrapping her hands in the folds of her skirt. "Nor to the Canton name, Father."

"But you didn't think, Phillip said."

Emily snapped her eyes to him. He must stop insulting her. One more time and she'd—

"Tell them the rest, Emily," he said, taking a cigarillo from his waistcoat pocket. "Tell them you didn't go alone."

"Indeed I didn't." Emily stood as Phillip prepared to strike his match. Gently she cupped her hands around his, took the match, and lit it for him. Smiling, gazing into his eyes, she touched the flame to his cigarillo. "I had an escort."

"A *male* escort." Phillip lowered his lit cigarillo, holding on to the cold glint in his eyes. Emily blew out the match, squeezing his hand. She didn't know much about men, but she'd learned a few things about Phillip. Without fail, he responded to her touch. To her batting eyelashes. "Y-you worsened the situation, Emily." Phillip's handsome features softened. "When you travel with a man we do not know."

"Who was your escort?" Father asked, his tone low and steady.

"A kind old man I met on the street corner after Mother took the trolley. I called him Mr. Oddfellow because he never gave me his name." Because his name was divine. Something beyond earth. At least that's what Emily surmised on the ride home.

"Emily, what has gotten into you?" Mother's tone sounded exasperated. "It must be the stress of the wedding." She slipped her arms around Emily's shoulders. "Maybe you should go lie down. I'll have Molly bring up a cold cloth for your head."

"I don't need to lie down, Mother." Emily turned to Phillip.

"How did you know I went to the colored district? How did you know about Mr. Oddfellow?"

"I have my ways." Phillip dragged on his cigarillo so the ashes on the end burned a bright orange. "But if you must know, I saw you with my own eyes."

"Were you following me?" Emily gently pushed him around to face her. "For what reason?"

Father stepped close. "Phillip?"

"I have people, friends of the Saltonstalls, employees and workers. They watch out for us."

"But you said *your* eyes saw me." Emily narrowed into him.

He grinned, a cocky, sideways grin that caused bubbles to rise in Emily's middle. "I saw you enter the cab, alone, with your Mr. Oddfellow. He wore a hideous purple ascot."

"What were you doing downtown at two o'clock in the afternoon?" Emily said.

"I was on an errand."

Mother sighed and collapsed into her chair. "Was everyone on errands this afternoon that took them to another part of town? Howard?"

"Not me, Maggie. I was in my office as usual."

"Phillip, what kind of errand?" An image of Emmeline filled her thoughts. "There's nothing in that part of town but a print shop and furniture store. You send your *people* to do menial tasks."

"I occasionally do my own bidding. Do you think I just sit in my office and make demands of others?" He planted the cigarillo between his lips, smoke puffing about his face, his chest rising and falling with each shallow puff.

"If you saw me, then why didn't you call out to me?"

"It was too late."

"Emily, stop badgering the man." Mother stood, smoothing her hand over her skirt, plumping her hair. "I don't know why you have to be so defensive."

"And I don't know why you have to defend him instead of your own daughter."

"All right now." Father stepped between Emily and Phillip. "This sounds like a young couple's quarrel. Phillip, Emily is a fine, levelheaded girl. Even more so than some men I know."

Thank you, Father. Emily glared at Phillip. He was hiding something. Something deviant.

"Phillip, I'm sorry for the trouble Emily may have caused you."

"Not to worry, Mrs. Canton. We have connections. We'll make sure any rumors are squelched." Phillip sauced up his grin and Emily felt weak. When he shot her a brown-eyed wink, she breathed deep, tucking in her shirtwaist and smoothing a wild hair away from her face.

"Good, good." Mother patted Phillip's arm. "Now, Emily, I want to settle the issue of the dress. You will wear the gown Mrs. Caruthers made. As will your bridesmaids, I don't care the cost. That is the end of it." Mother started for the door, hitting the carpet hard with her thick heels. "Howard, I'll see to supper. Phillip, you'll dine with us, of course."

"Thank you, but not tonight, Mrs. Canton. I'm otherwise engaged. Perhaps tomorrow."

"Otherwise engaged? On a Thursday evening?" Emily watched as Father closed the library door behind him and Mother. "Are you going to the Phoenix Club?"

Hues of the pink and orange sunset broke through the shade tree limbs and settled in the tense pockets of the library. The breeze snuck through the open window and inspected Father's papers, lifting them from his desk, then back down again.

"I've made arrangements with some friends. Wainscot and

Powell. We're having a gentlemen's night. I'll not have many once we're married. We're coming up on the social season, then the holidays, and our wedding will be here before we know it. This might be my last chance."

Wainscot, the friend of willowy Emmeline. "I see. I didn't know you regarded marriage as such a killjoy. Whatever made you propose in the first place? You're getting married, not being carted off to prison."

"I didn't mean it like that, Emily, and you know it."

"I know nothing but you barging in here and accusing me of all kinds of misbehavior. I know nothing but you dancing in the shadows with—"

"Not that again. We've been over and over the dance with Emmeline. She was feeling faint and wanted fresh air." Phillip tightened his words. "Do you believe you're marrying a fool, Emily? If I did fancy that narrow waif, and I do mean if, I'd hardly carry on with her at my own engagement party."

"No, I suppose not." See, she was being girlish and immature. How could she doubt him?

Phillip's eyes flashed as he grabbed Emily and pressed himself into her, drawing her up on her toes, kissing her with a consuming fervor. He held her so tight she couldn't inhale. Or escape his hold.

His lips explored hers until Emily couldn't tell where hers ended and his began. "Come away with me tonight, Emily. Be with me."

"Phillip—" She pressed her palms against his chest. "Remember your good Christian upbringing. I'll be yours soon enough. Nothing good will come from sneaking off with you."

"Besides appeasing my hunger?" The fierceness of his tone cooled Emily's passions.

"Phillip, I'm not a two-bit dance hall girl. We'll be married soon enough."

"I'm sorry, you're right." He released her and fell back against the window. "I apologize, my love."

"Goodness, what will come over you when I'm completely yours and we're not arguing but speaking sweet nothings?" Emily bent forward to see his face, smiling.

"Yes, well . . ." He stared at the cigarillo burning between his fingers, reaching for Father's ashtray. He dashed out the smoking stick. "I must be going." Phillip took her hand into his. "But, Emily, do not go to the Gaston Hotel again. There are laws, dear, laws we must abide by, whether we like them or not."

So, the conversation had come full circle. Emily withdrew her hand from his and moved behind the wingback chair.

"Do you know why I was so long at Miss Hayes's this afternoon? Because she felt like a sister to me. As if I'd known her my whole life."

"I can't believe what I'm hearing. What on earth could you have in common with a colored dressmaker?"

"Fashion and fabric. Books. Music. Jesus. We spoke of fall afternoons and love for our families. We're both sad over the injustices in our city, with chain gangs, with women's votes, with separate but equal. We talked about weddings, marriage, and babies."

Phillip laughed, slipping his arm around Emily and twirling her around the room. "Now you're talking. Marriage and babies."

As the issues of her heart came alive with her words, Emily felt open and vulnerable to Phillip. Though she'd known him her whole life, she'd never expressed her fears and dreams to him. Or shared her thoughts on the world, people, faith.

"You're trembling." Phillip stopped turning about, his voice soft and a bit bewildered.

"Phillip, do you truly want to marry me?" She kept her right hand locked in his, her left arm looped about his neck. "Do we truly *know* each other?"

"Emily, oh, sweet Emily." Phillip cupped the back of her head and kissed her forehead. "You're something else, Emily Canton. Of course I want to marry you. But I must stand by my own conviction. I can't have my fiancée going to a colored man's hotel or working with a colored dressmaker. People talk. It's bad for business."

"I won't change my mind. Miss Hayes—Taffy—is making my gown. Phillip, it's beautiful. The one Mrs. Caruthers made is horrid."

"Then if you don't care about me or yourself, consider Miss Hayes and old man Gaston." Phillip lowered his hands, letting Emily go. "People will think you're breaking the law, maybe even stirring up the Negros against the whites."

"That's outlandish. Why would I do such a thing?"

"You went to a suffrage meeting, didn't you?"

"Suffrage is not about stirring up riots." Emily paced the room. "What is wrong with people?"

"Nothing. We simply like our boundaries and we have the community and the greater good to consider. Phillip and Emily Saltonstall can make great strides in Birmingham *if* we play the game right."

"I'm sorry, Phillip. I didn't realize how much it would upset you and your business." Emily fit her head against his shoulder as he smoothed his hand down the length of her spine. "I'll not go to the Gaston Hotel again."

"That's my good girl." Phillip lifted her chin with the tip of his finger and lightly brushed his lips over hers. "I came in angry but, Emily, you make me forget myself."

Emily shied away from his second kiss, pressing her cheek to his chest. Emily had experienced a bit of heaven on earth in the company of the seamstress and she'd not deviate from her course. If she couldn't go to Taffy, she'd have Big Mike bring Taffy here. To Highland Avenue.

Chapter Twelve

Charlotte

*C*harlotte woke from a sound sleep. Kicking off the covers, she wandered to the kitchen for a glass of water. When she returned to her room, she crawled onto the bed, cupping her glass in her hands, and stared at the dress hanging in the corner.

She batted her eyes, clearing away her dreamless sleep, and squinted across her dark room. The glow of the city lights burned between the edges of the blinds, framing the bedroom window with gold.

But the dress appeared, in some odd way, to have its own luminous energy. Charlotte plumped her pillows behind her back and stared at the dress. She had to be imagining the gown's light. Perhaps it was bouncing off of her mirror and onto the dress.

But the gown hung on the dress form in the corner, away from the window. Away from any mirror or any other light.

Charlotte sipped her water. Tim sure looked like a kid caught breaking the neighbor's window with his bat and ball when Charlotte lifted the dress from the bag.

A wash of emotion hit her eyes. He really *didn't* want to marry her. But now Charlotte had a purpose. Find out who belonged to this dress.

The next time the man in purple walked into her shop, *if* he walked into her shop, Charlotte planned to pounce.

"What's your story, dress?" Charlotte whispered. "Where'd you come from and why'd you come looking for me? One orphaned girl seeking another?" She crawled off the bed and sat on the floor, running her fingers over the silky fabric, feeling like she'd met a new friend.

Old trunk, purple man, magic gold gown. Something was up. But what?

"Help me find your bride."

Charlotte rested against the foot of her bed. Tim's fragrance lingered in the room. She tipped her head back for a long inhale, but the thick floral spice wasn't Tim's. It wasn't lingering in the room. It hovered right in front of her nose. Heavy. Oily. Unadulterated.

"Okay, God, what's up?" Charlotte drew her knees to her chest and waited.

She'd first heard God was her heavenly Father at a church youth rally when she was sixteen, four years after Mama died. Having grown up without a daddy, she thought it impossible and improbable she'd ever have someone to call Father.

But the last night of the rally when the youth speaker referred to God as Father, something changed in Charlotte's heart. And she smelled the same fragrance that now hovered in her room.

Only then, the scent was thicker, weightier, and nearly pressed her to the ground. She clung to the girl beside her to keep from crumbling. When she could think clearly, she understood God as her Father and *believed*. She couldn't have dreamed up a cooler dad.

But then, the next youth speaker hit the stage and said the only way to get to the Father was by believing in Jesus and the Cross. *No man comes to the Father but by Me.*

That option didn't thrill Charlotte at all. Jesus? Cross? Blood and dying? Sacrifice? Not for her.

A blast of cold air from the AC vent jolted Charlotte back into the present. She flipped on the bedside light and set her water on the nightstand. She hadn't thought of that youth rally evening in a long time. But it was a worthy memory.

By the time the youth pastor, Tony, finished his "Love of Jesus" message and asked if anyone wanted to know Him, Charlotte bolted down the aisle. Just closed her eyes, shut off her mind, and ran, listening to nothing but her heartbeat.

She had no idea what *saved* meant. She didn't care. All she knew was the thundering passion in her chest, the wild tremble in her legs, and that *God* was her Father. *Hello, Jesus, show me the way.*

That salvation summer she drank up, devoured, lived the reality of God's love and *desire* for her. She had a Father.

And the Cross she'd once disdained was exhibit A of Jesus's fierce love for her.

"Hey, dress, do you know God?" She laughed softly, stretching her legs over the edge of the bed so the tips of her toes touched the silky sheen of the dress. "No, I reckon you don't."

But the gown felt alive to her. She loved it already, even though she didn't understand why the gown had fallen into her hands. Or why the purple man handed her a bill of sale stamped REDEEMED.

Wednesday the shop fell quiet after a noontime rush and an appointment with a new bride-to-be and her maid of honor on lunch break. Charlotte ate half a sandwich at her desk, paying bills online and checking e-mail.

The kitchen door slammed. Charlotte looked up, listening. "It's just me." The soft lilt of Bethany. "Bringing back dresses." The seamstress angled around Charlotte's office door. "Tawny's dress is done, plus two of her bridesmaids'."

"You're the best, Beth." Charlotte smiled. "Say, what are the odds of a dress fitting without being altered?"

"It's possible. But in the bridal world, something will change. The bodice, the hem, adding padding. You know the score. Why do you ask?"

"What about a dress remaining in perfect condition for something like a hundred years? Does that ever happen?"

Bethany leaned against the door frame and laughed. "What are you up to, Char? A hundred years?" She arched her brow. "For real? Depends on how it was stored, but even if it was stored well, there's a good chance something would be tattered or yellowed."

"Yeah, that's what I thought." Charlotte rolled her desk chair over to her purse sticking out from the bottom drawer of the file cabinet. "Can you duplicate this?" She held up the silk sachet Tim found in the trunk. "I'd like to sell these."

Bethany adjusted the load of dresses in her arms and reached for the small white pouch. "Don't see these anymore. Very old style. Where'd you get it?"

"It was in the old trunk. Along with a wedding dress in perfect condition. Never altered. Not that I can tell, anyway."

"Never altered? Probably never worn then. You said it's in perfect condition?"

"Like it was made yesterday."

Bethany grinned, but Charlotte saw the invisible "impossible" on her lips. "Then it probably *was* made yesterday. But these I can make, sure. How many do you want?"

"Let's start out with ten. Mix up the colors. Maybe modify the design for brides and bridesmaids, mother of the bride, mother of the groom. I'll pitch them with the gowns. How about doing some monogramming to show what we can do with them."

"I'm on it." Bethany lifted the sachet to the light. "Pretty nice work. In fact, excellent stitching. Where'd you get this again?"

"The old trunk." She left out the Tim part. Charlotte didn't feel like hashing it out. She'd have to do a lot of explaining when she told Dixie.

"There's something in here." Bethany's fingers moved over the bottom of the sachet.

"Really? We, um, I looked but didn't find anything." Charlotte took the bag when Bethany offered it and pulled open the top drawstring.

Thrusting her hand into the bag, Charlotte landed on a cool metal plate. When she pulled it free, a set of dog tags swung from her fingers.

"Didn't expect those." Bethany stretched to see the tags. "My father was in Viet Nam. I've seen his tags a dozen times, and these look exactly like his."

"What are dog tags doing in the sachet?" Charlotte moved closer to the light on her desk to examine the engraved name.

"Got me." Bethany retrieved the sachet and backed out of the office. "I'm running these upstairs. I need to get going and pick up my kids, but I'll work on replicating this sachet tonight."

"Yeah, thanks, Beth." Charlotte sat at her desk, the tags splayed against her palm, cool and smooth.

Joel Miller

1271960

USMC - M

Protestant

The soldier had a name. And for the moment, so did the dress. Charlotte fisted her fingers over the tags, tears surprising her eyes.

Joel Miller. Was he the husband of the woman who wore the gown? Was she TH? If so, how could Charlotte find out?

A small bubble of joy bounced against her heart. God heard her prayer. He was guiding her toward the dress's destiny.

Dixie came in, a flush on her cheeks, her hair windblown, startling Charlotte from her contemplation.

"I just love that man of mine." Dixie sighed and dropped her purse on top of the file cabinet. "He was so sweet at lunch, telling me how much he appreciated me putting up with his schedule and standing with him, going without the little things and not complaining. I said, 'Yeah, well, be glad the steering wheel of my car can't quote me.'"

Dix fell against the desk and swigged from Charlotte's water bottle. "What's in your hand?"

"Dog tags." Charlotte lifted her hand and let the tags drop in front of Dixie. "They were in the sachet."

"You know, Jared just couldn't believe you got that trunk open with a hammer and screwdriver." Dixie examined the tags.

"Bethany said the tags are exactly like her dad's. He was in Nam."

"Uh-huh. How'd you get the trunk open?"

"I wonder who Joel Miller is—"

"Me too. How'd you get the trunk open?"

"Screwdriver and hammer, just like Jared said."

"Charlotte, Jared knows darn well you didn't open that trunk with a hammer and screwdriver."

"Tim. All right." Dixie could be so unrelenting. "Tim came over and cut the lock open."

"Tim, as in the guy who dumped you Tim?"

"My friend Tim. Not the mean, evil fiancé Tim. My friend Tim has tools. Real tools."

"He was there when you found the dress?" A smirk tipped Dixie's lips. A soft snort flared her nostrils.

"Well, we didn't know . . ." Charlotte read the tags again. *Who*

are you, Joel Miller? Was he still alive? If he was he'd be what . . . anywhere from sixty to seventy? If he was in Viet Nam, that is.

"What sweet irony," Dixie said. Tim helped his ex-fiancée dis-
cover a secret wedding dress. "What'd he say?"

"Nothing. Looked a bit panicked until I assured him it wasn't
some ploy to get him back." Charlotte fiddled with the dog tags. "He
did look a bit disappointed though."

"That you hadn't worked up some grand scheme to win him
back? Good grief, Tim Rose thinks too much of himself." Dixie took
another gulp of Charlotte's water. "Do you think this Joel Miller is
tied to the dress?"

"Maybe, but if he was in Nam as a young man, that'd make
him a groom in the sixties and that gown is not a sixties gown. I've
been Googling wedding dresses all morning, and I can't make out
the style or era of the gown from the trunk. Doesn't match the style
from 1912. In the teens the women wore ornate, lacy, high-collar
dresses with long court trains. Others wore more simple dresses with
hems to the top of their shoes and long tulle veils. The twenties was
the distinctive drop waist. After Bethany and I found the tags this
afternoon, I looked at dresses from the forties to the sixties and my
gown is way too . . . too . . ." Charlotte ran her thumb over her
fingers. "Rich? I can't find another word." She gazed at her friend.
"Dix, it's such a gorgeous gown. Wait until you see it."

"Brides after World War I didn't carry sachets either. I remember
a few things from my textiles class at Ohio State. And most women
of common lineage didn't wear a gown of silk or satin. They wore
muslin or cotton, even cashmere. Not until the fifties maybe, after
World War II, do you see silk and satin becoming common for weddings." Dixie popped her head out Charlotte's office door to check
on the shop. "Hey, Bethany. Bye, Bethany. That girl is like the wind,
sneaking in and out of here."

"She's going to make sachets for us to pitch with the dresses."

"Brilliant, boss. So, did you try it on?"

"The dress? No. And I'm not going to either."

"You're kidding me. Really? How can you resist? I'm itching to try it, and I'm already married." Dixie reached for Charlotte's water, but Charlotte grabbed the bottle and tipped her head toward the minifridge in the office corner.

"You do know we have a whole fridge of water, right?"

With a sigh and eye roll, Dixie stooped to open the minifridge. "Why won't you try it on?"

"Because."

"Because why?"

Charlotte turned the tags over and over in her hand, tears blurring her eyes for a moment. "I'm just not. What if it's never been worn? What if it's made for that one special bride? I'm not going to ruin it."

"Certainly someone has tried it on, especially if the dang thing is ninety or a hundred years old."

"My job is to find the woman that dress is looking for." Charlotte couldn't explain the special, hallowed reverence she had for the gown. It deserved her respect. It deserved more than an immature bride trying it on with a curled lip and a disdaining, "No, not for me." No, Charlotte's instincts would lead her to the right bride.

"It'll be like finding a needle in a haystack, but if anyone can find that wedding frock a bride, it's you." Dixie squeezed Charlotte's shoulder, then twisted open her water bottle. "In the meantime, what can we find out about the dog tags?"

"Back to Google," Charlotte said.

The search engine provided a quick answer. The tags were definitely not World War I. Nor from the Second World War—those tags were notched.

"The last notched dog tags were issued in 1964. Joel Miller's don't have the notch so they might be from the last years of Nam?"

Charlotte typed "Joel Miller" in the search bar. It was a start. A list of names splashed to the screen. Charlotte scrolled past a New York lawyer, a politician, an actor. But who or what was she looking for, expecting to find?

The front bells chimed and Dixie moved toward the door. "Keep looking," she said. "I'll take care of the customer."

Charlotte detailed her search. "Joel Miller+Birmingham." A list of names returned. After scrolling through a few pages, she refined her query just a little bit more.

Joel Miller+USMC+Viet Nam+Birmingham

The discovery of the dog tags generated a lot of questions. How did the tags get stuffed into a bridal sachet? Did Joel dump his bride before the wedding? Charlotte envisioned an angry, wounded bride taking a blowtorch to the trunk lock.

If so, then was the dress ever worn? And how had the dog tags been sealed inside?

Google's first hit brought up The Wall, a memorial site dedicated to Viet Nam veterans. *Oh, Joel Miller, are you in here?*

Charlotte entered the site, her fingers stumbling over the keyboard as she typed in Joel's name and serial number and state. An icy sensation swirled around her heart and down to her belly.

Holding her breath, fingers pressed lightly to her lips, she waited for the search to return. When it did, her eyes misted.

Joel C. Miller, Marine Corps, 1LT, 02, age 22, born September 4, 1946, in Birmingham, AL. Casualty date April 14, 1969.

Oh, Joel Miller.

And he was . . .

Married.

The words on the screen blurred together. Charlotte's heart kicked into high gear as she clicked on his info tab. His tour began on September 11, 1968. On April 14, 1969, in Quang Tri, South Viet Nam, he died from hostile fire . . . ground casualty, body not recovered.

Not recovered. Not. Recovered. What did that mean? Was he lost, left to die alone? Blown to pieces, so it was impossible to—

Mercy, mercy, Lord have mercy.

Another button took her to a bevy of postings to Joel C. Miller from friends and family and fellow marines.

"I was there the day you died. I'll always remember you, JC. Semper Fi."

"Thinking of you, Miller. Remember how we took the baseball championship our senior year at NC State just before we took off for the marines?"

Dixie returned and propped on the desk next to Charlotte's screen and leaned to see. Her ponytail swung down over her shoulder.

"Find anything?"

"He was killed." Charlotte looked up at Dix. "And he was married."

Dixie straightened, her eyes shining. "She put the dress in the trunk and sealed it shut."

"That's what I'm thinking. Listen to his bio, Dix. Joel was military honor society at the University of North Carolina, the Semper Fidelis Society, and the Scabbard and Blade. A recruited baseball player."

"Is there a picture?"

"No, no picture." But Charlotte started missing a man she'd never met, envisioning a clean-cut, rawboned, steely eyed marine.

Scrolling through the pages of messages, eyes filled with tears, she searched for a hint of the woman who might have loved him. The one who tucked his dog tags into a silk sachet before sealing them away forever.

There were only three postings on the last page and one caught her eye. It was posted three weeks ago, April 14, the anniversary of the day Joel Miller died.

"It's been over forty years, but I still think of you. You're not forgotten. I miss you, Joel C. I'm not sure my heart has ever healed. With love, Your Wife."

"Oh my gosh. She posted a note." Dixie stepped back with a sigh. "Wow, can you imagine?" She dropped a tissue over Charlotte's shoulder. "War stinks."

"Death in general stinks." Charlotte blotted the tears from under her eyes and stared at the screen, a cold, weighty realization sinking through her. "Dix, April 14 is the day I went up to the ridge to think and wound up at the Ludlow auction."

"The day you bought the trunk."

Charlotte shoved out of her chair, her thoughts rattling into place. "So, this grieving widow of forty-some years posts on Joel's wall the same day I buy the trunk with a wedding dress, her wedding dress maybe, and his dog tags shut up inside it."

"I just got chills." Dixie shivered, rubbing her hands over her arms.

"Did she leave an e-mail address?" Back at the computer, Charlotte scanned the woman's post. Yes, she'd left an e-mail address.

Charlotte clicked on the link and typed in the subject line: *Did you weld shut a trunk forty years ago with Joel's dog tags inside?*

"Charlotte, stop, you can't do that." Dixie pulled Charlotte's hand off the keyboard. "She might not want to hear from you. Or bring up memories of Joel. She put those tags in the trunk and torched it shut for a reason."

"Then why did she just post on his wall? She's obviously not afraid to think of him or read about him." Charlotte scrolled up to the last post before "Your Wife" posted. "It's been over a year since anyone else visited here. *She* posted three weeks ago." Charlotte went back to her e-mail. "I think she wants to touch him in some way. She's missing him. The dress was probably her mother's or grand-mother's, and she wore it for their wedding."

"Yes, then he died and she stored all their memories in the trunk. Charlotte, just because she posted doesn't mean she wants you to unearth her past. What looks like a painful one too."

Charlotte sighed and sat back, gazing up at Dixie. "I hate when you make sense." She combed her finger through her hair and stared at the screen. "I have to send it, Dix."

"I know you do."

Charlotte pressed Send. Now all she had to do was wait. And pray she didn't open a sealed tomb that awakened the memories of a broken heart.

Chapter Thirteen

The aroma of garlic and basil lingered in the loft long after Charlotte and Dix sat at the table with empty bowls of spaghetti and salad. Dixie had left for a movie with Jared's sister.

"Sure you don't want to come?"

"No thanks. The last time I went with you and Sally somewhere, your razor-sharp bantering sliced me to shreds."

Charlotte cleaned the kitchen, then made a cup of tea and wandered to her living room. She'd brought the dress form out of the bedroom and put it by the sofa. Sitting next to it, she aimed the remote and turned on the TV.

"This is a TV, dress. Have you ever seen TV before? Bunch of junk on nowadays."

Charlotte surfed a few channels, blowing past movies that starred geeky men winning the affections of gorgeous women who sported unrealistically perfect bosoms.

Every so often, her gaze jerked toward the dress. She could swear the thing was moving. Even glowing. Shutting off the TV, Charlotte faced the gown, sitting cross-legged on the couch.

"What? Tell me the story in your threads."

Her email to Joel Miller's wife was returned by MAILER-DAEMON. Which Charlotte found odd, because the address was just posted three weeks ago.

Did "Your Wife" delete her account so soon after posting?

Charlotte sipped her tea, compiling options, figuring ways to find out just who loved and missed Lt. Joel Miller.

As if trying to get a visual of the puzzle, Charlotte had draped the dog tags around the neck of the dress form. They rested in the swag of silk draped across the neckline.

Sliding off the sofa, she stood by the dress form, shoulder to shoulder, wiggling her toes under the hem. The skirt length fell to the top of her toes.

Maybe if she tried it on, it would fit. Maybe. But she didn't dare. Her heart didn't need the hope of a wedding or an amazing, storied gown. Charlotte moved away from the dress. It had to be a second or third generation, handed down from mother to daughter. The time-less style and the enduring fabric were incredible.

What she needed was another clue. But Charlotte was horrible at mysteries. She hated games. Mama had loved them because Mama had always won.

She could go through all the Millers in the Birmingham phone book. Might take her months to call all the names. There had to be over a thousand Millers crowded together across four pages. She'd looked for the obvious, Joel Miller or Joel C. Miller. Maybe there was a senior or a junior. But in all of Jefferson County, there was no Joel Miller.

Oooh, could there be something else in the trunk? Charlotte dashed back to her room and knelt to the floor. One by one, she removed the pieces of tissue paper, smoothing, folding, and stacking them. She felt around the bottom like Tim had done, knocking on the sides of the smooth and fragrant cedar.

When she found nothing, she called Bethany. "Was there any-thing else in the sachet?"

No, nothing else. Charlotte looked in the linen bag where she found the gown. Nothing. She shook the piece as if the threads were purposefully keeping her from answers. Then, on an impulse, she reached deep and turned the bag inside out.

A rectangular business-sized card floated free and landed by her foot. It was faded pink, with embossed magnolia petals in the corners and raised lettering across the middle. *Mrs. Lewis's Famous Pie Co. 2nd Avenue North. Downtown Birmingham.*

Mrs. Lewis's. Charlotte ran her finger over the letters. She knew this place. Tim did a fabulous remodel of the corner building that had once been the pie company.

He had turned it into an office space with upstairs lofts. Charlotte almost bought in there before she found her place in Homewood.

She auto-dialed Tim without considering the cost or implications. She needed answers. To sound this out.

"You know that building you remodeled on 2nd Avenue? You showed it to me when we walked downtown on New Year's." That had been a fun night, their sixth date but their first kiss. Standing under a string of red, blue, green, and orange lights.

"I remember." He cleared his throat.

"Didn't it used to be a bakery?"

"Yeah. Mrs. Lewis's Famous—"

"Pie Company. Right. Gert used to talk about them."

"My grandma worked there when she graduated high school. The Lewises also had the Lewis Bakery. So, what's this sudden interest in Mrs. Lewis?"

"I found her card in the trunk. In the linen sack." Charlotte waved it in the air as if Tim could see it.

"The plot thickens." Now he sounded relaxed, fun.

"Tim, oh, I'm sorry. I didn't even ask if you were busy. Are you busy?" Charlotte dropped down to her bed. Broken or not, talking to him always felt like home.

"I'd have told you if I was. So, you think Mrs. Lewis owned this dress?"

"Good question. Her daughter or granddaughter. And oh, I have dog tags."

"Dog tags?"

"I know, crazy. I found them in the sachet." Charlotte gave Tim the brief history, to which he whistled and said, "Man, that's incredible. When I searched the sachet I found nothing. Weird."

"Tim, do you think you can find out who owned the pie company building last? Or who might have worked there? Is there anything in the city records?"

"Yeah, there's plenty of buying and selling info in the records. Let me see what I can do."

"You're my hero. Let me know." Even in jest, the words "you're my hero" carried a weight she'd not intended. She coughed, slid her foot over her polished hardwood, and figured to end the conversation quick. "Thanks. Call me if you find out anything. Or e-mail. No rush. I know you're busy."

"I'll check tomorrow."

Hanging up, Charlotte wandered back into the living room and tucked the pie company card in the empire waist's sash. She dropped to the sofa and pointed her phone at the dress. "I'm going to help you find your way home. You just wait and see."

Emily

In the upstairs sewing room of the Canton home, Emily stood on a stool in her bloomers and corset while Taffy Hayes slipped the unfinished gown over her head. Mother stood vanguard, arms crossed, lips pursed.

The western windows were ablaze with the glory of the setting sun, which warmed the chilly October air in the room.

"I just love to see the fabric against a girl's skin." Taffy's slender, dark hands tucked and pinned with quick skill. "What do you think, Mrs. Canton? This ivory satin is lovely with her skin tone and the rich chestnut color of her hair."

Taffy spoke so respectfully, kind and gentle. Not like that boisterous, arrogant Caruthers woman.

When Taffy stepped aside, Emily caught her reflection in the mirror. The dress, her wedding dress, came to life. This was exactly how she pictured herself as a bride. The gown was light, easy on her shoulders. The round neck sat just below her collarbones. Not up under her chin, desperate to cut off her wind.

The skirt, or what Taffy had fashioned so far, just barely touched her shoes in front while the back swept around to a petite train.

"I have in my mind to add two flounces over the skirt, like this." Taffy demonstrated with a run of fabric. "Sort of swag down to give the skirt some character and depth. I figured an empire waist will accentuate your figure"—she smiled softly—"and I'll sew it up with pearls."

"And the bodice?" Mother's condescending tone drew a sharp glance from Emily.

"Same material as the skirt but with lace. The sleeves will be lace and silk. I do love to work in silk. My, my, Mrs. Canton, Miss Canton is as pretty as a Gibson Girl, even more so, I declare, with that thick hair and hourglass figure."

"The gown is lovely, Taffy," Mother said. "What I can see of it."

"I'm glad you like it. I haven't sewn for a—" Taffy pursed her lips. "For a wedding in a while."

"What color gowns do you sew for colored brides, Taffy?"

"Emily." Mother snapped her shoulders back, dropping her folded arms.

Emily looked at her mother in the mirror. "I mean no disrespect. I've never been around a colored girl before."

"Colored girls what can afford a wedding dress, and there ain't many, like white satin or taffeta. Some choose ivory. Most of them get married in their church dress. If they have a little bit of money, they might get married in a new walking suit."

There was no envy in her voice. Just a resolve, a resolution, to the way life was for colored girls in Birmingham.

"Most of the poor girls in this city marry in their church dresses," Mother said, as if to minimize Taffy's confession. "It's not restricted to coloreds."

"I didn't say otherwise, Mrs. Canton." Taffy stood back, taking in the shimmering fabric. "Mr. Saltonstall will be weak-kneed when he sees you walking down the aisle."

Mother ran her hand along the skirt, taking in the dropped neckline. "It'll make more of an evening dress." Her gaze lowered to the straight skirt. "Maybe you can change into it for the reception."

"Mother, no—"

"Emily, we can't tell Mrs. Caruthers 'never mind,' now."

"Caroline Caruthers? She's a fine seamstress. We were taught by the same woman, Madam Sinclair."

"See there, Mother." Emily ran her hand over the silk waist. "Mrs. Caruthers's dress makes me feel as if I'm carrying the weight of the world on my shoulders. I'll suffocate in it. Faint on Father's arm."

"Don't be so dramatic, Emily." Mother walked to the sewing room door. "Taffy, please excuse us. I'd like a moment with my daughter."

"Yes, ma'am." Taffy walked to the door with her measuring tape around her neck, stabbing the straight pins into the cushion strapped around her wrist.

"There's cake and milk in the kitchen," Mother called after her. "Tell Molly I sent you down."

Emily stepped off the stool when Taffy closed the door. "Don't, Mother. I know what you're going to say."

"Then why are you behaving like this?"

Emily walked to the window and peered out. She wasn't sure she knew the answer. In the yard below her window was the tree where Daniel surprised her two months ago.

Since seeing him at Newman's, she thought of him now and then, just memories she'd shove aside. But with her next breath, Emily knew she missed him. Something about the day, about being fitted with Taffy's dress, stirred her longing for him.

When she looked at Taffy, listened to her talk, Emily felt a kinship with the older colored woman. More than just a common faith in Jesus, but a sense of feeling . . . trapped. Locked in by society, expectation, and the wants of others.

"Emily." Mother touched her arm and bent her head to see Emily's face. "Tell me, dear, what are you thinking to have that expression on your face?"

Smiling, Emily tapped the windowpane. "Remember when we first moved here and Howard Jr. and I dug up the backyard to make a fort?"

"Mercy, I do." Mother pressed her hands to her cheeks. "I'd just joined the garden club and was to host my first meeting. My prize lawn and roses were destroyed."

"We were terrified." Emily laughed, pointing to a far willow tree. "We hid up there trying to decide if we were going to run away or not. We just knew Father would strap us."

Mother smiled. "But you two didn't mean it. I knew you didn't."

"You told Father you handled it and he merely gave us a stern look at dinner and reminded us to behave, that we lived among a different kind of people."

"Something we can never forget. Something you must remember now, Emily. Is it our society that's bothering you? Our friends?"

"I do admit, Mother, it feels as if you and Phillip, even Father, are trying to fit me in a mold so society will like me." Emily moved away from the window, the soft swish of the silk around her legs. "It's my wedding. I want to wear a gown I love. I don't care if the seamstress is the one the Woodward or Campbell girls used. Or if she's colored."

"Now, you listen to me." Mother's heels thudded as she crossed the floor. "You will wear the gown Mrs. Caruthers made, and that is the end of it. As soon as the wedding is over, you may change into this gown Taffy is making."

Emily faced the mirror, sighing. She'd met defeat. "Mother, are you happy?"

"You're vexing me a bit at the moment." Mother's light tone betrayed her scowl.

"Are you happy with Father?"

Mother's cheeks pinked. "Don't I look happy?"

"Has he ever been unfaithful to you?"

Mother inhaled sharply. "Mercy, girl, what a thing to ask. Certainly not." She fussed with the satin and silk still draped over Emily. "Your father and I were cut from the same cloth. He escorted me to my debutante ball, and I don't think he ever left my side. This gown *is* quite lovely. Gracious, I believe Taffy sewed with gold thread."

"Do you think I'm cut from the same cloth as Phillip Saltonstall? Is he a man like Father?"

"He's a very powerful man from a very powerful family. He adores you, Emily. I'm very proud and happy for you. This is a good match. For you, for our families. Even for Howard Jr. You and Phillip will be quite the couple of our Magic City. In fact, I was speaking to Della Branton at bridge club and she's decided to attend suffrage meetings with her daughter because of you. If the future Mrs. Saltonstall believes in suffrage, she will too."

"How foolish. I've been to a few meetings. I'm not even sure I believe in suffrage. She should believe in a cause because her heart tells her, not the future Mrs. Phillip Saltonstall." So now she was responsible for the convictions and actions of others?

"Oh, my dear, you are your father's daughter." Mother softened, her smile fresh with love. "So forthright at times." She kissed Emily's cheek. "You're going to be very happy with Phillip. He'll be a wonderful husband. He's quite handsome, don't you think?"

"Mother, I saw him with another woman." The confession released a valve in her heart. "The day we first met with Mrs. Caruthers, when I leaned out Loveman's window."

She'd been pondering Phillip and Emmeline for quite a while. In the evenings Daniel's letters tucked under her bed called to her. But she could not very well read them if she didn't want Phillip involved with another woman. Weren't love letters the same? Emily involved with another man? Daniel? Even if it was only in the privacy of her own heart?

"Goodness, Emily. Phillip knows everyone. He's twenty-eight years old, with friends all over the city."

"It was the woman who attended our engagement party with Herschel Wainscot. Emmeline Graves."

"Emmeline Graves? Why, she's barely off her mother's bosom. Never you fear. A man like Phillip is looking for a woman, not a girl."

"Mrs. Canton, Miss Canton," Taffy called from the other side of the door. "Might'n I come in? If Miss Molly served me any more cake and milk, with such kindness, I might never leave."

"Yes, do come in. We're ready. Now, please fashion this into a reception gown for Emily." Mother headed to the door. "I'm going to check on luncheon."

Taffy went to work with a glance at Emily as she stepped up on the stool.

"Fashion this into a wedding dress, Taffy."

The colored woman worked in silence for a moment, pinning and measuring. "What situation have you gotten yourself into, Miss Canton?"

"I'm sure I don't know what you mean."

"Once in a while, the Lord gives me night visions—"

"A dream?"

"A dream . . . yes. I see dresses. Made one for Mr. Gaston's daughter a few years back. The night before you visited me, I saw a gown. When I woke up, I put it down on paper. You're wearing it right now."

"What do you think it means, Taffy?" Emily bent to peer into her eyes, her heart trembling in her chest.

"I'm sure I don't know. I can only guess that you're going to need the courage of heaven to wear this dress."

Chapter Fourteen

Daniel

*I*t was late. Friday night. After a long, hard week at school, Daniel arrived at the Italian Garden, comforted to find his friends gathered at a table in the corner. With a nod at the maître d', he started toward them.

"Daniel." Ross shook his friend's hand. "We thought you forgot us, chum."

"Midnight, Ross? Can't you find a more decent hour to socialize?" Daniel took his seat, then greeted the man on his right. "Alex, can't you talk sense into him?"

"No, and seeing as you've been his friend longer, you should know better." Alex smiled, clapping Daniel on the back. "Besides, the theater has just let out as well as the symphony." He nodded toward the front of the restaurant. "All the pretty ladies should be coming through that door any moment."

"With their escorts, I imagine." Daniel barely glanced at the couple entering the restaurant and instead, reached for the menu. "I'm famished." After the school week, he'd spent his Friday evening not in the company of a soft, lovely dame but attempting to launder his own clothes. He was exhausted. But his compassion for the "weaker" sex, who tended such arduous chores, rose ten notches.

Ross zipped the menu from Daniel's fingers. "Escorts can be fathers, brothers, uncles. Don't keep your mind so closed, Ludlow."

"I'll keep that in mind if a girl enters who's so gorgeous she makes my heart forget my stomach." He snatched back his menu, flopped it open, and started to read. *If Emily Canton walked in . . .* "I warn you, my stomach is very important to me."

"How's life at the Ridley, chum?" Alex said.

"Decent. There's a grandmotherly lady who likes to bake me cookies. Leaves them at my door for when I come home from the institute."

"There you go. You don't need a wife now." Alex motioned for the waiter. "A round of waters and some bread to start with—give us a minute to figure out the rest."

"Starving, Al?" Ross put away his menu.

"You made Danny and me wait until almost midnight to eat, Ross. What do you figure? I could eat a horse."

Ross smacked his palms together. "I'm going to polish off a large plate of spaghetti and meatballs, then I'm going to dance the Navajo Rag with the cutest girls in the joint until the sunlight glints off the top of Red Mountain."

"I'm not dancing with no glue shoe." Alex sat back, took his pipe from his jacket pocket, and propped it between his lips without lighting it. "I don't care how pretty she is. She's got to know how to dance."

Daniel grinned. "That pipe makes you look like your father, Alex."

"Good, I hate being twenty-three. You should hear the way the senior bank managers talk to me. Like I was a snot-nosed child. The other day one of them patted me on the head."

Ross tipped back his chair as he laughed. "Bide your time. In a few years you'll be patting the new tellers on the head."

"I pray not." Alex slipped his pipe back into his pocket. "It's humiliating."

"How's it with you and Georgette, Alex? Are things getting serious?" Daniel closed his menu, deciding on the linguini dish. He moved aside for the waiter to set down the bread basket and the waters.

"I think so. But who knows? How can you tell who's the one?" Alex took a slice from the basket and bit off an entire half. He gazed at the boys and tried to speak while chewing. "I told you I was hungry."

Daniel took a piece of bread and set it on his plate. "If you find the answer, let me know."

"Cheer up, chum, there're other women besides Emily Canton." Ross craned his neck to see the girl sitting at the neighboring table. "She's a looker there."

Daniel didn't bother to inspect Ross's choice—every gal in a gown was a looker to him. As he buttered his bread, he took a coy survey of the room.

The Italian Garden was a soft lit, romantic place, with an Italian band playing songs from the home country. But at midnight the joint went ragtime and jazz. There were quite a few lovelies around, but most seemed connected to a fella.

"Can't believe you quit baseball to marry Emily and she dumped you for Saltonstall." Alex shook his head. "Don't envy you, son."

"Worse, the society sections of the *News* and the *Age-Herald* report practically every blade of grass crushed under their feet." Ross squinted down his nose, raising his chin. "Mr. Phillip Saltonstall and his fiancée, Miss Emily Canton, attended a dinner at the Strasburg home in Red Mountain in honor of their engagement. Miss Canton wore a lovely evening gown of—"

"Chum, have a heart. We get it . . . you can read." Daniel stuffed his bread in his mouth, then punched Ross's shoulder.

After Emily's engagement he'd avoided the society section,

even the business pages where some article usually focused on the Saltonstalls. Or Howard Canton.

"Have you met Saltonstall?" Alex said, intrigue in his voice.

"Not in person. Just read about him. Did you hear Saltonstall mines had the largest number of labor gang deaths than any of the other mines? Can't find that in any of our fine newspapers. Why don't you do some digging on that, chum." Daniel motioned to Ross.

"If it's not in the papers, then how do you know?"

"A friend of Dad's is a guard at one of their mines," Daniel said.

"When you got that kind of money"—Alex tore off another bite of bread, elbows on the table—"you can get away with whatever you want."

"You got that." Ross swiveled around when the music started, snapping his fingers to the ragtime beat.

"Enough to make a man think women do need the vote." Daniel raised his voice above the music.

Ross snapped his head around, eyes wide. "Now you're just talking nonsense, Ludlow."

"I'm just saying *maybe* suffrage makes sense." He reached for more bread, resisting the urge to consume the remaining slices. The years his mother spent drilling manners into him had permanently stuck.

"Call the doctor, Alex, Ludlow's lovesickness has muddled his brain." Ross tapped his temple.

"I'd love for a dame to come around and muddle my brain," Alex said, shoving bread into his mouth, trying to catch the attention of the women sitting at the neighboring table.

"I'm neither muddled nor lovesick," Daniel said. "I'm a thinking man."

"Oh, come now, chum—" Ross scoffed.

Their banter worked its way around the table, back and forth, moving from suffrage to sports and the end of the Barons' season. When the waiter arrived with their food, Ross sat back, patting his belly. "Delightful, Angelino. How about a round of vino?"

"Certainly, Mr. Kirby." The waiter backed away, his olive skin, dark eyes, and thick hair revealing his Italian lineage.

Daniel picked up his fork and twirled his noodles into a thick ball, inhaling the aroma of garlic and tomatoes. The first bite—hot and delicious—warmed his bones and energized his emotions. But talk of Emily only made him miss her more. A dozen times he'd gone to the phone room at the Ridley House to place a call to the Cantons, but hung up before the operator could take his request.

"Tonight, we get you dancing, Ludlow. On your feet, twirling over the dance floor with a pretty belle in your arms. Yes, we will." Ross cut up his meatballs.

"So you've said."

"Nothing like a gal to make you forget another."

"Unless the first one is unforgettable."

Ross made a face at Alex. "I told you, pal, call the doctor. Danny-boy is lovesick."

Daniel released his angst with another forkful of pasta and a slow grin at his buddies. Ross had been his best friend since their Phi Delta pledge days at the university. More than anyone, save God, Ross understood Daniel's struggle over Emily. He'd been the first to hear the news when Daniel returned to their quarters after his first date with her. "She's the girl I'm going to marry."

Ross kindly listened, without snickering, and did not consider him a fool. Even now, he didn't recall Daniel's silly, failed, romantic notions in front of Alex. The dinner talk moved to work—Daniel's students and his position at the Institute, Ross's reporting at the

Birmingham Age-Herald, and Alex's banking aspirations—then back to the true longing of the gents' hearts.

"The only feminine thing I touch these days is the tip of a woman's glove as I pass her money across the counter at the bank." Alex brought his fork to his lips for an exaggerated kiss. "How'd I do, boys? Think I can remember how? What's a fellow to do for a date these days?"

"Have money," Daniel confessed before he'd considered his words. But he didn't repent. It's what won Saltonstall Emily Canton's hand.

"Look at it this way, Danny boy. If all it takes to win Emily is money, what kind of girl is she anyway? Deep down where it counts? What kind of wife and mother would she be? What would happen if you fell on hard times? The first rich, debonair man to come along would steal her affections while you were out breaking your back to make ends meet." Ross stabbed the air with his fork, his dark hair falling loose from his hair cream and flopping over his forehead. "No, no, you're better off, chum. Believe me. Best you find out now the kind of woman Emily is."

"That's the thing. The Emily I knew *wouldn't* marry a man for his money."

"That's what she had you believing, chum. I see it like this . . ."

Back and forth, debating, laughing, deciding if one married for love or money or beauty. If a woman could marry for money, why couldn't a man marry for beauty?

"The more money in a chap's bank account, the lovelier his bride. It's the way of the world," Alex insisted. "I see it every day."

Talk of love somehow morphed to talk of sports. The discussion was serenaded by the clink of glasses and the clank of silverware against porcelain plates, scented with the aroma of melting candle wax, garlic, hot bread, and fruity wine.

The warm room, with music and laughter, sank into Daniel's soul, lifting his tired spirits. Ross and Alex proved to be far better chums than he'd been lately. They were right. Emily wasn't the only beautiful, kind, smart, loving gal in Birmingham.

It's just . . . Daniel downed the last ounce of his wine. It's just that the melody of her laugh still sang him to sleep at night.

She'd been the center of all his dreams and plans. Sometimes when he looked up from grading papers by the evening gaslight, he felt as if only half his heart were beating.

As the waiter cleared away their plates, Ross mused over his life plan and what he might do for his future. Daniel mentioned rather off the cuff he might continue his education, perhaps seek a professorship. Politics interested him.

Yet no matter how hard he tried to envision the future, Emily's face proved to be the most distracting roadblock.

In the middle of Alex's dissertation on rising through the banking ranks, he let out a low, slow whistle, nodding toward the door. "Now there's a blessed feller. Moneyed, by the cut of his suit, and escorting a goddess of a woman. I've just got to get some of my own money to flash around."

"Chin up, Alex, it's not all about—" Daniel's exhortation ceased as he turned toward the door, his eyes landing on the man beneath the top hat and tuxedo. All the light in the room narrowed onto his face. "That's Saltonstall," he whispered.

What was he doing here after midnight? And with *her*. He'd not seen them on the street since the day he spoke with Emily at Newman's and tipped her off.

Nor had his police officer father and brother seen or heard anything of Phillip Saltonstall's extra activities.

"Saltonstall? Which one—the father or the brother?" Ross angled around for a better look.

"That's not a brother. Or father." Daniel quick about-faced, putting his back to the door. What a lowdown scum. "That's Phillip."

"Phillip? The one engaged to your gal?" Alex whispered far too loud, rising up, craning his neck to see. "So that's Emily? No wonder you're lovesick, chum. I'm sick for you."

"That's *not* Emily." Daniel shoved his wineglass out of the way, reaching for his water goblet. His mouth was a desert and his heartbeat shoved his nerves to the edge.

"Are you sure that's Phillip? You said you never met him." Ross glanced again at the door.

"Not in person, no." Daniel pressed his hands on the table and stood. "But that's him." The linguini had cemented in his belly so all of his movements felt slow and stiff, but he'd not let Saltonstall get away with his deceit. "And it's high time I did."

"What are you going to do?" Ross said.

"I don't know." Daniel maneuvered through the check-clothed tables and long, thin candlelight.

Across the front of the restaurant, the maître d' led Phillip and the woman through the low shadows. For a moment Daniel considered giving Phillip the benefit of the doubt. Perhaps the woman from the street was indeed a cousin or a friend. Yet the intimate position of his hand on her hip told him otherwise. Drawing close, Daniel cleared his throat.

"Paul! Excuse me, Paul. It's me, Daniel."

Phillip drew up, glanced back, moving his hand to caress the woman's bare shoulder.

"Paul, don't you remember me?" Daniel smiled large and offered his hand.

"I'm afraid I don't. You confuse me with my brother." Phillip shook Daniel's hand in one hard clasp.

"Yes, of course, Phillip. Begging your pardon. I'm Daniel Ludlow."

"The ballplayer with the Barons. I've seen you pitch."

"Have you now?" Any other time, he'd be flattered. But not tonight. "Shall I bow in triumph or shrink away in shame?" Daniel hooked his thumbs into his vest pockets, bowing toward the woman. She was beautiful, willowy, and fair, with crystal blue eyes and ruby red lips.

"Take a bow. You pitched a no-hitter," Phillip said with a trumpet of admiration.

"Then it was a good game." He turned to the woman. "Sorry to have disturbed you, miss."

"Not at all," she said with refined Yankee diction. "Phillip and Paul do favor one another. They're both so handsome." She snuggled into Phillip and Daniel expected to see him stiffen or move away, but he only drew her in closer.

"Come along, my dear." Phillip turned her toward the waiting maître d' and the open door of a private side room. "We've a table waiting."

"It's a pleasure to meet you." Daniel reached for her fingers, bowing to kiss her hand. "Miss . . ."

"Graves. Emmeline Graves."

Emmeline. "I hope to make your acquaintance again sometime."

"Of course, Phillip, maybe he could join us?" She giggled as Phillip squeezed her and inched her toward their private room, protesting her suggestion with a husky whisper.

Back at his table, Daniel yanked out his chair so the legs rattled against the stone floor. The band played a slow dance number.

Alex looked up from reading the dessert menu. "Is she a vision up close?"

"Quite becoming." Daniel peeked back to the spot where he'd met Phillip and Emmeline. "He, however, is a prig."

"So, what are you going to do, chum?" Ross's expression matched the shadows in the room. "Sit there and grumble?"

"You have to tell her. Emily, I mean." Alex hammered the table with his fist. "Be her hero. Win her back. Let her know what a scoundrel she's marrying."

"She already knows."

"She knows? Then why is she with him?" Alex spoke too loud, gesturing to the waiter as he passed by. "Three slices of chocolate layer cake please."

"I saw him with her on the corner of 19th a few months back, getting a little cozy. In broad daylight, mind you. Then I ran into Emily. Turns out she saw him too. She asked me if Phillip had a mistress and I said yes. Then she called me a liar." Daniel surveyed his friends. "So I tell her about tonight? She doesn't want to know. Besides, it'll humiliate her and gain me no favor. 'Hello, Emily, I was out with Ross and Alex last night and saw Phillip with a strikingly beautiful woman named Emmeline. Would you like to go to the Strand for a picture show?'" Daniel shook his head, running his fingers over his curls. "No, I can't do it."

But he had to do something. *Lord, what am I to do?*

"I suppose you're right. Can't win there, can you?" Ross said.

"Not one iota." Daniel was trapped. Darned if he did. Darned if he didn't. "I can just hope she finds out, right?"

"More like pray she finds out," Alex said.

Daniel sat back, considering the evening, a sudden, warm smile tapping his soul. If he'd had his way, he'd have stayed home tonight and read a book. But instead, he yielded to Ross's insistence that he get out, have some fun. Daniel clapped his friend on the back. "I owe you, chum. For making me come out tonight."

Sometimes luck put a man in the right place at the right time. Sometimes, a good friend. But more often than not, Daniel mused, it was the providence of God and His never-ending grace.

Charlotte

The clatter of teacups came from the other side of the wall. Mrs. Pettis insisted on making tea.

"Can I help you?" Charlotte called as she shifted on the edge of a worn mohair sofa. Her knee cracked the sharp-edged coffee table. Furniture was jammed in every space from one end of the room to the other. Charlotte didn't know how the old baker got around without running into a chair or table.

The long, narrow room smelled of lemon drops. Lace curtains hung limp at the windows and grayish white doilies covered the arms of every chair and the back of the sofa.

Across from Charlotte, Tim sank down into a tired wingback. Using his city connections, he'd found out the last owner of Mrs. Lewis's Famous Pie Company was Aleta Pettis. Tim called her Monday morning, and by Monday afternoon Charlotte was riding with him down I-20 toward Irondale.

"Sure you don't mind me being here?" he said, pulling himself out of the soft cushion and perching on the edge of the seat.

She shrugged, taking in the pastoral pictures on the wall. She kind of minded, but . . . "You might as well see the fruit of your labor." Charlotte peered at him. He'd practically insisted on driving her to meet Mrs. Pettis. But what was he really doing here? Was he *that* curious about the wedding dress?

Pieces of her lunch conversation with Dix flitted around Charlotte's head.

"Careful, Char, you'll start thinking he's into you."

"How do you know he's not?"

Dixie lifted Charlotte's bare ring hand. "Exhibit A."

"I'm the one who returned the ring. He didn't ask for it."

"Of course not. He's got some kind of heart. Can't call off a wedding and ask for the ring back on the same night. Got to do it in stages."

"Dixie, he wanted to stay engaged."

"But not get married? Hello, Charlotte, if he's not marrying you, he's not into you. No man gives up a girl he really wants."

"How do you know?"

"Jared. He spilled the guy code on our honeymoon."

So Charlotte shifted her body at an angle, away from Tim. *If he's not marrying you, he's not into you.*

"Here we go, young people. Tea. Oh, the cookies, I forgot the cookies." Mrs. Pettis wagged her finger in the air as she headed back to the kitchen. "They're not homemade, sorry to say. I had to give up baking. Now where are those cookies?" Cupboard doors opened and closed.

Tim sniffed his tea. "She seems nice enough."

"Don't you mean safe enough?" Charlotte inhaled the hot, sweet scent of brewed tea. "Tim, there's no way she's going to remember a cake she made in 1968. Or '67. Or whenever Joel Miller got married."

"You have a name. That'll narrow it down."

"A name. The groom's. You really think she'll remember the groom? She probably never met him."

"Let's just ask. See what she says."

Faith. Tenacity. Maybe that's why he came along.

"Here we go. Cookies." Mrs. Pettis held up a rubber-banded package of Oreos. She wobbled, reaching to hold on to a chair. "I lose my balance from time to time." She unwrapped the green rubber band and slid the cookies onto a china plate matching the cups, both with a faded baby's breath pattern. "So, you want to know about Mrs. Lewis's?"

"Yes, ma'am." Charlotte set her cup and saucer on her lap and reached for the pie company's business card in her purse. "I found this card in an old trunk, along with a wedding dress and a set of dog tags."

"Oh my." Mrs. Pettis ran her finger over the raised print on the card. "Haven't seen one of these in years." Her gaze glistened when she looked up.

"Do you know the name Joel Miller, Mrs. Pettis? It's the name on the dog tags I found. Is he related to you? Maybe married to your daughter?"

"I never had a daughter. And my son is a Pettis, naturally. I don't know any Millers. At least not a Joel. 'Course, my memory ain't what it used to be."

"He died in 1969. Killed in Viet Nam."

"Oh my, oh mercy, that is sad, right sad."

"Do you think maybe you made a cake for his wedding? Based on his birthday and death, I think he might have married sometime in '68?"

"I suppose that's possible. I made a lot of wedding cakes in my day. First working for Mrs. Lewis, then when I owned the place. We had so many, many customers. They all knew our names, naturally, but we smiled and called everyone Jimmy. Even the ladies." Mrs. Pettis laughed behind her hand, chewing on her cookie. "Do you know I calculated how many pies I made in my forty years as a baker. Two hundred and twenty thousand pies. My land, I about choked on my own gizzard."

"How many wedding cakes?" Charlotte wanted to get a feel for the odds of her making Joel Miller's cake. Maybe that would lead to finding his bride. How, Charlotte had no idea. If she fished with enough questions, maybe something would bite.

"Oh sure, about twenty thousand cakes." She chortled. "Makes me feel kind of like I accomplished something. Didn't feel so important doing what any woman could do in her kitchen. But I took pride. Made each pie and cake with care. I loved the bakery. It was such a sad season when all the businesses shifted away from downtown. All those great buildings, great stores like Loveman's and Pizitz just closed up and vanished, as if they never existed."

"Would you like to keep this card, Mrs. Pettis?" Charlotte offered the woman a remnant from her glory days.

Her hand trembled as she reached for the card and her eyes glistened. "Now, what can I do for you young people? Are you getting married?"

"No, no," Charlotte said, "we're just friends."

"We were going to get married, but—"

"We're just friends." Charlotte shot Tim a look.

"Did he cheat on you, sugar?" Mrs. Pettis reached for another Oreo. "I'm sorry, son, but you seem like the cheating kind. Handsome men with long hair usually are, you know."

Charlotte wanted to laugh, but Tim seemed rather taken aback. Served him right. "He didn't cheat, Mrs. Pettis. Just decided he wasn't ready for marriage. He's only thirty-two." Those Oreos were looking better all the time. Charlotte reached for one. "He waited a full twenty-four hours after he broke my heart to go on a date."

"It wasn't a date. Just a friend dining with a friend."

"My," said Mrs. Pettis.

"His ex-fiancée." Charlotte wrinkled her nose at the older woman as if they shared something in common, something womanly. And she liked watching Tim squirm.

"My, my." She waved her half-eaten cookie at Charlotte. "It's the good-looking ones with the hair you got to watch, I'm telling you. It was the same in my day."

"Can we please just get to the business at hand?" Tim ran his palms over his hair, picked up his petite teacup with his large hand, then put it down. "Mrs. Pettis, is there any way we could find out about Joel Miller? Who he might have married? Do you remember him? He was a soldier, a marine."

"You say he died in the war? So many good men lost in wars. My own brother died in the war. The big one. My father was never the same afterward. He'd come home from the steel mill, sit in his chair and read the paper, then he'd go out to the front porch, lean against the post, and stare beyond the neighbor's yard like he was waiting for his son to come home. Sometimes I think he longed to be with him, away from the stinking mill. He died himself about ten years later. Consumption got him like so many of the mining men. There used to be a ring of smog hovering over the city. Do you kids remember? I suppose you're too young. My mother couldn't even hang out her clothes on the line without getting them smudged."

"Mrs. Pettis." Tim stood. "Thank you for your time. Charlotte, I need to get back to the office."

What office? Charlotte gave him the sit-down eye.

"My old bakery is an office space now, you know."

"Yes, and loft living on the second floor," Tim said, sinking back down to his chair.

"Well now." Mrs. Pettis sniffed the air, wrinkling her nose. "I wonder if folks can still smell the baking pies in the old bricks. We used to say baking was the aroma of heaven." She laughed, strolling down her private memory lane, consorting with people alive only in her heart. "We used to do it up for Christmas too. Decorations and candies. We had a little contest with Newberry's and Mary Ball

Candies. Downtown was the happening place. 'Course, in the days you're talking about, racial tension was mighty high. Downtown became right scary what with the church bombing and police dogs being let loose on folks. But those days are behind us now. Hallelujah."

Charlotte peered at Tim. Mrs. Pettis wasn't going to help them, was she? "Thank you again, Mrs. Pettis." She carried their teacups to the kitchen. When she came out, she joined Tim near the door. "We enjoyed meeting you." Her heart sank a bit. Now what? Where could she find Joel Miller? Hire a detective? She hadn't even done that to find her own father.

"Mrs. Pettis, we need to get going." Tim twisted the door knob. Charlotte slung her handbag under her arm with a final glance at the old baker.

"Too bad. I got a whole attic of bakery records going back to 1939. Your Joel Miller and his bride most likely will be in there."

"How'd you like that routine?" Tim said when they landed at the top of the attic's narrow staircase. He shoved boxes aside to make a path. "'Oh, you kids, I don't remember any of my customers, called everyone Jimmy. By the way, I have sixty years' worth of records in my attic.'"

"Stop. You're just sore because she said men like you are unfaithful."

"She said men who *look* like me are unfaithful." Tim kicked a box out of the way.

"That's it, take it out on the box."

"It's hot up here. Can we just find the"—he moved to the wall shelves loaded with boxes—"whatever we're looking for and go?"

"Hey, you're free to go anytime, Tim. I'm going to look for the invoice or something with the name Joel Miller and his bride. Go if you have to go."

"And how will you get back?"

"Bus. Cab." Charlotte surveyed the room under the warm eaves. Small sailors' windows on either side of the attic let in enough light for them to see. Tim was working his way through the furniture to turn on a Tiffany-looking floor lamp by a wide-seat willow rocking chair.

"Look to your left, Tim. Isn't that a Victrola? And a Westinghouse radio."

"My grandpa had one of these in his garage." Tim absently turned the radio knobs.

Old suits, faded dresses, and a coat with the scarf and gloves stuffed in the pockets hung on a line strung from one pitched corner to the other.

"And people wonder if time travel is possible. They should come here." Charlotte unbuttoned her Malone & Co. jacket and slipped it off, draping it over the stair rail. "I think what we want is on those shelves, Tim." She pointed to the far wall. When she looked around, he was watching her. "What?" She nudged aside a box of folded clothes.

"When I told Mrs. Pettis we were going to get married, I didn't mean to upset you."

"Can we just find the bakery records?" Charlotte motioned again to the shelves. "These boxes look official, don't they?"

"That's what I was thinking." Tim crossed over and pulled out the first box from the bottom shelf. "Yep, bakery records and they're dated. The box is marked 1959." He pulled the lid off and took out an invoice. "December 1959. All of these are 1959."

"Okay, so let's find '67, '68, and '69 and see if we can find Joel Miller." Charlotte reached for a box on her far right, two shelves up from the bottom.

It was marked 1967. She dropped it to the floor and knelt beside it.

"Man, she made a lot of pies and cakes." Tim checked over his shoulder from his spot by the shelves. "Did you find something?"

"Maybe," Charlotte said, her fingers flying through the invoices. "She separated them by months."

Tim reached for the box marked 1968. "It feels so normal with you. I forget we're . . . you know. Broken up."

"Try to remember, will you?" On top of filing the invoices by month, Mrs. Pettis had alphabetized them. "Looks like she filed wedding cake orders by the bride's last names."

"But we don't know the bride's last name."

Charlotte looked up, smiling. "But we know the groom's, and Mrs. Pettis wrote the groom's name below the bride's."

"Jackpot. Now, if we can find Joel Miller . . . Charlotte, what if Mrs. Pettis didn't make their cake?"

"Shh, don't say that out loud. You'll jinx us." Charlotte fingered through July and August of '67. Nothing. "Is it because of *her?*" she braved to ask, but without looking at Tim.

"Her? What are you talking about?"

Charlotte sighed. Loud.

"Kim? No, I didn't postpone our wedding because of *her.*" He mimicked Charlotte's inflection. "I told you she didn't call until after we . . . talked. I just need to sort some things out, Char."

She turned her face to him. His blue eyes peered at her from under his dark brows and seemed to gaze straight into her heart. "I'm sorry I hurt you. I really am."

"I believe you." Charlotte went back to her box, flipping through the invoices. "But we're over. Moving on. Better to find out we're not right for each other before the wedding than after." Why couldn't she be mad at him? At least keep a wall built between them. Instead, he melted her resolve at the very hint of his sweetness.

Tim took the top off his box. "I never said we weren't right for each other. I think we fit pretty good. I just—"

"Tim, we came here to find out who Joel Miller married. Let's just do that." Charlotte went back to the invoices. As if she could read the handwriting through her watering eyes.

In contemplative silence they worked through the boxes. Then the crackle of thin paper suddenly ceased from Tim's box.

"Hello, pot-o-gold." He held up an invoice to the hot, hazy light fitting through the small windows.

"You found it? Really?" Charlotte stooped to see over his shoulder. His cologne seeped through the oxford threads of his shirt as she rested her palm on the familiar muscled curve of his arm.

She let her hand fall away. Breaking up had ended her time with Tim, but not the longings of her heart.

"Here we go," Tim said, looking up at her, his eyes full of comfort. Charlotte dug her fingers into her knees. If she wasn't careful, she'd trip and fall in love. "Bride. Hillary Saltonstall. Groom. Joel Miller. They ordered a coconut cake with lots of icing. Look, *lots* is underlined three times." Tim tapped the paper, his smile a white beam. "Pick up the morning of the wedding. September 8, 1968." He stood, slinging his arm around her and kissing her forehead. "We found our bride."

Then he realized what he'd done and released her with a sheepish, "Sorry," and offered Charlotte the invoice.

"No . . . no worries." She rubbed the fiery burn of his lips from her skin. But nothing could remove it from her heart. Stop. Focus. Think. The dress. *This is about the dress.* "Joel Miller, Hillary Saltonstall. Here's a note at the bottom. 'Rush order, groom leaving for Viet Nam.'"

That moved her heart away from Tim. Joel Miller rushed to his wedding before going off to war.

"When did you say he died?" Tim asked.

"April '69."

"Six months later." His eyes remained fixed on the invoice as if it could somehow show him the past. "Do you think they actually got married? You said the dress didn't look worn."

"Or altered." Charlotte took the invoice from Tim. "It's possible for a gown to fit from one bride to the next without alterations, but it's highly improbable. Something has to be changed. The hem. The bodice. Something. Unless the dress wasn't really made in 1912 and the auctioneer just made up a story to trick me into buying it." She was shaking. While she was further down the trail of discovering the heritage of the dress, she felt miles away from the truth.

But in her hand she held a piece of a man's life that history and time had forgotten. Except "Your Wife," who'd posted on Joel's wall. Except God. "Do you think Mrs. Pettis will let me have this? At least borrow it?"

Tim fit the lid on the box and returned it to the shelf. "Why not? It's the reason we came."

At the stairs, Charlotte picked up her jacket and draped it over her arm. "On the wall where I found Joel's name, it said his body was never recovered."

"Bet that would be hard on a new bride." Tim walked over to her and brushed her hair off her shoulders, then quickly stuffed his hands in his pockets. "Ready?"

"Ready." It was getting hotter and hotter in that old attic.

Chapter Fifteen

*S*aturday just before noon, Charlotte pulled into Hillary Saltonstall's Crestline driveway. It curved like a concrete river past the front of her terra-cotta brick home and cut through the plush, manicured lawn. Shading oaks and elms canopied the house and cooled away the noonday sun and the rising May heat.

Charlotte stepped out of her car, her low-heeled pumps tapping on the driveway. She removed her suit jacket, tossing it into the passenger seat.

The clear-blue-day breeze shifted the light and rearranged her emotions. On the drive over she'd mentally worked out a pragmatic interview with Hillary, planning how to forge into the woman's past. Which enabled Charlotte to ignore the fact that she herself was driving into her own past—her old Crestline neighborhood.

To get to this place and time, she'd called every Saltonstall in the Birmingham phone book until she found Hillary's elderly aunt, who graciously listened to Charlotte's story and after a few questions, passed along Hillary's phone number.

The fact that Hillary lived in Charlotte's childhood neighborhood where she played with her friends and rode her bike, the fact that Hillary might have waved at Mama as their cars passed in the street didn't register on Charlotte's emotional scale. Until now.

She walked to the edge of the drive and stood at the apex where Baker Street met Monarch. Seven houses on the right sat a little white house with redbrick trim, a concrete porch, and a wood-slat swing.

Charlotte strained her senses to hear, to see, to smell the essence of that house. But all that came to her were a few faded snapshots.

The upstairs, the alcove room that once had been pink with yellow daisies growing up from brown "dirt" baseboards.

Mama, standing in the driveway, dressed in her tight jeans and midriff top, hollering for Charlotte to hurry home, supper was on.

Charlotte squinted into the waving noon light. Seven houses down, only the walls remembered Mama's voice.

Glancing back at Hillary's, the wind coiling her hair about her face, she wondered how long Hillary had lived here. Had young Charlotte ever encountered Mrs. Joel Miller, the grieving war widow?

Only Hillary was a Warner now. Not a Saltonstall. Nor a Miller.

Taking her phone from her bag, Charlotte dialed Dix. But the call went straight to voice mail. Dixie had a consultation with a new client this afternoon so she must be getting ready. Charlotte hung up without leaving a message, stared at her phone, then dialed Tim.

"Hey." Hesitant. Expectant. Revving motorcycle engines in the background.

"Where are you?" Charlotte scooped her hair away from her face.

"At the track. Where are you?"

"Standing at the curb of Baker and Monarch."

"So you called her?" Tim's voice grew louder as the background engine rumble faded.

"She lives seven houses down from where I grew up. The house where I lived when Mama died."

He whistled. "Did you know that going over?" The creamy tenor of his voice sank through Charlotte like sweet caramel.

"Didn't really think of it until now. It's weird being here, Tim. I haven't been here since Mama died."

A thick, muffled knock resonated from his end of the phone.

"Hey, Charlotte, can you hold for a second?" She heard rustling, then, "I'm on the phone, man."

The muted, distant conversation revealed Tim needed to get off and head to the track. His heat was coming up.

"Char, I'm sorry, but I need to go in a second. So—it's weird?"

"In a way, like Mama should be here. In that little white house with the bricks. But she's not. What's worse is I can't remember much of anything about living here."

"She's been gone a long time, Charlotte. You were a girl who lost her mother. Now you're a woman, making your way in life and succeeding."

"But a girl should never get over needing her mother."

"Who said that? Charlotte, every day people get over their mothers and fathers, siblings, friends leaving and dying. Getting over things is part of life."

"It's different with death. I've lost my memories of her, Tim. I wonder if what I remember about her is just some picture or ideal I've made up. I'm trying to see something clearly from my past and I just can't. There's no sense of her."

"Maybe that's a blessing." The heavy clap of the truck door closing warned Charlotte the call would end soon.

"But memories are all I have. For all practical purposes, *they* are my family."

"You'll make new memories. Have a new family . . . someday." His words tumbled a bit. Friend Tim wrestling with fiancé Tim.

"Hey, you need to get going and so do I. Thanks for answering."

"Yeah, Charlotte . . . any . . . anytime."

"Have fun. Be safe, okay? Now that you're my friend and not my fiancé, I don't mind telling you I hate your passion for racing those bikes over dirt tracks. It's so dangerous."

He laughed and the tenor of it boosted her courage. "Now you tell me. So you were going to let fiancé Tim risk his neck but tell husband Tim, 'No way, bubba'?"

"I hadn't gotten that far. But, yeah, probably. Something like that."

"You should've told me." The humor in his voice sobered. "Those are things a girl should tell her guy."

"When would I have done that? We met, we talked, we kissed, we were engaged."

"Don't look now, Charlotte, but I think you're making my point about postponing our wedding."

"I'm hanging up now. But, Tim, be careful." The sun's yellow hue paled as a gray cloud drifted by and marred the blue sky.

"Good luck with Hillary. Just be yourself. She'll love you."

Charlotte tapped End and tucked her phone into her purse. When she turned around, a tall, slender woman with salt-and-pepper hair was watching her from the edge of the lawn.

"Are you Charlotte?"

"Yes, and you're Mrs. Warner?" Charlotte moved to shake her hand, surprised by the sheen of tears in the woman's eyes.

"Please, call me Hillary." She wore jeans and a blouse and white canvas sneakers. Her short hair blew free in the wind and curled about her face. Kindness radiated from her brown eyes. "Can I ask what's so interesting down the street?"

Memories. "I lived in the white house down on the right—the one with the bricks—when I was a girl." The sun's golden rays fought back the drifting rain cloud.

"Did you, now?" Hillary stepped into the street, leaning to see around the trees and a passing car. "Greg and I moved in twenty years ago, and there were a lot of children running around these streets, riding bikes. They're all gone now. In fact"—she pressed her fingertips against her lips—"there was a skinny dark-haired girl who used to ride a purple bike around the neighborhood. She peddled *zip-zoop.*" Hillary smacked and slid her palms. "I used to tell my husband if we had a girl—"

"I had a purple bike," Charlotte said. "And long dark hair."

"Down to your waist. Never could keep it in a ponytail." Hillary peered at her.

"Never."

"Well, now"—her gaze narrowed—"so that was you. How do—"

"Small world." Charlotte's pulse raced.

"I told Greg, if we ever have a baby, I'd want her to be a girl like that one. On the purple bike."

Charlotte warmed at the idea. "I remember in the summer the smell of barbecue coming from your backyard. And at Christmas, your house had the prettiest decorations and the most lights."

"My husband loved to cook out on the grill. I wasn't much of a cook myself, so it was a win-win. But Christmas, that was all me." Hillary motioned toward the house and started walking. "Your mother died, didn't she?"

"When I was twelve. In a car accident."

Hillary stopped in the shade of the front walk. "I'm sorry. What about your father?"

"Never knew him. Still don't. I went to live with Mama's friend Gert."

"I had no idea." Hillary hesitated, staring out over the lawn. "I had no . . . idea." She peered at Charlotte for a long moment, then turned for the house. "I baked cinnamon muffins."

The inside of the house matched the outside. Neat, inviting, homey. The carpet was new and thick, the furniture modern. The air was tinged with the scent of fresh paint with a touch of cinnamon. Hillary crossed the living room to a bright enclosed sunporch.

"Sit here," she said, patting the top of a burgundy rocker. The matching one sat on the other side of the end table. Both faced the windows and the yard. A bird book and pair of binoculars sat on the table.

Charlotte tucked her purse beside her in the chair. She'd seen this room many times from the outside. So Hillary had watched her ride her bike. It was her last big gift from Mama. A year later Charlotte was an orphan living with Gert—who backed over Charlotte's bike the week she moved in.

"Here we go." Hillary set a white plate with steaming muffins on the table. "What's your pleasure? Milk, coffee, tea, water, Coke. No diet. Drink the real stuff 'round here."

"Milk, please." Sounded good. Charlotte squeezed her arms against her sides, warmed by Hillary's frank but tender demeanor.

Over glasses of milk and cinnamon muffins, the women chit-chatted, getting to know each other. Hillary had been a nurse in the navy, then at St. Vincent's.

Charlotte owned a bridal boutique.

Hillary had married Greg when she was in her forties. He was a retired naval officer who worked as a civilian contractor.

Charlotte was thirty and still single.

They both loved sunny, hot days. Dogs. And Michael Bublé.

"Are you successful?" Hillary leaned on the chair's arm. "Your shop, I mean."

"Five years and counting. I'm in the black most of the time. Tawny Boswell recently bought her wedding dress from us."

"Tawny Boswell. Miss Alabama? Well, well."

Charlotte smiled. Hillary didn't seem the kind to know about beauty queens.

"I can tell by your face you're surprised I know about Miss Alabama." Hillary rocked back in her chair, bringing her coffee mug to her lips. "I was a Miss Teen Alabama finalist in 1962."

"Really?" Charlotte said, smiling. "You just don't seem like the beauty pageant type." Why did it sound like an insult? "I mean, the fuss and pretend. The phoniness."

"Twenty years as a navy nurse will get the frippery out of you." She drank her coffee. She didn't sip. She drank. "You don't have to look sheepish. I'm not the same woman I was then. Nor the woman I thought I'd be when I reached sixty-five. So tell me, why'd you come? You said you found something that belonged to me?"

"I was hoping you could help me solve a mystery." Charlotte took the silk sachet from her purse and handed it to Hillary. Bethany had returned it, sample sachets already made, and Charlotte tucked the dog tags back inside the original. "I found this in a trunk I bought at an auction."

At first Hillary didn't show any recognition. But when her fingers touched the silk, they were trembling. Her nose and eyes reddened. "Well, mercy—" Emotion watered her voice and her eyelids fluttered. "I didn't ever expect to see this again."

"The dog tags are inside. Did you put them there?"

"I take it you finagled a way to open up that trunk?" Hillary poured the tags into her hand and closed her fingers over them. "I wanted to burn the whole kit and kaboodle the night after his funeral."

"I read his body was never recovered."

"He was blown to pieces. There was no body *to* recover." Hillary reached down beside her chair for a tissue. "I didn't think anyone would ever get into that trunk after I torched it closed."

"It wasn't easy. My friend had to cut it open."

"Guess I'm not the welder I thought I was." The soft curve of Hillary's smile caught the slow drift of a solo tear. She caressed Joel's dog tags. "I still miss him. Forty some-odd years later, I miss him."

"You were married before he left?"

"We had the loveliest backyard wedding at my parents' home—not far from here, actually. Joel was set to leave and I wanted to marry him so bad. I had a year left of college, but he'd be in Nam. I thought we should seal our love with a wedding. I just knew our love was stronger than death."

"Maybe it is, Hillary. You still love him, right?"

Hillary wiped her cheeks with the back of her hand. "Our love wasn't bulletproof. It didn't keep him alive. I don't know how it was with losing your mama, but with Joel I found it awfully hard to have closure on a life that never got started. All our dreams were on hold while he did his tour." Hillary rocked back in her chair. "And there they are now, still on hold. Rusty and dusty on the shelf, lonely 'cause I never look at them anymore. He didn't want to get married, but—"

"What happened? I mean, you got married, right?" Charlotte pictured Hillary's and Joel's names on the brittle cake invoice.

She smiled softly. "I'd already decided to throw him a party before he shipped out. We talked and argued about getting married, but Joel insisted he didn't want to leave me alone, didn't want the possibility of leaving me a widow at such a young age. The going-away party was fine, but not a wedding. I invited all our friends from college, our families. I was cleaning out the basement when I found the trunk and the dress."

"You didn't know it was there?"

"I had no idea. Neither did my parents. Boy, if I didn't take that gown as some kind of sign."

"What did Joel say?" Charlotte leaned into Hillary's story.

"I didn't tell him. About killed me to keep my mouth shut." She smiled, a wrinkled nose smile that Charlotte felt in her spirit. "I wanted our last couple of weeks to be happy. Not arguing about weddings and marriage. But"—Hillary speared the air with her finger—"what I didn't know was Joel had changed his mind about waiting.

We were about halfway through his party when he got down on one knee and proposed in front of our family and friends."

Tim had proposed in front of his family and friends too. But that story was for another time.

"The next week was a blur of wedding preparations. We got married on a Friday night, he shipped out the following Friday, and that was the last time I ever saw him."

Charlotte sat back—no words she could conjure would fit the moment. Then, at last, "Hillary, I have the dress."

"If you opened the trunk, then I guess you do. Please tell me you're not getting married in it."

"No, I'm not getting married. But the gown is . . . like new." Charlotte started for another muffin but drew her hand back. "It's like it's never been worn."

"I wore it, Charlotte." Hillary eyed her, brows raised.

"Did you alter it?"

"Didn't have to. That was the strangest thing. My mother and grandmother couldn't get over it. The dress fit like a glove. Like it was made for me." Hillary cradled her mug against her chest. "The style was timeless. I loved it. Tell me, does it still have an empire waist with pearls and—well, I guess it does if it's been in the trunk all this time."

"Yes, it does. It's perfect."

"I wanted to burn that dress. But Daddy wouldn't let me. I was just about to set fire to the trunk, the dress, and the dog tags when he caught me. I was crazy with grief. I didn't even get to see Joel's dead body, to kiss his cold, blue lips. I would've too. I wouldn't have cared if his spirit wasn't really there. After the funeral I fired up the blowtorch and welded the lock. I didn't want anyone to ever, ever wear such a sad gown again." Her gaze snapped to Charlotte. "I never thought I'd find love again. Then I met my husband, Greg, right after I turned forty. He saved me. I tell you, he saved me." Hillary opened her fingers and peered at the dog tags. "It's incredibly hard to be wedded to a ghost."

"Hillary, where did the dress come from? Do you have any idea?"

"The house. The trunk and the dress belonged to the house."

"To the house?" Charlotte turned slightly in her chair for a better angle at Hillary.

"I found it in the house. I left it in the house. It belonged to the house. How did you find it?"

"I bought it at the Ludlow Auction. Up on Red Mountain."

"Forty-four years later, that dang trunk makes its way up to Red Mountain." Hillary squeezed her fingers around the dog tags. "We moved when the house was razed to make room for a shopping center. I never asked Mama what she did with the trunk. I was gone, half crazy by then."

"So you have no idea how the trunk wound up at the Ludlow auction forty years later?"

"None whatsoever."

Dead end. And she'd been doing so well. Charlotte jumped when her phone broke the contemplative moment. She fumbled for it, not recognizing the number that paraded across the screen. "Hello?"

"Charlotte, it's Jared." Dr. Hotstuff. "Dixie gave me your number."

"Jared, is everything all right? Is it Dix? The shop?" Charlotte turned cold in the warm, bright room.

"Dix is fine. She's too stubborn to get hurt. The shop is fine as far as I know. But again, you left Dix in charge." He sighed in a way that raised chills on Charlotte's arm. "I just arrived for my shift and, Charlotte, it's Tim. He's been airlifted to the hospital. I thought you'd want to know."

Chapter Sixteen

Emily

*T*affy slipped the final fitted gown over Emily's head. She closed her eyes, letting the sensation of warm rain on a hot summer afternoon wash down her arms and swish into a pool about her feet.

"I don't know that I feel altogether right about this, Emily. Your mother seemed rather insistent about wearing Caroline Caruthers's gown."

"I feel perfectly right about this. I'm the bride. Not my mother. Isn't this my day?"

"You're not so naïve as to believe it's not about families too."

"No, but this is a simple little thing. I'm not stubborn, Taffy. But this is my wedding day, my wedding dress. I'm. Choosing. This. Gown." Emily gazed into the seamstress's mirrors. "I feel loved in this dress."

"And is your man the one who loves you?" Taffy knelt to measure the hem, coughing over her shoulder. She'd canceled her visit to the Cantons' due to sickness. So Emily found Big Mike and made the trip to 5th Avenue. "Miss Emily, hold still so I can get this done. And get you on out of here. I don't want anyone catching us together, getting you in trouble. Plus, I don't want you carrying my sickness to your mama's house."

"I won't get in trouble." Emily smoothed her hand over the bodice. Yes, her man loved her. Didn't he? The dress was beautiful.

202

Shiny, silky, and if possible . . . "Taffy, I do declare this dress appears to beam light."

"I sewed it with gold thread."

"Gold?" Emily examined the hem of the fitted lace sleeve. "What on earth? Real gold?"

"I get it here and there. I save it from some piecework I do. Things can be had in this city, even to a colored, if she wants it and knows how to get it. Sometimes I just ask the Lord to bring me what I need."

"What did you ask Him for while sewing my dress, Taffy?"

"To bring you what *you* need." Taffy patted Emily's leg. "Turn so I can keep pinning." She bent away again, coughing, her chest rattling.

"You should see a doctor." Emily stepped around so Taffy could finish the hem.

"White girls see doctors. Old colored ladies kneel and pray."

Emily gazed down at her. "I wish I had your faith and courage."

"That's what I've been praying for you to have, Miss Emily. Courage and faith."

Emily peered over her shoulder into the mirror. The back of the gown scooped down her shoulders. The skirt fitted smoothly to her hips and flowed like milk over the stool to a chapel train. She felt as if she could float in this gown. She never wanted to take it off.

"Courage and faith, you say?" Emily gave her attention to Taffy. She'd need both, no doubt, to marry Phillip, the stubborn man. She'd realized since their engagement it would be no small task to bear the Saltonstall name. Women like Emmeline didn't care a wit about marital vows. They'd always bat their eyes and shove their bosoms at men like Phillip. ". . . He's too much about himself, too stupid, not to be flattered."

"Come again, Miss Emily?"

Her cheeks burned. "Just talking to myself."

Taffy grinned and plucked another straight pin from her lips. "I talk to myself all day long 'round here."

"Taffy, why do you think I'll need courage and faith?"

"Because . . ." The woman exhaled as she pinned the last length of hem. She stood to her full height and gazed into Emily's eyes. "You'll need it to marry the right man."

Soft pockets of mud sloshed over Emily's shoes and dotted the hem of her skirt as she cut through the neighbor's yard toward her own kitchen door. Big Mike had dropped her off at Taffy's but he couldn't stay. Father had a list of chores for him to attend so she rode the trolley home.

"Aye, there you are, miss." Molly pushed through the kitchen door, her brow arched. "The missus has been looking for you. Decide to take a romp in the mud, did you?"

"I walked from the trolley." Emily started for the back stairs. "Where's Mother? Can you launder this before she sees it?" Emily unhooked her skirt and stepped out, stepping around the pantry door in case Father's man, Jefferson, walked in while she was in her bloomers.

"Leave it in your dressing room. I'll come for it." Molly dropped a mound of bread dough onto the work table. "And just where were you this afternoon?"

Emily blushed under Molly's quizzical stare. The woman knew her better than some of her school friends. "I went to Taffy's. She sent word the dress was ready for hemming."

"Why didn't you tell her to come here? You know how your people feel about you going to the colored neighborhood."

"She wasn't feeling well." Emily walked over to the worktable. "Besides, I had to make sure Taffy made a wedding dress, not an evening gown as Mother insisted. I'm going to figure out a way to wear Taffy's gown at my wedding, Molly. You watch. When I tried it on today, I actually felt . . . loved."

"Loved?" Molly made a face. "Are you *not loved*, miss?"

"Mind your tone, Molly." Since Charlotte's confrontation with Phillip over her first visit to Taffy's four weeks ago, he'd become the most attentive and affectionate fiancé. His passions were tempered and controlled, as if he remembered whose lips he kissed. His future wife's. Not a subservient mistress who served to quell his lusts. "I'm loved, certainly. It's just that the dress makes me feel . . . so good. So clean." Emily struggled to find words to match her feelings.

"Ah, the kind of feeling I get at church when the Spirit moves."

"What does the Spirit do when He moves?" Emily stood by the kitchen stairs, eyes fixed on Molly. She'd heard of signs and wonders in some of the churches. Her minister passed it off as emotionalism. But Molly was a steady girl, not given to demonstration.

"What does He do? Whatever He wants, miss. Do you know how you sometimes have to take all the linens out of the drawer to get it straight and orderly again? The Spirit sometimes does the same with our sins."

"Put all your sins on display?" How horrifying. Emily shivered from the idea. And from the cool evening air seeping into the kitchen from the window Molly kept cracked open.

"Only to you. Not everybody. But a person might weep. Or shake. Or blubber for forgiveness. Then in two shakes of a lamb's tail, the Spirit has righted things and the person is back in business, all clean and orderly inside. Joyful."

Did Emily feel clean and orderly inside? Joyful? "Don't tell Mother I went to Taffy's." When was the last time she laughed? Really laughed. It was with Daniel that time he—

"What if Mr. Phillip's people saw you again?"

"I was careful." Emily had counted the cost, but now that she was home, cold shivers wrapped around her torso. "He'll just have to understand. I needed the dress fitted and hemmed."

"Emily, are you in here?" Mother emerged from the other side of the kitchen door. "Mercy, you're in your bloomers. What have you done to your skirt?"

"Mud, Mother, it's not the end of the world."

"Certainly not. But why is your skirt covered with it?"

"It's been raining . . . the streets are muddy." Emily dashed up the stairs with a backward glance at Molly before Mother could probe further.

"Would you like some cake, Mrs. Canton?" she heard Molly say. "The last piece of chocolate is under the tin."

Oh, thank you, Molly. Mother would do just about anything for chocolate cake. Especially yours.

Emily washed and changed, her thoughts wandering to a thick slice of jellied bread, when she heard the front bell chime. She peered out her window. A police wagon waited in the circular drive. *Father? Or . . . Big Mike?* Mother was right, she was going to get someone hurt by going to the coloreds' district.

Emily hurried from her room and down the stairs.

"Good evening, we're sorry to disturb you." Somber male voices swept through the foyer.

"Officers." Jefferson held the door open for them. "How may I assist you?"

Emily stepped off the bottom stair into the foyer. "Is everything all right?" She gazed from one officer to the next. "It's not my father, is it? Or Big Mike?"

"No, ma'am." The officers exchanged a joyless glance. "We're here to see you."

"What's all this?" Mother came out from the kitchen. "Officers, please, won't you come in? Can I offer you tea or coffee? Mr. Canton isn't home but we do expect him soon."

"Ma'am." The tall one with serious blue eyes removed his cap. "We're here on official business."

"What sort of official business?" Mother faced them, hands grasped at her waist.

"We have a warrant for the arrest of Miss Emily Canton."

Emily froze, her heart careening to a stop. "Me?" The word exhaled on a thin, weak breath.

"Arrest my daughter? On what charge?" Mother stepped in between Emily and the officers. Emily collapsed to the step with a thud. Jefferson pressed his hand against her back, kneeling on the step beside her.

"Violation of the law, ma'am. She was seen down at the Gaston Hotel this afternoon. The charge is fraternizing with the coloreds, threatening to stir up insurrection."

"Insurrection." Mother stomped her well-heeled foot. "Taffy Hayes is my seamstress. Are you saying we can't do business with my seamstress because she's colored?"

"Not when it's believed trouble's brewing. There are some who want to remind us whites and coloreds are separate but equal."

"So they make a spectacle of my daughter?" Mother's words fired like a Fourth-of-July canon.

Emily clung to Jefferson as the tall, leading officer produced a warrant. She tried to read the document but the words simply swam. Mother snatched it from the officer.

"I don't believe it. I don't believe it."

"Miss, you'll have to come with us." The officer reached for Emily but Jefferson held on. *Don't let me go, Jefferson.*

The officer apologized with his eyes as he wrenched Emily from his grasp. "Mother?"

"This is an outrage." Mother followed them down the porch stairs. "Jefferson, telephone Mr. Canton's office. Now."

Emily tripped toward the wagon, her legs out of her command, the toes of her shoes dragging along the pavement, her thoughts like dead leaves in the fall wind.

Mother ran alongside. "Now you listen to me." She gripped Emily's face in her hands. "You are a Canton with Woodward blood. Be strong and courageous." Mother's eyes glowed with anger at the officers. "I'm sure these men will treat you as the lady you are. I'm right behind you. Jefferson will drive me in the car."

"Oh, Mother." Emily collapsed against the officer, going limp as he steered her into the wagon. "I just wanted a wedding gown that made me feel free, and loved. Beautiful. Like a princess."

"Emily, be strong." Mother raised her up straight, shaking her shoulders. "This will be over by dinner."

The officer helped Emily into the backseat of the wagon. When the driver chirruped to the horses, Emily's hot tears burned a trail from her eyes to her chin, dropping like hot coals to her icy hands.

Chapter Seventeen

Charlotte

The waiting room needed more light. Why did architects insist that grieving, scared, nervous people sit in the dark? Charlotte walked to the window overlooking the city, grateful for the lingering sunlight claiming the early evening hours.

She arrived at the hospital the same time as Mr. and Mrs. Rose and Katherine. While they talked with the doctor, she stood by the chairs, waiting. The brothers, David, Jack, and Chase, were on their way, bringing their bikes home from Huntsville.

Tim was wheeled into surgery, and in a punctuated silence, Charlotte waited with the family for more news, making small talk, trying to piece together details from David's scattered, anguished call.

Hit a double. Came down wrong. Landed on another bike. Tim's bike went airborne and landed *on* him. He was pinned between the two in a painful heap.

The news made Charlotte crazy. Why did grown men behave as if they were invincible boys? Mrs. Rose, who had lived though many accidents with her sons, patted Charlotte's arm.

"Tim will be fine."

But this was new to Charlotte. Deadly sports and men who loved them. She'd just told him to be safe.

Around six the brothers arrived, still in their dusty racing gear. Around seven Tim was moved to a room. As soon as the doctor gave permission, the Roses flooded down the hall to see him.

Katherine held back for a moment. "I'm sorry about you and Tim, Charlotte."

"It's old news, Katherine. If you were sorry, you'd have called me weeks ago." She wasn't in the mood for games.

Her almost sister-in-law started to speak, then hesitated. "I want him to be happy."

"That makes two of us."

Charlotte continued to wait. The family had dibs on Tim first. Not the ex-fiancée. She wouldn't be comfortable with them anyway.

Watching them pile into Tim's room, Charlotte ran her thumb over her bare ring finger. Family. She wasn't sure she'd ever known what *that* felt like.

With Mama it was "us girls" or "us two." For birthdays. For Christmas. For Thanksgiving. When Mama died, Charlotte was the only relative listed in the obituary.

Moving to the window, she rested her forehead against the sun-warmed glass and exhaled her pent up emotions. *Please, Jesus, be with Tim.*

"Charlotte, hey—" She looked up as Jared approached, dressed in his blue scrubs and white coat. "Dix said don't worry about the shop. She's got it."

"What's the word on Tim?" Charlotte sank her hands into his. They were smooth and strong. Healing.

"Good for a man who landed on top of a bike, then had his five-hundred-pound bike land on him." Jared squeezed her fingers. "He's bruised and banged up. Had his spleen removed, and we have a tube in his chest to help reinflate his left lung. We'll keep him a few days. He's lucky he's alive. If he'd landed an inch or two higher on his neck, he'd be paralyzed or dead."

He's lucky to be alive. The confession swirled in Charlotte's head. What would she do without Tim? Friend Tim. She loved and needed him. She depended on him in a way she didn't realize until now.

Jared drew her into a hug. "We're here for you."

Charlotte exhaled, releasing some of her burden on him, Dixie's Dr. Hotstuff. If she had a brother, she'd want it to be like this.

"Charlotte?" Jack came from Tim's room. His face was ringed in dirt. His tone, somber. "Tim's asking for you."

"Oh?" She gazed around Jared, down the hall.

"I'll be back later." Jared turned to go, and for a blip of a second Charlotte wanted to cling to his brotherly warmth. "I need to check on a few other patients."

"Thanks, doc." Jack watched him go, then looked at Charlotte. "Tim couldn't care less about the rest of us. Just keeps asking about you. He's in and out, so . . ." Jack motioned for her to follow him.

When Charlotte entered, the family exited, each one giving her a light embrace. "Darling, come by for dinner if you can." Mrs. Rose, always the matriarch, smoothed her hand over Charlotte's hair, like she'd done numerous times when she was in Tim's life. "We're going to be at the house."

"Thank you." *But no.* Charlotte stepped aside for Katherine to pass.

Tim's room was quiet, lit with a soft lamp attached to the wall behind the bed. His window framed the last hurrah of the sunset. Charlotte leaned in to say "I'm here," but he was sleeping.

Slowly, she sank to the chair by his bed. "Crazy boy, almost got yourself killed."

Hooked to tubes and machines, he appeared peaceful in his sleep, a sweetness to his bruised, handsome face.

Hideous dark blue and black marks ringed his neck and ran down his right arm, straight through the cast and out the end to his fingertips.

"Oh, Tim, you have to be all right." Charlotte rested her forehead against the edge of the bed and whispered, "What would I do without you?"

A soft touch on her head sent chills down her arm. Gently, Tim stroked her hair. "Tim . . ." she lifted her head.

"I'm sorry." Tim swept his thumb over her wet cheeks, his voice a whisper, breathless.

"Sorry? For what? Being you? You don't owe me—"

"For thinking there was anything in this world I loved more than you." His words ebbed and flowed with his strength.

Charlotte pressed her lips against his palm. "Just don't die on me. If you do, I'll be mad."

He smiled, then winced. "Everything hurts. Even the tips of my hair."

Charlotte rose up and leaned against the side of his bed. "Sleep, rest, tell your lung to get back in shape."

"Banged myself up pretty good, didn't I?" Tim bent his not-so-banged-up arm until his fingers touched his lips.

"What? Do you need something? Water?"

"Kiss."

"A kiss?" Charlotte brushed his sweaty, matted hair from his forehead.

"Makes the wounds feel better, right?"

"I can't deny a wounded man, can I?" Charlotte stretched to kiss the side of his mouth. His eyes closed and his warm breath brushed her face. She slid her lips over his with another light kiss. Tim wrapped his good arm behind her back.

Charlotte lifted her head, and when their eyes met, she kissed him again, her light touch tasting his passion.

"I love you, Charlotte," his lips whispered against hers.

"Lord help me, but I love you too." Gently, she stroked her fingers over his forehead. It was the one place where he wasn't bruised. "I don't want to, but I do."

He slipped his fingers though the ends of her hair. "When I came to after the crash, all I could think about was you. I didn't know where I was, and for a few minutes, who I was, but I knew there was you."

"Good friends are hard to find, you know." She smoothed her hand down his chest between the tapes and the tubes.

"I have good friends. But a woman I love who's also the hottest thing I've ever seen and happens to be my best friend too—that's darn near impossible to find. Charlotte—" He seemed awake now, peering at her, his voice unwavering.

Behind them, the door swung open. "Goodness, Tim, I got here as fast as I could."

Charlotte jumped back as Kim, the blonde from the restaurant, barged across the room.

"Katherine called hours ago, but I was in a commercial shoot. Oh, darling, are you all right?" She walked around the side of the bed and kissed him full on the lips.

The lips where Charlotte's had just been.

"Kim." Tim winced, tipping his head away from her. "This is Charlotte Malone."

"Nice to meet you." Kim offered her hand, then set her handbag on the nightstand and slung her sleek, gorgeous hair over her shoulder. She bent her sculpted face over his and leaned close with her taut, perfect body. "I canceled our dinner reservations, babe. George and the gang send their love."

Charlotte stumbled over her chair as she backed away from the bed.

Kim looked up, frowning. "Goodness, are you all right?"

"Yeah." Charlotte contracted her ribs, holding the roiling

emotions in her belly. If she let loose, she didn't know what would come out of her. "I'll see you, Tim."

"Charlotte, wait—" His voice weakly trailed her out of the room.

She was halfway down the hall, her throat thick with swallowed sobs, before she realized she'd left her purse in the chair by Tim's bed.

But there was no way she was going back to get it now.

Sunday morning Charlotte woke up early, the sunrise bright over the mountains, and for a second all was right with the world.

For a second.

Then she remembered. Tim and Kim. Cute, huh? Tim and Kim. They deserved each other.

She popped out of bed, without allowing herself to dwell on the pain in her heart, and showered for church.

Finding a seat in the back, she worshipped with the early service congregation, eyes closed, arms held wide, her heart offering it all to the One who wooed her with love and grace. Unconditional and uncompromising. Perfectly done on His part, not so much hers.

But she could trust Him. He'd not switch His gaze from her when another walked into the room. It was the miracle and beauty of Jesus—fixed, unwavering affection. A smile started in Charlotte's belly and floated to her lips. She was His favorite one.

I am Yours, I am Yours

She opened her eyes when a masculine body scented with sandalwood took the seat next to her. "Hey, Jack."

"I heard."

"Heard what?"

"Kim showed up."

"Thanks to Katherine."

Jack heaved a sigh as the music faded and the woman in front of them scowled over her shoulder. "He wants to see you," Jack whispered in Charlotte's ear.

"He *saw* me. Yesterday."

"Charlotte, come on, don't let Kim kick you out of the race."

"Never fear, Jack. Kim can't kick me out of the race." She patted his shoulder and bore her gaze deep into his. "Because I'm not competing."

She faced forward as the next song shifted from verse to chorus. Jack didn't move.

Saturday night Charlotte had spent the evening munching on a bag of baby carrots, resisting the overwhelming urge to order a large pizza and eat the whole thing herself. With her carrots-of-comfort, she watched movies and talked to the dress. Hillary's dress. The dress from the trunk. The dress she was charged to care for until she could find its next bride.

"Then this Kim chick comes into the room. Dress, are you listening? Comes in like she owns the place. A second earlier she'd have caught us kissing. Yeah, I know. He asked me to kiss him, but he had a date with her."

"What do you want me to tell him?" Jack said as the worship song rose in power, the chorus transitioning to a glorious tag. *Our God reigns, our God reigns.* The band drove the music hard and tight, and Charlotte wrapped her heart in the power of the melody.

"Tell him to get well." Charlotte closed her eyes, feeling the drums and bass in her chest, prophesying to her spirit, encouraging her soul.

Our God reigns. Our God reigns.

"He loves you." Jack's declaration wrenched Charlotte's soaring spirit.

She popped open one eye for Jack. "He has a funny way of showing it."

"Tell me about it. You're the best thing that's ever happened to him." The third oldest Rose boy hooked his arm around Charlotte's shoulders for a one-arm side hug, then slid out of the row.

Trembling, Charlotte sank to the pew. She'd been in a good place, enjoying God and worship. Now she was back to the swirl and whirl of heartbreak and the other woman. She picked her bag off the floor—asked a nurse to retrieve it for her—grabbed her Bible, and headed out.

When she pulled into her Homewood loft, thinking today would be a good day to eat a whole cheese pizza, a woman called her name. She turned to see Hillary hurrying toward her, a tan leather messenger bag slung over her shoulder.

"Hillary? What are you doing here?"

"I couldn't stop thinking about you. I called your bridal shop after you left yesterday. Your friend told me where you lived. I hope you don't mind." She met Charlotte at the building's entrance wearing Joel's tags around her neck. "My mind was reeling with thoughts of you, the dress, Joel and me. When Greg came home, he found me sitting in the middle of pictures, reliving the whole ordeal, crying. I just never figured out why. Why did I marry Joel, only to lose him? I didn't realize I was still so angry." The truth of her confession sat in the taut and deep lines of her face.

"Hillary, I should've never come to you. I was so wrapped up in needing to know about Joel and how he related to the dress, I never considered how it would impact you. Not really. I was a bit obsessed." Charlotte pressed her hands over her middle. Dix had tried to warn her. "One day I had an old gown in my possession. The next I was deep into this mystery of a man whose life was summed up in five lines on a dog tag and a few details on a website."

"I'm glad you came to me, Charlotte. I needed you to come to me." Hillary's hair buoyed in the wind. She wore a long-sleeved t-shirt, Go Navy, and khaki shorts with the same white sneakers from yesterday. "Even my husband knew this day of reckoning had to come. He said he's known for years I wasn't finished saying good-bye to Joel. Maybe now I have a chance to find that elusive closure."

Charlotte jiggled her keys in her hand. "I was about to order a thin-crust cheese pizza."

"Are you informing me or inviting me?"

Charlotte watched her through narrow eye slits. "Depends on your answer. Do you like pizza?"

"I love pizza. Any kind."

"I'm on the fourth floor."

"Lead the way, my dear."

Taking the stairs to the fourth floor, Charlotte unlocked her loft, remembering the gown was in the living room as Hillary rounded the short hallway wall. She gasped, one hand cupped over her mouth. The other over her heart.

"I'm sorry, Hillary. I forgot the dress was out in view."

"I never thought I'd see this thing again." She circled the gown, brushing her cheeks dry and gently lifting the silky folds of the skirt. Lowering her face to the material, she closed her eyes and inhaled. "The skirt always smelled like a thick fragrant oil to me."

"It seems to always catch and hold the light to me." Charlotte lightly slipped her hand along the sleeve. "I love the gold threads."

"It's *still* the most beautiful gown I've ever seen."

Charlotte sat on the edge of the sofa, crossing her legs, relaxing into the moment. "I've seen a lot of wedding gowns, many of them exquisite, but none compare to this one."

"It's special," Hillary said, her voice and eyes filled with emotion.

"Why do you think it's so special, Hillary?" Charlotte propped her chin in her hand. Seeing the gown through Hillary's eyes broadened Charlotte's heart and determination to find its next bride. She must be a special woman indeed.

"Because it's only for those who accept it. Who can wear it."

"What do you mean? Only for those who accept it?"

"I don't know what I mean . . . it's just here." She tapped her heart. "You have to accept this gown, to believe in it. Have faith, if you will."

"It's just a gown."

"No, it's a destiny." Hillary's face brightened, the hue in her eyes the same as the hue of the threads. "I'm so glad you found the trunk, Charlotte. Oh my—" She pressed her hand over her heart, letting her eyes water and leak down her cheeks.

Charlotte swallowed the emotion rising in her chest. "The man who sold me the trunk mentioned something about 1912 and a bride. He handed me a receipt stamped REDEEMED. Do you know what that means? Do you know if you're the only one to wear it, Hillary?"

"I don't know for sure, but I had this feeling when I put it on, I wasn't the first bride to wear it." She peered over at Charlotte, hard. "And I have a pretty good idea who might wear it after me."

"Ho, not me." Charlotte stood, hands surrendered. "I'm going to find the right bride, but trust me, *she* is not me."

"Mercy, you protest so loudly."

"When people talk crazy, I have to speak up. Now, let's order pizza."

Charlotte snatched up her cell and phoned in their order, then changed into jeans, leaving Hillary alone with the dress, alone with her memories.

When she came out of her room, Hillary stood by the window, staring northwest toward the city. She cradled a black framed picture against her belly.

"You have a great place here, Charlotte," she said, turning back into the room.

"The west edge of the mountains have some lovely sunsets. But you said you were in the Navy—did you live on a ship? You must have seen some great sunsets."

"I lived in quarters smaller than your closets. But, yes, I saw some spectacular ocean sunsets. And sunrises. Even an ocean storm is fiercely beautiful. Been through a few of those." Hillary crossed over to Charlotte. "I have something for you." She offered her the picture. "Joel and me on our wedding day."

"Hillary—" It was a color-faded snapshot. The background images were fuzzy and grainy. But in the center of the eight-by-ten photo stood a handsome, athletic-looking lieutenant with his arm curled tight around his bride, a beaming, bright-blond Hillary, perfectly sculpted into the wedding gown that now hung on the dress form. Charlotte glanced across the room and if she didn't know better, she could've sworn the gown exhaled. Must have been the shift in the late-morning light falling through the window. "You're so beautiful. Joel looks just like I imagined."

They were young with their chins held high and eyes aglow with big love. Their smiles wide with big hope. He, a conquering hero. She, a conquering Southern beauty queen.

"Keep it. Please." Hillary pressed the frame toward Charlotte when she tried to give it back.

"No, I couldn't." Charlotte traced her finger over Joel's face, forever young. "Don't you want it?"

"I want you to have it. Joel belongs to both of us now. You brought him back to me. For all the good reasons. He captured you the same way he captured me." Hillary's countenance softened as she spoke. "For the first time since he died, I was glad I married him. I remembered all the good and happiness. And I owe that to you."

The doorbell rang, the delivery of pizza interrupting the moment. Charlotte paid, refusing the money Hillary held out.

"Smells good." Hillary opened cupboards. "Um . . . plates and glasses?"

"By the sink." Charlotte pointed from the pantry where she gathered napkins. "I have iced tea, water, milk, juice, Diet Coke. I drink the fake stuff around here."

"I'll have iced tea." Hillary stopped. "Is it sweet?"

Charlotte grinned, opening the pizza box on the dining table. "In a manner of speaking."

"Good enough. I don't want to know more."

The women ate the first few hot bites of cheese and sauce in peace. Then Hillary reached for a napkin. "How's your friend in the hospital?"

"We're talking about me now?"

"Might as well. That dress practically makes us family."

Family. The word smacked Charlotte's chest and burned through to her heart.

"He's fine. Had an accident racing motocross." Charlotte wiped tomato sauce from her fingers.

"Is he someone special?"

"He was. We were engaged, but he called it off." Charlotte reached for her soda. "Well, he wanted to postpone the wedding. Said he wasn't ready. But how do you go from being engaged and planning a wedding to just . . . waiting. Being in limbo." Charlotte swigged from her Diet Coke. The drink, the conversation, went down well with pizza. "We moved too fast. Engaged two months after we met."

"Some of the world's best loves stories are about men and women who met one day and married the next."

"Yeah, like who?"

Hillary balked. "I don't know, you're the wedding consultant. But I'm sure it's true."

Charlotte laughed. "You're a horrible liar."

"Maybe I am, but you know you've heard the stories of fast love. And I get the feeling you don't really want to say good-bye to this fella." Hillary chose a piece of pizza from the remaining slices.

"Didn't want my mama to die at thirty-five either, but she did. Can't always have life the way we want it. But there's always pizza." Charlotte took a big bite of a small slice. By forging into Hillary's past, she'd given permission for Hillary to forge into hers.

"Before Joel was killed," Hillary said, "we'd write letters and pick a day to look at the moon together. We were twelve hours apart, so one would look at the night moon, the other during the day, if we could find it. The night of his funeral the moon was bright and full, like a dancing globe in the sky. How dare the moon shine when my heart was so dark. I lost it, ran up to my room, tore the dress from the hanger, scooped up Joel's dog tags, and headed down to the basement. I had no idea what I was going to do until I spotted the trunk. I threw the dress in, back where it came from, stuffed Joel's dog tags into the little bag, and dragged it outside. I had every intention of burning it to ashes. Then I ran right into my daddy."

Charlotte brushed crumbs from her fingers and listened.

"'Shug,' he said, 'I don't think you want to do that.' But I didn't listen. I was going to burn that stupid trunk and everything it represented. I wanted nothing that reminded me of Joel. Daddy talked for a while. 'Now you listen to me.'" Hillary wagged her finger as her father might have done that night over forty years ago. "'You're hurting now, but you won't always feel this way. You just might want this dress again. Another Joel will come along.' Oh mercy, that sent me right over the edge. How could he say such a thing? There was only one Joel. Only one man for me. But some bit of reason sank in, so after Daddy left, I went to his workshop and found his blow-torch and fired it up. Teach him to make me take shop class in high school. I welded the lock until it glowed like the fires from the Sloss Furnaces. Then I collapsed. Woke up in my bed in the morning with bandages on my hands from torch burns."

Hillary got up from the table for her black bag and pulled a picture from the front pouch. "I found this when I was going through all the photos." She offered Charlotte a black-and-white image. "That's my mama and daddy, and next to them, the previous owners of our house."

"The one where you found the trunk?" The woman, perhaps in her midthirties, was beautiful in her Sunday suit. "Do you think they're connected to the dress?"

"I have no idea. Their names are on the back. Thomas and Mary Grace Talbot. That's my mama's handwriting. Darn near perfect, isn't it? I remember Thomas was a preacher, and they'd just purchased a big tent to hold revival meetings across the country. He told Mama he had the gift of healing. I thought he was the weirdest man I'd ever met."

"Really? Because of the healing thing?"

"I was a future nurse, so yes, even at ten, I didn't believe any man could *heal*." Hillary arched her eyebrows. "What do you think?"

"I think God uses imperfect people to do whatever He wants. He uses me to help brides get ready." Charlotte gazed at the picture again, touching their faces with the tip of her finger. "Thomas and Mary Grace Talbot. Where did you wander to?"

"I guess they'd be in their late eighties or early nineties now."

"If they're alive."

Hillary took up a piece of pizza. "They're alive." She grinned. "And I think I can find out where they live."

Chapter Eighteen

Charlotte unpacked a new shipment of dresses Wednesday after lunch. The winter gowns she'd ordered were beautiful. Dealing in her treasured merchandise always righted her tilted emotions.

Jesus Culture played from her iPad dock, and on days like today, Charlotte believed the storeroom of her shop was her most holy sanctuary.

Footsteps echoed over the shop's hardwood floor. "I'm here." Dixie. "Your relief." She came into the storeroom and sat on the old wooden packing and shipping desk, gathering her hair into a ponytail. "Jared said Tim is doing well, by the way. He'll probably go home today."

"Good, I'm glad." Monday, over a two-hour lunch, Charlotte had delivered the weekend details to Dixie—who demanded to know everything, starting with the first *H* in "Hey" to the trailing "e" in "Good-bye."

"Jared said Tim's blond restaurant girl has been there every day."

"It's nice to have someone care for you when you're hurting."

Dixie slammed her hand on the desk. "Would you stop being so nice? Get angry. Blow up. Shake your fist. 'I'll never go hungry again.'" She put on her best Southern-belle tone. "Fight for him, fight for what's yours."

Charlotte smirked, rolling her eyes. "Very dramatic, Miss O'Hara. Where would shaking my fists get me? Just riled up about something I can't change." She'd done her share of fist waving, and it only made her more mad and more sad. She had peace at the moment, and she'd kind of like to ride that river for a while. "I can't fight for a man who doesn't want me."

"But you said he—"

"Yes, he said some stuff. But when she walked in it was like I faded into the shadows." Charlotte held up a new Bray-Lindsay. "How do you like the dresses? I love every Bray-Lindsay gown." She wanted to hold it to her and meld with the silky threads and pure, creamy whiteness.

"They do exquisite work. Don't let Tawny see them. She'll change her mind."

Charlotte shook out the next gown, a new one from a local designer, Heidi Elnora.

The front chimes pealed through the shop followed by a high pitched, "Hello?"

"I got it." Dixie stepped out of the room, returning a few moments later with Hillary.

Charlotte hung the gown on the rack. "Hillary, hey, what are you doing here?" She motioned for her to come in. "Dixie, this is Hillary."

"I know. We just met." Dixie slid back onto her perch, the old desk. "So you're the Hillary who wore the dress? Who sealed it in the trunk?"

"Guilty. But I'm indebted to this woman, who redeemed it. Redeemed me." *Redeemed.* The purple man's word. For a moment it reverberated in Charlotte's soul. "Charlotte, are you free for a few hours?" Hillary asked.

"I could be if you need me. Is everything okay?" She checked with Dix, who nodded. She'd cover the afternoon.

"I called Thomas and Mary Grace Talbot. They're up for an afternoon visit if you're game to go."

"Now?"

"Now."

"Whoa, back up, y'all. Explain to ole Dixie what's going on. How did you get in touch with the Talbots?" She wagged her finger at Charlotte. "You didn't give me this piece of the story."

"I didn't know it myself until yesterday." Charlotte gave Dixie the Twitter version. "Hillary worked with a doctor at St. Vincent's named Talbot. When she came across Thomas and Mary Grace's name, she called him on the chance there might be a connection."

"And?" Dix said, rotating toward Hillary.

"Never heard of them." Hillary took up the story. "But he went to school with another Talbot. When you're in the same homeroom with a guy from first grade to twelfth, you find out things. The Dr. Talbot I knew put me in touch with Harry, who is Thomas and Mary Grace Talbot's great-nephew."

Dixie whooshed a "wow" from her desk perch. "Do you think Mrs. Talbot wore the dress before you, Hillary?"

Charlotte hung up the last dress in the shipment. "Let's go find out."

Kirkwood by the River was a retirement village nestled on wooded acreage by the Cahaba River. As Charlotte parked and walked with Hillary toward the main entrance, Hillary talked.

"He's ninety-four, suffers with some dementia. She's ninety-three, sharp as a tack. At least, according to Harry."

Passing through a golden sun spot on the stone patio, Charlotte stopped. "I'm not sure I want to go in."

"What? We came all this way. Isn't this why you found *me*?" Hillary sat on a wrought iron two-seater with flowered cushions.

"What if she knows nothing about the dress? What if this is a dead end? You were the last one who wore it and we have no idea who came before. We won't know if the bride before you was in love or if she married out of convenience. Or if she was made a widow like you. There are three more wars to contend with here. I'm not sure I want to reach the end of the line. To know *I'll never know*. There's too much unknown in my past already. I don't want to add the dress."

"Charlotte, it's not the asking that leaves us in the dark—we're already there, right? If we come to a dead end in the history of the dress, then at least we know we tried. No guarantee of answers in life."

"But I can pretend." Charlotte eased down next to Hillary. "If I don't talk to Mrs. Talbot, then I can make up the rest of the story. A lovely girl, a handsome groom, a simple wedding. And she's wearing your dress."

"And *your* dress." Hillary started for the entrance. "You missed your calling, Charlotte. You should've written romance novels."

"It's not about romance, Hillary. It's about life. Who doesn't want to be loved? To be safe? To have a place called home and family." Was that what she wanted so desperately? To be safe? To have a home with a family? Charlotte had never framed her fear with words before. Was that why she harbored doubts about marrying Tim? Because she wasn't sure her heart would be loved with him? Or that home meant family? Katherine sure didn't see her fitting in.

"Sounds like you want perfect love, Charlotte. The kind that doesn't mess with your heart or your fears. Let me tell you, that love doesn't exist. Let's say we walk through those doors and find that neither of the Talbots has recollection of the dress. Know nothing about it. Do you know they've been married seventy-two years? Seven decades plus two. That's twice your age and then some. Maybe we don't find another woman who wore that gown or find out how it got in my parents' basement, but we will find someone who knows how to love. It's that kind of love that'll drive out your fears. Not the kind you think you'll find by running and hiding." Hillary shoved her shoulders back, navy square. "Now let's go."

Without a word, Charlotte followed. A young, dark-haired resident assistant met them and escorted them down a long hall, past the TV and dining rooms, to Thomas and Mary Grace Talbot's door.

"Are they expecting you?" He knocked lightly. "Mary Grace? Thomas? It's George. You have visitors." He twisted the knob.

Around the opening door, Charlotte spotted Mrs. Talbot, thin and lost in her sweater and slacks, moving across the room with her cane. "Let them in, George." Charlotte's heart swelled with expectation. Mrs. Talbot smiled, and Charlotte recognized the aura of the younger beauty in the photograph. "Come in, come in. Thomas, our guests are here."

George quick-stepped across the room, offering aid to a frail man coming from the bedroom. "Darn legs giving me fits. Don't get old, young ladies." He wagged his finger, bending to sit in his rocker-recliner. "It don't pay. It don't pay. I'm good with the Lord . . . don't know why He won't come get me. Ain't no use to Him no more down here."

"Except to keep me company." Mrs. Talbot moved back toward another chair, George lending a support hand. "You'd miss me if you went on to glory, Tommy."

"Sweetheart, I wasn't planning on going without you. You've been with me through it all. The spoils are yours as much as mine." His spotted, veined hand dropped over the side of his chair and grasped hers. "Now, what can we do for you young ladies?" The light in Thomas's eyes was kind. Wise and patient. Charlotte loved him at once. If he suffered from dementia, it hadn't surfaced today.

"I'm Charlotte Malone, Mr. Talbot. This is Hillary Warner."

"We go by Thomas and Mary Grace around here."

"I'm the one who spoke to you on the phone," Hillary said, half rising as Mary Grace started to exit from her chair. George had gone, and it wasn't clear what the older woman wanted. "Can I help you?"

"There's hot coffee brewing in the kitchen. Can you bring it 'round? I'd do it, but by the time I shuffle there and back, it'll be dinnertime." Her laugh denied her age.

Hillary moved toward the kitchen, pointing to Charlotte. "Start the story."

Charlotte angled a bit more toward the couple, leaning on the arm of the sofa, meeting Mary Grace's eyes, blue and clear as a southern summer sky.

"I found a wedding dress." The air of the room shifted. Charlotte's eyes watered with unbidden tears. "In a trunk I bought at an auction."

"So, you found the dress?" Mary Grace's fingers remained linked to her husband's. "The silk one with the satin skirt, pearls about the waist, and the shimmer of gold thread."

Hillary darted out from the kitchen, a coffee cup in each hand. "Yes, that's the one. Who takes cream and sugar?"

"Black over here." Thomas raised his shaking hand.

"One dollop of each for me." Mary Grace scooped an invisible spoon through the air, her spirit, her youthfulness, threading through Charlotte.

"Charlotte?" Hillary said.

"Water for me." Caffeine would only jack her up. Her nerves were buzzed enough from the excitement and trepidation of this meeting. "Mary Grace, you know about the dress?"

"Surely. I wore it for my own wedding."

"Prettiest bride Birmingham ever saw," Thomas said, clear and strong.

"Hush, Thomas." Mary Grace took the cup Hillary handed her. "He still plies me with sweet nothings. Tell me, what do you do, Charlotte?"

"I . . . I own a bridal shop in Mountain Brook." Mary Grace wore the dress. Charlotte reached for the water Hillary offered. The cool ceramic cup felt good against her hands.

"And you found my gown." Mary Grace smiled, then let it fade. "But that gown is not to be sold. It must be worn by the one who finds it."

"Well, yes, you see, Mary Grace, I think I'm the one to *find* the next bride." Charlotte brought the mug of water to her lips and took a sip. "Perhaps someone will come into my shop and I'll know she's the one."

"You're the bride." Mary Grace pointed at her, slow and deliberate, almost like she was poking something invisible and buoyant.

"Told you," Hillary whispered out the side of her mouth.

"Hush." Charlotte slid to the edge of her sofa cushion, fixed on Mary Grace. She'd help her understand. "My job is to help brides get ready for the biggest day of their life. It's my gift, you might say. I'm good at what I do." Even to her own ears, her argument sounded shallow. Who was she kidding? She had no idea why she *redeemed* the dress.

"I'm sure you are, but that gown has never been for sale. It's been gifted from one bride to the next."

Hillary froze with her coffee mug in the air. "But I found the trunk in my parents' basement."

"I know." Mary Grace rocked gently in her chair. "I left it there for you."

"You left it there . . . I was ten years old." Shock and surprise blended over Hillary's angular face.

Charlotte could see that Hillary still hadn't completely settled the issue of Joel in her heart, so she moved the topic away from the dress for a moment.

"Thomas, I hear you were a preacher."

"Yup, yup, fifty-two years. Preached the gospel of the kingdom from Maine to Hawaii, down on into Mexico and Guatemala. Up to Canada and Alaska."

"He still preaches," Mary Grace said. "To me and all the residents here. Our poor cleaning lady gets a sermon every week for sure. And the man who brings our groceries is about to get born again, I know it. Then there's our dear George who insists he's an . . . what's he again, Tommy?"

"Agnostic."

"Yes, that's what he says he is. Imagine, believing in nothing. What hope is there in that?"

"Exactly. If you got good news, you best tell it." Thomas laughed softly. "Don't make no sense to be quiet."

"He's a gifted preacher," Mary Grace said. "He led many a lost soul to the foot of the Cross. Why, there was the time we were preaching in a tent out in the middle of a Kansas prairie and—"

"Mary Grace, where's my coffee?"

She picked it up from the table between them and handed it to him. "It was hotter than anything that summer and the flies were just thick as could be. Let me tell you, no wind was sweeping down the plain that night. But the folks came out to hear the preaching."

"Most folks didn't have TV in those days." Thomas sipped his coffee and set it back down. "It was right after the war and the country was ready for some good news. A message of hope."

"But the heat just melted folks right in their chairs. Hand fans were just a-going, then Thomas started preaching and fifty words into his message he suddenly stopped." Mary Grace pressed her palms against the air, her eyes on her husband. "He stood right in the middle of the stage, spread his hands, tipped back his head, and closed his eyes."

Mary Grace's story stirred a bubbling sensation spreading in Charlotte's chest. The Talbots spoke like young, energized believers. No sign of fading. Of dementia.

"There Tommy remained, center stage, arms spread, face toward heaven, and he said in the most even, calm, but oh-so-sure voice, 'Lord of heaven, who calmed the seas and rebuked the storm, I ask for Your mercy on these humble folks who drove for miles and miles to hear Your Word. Please send us a cool, gentle rain.'"

"Some folks on the front row snickered." Thomas shook his head.

"Yet he didn't let it bother him or break his concentration," Mary Grace said. "Time ticked on. Thomas didn't move, and nothing happened."

"The sweat under my shirt started soaking through. I'd just put my entire reputation and ministry on the line with that crazy request."

"So, what'd he do? He requested it again." Mary Grace popped the air with her lightly fisted hand. A don't-you-just-know gesture.

"Just in case the folks in the back wanted to snicker too." Thomas and Mary Grace told their story like a well-danced waltz.

"'Lord,' he said, 'Master of the wind and the waves, Creator of all things, Lover of our souls—'"

"If you're going to go down, go down praising His good name." Thomas raised his hand, waving toward heaven.

"'Send us a cool, gentle rain,'" Mary Grace finished.

"The chairs were creaking," Thomas said. "Men were clearing their voices, tugging on their sweaty collars. Babies cried and mamas tried to cool themselves by waving fans."

"It was the longest minute of our lives, waiting to see what Thomas, or God, would do. Then . . ." Mary Grace paused, eyes sparking. Charlotte leaned toward her, hand gripping her water cup. Hillary hovered close. "Then the tent shook a bit."

"The air stirred."

"And the sweetest cool breeze rushed right under the tent, around our chairs. Through people's hair. You could see the ends flutter."

"It smelled like new mown grass. Folks rose to their feet, started praising. Just when their voices hit a crescendo, the softest rain pitter-pattered on the top of the tent. It rained the rest of the night and all the next day." Thomas sat back, a smile on his lined face, his coffee cup shimmering in his hand.

"I tell you," Mary Grace said. "There were no atheists in the crowd that night. We had a ton of folk who gave their hearts to the Lord. Even had a couple of healings. Remember the boy with polio, Tommy?" Her dark eyes sparkled. "Threw down his crutches, snapped off his brace, and ran around the tent like a freed man. His daddy finally caught him and let a doctor in attendance examine him. He determined the boy had a whole new leg."

"A boy was healed of polio?" Hillary set her coffee down with a snort. "Just like that." She snapped her fingers. "I've been a nurse for almost forty years. I've never seen anyone healed of anything like polio."

"I see. So your faith is based on your experience? What you've seen? Won't get you very far." Thomas was no longer an old man. He spoke with authority. "Without faith it's impossible to please God."

"Thomas, please." Mary Grace squeezed his fingers, gentling her way into his sentence. "It was a bona fide miracle, medically proven. Now, darlings, what was it you wanted to know from us?"

Yes, back to the dress. Charlotte cleared her throat and smoothed her hand over her Malone & Co. skirt.

"Mary Grace, Hillary found this picture in a box of her parents' things." Charlotte indicated Hillary should pass over the picture of the Talbots with her parents.

"On the back it has a date," she said. "The day my parents bought the house from you."

"Oh my." Mary Grace pressed her small, spotted hand to her chest. "That was so many years ago."

Thomas put on his glasses and leaned in to see the photograph. "Who's the young, beautiful lady I'm standing next to?"

Mary Grace chortled. "I was in my late thirties and dreading turning forty, thinking it was so old."

"Bet you'd trade now if you could, wouldn't you, love?" Thomas said.

"In a gnat's breath."

Maybe they'd want to trade with Charlotte or Hillary, but Charlotte wanted to trade with them. Even for a moment. To know what it felt like to love for seventy-two years. To tell a story in perfect harmony. To still hear she was the prettiest bride in Birmingham.

"You're with my parents. Lindell and Arlene Saltonstall." Hillary moved over to Thomas, who held the picture. "They bought the house from you in '57. I was ten. I had an older brother. We called him Shoop."

"Hillary, you were the young girl I left the dress for." Mary Grace sat back, sighing, and closed her eyes. "Tell me, were you any relation to the Saltonstalls who owned the mines? My father worked their mines for thirty years."

"My great grandfather was one of the brothers. But my grandfather, Paul Saltonstall, didn't want anything to do with the family mines. He went in another direction. Wanted to be in engineering."

As Hillary spoke, Mary Grace tipped her head back. Her eyes fluttered closed.

"Mrs. Talbot?" Charlotte started to get up. Was the woman all right? Thomas didn't seem alarmed. Or very awake himself.

"Dear, call me Mary Grace." She opened her eyes. "I was just remembering my father. So, Hillary, tell me, did you wear the gown?"

Hillary flowed with the stilted conversation. "Yes, yes, I did."

Charlotte could hear Hillary's heartbeat in her words.

"I married my first husband in that dress. Six months later he was killed in Viet Nam."

"Oh dear, I'm so sorry." Mary Grace worked her way forward, out of her chair. She reached for her cane, steadied herself, and moved to the small breakfront drawer. When she worked her way back to her chair, she held a photo.

Through the reflective light, Charlotte could see the smiling, newly married Talbots.

"This is Tommy and me on our wedding day."

Charlotte held the picture, a touched-up black-and-white. An artist had brushed a pink hue on Mary Grace's cheeks. Reddened both of their lips a bit. But there was no mistaking her beauty and his handsome youth. And she was wearing *the* dress.

"We met in elementary school. I fell in love with him on the playground."

"She was the preacher's daughter and I wanted nothing to do with her."

Thomas rocked in his chair and Mary Grace's eyes had closed again. Charlotte glanced at Hillary. If they didn't find out about the dress in the next few minutes, they might not find out at all. At least not today.

"Mary Grace." Hillary moved to kneel by her chair, squeezing her hand. Charlotte guessed she was half checking to see if she was awake and half checking her pulse. "How did you get the dress? Was it made for you?"

The older woman sat forward a bit. Her shaking hand reached for her coffee. "I was given it by the woman who wore it first."

Her statement, so profound and clear, opened the door to a bevy of questions. Charlotte's nerves prickled and she scooted forward with a glance at Hillary, who was frowning.

"So why did you leave it at the house?"

Okay, good question, but not the one Charlotte would've asked. *Who* gave the dress to Mary Grace? Who was the first woman to wear it? But today seemed to be about Hillary's journey. Charlotte sat back and sipped her water.

"We sold the house to your mama and daddy, and when we were all packed up, ready to go, the trunk with the gown was one of the last items to be loaded."

"I was about to carry it out to the moving truck," Thomas said from his reclining position, eyelids at half-mast, "when Gracie told me, 'Tommy, leave it. For that young girl.'"

"So you really left the trunk just for *me*?" Hillary's voice trembled. Her countenance wavered.

"I felt I was to leave it for you."

"She loved that dress too. But when the Lord gives Gracie a nudge, she responds."

Hillary stood. "God told you to leave *that* trunk in the basement for me?" Incredulous. Doubt. Awe.

"I think He did. I believe He did. And you found it. And you wore it."

"Yes, yes, I did. On the happiest day of my life. Which led to the worst. I wore it for a groom who was killed six months later." Hillary was up and out the door before anyone could say another word. No excuse me, no thank-you, or good-bye.

"Hillary." Charlotte stepped out the door into the hall. But her new friend was gone. "Mary Grace, Thomas, I'm so sorry." Charlotte gathered her purse and Hillary's. "She's just working through old memories. Thank you for your time. May I come again?"

"Please, come and see us. Don't worry about Hillary. She'll fare all right. She'll fare all right."

From Mary Grace's lips to God's ears. Charlotte caught Hillary just as she got to the car.

"Hey, you run fast for an old lady." Charlotte worked up a laugh, aiming her remote entry key at her car. Hillary stood by the passenger door with a stone expression. Charlotte slid in behind the wheel, dumping their purses in the backseat. "What's going on?"

"Just drive." An ashen-faced Hillary rolled down her window and hung her head out. Her left hand crossed her body and white-knuckled the door handle. "So God set me up in 1957 to be a widow? To marry a man six months before his end-of-life number was called?" She smashed the door with her right fist. "I am never going to step inside a church again."

"You think God only hangs out in church? He was in that room with us five minutes ago. He's everywhere." She'd learned of His every presence that summer at youth camp. And dozens of times since. Charlotte backed out of the parking spot but stopped the car in the middle of the lane. "Are you okay?"

"He knew, He knew Joel was going to die." Tears slithered down Hillary's high, pink cheeks. She gulped the fresh air out her window. "And He let me marry him."

Charlotte sighed. *God, help me. What do I say?* "Hillary, maybe God—"

"Is there a reason we're stopped here in the middle of the parking lot?"

"Hillary." Charlotte gazed out her window. The wind raced

through the trees. Her thoughts raced through her mind. "What if marrying Joel wasn't about you? What if marrying Joel was about him?"

"Getting married was about both of us."

"But only one of you, using your theory, was slated to end his life in six months. What if marrying Joel was about sending a young man off to war, loved, happy, comforted by the idea of warm fires and a beautiful wife waiting for him at home? What if thinking of you, remembering your wedding, making love, your friendship and laughter"—Charlotte's thoughts formed words faster than she could speak them—"were the only things that kept Joel going on those nights he was scared and lonely, cold and hungry, miserable as I'm sure only a man at war can be?

"What if your letters were the only grounding to sanity he had in the midst of battle? What if marrying Joel wasn't about you, Hillary. What if it was all about Joel? Only for Joel? What if God loved him so much he gave him a bride before he died? Would that be okay with you? Would it?" Charlotte shifted into gear and off the clutch. The car surged forward, the road ahead blurry.

Hillary tucked forward and muffled her weeping with her face in her hands, her shoulders shimmering with rolling sobs.

Charlotte braked at the residence entrance and smoothed her hand over Hillary's back. "I'm sorry. I'm so sorry, I don't know what came over me." She waited, whispering, "Jesus, Jesus," every now and then.

The breeze through the trees whistled comfort through the car. After a long while, Hillary sat up, wiped her face with the back of her hand, and gazed out the window.

Charlotte shifted into gear and eased on the gas. As she turned onto the road, Hillary reached over and squeezed her hand.

Chapter Nineteen

Emily

*E*mily sat alone in the downtown holding cell, waiting for Father or Phillip, *someone*, to rescue her. The block room with a barred door was cold and dark, chilling Emily to the bone. And to the heart.

Mother had come with Jefferson and demanded her release, but the warrant officer said bail must be posted. A thousand dollars. *A thousand dollars.* A working man's annual wage. Of course, Father could afford it, but with the banks closed for the day, would he be able to get the money?

As Emily was escorted to her cell, Mother insisted—demanded—the officer give her the cloak she'd brought for her. "I'm off to find your father. Emily, be strong, you're a Canton."

But Emily had crumbled, weeping, so limp the officer had to drag her to the holding area.

When the iron door clanked behind her, she collapsed, barely landing on the worn, moldy cot. For long, sorrowful minutes, she heard nothing but her own sobs.

Now she sat against the stone wall, drawing her cloak around her shoulders. The November chill seeped through the concrete wall and gathered around her arms and legs.

She'd envisioned many things about her future. But being arrested and locked in a cell was never one of them.

How humiliating. Devastating. If only she were as strong and courageous as Mother implored her to be. She wanted to quit, promise to never visit Taffy Hayes again. She wasn't a Canton. She was a coward.

Moving to her feet, Emily gripped the cell bars and pressed her face through a small square, trying to see down the dark corridor. "Hello. Somebody, please. Hello?"

Would they ever come for her? Or leave her to rot, trapped and forgotten?

With sagging shoulders and a weary heart, Emily dropped to the cot again and drew her legs to her chest, trying not to dwell on the dark walls inching in around her. But she could think of nothing but the stony chill in the claustrophobic box.

Who had done this to her? Who hated her so much to swear out a warrant for her arrest?

Emily tossed off her cloak as her thoughts began to boil. This whole ordeal was unthinkable. Downright absurd.

She had no enemies that she knew of. Back on her feet, she wrung her hands, her thumb pressing against her bare ring finger.

The officer took her engagement ring. For safekeeping, so he said. If she'd known she would be held for so long, she'd have demanded the ring be her ransom.

It was certainly worth a thousand dollars. Emily exhaled at the amount. One thousand dollars. Even her bail seemed of absurd proportions.

A steel door slammed. She jumped to the bars and angled her face to see the single gas light glowing on the far wall. Voices drifted toward her, then faded.

"Hey there . . . hello? I'm Emily Canton," she shouted from the bottom of her belly. "Please release me."

The voices faded, then disappeared. She sighed. They weren't coming for her.

What the dickens happened to Mother? To Father? Why wasn't Phillip racing to her rescue? Hours had passed since she arrived at the jail. Night darkened the street-side barred window and the sounds of commerce had long since faded.

Emily retrieved her cloak and wrapped it around herself. How could they just leave her in here?

A door clicked. Emily jumped up and angled again to see down the corridor. A bright light broke against the wall. A double set of footfalls echoed. The gait and stride didn't ring familiar. But then a face, a *very* familiar, handsome face rounded the corner.

"Daniel." Emily stretched her hands through the bars, her pulse drumming in her ears. "What are you doing here?"

He gathered her hands in his. "I was going to ask you the same."

"I'm accused of breaking a Jim Crow law."

He laughed, removing his cap, bunching it in his hand. "What Democrat did you make angry, darling?"

"Do you think this is funny, Daniel Ludlow? I'm behind bars. Look around. I'm locked in this dank, dark, cold place. For what? Hiring Taffy Hayes to make my dress and visiting her shop."

"Now you know what it's like to be on the other side. You'll have deeper compassion for others who are falsely accused."

"I do have compassion for them." Though in recent light, she'd doubted the depth of her commitment. "Did you come here to make fun of me?"

"I came to help you." He reached through the bars and traced his finger along the curve of her chin. "Ah, Emily, even in jail you're beautiful. Especially when you're mad."

"Keep taunting me, Daniel Ludlow, and you'll see a beauty mankind has never beheld. Can't you get me out of here?"

"I'm trying. I visited your father's office, but he'd already left for the day."

"It's Thursday. He goes to the club. I'm sure that's where Mother's gone. But the banks are closed and I'm not sure he keeps a thousand dollars on hand. Oh, Daniel, I can't spend the night here." Emily drew her hands from his and folded her arms under her cloak. "How did you know I was here? Is it all over Birmingham? Did I make the evening paper? There was a photographer outside the jail when I arrived. Oh my, it's all so humiliating."

"It's not in the paper, Em, not as far as I can tell. I found out you were here through Father's friend, Lieutenant Flannigan. He sent word and I came as soon as I could."

"Lieutenant Flannigan sent word to you?"

"He thought I'd want to know." Daniel looped his arms through the bars and grabbed hold of Emily. The strong press of his hands on her waist gave her comfort. She wasn't alone now. "It's not hard for anyone, even a man's friends, to see when a fella's in love."

His confession tied up her heart with soft ribbons. "Don't say that, Danny. Ours was a most sincere friendship, and I adore you, but when you left to play with the Barons, it was over. Your kind way of saying good-bye to me."

"Kind way of saying good-bye? I had no intentions of choosing between baseball and you. How was I to know you'd engage yourself with that blowhard Saltonstall? Now if you'd read my letters—"

"I found your silly ole letters." She was in jail, why not confess everything? "Father hid them in the stable."

"Why would he do such a thing?" Daniel released her, stepping back.

"Never mind why. He just did. I started to read them but changed my mind. I'm engaged to another man, and I shouldn't read my former beau's letters. It wouldn't be right. I wouldn't appreciate Phillip—"

"Going around with another woman?"

241

Emily twisted sideways out of his hands, ignoring the shivers-of-truth crisscrossing her tired form. "There you go again, accusing the man I love."

"I didn't accuse him of a thing, Emily."

She gripped the bars and stuck her chin through them, facing Daniel nose to nose. "Do you know something else?" She fisted his coat collar. "Do you?"

"Don't ask the question if you don't want to know the answer. We've been around this mountain once before, Emily."

"For all that's decent, Daniel Ludlow, tell me the answer." She pulled his face into the bars. The cold steel pressed against his cheek, but he didn't flinch or break free, holding his gaze steady on her face. "If I mean anything to you, if your lovesick confession carries any truth, then tell me what you know. You're my friend, aren't you?"

"I've seen him. With her."

"Besides that day on the street, you mean." Emily released his collar and Daniel rubbed his cheek. "He was with her? Emmeline?"

"At the Italian Garden, during the midnight supper."

"She's quite beautiful, isn't she?" Emily turned toward the back of the tiny cell, feeling weak and dull, a lawbreaker, shamefully arrested. A poor, wretched sight compared to the striking Emmeline Graves.

"She's nothing compared to you, Emily."

She brushed the string of tears from her cheeks. "Can you believe he goes around with a girl who has nearly the same name as I do? Probably so as not to confuse us."

"She doesn't have your character. Look at you, in jail for sticking to your convictions."

"Lot of good it will do." Emily whirled around. "Taffy. Oh mercy, Daniel." Back at the bars, she grabbed his collar again. "I'm so selfish . . . only worried about myself, but what will they do to Taffy? Please tell me she's all right."

"As far as I know, she's fine. Flannigan said he was directed to merely send word for her to stay away from you."

"Stay away from me? This makes no sense. None at all, Danny. Who would order such a thing?"

"Emily, you're not so naïve to the ways of this city, are you?"

"No, but—"

"Tell you what . . . Remember my chum, Ross? He's writing for the *Age-Herald,* and I can ask him to check into your arrest."

"Please, Danny, would you? Help me find my accuser."

"Now how can I deny such a sincere plea?" He reached for her hands. His thick, floppy bangs curved over his forehead, drawing Emily into his blue eyes. "I miss you."

"Danny, don't. It will do us no good to remember what we were. We must go forward with who we are, who we'll be. I do want to be friends."

"But I love you."

Emily drew her hands back. "Then you should've spoken to Father. If not before you left with the Barons, then the moment you returned home."

"I'd not even spoken to you, Emily. You'd not returned one of my letters. What was I to say to your father? 'Hello, sir, I'd like to marry your daughter, even though I've not spoken to her in five months.'"

"Yes, Daniel, for pity's sake, yes."

He sighed and faced the dark clouds of the corridor. "Then why are you marrying Phillip Saltonstall?"

"I'm in jail, Daniel." Emily let her hands fall from the bars and grabbed her cloak as it threatened to slip from her shoulders. "I don't want to have this conversation. I can't think about it now. I just want to get out of here."

"I'm sorry, you're right." He slapped his cap against the bars. "Let me go see what I can do."

"Thank you. And, Daniel?"

"Yes?"

"That night, at the Italian Garden. Who were you with?" She didn't have a right to know but she asked anyway.

"My chums, Ross and Alex."

"Did you dance?"

"Once, but only to save Ross's neck and not embarrass the poor girl he dragged over to our table." He fitted his cap on his head. "Are you hungry?"

"Famished."

"I'll be back with food and hot coffee, and hopefully news about your release."

"Daniel, you're so kind and I'm behaving so rudely. I'm sorry, but this is my first jail experience. I'll be more cordial next time."

She loved the timbre of his laugh. It cushioned her pain. "I'm sure you will." He reached his hand through the bars and smoothed the back of his fingers over her cheek. "Emily Canton, you can air your frustration to me anytime." He bowed as he backed down the corridor. "Sparring with you is more fun than frolicking with any other girl."

Emily leaned against the bars, staring at the spot where Daniel had been, inhaling his subtle, clean fragrance. Did she love him? Oh, that man could get under her skin, make her blood boil. But she loved sparring with him too. He made her heart and mind race. Unlike Phillip, who seemed only interested in . . . her body? He spoke constantly of her charm and beauty. And of her family's name. But rarely commented on her stories or laughed at her anecdotes.

Did she love Phillip? At the moment she couldn't think about anything but being freed.

Oh, what did it matter? She'd pledged Phillip her love, accepted his ring. What good was her word if she didn't honor it when the day seemed difficult and fruitless?

Even if she loved Daniel, she was given to Phillip. Like it or not, she was bound by her own actions and confession.

Oh mercy. Emily yanked on the bars. "Let me go!"

The far steel door clanged again and her heart jumped. *Daniel.* Emily's mouth watered in anticipation of food. Her pulse pumped in anticipation of Daniel.

But it wasn't Daniel who came around the corner.

"Phillip." She stretched her arms through the cell, her heart beating against the bars. "You came." He walked beside the officer, his chin raised, his back straight, shoulders wide.

"As soon as I could, dearest." He held her face and tipped her forehead toward him for a kiss. "I'm so sorry, Emily, so sorry. You can trust I'll be speaking to the chief of police and the mayor about this miscarriage of justice."

"Bail's been posted," the officer said. "You're free to go, Miss Canton."

The cell door opened and Phillip drew Emily into him, caressing her, whispering, "I'm here now. This will be handled. Trust me."

"Oh, Phillip." Tears soaked up the rest of her words. She felt weak and womanly, needing the arms of her man. How could she have flirted with Daniel only moments ago? How dare he deposit doubt in her heart? *Again.* Emily gazed up at Phillip. "I don't want to wait."

A saucy grin tripped a light his eyes. "Darling, I've been saying that for a while but we can't"—he gazed around—"the officers might come upon us." He raised her hand and slid her diamond down her finger. "I believe this belongs to you."

"I mean let's get married, Phillip. I don't want to wait until spring. Let's get married on New Year's Eve. Let's end 1912 in each other's arms."

"Are you sure? What about Europe for our honeymoon?"

"We'll go to Hot Springs or Florida. In the spring we'll sail to Paris. Doesn't it sound lovely, Phillip?"

"It sounds divine. New Year's Eve you'll become my wife. I'll speak to your father and mine."

"What about our mothers?"

Phillip wrapped his arm around her, kissed her forehead, and escorted her out of her cell. "That, my sweet chickadee, is a chore for you."

She laughed. A hearty, free laugh. "You send me to the wolves while you handle the lambs, I see."

"A man's got to do what a man's got to do."

As they rounded the corner, Daniel stood in the corridor, a basket in his hand. His eyes roamed from Emily's face to Phillip's. Without a word, he turned on his heel and left.

Phillip shook his head. "Such an odd fella," he said, chuckling, mocking.

"Do you . . ." Emily cleared the clutter from her voice. "Know him?"

"In a manner of speaking. I met him." Phillip removed his arm from around Emily. "Out on the town . . . you know how men do."

"Phillip." Emily slowed her step, touching his arm. "Might I ask a question and request a true, honest answer?"

"And risk your anger with a lie?"

"Once we are married . . ." Keeping her eyes averted, she brushed her hand over his jacket. The fine wool released the thin residue of a woman's perfume. "There'll be no more Emmeline. Right?"

"Emily!" Phillip jerked back, shoved aside his blazer, and tugged on his waistcoat. "What prompted this line of questioning? We've been over this. I feel lost how to answer. Why do you want to marry me if you believe me unfaithful? Was it him?" Phillip pointed to the door. "Did that cretin fill your head with lies?"

"Just be clear and honest, Phillip. Are you being unfaithful? Have you been with Emmeline?"

"Might I ask *you* a question?"

Emily exhaled. Phillip seemed to always answer her questions with a question. "Yes, what is it?"

"Will this be the last time I spring you from jail? I had a time settling Dad down once he heard the news. We phoned the paper to remove your name and paid a pretty sum to assure there will be no photograph. I don't want our wedding to be overshadowed by the sight of you in a paddy wagon."

"I never intended to be arrested in the first place. I merely went to Taffy's for a fitting."

"What did I say to you about going to the colored section of town?"

She held her answer, tired of arguing the same thing over and over.

"Emily, darling." Phillip clasped her chin. "We are Saltonstalls. We do not go to people, they come to us. We do not do business with coloreds."

"Ever?"

"There are plenty of white men and women in need of jobs. Any job I'd hire a colored to do I can find a poor white to do for the same price."

"Except in the Saltonstall mines. How does your theory work there, Phillip? The colored convicts seem to get the job done. You don't mind finding ways to extend their sentences so they can continue to work without pay, now do you? *Then* a colored worker is just fine for your needs."

"We're giving convicted criminals jobs and skills, so when they are released, *at the proper time*, they can get hired for pay."

"When was the last time Saltonstall mines hired a colored ex-con for a paying job?"

Phillip bit his bottom lip and gazed at the ceiling. "Five minutes ago I could've made love to you in a jail cell. You were a rose in my palm." He peered down at her. "Now you're a thorn in my flesh."

"Then shall we return to the original question?"

Phillip scooped Emily into his arms and, bending his lips to hers, kissed her with passion and fire, leaving her breathless and nimble. When he raised his head, she swallowed a moaning yearn for more.

"Would a man who kissed you like that be burning away his desires with another woman?"

"I reckon not." Truthfully, Emily had no idea. She had much to learn about men. Her man. But for the moment, the heat of his ardor was enough to convince her. Phillip Saltonstall belonged to her. And her alone.

Chapter Twenty

Tim

He'd wrecked before. Crashed and burned. Broken bones. Cracked ribs. Knocked his noggin. But never broken his own heart. No sir, he was careful about that precious beating thing.

The image of Charlotte backing out of his hospital room as Kim hovered over him sped around in his mind without stopping. Without mercy. Tim winced. *Stupid. Stupid. Stupid.* But to save Charlotte would have meant humiliating Kim, and she'd done nothing wrong—her attentiveness was in response to his own overtures.

Tim tugged on his jeans, jammed his feet into his Nike slides, then slowly slung his shirt over his shoulders. Ten days after the accident, he still hurt. Pain beginning in his waist, shot up his torso and down his arm. Sometimes at night he could feel the bone moving under the skin. Or so it seemed.

The bruising, still evident on his neck, chest, and arms, made showering and dressing a pain and taxed him like a five-mile run. Uphill.

His entire body was covered with deep tissue bruises. The doctor ordered him home only if he promised to lay low, rest, stay away from work. No driving. And well, no racing. As if he needed to be told. But praise heaven, he could live on his own.

"Tim?" The kitchen door slammed. "I brought breakfast." The beams of the remodeled '20s cottage creaked as if responding to Kim's familiar voice. "Sugar, are you up?"

"Yeah, yeah, coming down the hall." Tim slipped his phone into his pocket and moved slow and steady down the wide passage.

"You should've seen the line at Starbucks," she called.

"Yeah? Not surprised. Popular place." Tim detoured into his office. Since he'd been home, he had more time than was comfortable to think about his life. His choices. His self-wounded heart.

"But if anyone knows how to work the line, baby, it's me, Kim Defario." Each syllable of her name was accented with her snapping fingers.

"So true. Doesn't need to be said twice," Tim called, breathing deep. It hurt to talk loud. He lowered down to his drawing table stool, wincing. He still liked to draw his first ideas and designs by hand. He liked the creative feel of pencil to paper.

"You coming? I need to go in about a half hour."

"Just one sec . . ." Tim ran his hand over his cracked, sore ribs. Man, it was hard to recover from a five-hundred-pound bike falling on top of you.

He hadn't intended to take up with Kim. Didn't even know she was in town until she called, wanting to get together and catch up. Nice and friendly, right?

Three weeks later she was a constant in his life, and he wondered how he got here, feeling more and more like a heel. More and more like the nincompoop who let go of the tender, beautiful, be-still-my-heart Charlotte.

Tim slipped his cell from his pocket. No missed calls. No Charlotte. She'd reinforced her feelings about him by not coming back to the hospital after Kim broke in on their tender moment. No calls or texts.

Tim had sent Jack. But even his charming little brother couldn't get her to budge. So why did he miss her? What he needed to do was move on, get over her. A gorgeous, loving, intelligent woman just brought him breakfast, so what was his problem?

His problem? The lingering taste of Charlotte's lips. The phantom scent of her skin. The light brush of her hair against his cheek. Her sudden laugh that always caught him off guard and made *him* laugh. The way her eyes danced with her words when she talked shop—wedding gowns and brides. Tim shuddered. *Get a grip, man.*

She was starting to invade his soul like when he'd first met her. She was an unexpected, beautiful thrill that made flying over a motocross track seem like a kiddie ride. Rather than winning a new job for the Rose Firm, he'd spent the days after their first meeting calculating ways to win her.

He and David had never argued so much.

"Get your head back in the game, Tim."

After two months, he'd proposed. Slept like a baby that night. Felt right. Moving on with his life, growing up. Thirty-two would be forty-two before he knew it and he wanted a wife and children. But as the wedding neared, the stark reality of merging two lives into one turned tranquility into tempest.

"Hey, Timbo, I'm eating my breakfast, and if you're not here in sixty seconds, I'll eat yours too."

"Kim, please, since when could you eat two breakfasts? I'll eat mine *and* half of yours."

Her laugh bounced down the hall. "You know me too well."

The nearer he got to June 23, the more he'd panicked. Stuck his head in the sand like a scared ostrich and let go of the best thing in his life.

"Let me make a quick call." Tim took his phone from his pocket and dialed the number he'd scrawled along the edge of drafting paper the day before the accident.

As the phone rang on the other end, he winced and hobbled to shove the door partway closed. He owed his friend Brooks in the county records office another huge favor for pulling the number Tim just dialed.

He jerked to life when a man answered. "Hello?" Tim said. "Monte Fillmore?"

"Speaking."

"You don't know me, but I'm Tim Rose and my fia—friend Charlotte Malone used to live with your mother, Gert."

"She certainly did. How can I help you?" His businesslike tone told Tim to get straight to the point.

"I was wondering if you knew her father's name."

"Charlotte's father? No. I wasn't that close to her, or her mother. I was married with kids of my own by the time Mom took Phoebe and Charlotte under her wing."

"Did your mother ever mention him?"

"Not to me. Phoebe might have talked about him to Mom, but names and news never made their way to me."

"Do you know of anyone else who might know Charlotte's father? Grandparents? Aunts, uncles?" Tim paced to the window. Beyond the glass, the June day was composed of blue and white hovering over the Birmingham skyline. "Anything left behind when she moved out, or when your mom died?"

"Don't know anyone who might have been that close to Phoebe. My mom took Charlotte in after Phoebe died because the girl had no one else. Foster care or an orphanage were her only choices. Can't think of anything left behind. We did a pretty thorough job of breaking down Mom's house. Gave away five rooms of furniture, clothes, and appliances. There wasn't much left. Why do you ask?"

"Just trying to do a favor for a friend. Thanks for your time,

Monte." Tim hit End. When he swung the door open, Kim stood in the hall, arms folded.

"You know, she might not want you digging around in her past."

"Maybe." Kim's eyes—hazel like a hawk's and twice as intense—bore into him as he headed for the kitchen.

"Sometimes not knowing is the only way to deal with hard stuff, Tim. You can't just pop into this woman's life with, 'I found your daddy,' and expect to be her hero."

"Never said I wanted to be a hero." Tim opened the cupboard for a bowl. He felt like cereal. But truth? He did want to be Charlotte's hero. He wanted to make up for his stupidity in some way. Do something lasting for her.

"Tim, what's going on?" Kim leaned against the counter, crossing her long legs at her ankles. Her tailored blouse fit her curves and her slacks hugged her hips. And her heart crawled out of her chest and perched on her arm.

"We're eating breakfast. That's what we're doing." Smart aleck. His turmoil wasn't her fault.

"Don't dump your attitude on me." She went to the table and snatched up her coffee. "I mean, what's going on with you and me? This? Us?"

"I think I still love her." Tim tugged open the fridge and reached for the milk, pouring it over his cereal.

"You think?"

"Know. I know." When he turned, Kim was slinging her handbag over her shoulder. "I never stopped," he said.

"Then go get her." Kindness undergirded the sadness in her voice.

"She doesn't want me. And I don't blame her."

"So what was this with me? Rebound?"

"You came back to town, gave me a call, we started going to

dinner." He peered at her. "Kim, I'm sorry. I never meant for us to be more than friends, but I've led you on. I should've . . ." He gazed at the milk, twisting on the cap. "I should've been up-front."

"You sure should've, bucko." Kim's heels resounded across the kitchen tile. "So don't be stupid with her, Tim." The door closed softly as she left.

Tim opened the silverware drawer and took out a spoon, scooping the first sweet bite into his mouth, a sad wash of emotion for Kim skimming his heart.

Lord, forgive me.

But joy. He was still in love with Charlotte.

Charlotte

Through June, Charlotte occupied her Saturdays with weddings. Just not her own. She and Dix prepared no fewer than twenty-five brides.

The best part of it all was Hillary. She came to the shop almost every day. Volunteered to run errands or help with inventory. Refusing all pay or reward. She brought in lunch dishes made in her own kitchen and bonded with Dixie over *Dirty Jobs* and Mike Rowe.

"Did you see what he did last night?"

"You know I did. Right when I was taking a bite of my dinner. I'll never look at spaghetti the same."

On Sundays, she saw Tim from a distance, arriving for the late service as he left the early. She'd park on the opposite side of the parking lot from his truck and scoot into the sanctuary's side door, but three out of four June Sundays she ran smack into him.

Hundreds of congregants, and she had to bump into Tim Rose. Usually one or two of the other Roses as well. She'd made every effort—short of being late for church—to miss them.

Yet, that's exactly what she did. Missed them.

Today, the Sunday after her supposed wedding day, Charlotte hurried toward the sanctuary, bleary-eyed, bone weary from wedding month, but grateful to be on her feet and moving.

She'd dressed seven brides yesterday, June 23rd, burying any threat of her soul remembering it was supposed to be *her* wedding day.

The ten a.m. sun burned high and hot from a wispy blue sky. Summer was sitting down hard on its first Sunday, stirring up the crickets' mournful serenade about the humidity.

Charlotte skipped up the portico steps when a familiar voice caused her to pause. "Where to for breakfast?" She looked back to see David passing by on the sidewalk, leaving the first service, with Jack and younger brothers Chase and Rudy. The rest of the Roses, Katherine with their two children and Mr. and Mrs. Rose, huddled in the middle of the parking lot.

Charlotte leaned against the guardrail. What did she want for breakfast? *That.* To stand in the middle of a family huddle. Or to walk up to the family, stick her head in the middle, and ask, "What's the plan?" No invitation required. No rejection expected.

Tim crossed the parking lot in a light, limping jog, his shirttail flapping over his jeans, his hair breezing past his jaw and shining in the sun.

A Rose by any other name . . .

He stopped just shy of the huddle and turned toward the church, squinting toward her. Her middle fluttered with the swirl of summer leaves.

"Hey." He stepped over to her. "How are you?"

"Tired . . . tired but good. You?" She smiled because he carried this aura of *it's all okay* about him. He was both confident and vulnerable. A combo she wasn't sure her heart could endure. "You look healthier than the last time I saw you."

"I feel better than the last time you saw me." He stopped at the bottom of the steps, hands at his waist. "So, yesterday was—"

"Busy-busy. Dix and I had seven weddings. Didn't get home until midnight. I fell asleep in my clothes." *Don't give him a chance to say it.* That today she would've been his wife.

"You look good." His intonation made her feel warm and admired.

"I don't have big bags under my eyes?"

"Not at all. Charlotte, I'm sorry about the hospital."

"What about the hospital? You mean Kim?"

"The kiss. And yeah, Kim."

The kiss? He was sorry about the sweet, tender, passionate kiss? The one that sashayed across her mind without permission whenever her day found a moment of silence?

"Listen, I'd better get inside. I can hear the music." Charlotte backed up the steps toward the sanctuary.

"You want to come to breakfast with us?" He motioned over his shoulder at the clan.

More than anything. "No, no, I can't. Better go hang out with Jesus and His friends for a bit."

"You sure?" He squinted at her, his brow in a deep furrow. "We can wait until your service is out."

"Really? No, I couldn't ask you to do that, Tim. That hungry huddle over there will turn into an angry mob if you ask them to wait."

He stepped forward. "Then I'll wait." He waited, breathing deep, his woodsy scent collecting in the air pocket between them.

"It's okay. I'm going to worship, then go home and crash."

"All right then. Guess I can't keep a girl from her Lord." He watched her for a long moment, then, "Oh, hey, how's it going with the dress? What happened with Hillary?"

"Pretty amazing." Charlotte smiled. The ends of her hair waved on the breeze at him. "She did marry Joel in the dress. When he was killed she sealed up the trunk. She also had a picture of her parents with the people they bought the house from and that led us to Mary Grace Talbot, who wore the dress in 1939."

"Wow. *Amazing* is an accurate word."

"Hillary helps at the shop all the time now. Just shows up—"

"Tim, you coming?" David called from the huddle. "Hey, Charlotte."

She raised her hand to wave. "Hey, David."

"Yeah, in a minute," Tim hollered over his shoulder.

"Listen, you go with your family. I'll see you, Tim."

"Can I call you?"

"No, Tim, please." Charlotte stared toward the western slope of the church grounds, hand on the sanctuary door.

"Charlotte, just so you know, friend Tim misses you."

"Yeah, but at the moment friend Tim and fiancé Tim still look an awful lot alike to me."

Chapter Twenty-One

Tim

One last time, Tim reviewed his plans for today's restoration pitch. The Rose Firm got the nod last minute and he wanted to bring his A-game.

Tim paused on a picture of a chain gang, black men in leg irons, conscripted by the convict-leasing program. He liked to add sculptures of remembrance to his restoration projects. Who worked and lived here before? How did they dress? What did they look like? How can we learn from history? Not repeat the mistakes?

He'd worked with his favorite bronze artist for a memorial plan to go with the restoration of a Saltonstall mine office. His memorial sculpture would commemorate the end of the convict-leasing program in 1928.

Rehearsing his conclusion, "Freedom, at all stages and by all means, must be celebrated," Tim surfed through his research material for the picture of the women who worked to end the program. He would hold it up and suggest an etching or bronze plaque with their image to be posted by the sculpture.

As he returned the picture to the stack, he reached for his water bottle, took a swig, and stared at the woman in the center. Emily Ludlow.

She stood out to him for some reason. Like he knew her. He certainly welcomed her passion and fire for justice.

The black-and-white image was tattered around the edges. It

had been borrowed from Cleo Favorite and the Ludlow estate by his assistant, Javier. He'd promised to return it as soon as he made the presentation.

"Booyah to you, Mrs. L., for fighting injustice. When it wasn't popular." He swigged his water again and leaned in for a closer look. He'd been a kid when she died but all through elementary school, his teachers taught civic lessons based on Mrs. Emily Ludlow and her husband, Daniel.

Something about her expression, her celebratory smile, her eyes. Tim snatched it closer and leaned toward the light.

Expressive eyes. Bow lips. Tall and commanding. Looked as if she could lasso the moon and ride it over the horizon. She looked familiar.

Tim glanced at the time. One o'clock. He needed to get his head out of this swirl, grab some lunch, and make sure the slides were good to go for his four o'clock meeting with the downtown restoration commission.

"Tim." Javier stuck his head through the door. "Someone to see you. Monte Fillmore?" He shrugged, making a face. "He said you'd know what it was about."

"He's here? Yeah, send him in." Tim crossed the room and greeted Monte with a firm handshake. "Please, have a seat." He offered one of the chairs around a small conference table. "Can I get you a cup of coffee? Bottled water?"

"Thank you, no, I'm fine. Don't reckon you expected to see me." Monte stood at the fifth-floor window and peered out over the city, a shoe box tucked under his arm. "Nice setup you got here. Good view." His strong tone reminded Tim of leaders and mentors he'd encountered in his life journey. "Used to have an office off 22nd North myself. Owned my own insurance agency for forty years."

"I remember your radio jingle. The tune kind of stuck in a guy's head."

The man laughed, a spark igniting his crinkled eyes. "Yeah, well, that was my silent partner's idea."

"Silent partner?"

He sat up with a huff. "My wife. She wrote that little ditty you heard. Listen, after you called, it got me to thinking." He shoved the Nine West shoe box over to Tim. "When we broke down Mom's house, we found this in the back of her bedroom closet. It's nothing much, just trinkets from Phoebe Malone's office. Guess Mom was saving it for Charlotte and I meant to take it to her, but in the busyness of her funeral, dealing with her will and accounts, keeping my own family and business afloat, I never got around to it. The contents didn't seem all that important. Mostly newspaper clippings and a few photos. I left the box on the kitchen counter for months until my wife went to bake Christmas cookies and moved it. Then we kept shoving it further and further out of sight. I thought I'd run into Charlotte one day and remember, but never did. Then you called."

Tim lifted the lid from the box. Yellow, crackling newspaper clippings floated free. He took them out one by one, scanning the headlines.

Ludlow Foundation Offers Its First Entrepreneur Grant
Emily Ludlow Celebrates Ninety
Professor Colby Ludlow Honored at UAB Banquet
Emily Ludlow, Dead at Ninety-One
Ludlow Estate to Establish Foundation for Business and Education

"Interesting mix. Wonder why Phoebe collected Ludlow articles? Was she related?"

"Not sure, but my wife's family came from the Canton line, Emily's family before she became a Ludlow. She doesn't know of any family with the Malone name. So we don't think Phoebe and Charlotte are part of the Ludlow-Canton tree."

Tim stacked the clippings, shoved aside pens and pencils, and found a picture of Phoebe and Charlotte. A chill ran through his chest.

Beautiful Phoebe with her long, thick, winged hair. Beautiful Charlotte, with a gapped-tooth smile, expressive eyes, and bow lips.

He looked up. The chill in his middle warming. Expanding. Tim flipped over the picture. *Our First Day in Birmingham.*

"Phoebe was rather eclectic. An artist. An engineer. Smart as a whip. I used to debate her politics once in a while, but it gave Mom high blood pressure, so we stopped. No flies on the woman, though."

"They don't dare land on her daughter either."

"Sorry I don't have more to give you. A name or a reason. Mom once said to me Charlotte's father was a nonfactor."

"Easy to say if you're not Charlotte." Tim studied the picture. Beneath their faces were a thousand conversations he longed to hear.

There was one more picture at the bottom of the box. A photo of a college-age Phoebe with a group of . . . friends? Fellow students?

Tim read the back. *Silver Lake Summer Project '81. FSU. Professor Ludlow's Geniuses.*

"Ludlow? Did you see this photo, Monte?"

Tim studied the image with Monte peering over his shoulder. In the center of the group was a handsome man with a cocky stance. The four-by-six picture made details hard to detect, but the man looked to be in his forties, corduroy blazer, long layered hair.

"When was this taken?" Monte said. "I see Phoebe, but I'm not familiar with the Ludlow in the picture."

"It was taken in '81." Tim sprang from his chair and grabbed the research folder.

"What'd you see, Tim?" Monte angled the picture toward the light of the window.

"I see a spitting image. Tell me what you see." Tim lined up the group picture of Emily with the group picture of the professor. "The professor here." He tapped the man's face. "And Emily Ludlow here."

"Well, I'll be. There's a bit of a family resemblance as well as the same name. You think Colby Ludlow was related to Emily?"

"Yep. And I think Phoebe Malone might have been in love with him. Just a wild guess." Tim collected his notes and research and closed his laptop, jamming it into the case, his blood racing. The familiar look of Emily's eyes in the picture. He'd seen that expression a hundred times. On Charlotte.

If he hurried, he could run up the mountain, check out the Ludlow estate for more clues, and be back in time for his meeting. "Monte, thank you. But I need to go. I appreciate you coming down." He grabbed his phone. His keys.

"Call if you find out anything," Monte said, following Tim out the door.

"I will. I will. You've been a big help." Tim knocked on David's door as he passed his office. "David, I'll see you at the meeting. Call my cell if you need me."

"Tim, where are you going? Did you go over the slides?"

"Yeah, no, but I will. See you at the meeting." Tim punched the elevator button, cutting a side glance to Monte, who was holding down a big grin. "So, what's so funny?"

"You," he said. "And pretty much all young men in love."

"Love? I'm just trying to help a friend." Tim stepped onto the elevator with Monte.

"Help a friend?" Monte punched the first-floor button. "That's what you kids are calling it these days? In my day, it was called love. Heart-thwapping love."

Emily

Mother set a beautiful Christmas table, with ivory china and hand-cut crystal and her own mother's silverware, buffed and polished to mirrored perfection.

The creamy linen threads of the tablecloth hosted the lamplight and the glow of the candles. On the crimson table runner, she'd placed crisp, fragrant fir boughs.

Father sat at the head of the table, Mother the foot. Phillip and Emily sat center, with Mr. and Mrs. Saltonstall directly across from them.

Howard Jr. dined on Mrs. Saltonstall's right. And his visiting lady friend dined on Emily's left.

Molly and Jefferson, with two additional servants, carried Mother's dinner of onion soup, roasted duck, mashed turnips, and gravy in and out of the kitchen. Along with Molly's heavenly bread and jam.

But of all the delectables, Mrs. Saltonstall raved over Mother's iced tea. "You must give me this tea recipe, Margaret. It's divine."

"It belonged to my grandmother." Mother blushed with the compliment. "Since we are family"—she gazed at Emily—"or soon to be, you shall have it before you leave tonight."

"I, for one, am glad the children moved up the wedding. Don't know where we got the notion long engagements were a good idea." Father spoke over his forkful of duck.

Under the table, Phillip squeezed Emily's knee, sending a fire-brand to her heart. She took an unladylike bite of her bread to hide her gasp. Since choosing not to wait until spring for their marriage,

Phillip had returned to his former ways, becoming more and more amorous.

Emily patted her mouth with her crimson and cream napkin. Greedy. He'd become greedy. She couldn't wipe the word from her heart. She'd been most grateful the other night for the complexities of her corset.

"Did Phillip tell you, Howard?" Mr. Saltonstall wiped his lips and chin with his napkin. "He cleared Emily of her charges."

"Our lawyer did quite the job." Phillip reached for his goblet. "The chief was most agreeable. He'll expunge the charges, but I think it's most clear, Emily darling, that you are to steer clear of the coloreds."

"Except I'm wearing Taffy's dress for our wedding." Emily adjusted her napkin on her lap as silence settled around the table. She peered from face to face. "I'm sorry, but I cannot be quiet about my choice. We can arrange for the dress to come here without infringing on any silly law or being accused of insurrection."

"I suppose the groom has no say." Phillip kept his eyes on his fork and knife slicing through his duck. "But I'd like you to wear Mrs. Caruthers's dress, darling. It seems to be the most pleasing to all. The most acceptable."

"You are correct, Phillip. Grooms have no say. I'm sure you do not want your bride fainting in the middle of the wedding because her gown cuts off all her air and blood flow."

"I have a say since I'm paying the bills." Father raised his voice. "Emily shall wear the dress of her choosing." *Oh, bless you, Father.* "Here's what I'd like to know. Who swore out a warrant against Emily? I've tried my contacts with the police and there seems to be a brick wall guarding the information."

"I found the same wall, sir. The only assurance I received through my barrister was that the charges would be expunged."

"Then we will be grateful for small blessings," Mrs. Saltonstall said. "Maggie, I declare, you and Molly outdid yourselves tonight. I never tasted a more succulent duck."

Jefferson appeared in the doorway in his waistcoat, his own dinner napkin dangling from his hand. "Begging your pardon, sir, but you have a visitor."

All eyes settled on the Irish butler.

"Might I ask who comes at dinnertime? Is it an emergency?" Father sounded annoyed.

"He says it's quite urgent, sir. He did not give his name. I told him you were dining with family, but he insisted."

"Excuse me, Cam and Henrietta." Father bowed to his guests, then to Mother. "My dear, begging your pardon."

"Hurry, dear. Molly's chocolate cake for dessert."

Emily watched Father go with a curious slither of *Who?* running across her mind. Rarely did Father's business come to the front door.

The chatter around the table moved to wedding details. There'd been much to do with the accelerated date. Mr. Saltonstall had secured the Phoenix Club for the reception. The gentlemen's club had a fine ballroom.

Mother made arrangements with the church and paid for extra seamstresses to sew the bridesmaids' gowns and the rest of Emily's trousseau.

"Oh, darling, I forgot to tell you." Phillip motioned to his father. "Dad and Mom have gifted us with the Highland home. No need to house hunt. We have a place all ready for us."

"That's very generous, Mr. and Mrs. Saltonstall." The Saltonstalls' home sat in the shadow of Red Mountain not but a few blocks from Father and Mother's. It was lovely. But not Emily's home. "But, Phillip, I thought we'd find our own home."

"Why? The Highland house is perfect." He took a bite of his duck. "And free."

"We are delighted for you to live there, Emily," Mrs. Saltonstall said. "The décor is practically new. We remodeled and never moved in."

Emily hid her emotions behind her glass of tea. But it was Mrs. Saltonstall's décor. Heavy and dark.

Father burst into the room, his face red, his eyes narrow beams of light. "Phillip, excuse me, but I require your presence."

"Is everything all right?" Phillip tossed down his napkin as he shoved away from the table.

Howard Jr. stood. "Do you need me as well, Father?"

Mr. Saltonstall joined the brigade. "May I assist?"

"No, no. Phillip is all I need."

Father's interruption popped the delight in the atmosphere, dimming the light and merriment. Emily visually checked in with Mother, who wore her usual mask of *all is well*. Especially in front of company.

The clock in the hall ticked off the time. The table conversation was thin and scattered—the lovely December weather, the Christmas program at church, Mr. Saltonstall's consideration of the newfangled invention of electric lights for the Christmas tree, then of Howard Jr.'s football prowess at Harvard. Mother inquired of his lady friend, Jennifer Barlow, and how she liked Birmingham compared to Boston.

On the half hour, when Father and Phillip had been gone a good twenty minutes, Molly appeared to clear the dishes. "Shall I cut the cake, ma'am?"

"No, we'll wait for Mr. Canton. But do bring the coffee, Molly."

Mr. Saltonstall shoved away from the table and started toward the door. "I wonder if I ought to see what's going on in there."

"Howard is dealing with this, Cam," Henrietta said. "Please don't pace."

Ten more minutes ticked off. Then Father entered the room with a serious, brooding countenance. "Emily, may I speak with you, please."

She gazed at him, hesitating, trying to ascertain what was going on. Then she, too, pushed away from the table.

"Certainly, Father." What could he possibly want with her? Her stomach knotted and cramped. Was she to be arrested again?

"In the library." Father stood aside to let Emily go first.

"Father, is everything all right?"

He halted her, lightly holding her arm. "You know your own mind, Emily. You always have. You're a smart girl, and your mother and I have taught you to be wise. To seek the good Lord for wisdom."

"Father, what is it? You're scaring me." Emily pressed her hand to her waist.

"Steady your heart. Listen. Don't respond until you've thought. Ask questions like I taught you."

"Yes, Father, I will." Emily entered the library, planning to remain at ease until she saw Daniel with his cap in hand. "What are you doing here?" He wore a thick, high-collared sweater and a Norfolk jacket. His eyes narrowed at her, shadowed with concern. But his smile warmed her through to her backbone.

"I came to speak to your father. I didn't realize you had guests. I'm sorry to intrude."

"But yet you did. What is the meaning of this?" She smoothed her hand over her silk gown embroidered with gold and trimmed in fur. The three of them, Father, Daniel, and Emily, stood in a loose circle. "You didn't answer my question." She flipped her gaze to Phillip, pacing and smoking along the back length of the library.

"I needed to speak to your father."

"So you said."

"He came to accuse me, that's what he came to do." Phillip hammered out his cigarette in Father's ashtray and joined the circle.

"Accuse you of what?" Emily glared at Phillip. He could be so dramatic and comical.

"He's got his cap set for you." Phillip waved his hand in Daniel's direction. "He's a liar. Howard, I believe I've had enough of this tomfoolery."

Phillip took two steps back before Father moved around to block him, his broad hand against Phillip's shoulders.

"Let's just sort this out. Daniel, why don't you tell Emily your story."

"*Story* is exactly what it is. A woman's novel. Full of foolishness." Phillip huffed and puffed like he was still smoking one of his cigarillos. "I think the innocent accused should be allowed to speak first."

"Phillip, you'll have plenty of chance for rebuttal once Emily hears the details." Father spread his hand as if to calm the air. "You both agreed to this method. Now, let's act like gentlemen. Emily, Daniel came tonight with news that concerned him. He asked to speak to me rather than you so he could obtain my counsel. Once I heard his dilemma, I asked Phillip to come and address him." Father scowled at the men. Though noticeably longer at Phillip. Emily eased down into a wingback chair. Her dinner churned in her belly. "I asked for them to tell their tales to you. You are of age. You can decide the truth for yourself."

"Then I am listening." She squared her shoulders and angled toward Daniel.

"When I came to see you in jail, Emily, the officers ignored me, refused to look at me when they talked to me. So I got suspicious. I know a good many of those chaps and their behavior struck an odd chord with me. I asked Dad to see if anything unusual happened the night of your arrest."

Phillip lit another cigarillo and blew smoke at Daniel. "This story is far more entertaining the second time around."

Daniel hesitated but went on. "It took Dad a few weeks, but here's what he's figured. Your fiancé was sick of you embarrassing him by going to the colored part of town, and there was some mess about who was making your wedding dress. He claimed you were ruining the family's reputation. Other society folk were claiming the Cantons were friends of the coloreds. Somehow it got suggested that the separate-but-equal law goes both ways. A little cash to grease a few palms down at the police station, and he had you charged and arrested."

"Do you think I would throw down good, hard-earned money to have my girl arrested? What kind of nimble-minded fool are you, Ludlow?"

"Not as big a nimble-minded fool as you."

Phillip exploded, threw his lit cigarillo to Mother's Persian carpet, and charged Daniel.

"Phillip." He ran into Father's tree-trunk chest. "Pick up your smoke, son."

"But you heard him, Howard."

"Pick up your smoke before you burn Maggie's good rug. I won't be able to help you if she finds a burn mark in it."

Huffing and red-faced, Phillip bent to retrieve the burning cigarette. Then he whirled around to Daniel. He pointed at Daniel with the lighted stick between his fingers. "Get out. If I ever see you near Emily again, I will have *you* arrested. And there'll be no mistake about whose name is on the warrant."

"He's in my home, Phillip." Father shot him a glance that used to make Emily run, trembling. "He leaves when I say. Now, Daniel, go on, explain the rest."

"Dad got his pal at the west precinct to look into your arrest. It took some doing . . . seems there was a big secret about it, but he managed to get a look at the record. Said the name on the warrant was Phillip Saltonstall. Then I talked to my chum, Russ, to see what he could dig up. He has a good nose for news. Russ looked up the lawyer on the case, asked a few well-placed questions as only he can." Daniel's lip curled in a cocky grin, sparking a zing through Emily's middle. "Sure enough, it was Saltonstall here. He had you arrested. Then he got to the police chief and bribed his name off of the record."

"He's lying, Emily." Phillip charged at Daniel, who remained planted, unflinching. "You think our police chief can be so easily bribed?"

"What on earth for?" Emily stood, grabbed Phillip's arm, and jerked him around to face her. "Did you do this? Don't lie to me."

"Have my own fiancée arrested? Do I look like an imbecile? How can you even ask?" Phillip's eyes were wild, his jaw taut and set. "Did you see my name, Ludlow? My signature? You've let your affection for Emily get in the way of good sense. You're upsetting her. Not for love but your own selfish gain. Foolishness."

Emily regarded Phillip, evaluated his tone and words. The man was strong, stubborn, and determined to get what he wanted, yes— but was Phillip a liar?

She knew Daniel was not.

"Emily." Daniel stepped forward, a pleading tone in his voice. "I don't mean to upset you. I'm sorry. But I couldn't live with myself if I didn't tell you."

"Sure you meant to upset her." Phillip laughed, mocking. "It's why you're here. To turn her against me. Are you denying that you love her?" He angled toward Daniel, puffed with his cocky composure.

Daniel bunched his cap in his hand. "No, I don't deny it." When he looked at Emily, his blue irises radiated a heat that made her lungs swell. "The only reason I'm here is because of love. But she's made her choice. You." He raised his gaze to Phillip. "I'm no threat to you, Saltonstall. But Emily deserves the truth."

"Your version of the truth is not mine." Phillip lit another cigarillo.

"Well, I'll be going. Mr. Canton, I came to talk to you. Didn't expect the privilege of accusing Saltonstall to his face." Daniel stepped backward to the door. "Just tell her, Saltonstall. About the arrest." He bunched his hat smaller and smaller in his hands. "And about the Italian Garden."

"The Italian Garden?" Phillip jerked forward, dropping ashes to Mother's carpet. "You!" His neck and cheeks flared red. "It was you. The ballplayer. You're the Daniel Emily went around with at the university?"

"One and the same. I saw you at the restaurant with Emmeline Graves. My friends have seen you with her twice since."

"Why, you lying—"

Not even Father could block Phillip's rage. He smashed his head into Daniel's chest, wrapped him up, and crashed over the chair, knocking over Mother's Tiffany lamp. The men hit the floor with a thunderous thud along with the shrill shatter of glass.

"Stop, both of you! Stop." Emily held her arms and fisted hands stiff at her sides, her heart careening, her eyes full of tears. "You are gentlemen."

Father grabbed her and pulled her back against the wall of books. "Let them go."

Daniel shoved Phillip off, scrambling to his feet, circling around the room. "I don't want to fight, Saltonstall."

"You started it with your words." Phillip ran at Daniel, aiming a blow at his eye, but Daniel ducked under Phillip's crossing jab and swerved out of his way, bouncing from side to side.

Phillip swung at Daniel again, tripping over the fallen lamp and landing on the floor face-first.

"Get up, Phillip," Father said with no mercy. "On your feet."

With a loud moan, Phillip shoved to his hands and knees, pulling himself upright. "Get Ludlow out of here."

Emily stood pressed against the bookcase, pulse throbbing, tears surging around her heart and behind her eyes.

"Daughter, you've heard both sides." Father righted Mother's broken lamp. "Ask your questions. Make your decision."

"I . . . I don't . . . know." Eyes on Father, she backed out of the room. Her whole body ached. Sharp pains shot through her chest. "I need to think, Father. You said to think."

"Emily." Daniel's jaw flexed, his eyes narrowed. "I wouldn't lie to you and you know it. Not for love. Or revenge. It's a cheap way to win a girl's heart."

"Daniel, you cannot accuse a man without proof. It's uncivil."

"I have proof." He nodded at Phillip. "Oh, I have proof."

"You have nothing. Don't listen to him, Emily."

"Silence, Phillip." She whipped around to him. "Daniel's never lied to me. But you . . . I'm not sure I can say the same."

"Emily! This is preposterous. How can you believe him?"

She didn't know what or who to believe. Whirling out of Father's library, Emily held her head high though her heart sank. Rounding the broad staircase, she scurried up the stairs. Below, Father's and Daniel's voices reverberated in the hallway. Then Mr. Saltonstall's and Phillip's.

Pausing on the second-floor landing, Emily peered down into the foyer. Daniel hesitated in the doorway, looking up at her. One second, two, then three. His steady gaze burned the truth into her soul. Her fiancé had her arrested.

"Good night, Emily," Daniel said. The closing thump of the front door vibrated in her chest, forming a wide canyon.

She spun toward the hall, starting for her room. If Daniel was right, then she'd be a fool to marry Phillip. But as much as she wanted to believe she was strong, like Mother insisted, and admit the truth, she was weak.

She'd given her word. Made a pledge. Not just to Phillip but to the Saltonstall family. The papers announced her engagement. Society waited. In ten days she'd become Mrs. Phillip Saltonstall.

Emily broke into a run. In her bedroom she sank to the floor. *Oh, Lord, what have I done?*

Chapter Twenty-Two

New Year's Eve

*S*teady now, Emily. Last photograph." The photographer
ducked under the black cover and snapped the picture. The
smell of sulfur burned Emily's nostrils.

Mother and Father had turned Birmingham upside down to
give her this day. Mr. and Mrs. Saltonstall ordered orchids from a
greenhouse in Florida and decorated the Phoenix Club with gran-
deur and opulence.

So why did Emily feel as if she were slowly sinking down a long
dark hole? She moved to the window and struggled to open it.

"Here, darling, what are you doing?" Her maid of honor,
Bernadette, raised the window. "You'll catch your death standing
in the cold air." She cupped her palm to Emily's forehead. "You look
pale."

"I'm so warm in this gown, Bernadette." After the confrontation
with Daniel, Emily surrendered all fight. She'd marry Phillip in the
gown Mother wanted. "I'm not sure I can make it down the aisle."
Emily stuck her head into the late-afternoon air. It was Sunday. A
day for love.

Loving the Lord. Loving one another. Loving Phillip. Tonight
she'd be Mrs. Phillip Saltonstall. Emily gave up her fight, and Phillip
turned into a crooning, wooing dream after the altercation with
Daniel. Kind, considerate, yielding. Tender.

He maintained his innocence. He did not have her arrested. Not now. Not ever. Emily drew a deep, cleansing breath. *I believe you, Phillip.* As for Emmeline? A thing of the past. Over. Done.

I believe you, Phillip. I do. I must.

The clank of chains drew her attention down the avenue. A line of colored men crossed the road, their stride burdened by the short length of their bonds.

Hopeless.

Emily stiffened at the sensation whirling in her chest and brought her head back inside. "Where's Father?" She put on a wide smile for Bernadette. "He should be here. He'll be giving his daughter away in a quarter of an hour."

Bernadette grabbed Emily's shoulders and kissed her cheek. "You're the most beautiful bride, Emily. You rest. I'll find your father."

Emily sat on the settee in the church parlor of the First United Methodist Church, shivering but perspiring under her thick satin gown. She tugged at the high, tight collar. Oh, to be free of this monstrosity. Taffy's dress hung on the coatrack in the corner, waiting for Emily after the wedding.

Just gazing at it made Emily's heart yearn, feel free, feel light, feel loved.

If she could do it all again, she'd forego this pomp and circumstance and marry at home with only friends and family. Molly, not Bernadette, would be her maid of honor. But Emily couldn't very well have the maid of the house stand up with her for the biggest society wedding of the season.

The door opened and Father stepped in, but not with a smile. Handsome and commanding in his black tuxedo and white carnation boutonniere, his high brow was furrowed and concern shadowed his eyes. "The church is brimming. The governor and his wife just arrived."

"Oh, Father, mercy." Emily's pulse fluttered. "So many people making time for us on New Year's Eve."

"It's a grand excuse for a party." Father kissed Emily's forehead and hugged her, then stood back, holding her at arm's length. "You are the image of your mother when I married her. Beautiful and sweet."

"Then why aren't you smiling, Father?" Emily pinched his chin. "You're not losing your girl but gaining another son."

"Yes, I know." Father walked to the window, his hands behind his back, and leaned out. "It's a clear, cold night," he called, his voice slightly raised. "A holy night."

Emily laughed low. "Father, who are you talking to, the street sweepers?"

He turned from the window. "Do you remember Ward Willoughby? Perhaps not. You were but a baby girl when I met him. I'd just started my exchange business and was in need of capital. He came along and offered to partner with me."

"I thought Uncle Lars became your investor." Uncle Lars wasn't really an uncle, just a wise man who believed in Father and invested in his future.

"He did, but not until I cut away from Willoughby." Father paced the length of the room, his hands clasped behind his back. He stopped in front of Taffy's dress draped over a dressmaker's form. "This is the one from Mrs. Hayes? Quite becoming."

"I'd rather be standing in it now than this gown. I declare, the weight is giving me a headache."

"Willoughby was quite the man about Birmingham in those days." Father went on with his words and walking. "Our city was young and eager to grow. He came down from Philadelphia, like your mother and I; a grad of Haverford, like me. He liked what I was doing, starting a bank. He wanted to join in, invest his money. He offered me a solid sum as an investor."

Something about Father's manner started Emily's heart churning. "Go on."

"He was the kind of man folks wanted to be around. Your mother and I would lie in bed at night marveling over our fortune of having made the acquaintance of Ward Willoughby."

"What happened?"

"The man came with conditions. If I wanted his money and support, I had to sign over Canton Exchange for the first three years. Or until Willoughby earned back his investments. But when it came right down to it, I just couldn't bring myself to sign the papers. I knew your mother and our small staff at the exchange would be disappointed. The city was growing so quickly. If I didn't move fast, I might lose a great opportunity. I went into town the next day, unhappy with my indecision, but I knew I had to turn Ward away. I couldn't give Canton over to his control. It was another five years before Lars came along. I didn't know if I could make my inheritance last long enough to keep the business going and a roof over our heads. But Lars rode up one afternoon, strode into my office with an expression that said, 'Well, I'm finally here.'"

"What happened with Ward, Father?"

"He'd planned to invest in the bank with worthless bonds. I'd have lost it all if I'd signed with him, Emily."

"Father, I'm about to be married and you're speaking to me of worthless men with worthless bonds." Emily crossed the room to stand with him by the window.

"Sometimes you have to trust your gut."

"What if that means letting a lot of important people down?"

"Occasionally, we don't care what others think. *You* have to do what's right for you." Father rocked back and forth on his heels, looking straight ahead.

"How can one tell the difference between cold feet and

trusting your gut, Father? How did you know your instincts about Willoughby were correct?"

"That's called faith. Trusting God." His voice waffled. "We must be ready to hear from Him and respond, at any moment, no matter what the consequence."

"Father, please." Emily pressed on his arm, turning him to her. "What are you really trying to tell me?"

"Emily darling, are you ready?" Mother swept into the room, pretty and young in her crimson and fur gown. She had a Christmas dress made every season and was delighted to wear this year's for Emily's wedding. "Howard, Bernadette has been looking for you. Oh, Em, you look absolutely divine." Mother's eyes misted. "Your gown is perfect."

"I'm not wearing this dress, Mother. Unhook me, please." Emily turned her back to Mother, reaching to remove her cathedral-length veil.

"Not this again, Emily. You're a grown woman. Stop acting like a child. I declare, you were more behaved when you were three." Mother fussed, grasping Emily's hands, then smoothing the veil pins securely in place. "Besides, it's too late to change."

Emily smiled at Father. "It's never too late to change."

Tim

The July sun seemed closer up on the ridge than down in the city. Tim's loafer heels clapped against the stone pathway as he walked toward the house through the cool rush of air up from Jones Valley.

It'd been a few years since he'd come up here, but the sight of the stone-and-beam structure got him every time. It was an extension of Red Mountain, coming out of the mountain rock and woodlands.

Skilled hands tamed the wild and crafted nature's elements into an architectural masterpiece.

He twisted the knob, the heavy walnut door opened, and Tim stepped inside the glass-and-hardwood splendor where natural light lit the entryway. The back wall was floor-to-ceiling windows overlooking the valley.

Tim gazed out over the treetops, smiling when his belly dropped, feeling as if he were floating high above the city. It must have been incredible to live here.

The place was an architectural marvel. He'd studied the design in college.

"Hello, may I help you?" Cleo Favorite greeted him. She was a classic southern woman with perfect blond hair and pearls about her neck. "Tim Rose, what brings you up here? Are you bringing my photo back?"

"Not yet. I'm heading to a meeting with it in a few hours." He knew Cleo from the city's restoration council. "I was wondering if I could ask you a few questions about Colby Ludlow."

"Don't see why not." She regarded him, waiting for more. "I don't get handsome men up here often. You still engaged?" She chuckled softly and motioned for him to follow her.

"No, ma'am." Tim followed her along a back hall that curved like a hideaway under the stairs, alongside the kitchen, then burst into a bright, windowed library. His stomach dropped again at the sensation of standing on treetops.

"I'm sorry to hear that. I saw Charlotte Malone up here not too long ago." Cleo leaned against her desk, crossing her ankles, folding her arms. "Lovely girl."

"I want to know about Colby Ludlow." Tim walked the perimeter of the library. The adjacent walls on his left were shelves, each one loaded with leather and gilded books.

On his right, the wall was a gallery of photos. In the center was a picture of Emily in her wedding gown. He stopped and stared.

Charlotte. How had he missed it? The resemblance . . .

"She's lovely, isn't she?" Cleo said. "That's Emily at the time of her wedding in 1912. She was twenty-two."

"She's beautiful." Clear, serene eyes held steady for the photographer. Her dark hair was piled in a high pompadour and crowned with a lacy veil.

"The story goes she didn't want to wear this wedding dress. She thought it was too bulky and heavy."

"But she wore it anyway." This was not the dress Charlotte found in the trunk. Not with the high collar and tight sleeves. Emily's hands were folded on her lap and a large diamond solitaire adorned her left ring finger. On her right hand she wore an oval stone set in diamonds. He leaned closer, wishing the image were in color.

"You were asking about Colby?" Cleo walked down the line of pictures and portraits, pointing to one near the end. "This is Colby Ludlow, Daniel and Emily's grandson. Emily's son, Daniel Canton Ludlow, was his father. He died at Normandy when Colby was a kid."

"Do you know about this picture?" Tim passed Cleo the shot of Phoebe Malone with Professor Ludlow's Geniuses.

"Professor Ludlow. Yes, indeed . . . Colby was tenured at University of Alabama, Birmingham." Cleo flipped the picture over. "Back in the eighties he took a sabbatical, but I didn't realize he'd worked at Florida State."

"Is that him? In the middle?"

"It is. Where did you get this?" Cleo crossed the picture gallery to a framed piece near the end. "This is Colby on his fiftieth birthday." She held up the four-by-six Tim found in the shoe box. "It's him. About the same age, I'd say. He has those Canton eyes." She handed Tim the picture. "Where'd you get this again?"

"From a box. It belonged to Phoebe Malone. Do you know that name?"

"Should I?"

"Her daughter is Charlotte Malone."

"The bridal boutique owner? Your ex-fiancée?"

"One and the same." Tim pointed to Phoebe in the picture. "That's her mother."

"Okay." She laughed. "How does Phoebe Malone being Charlotte's mother connect her to Colby Ludlow?"

"I wonder if . . ." Tim hesitated. Cleo didn't seem up for crazy today. "Did you know Charlotte found a wedding dress in the trunk she bought from your auction?"

"Interesting . . ." Cleo walked around behind her desk. "Is this your way of asking me where the trunk came from, Tim? We get items from all over the south for the auction. But we do keep an inventory list." Cleo worked the mouse, leaning down to view the monitor. She typed something and scanned the screen. She frowned and took a seat. "I'm not finding a trunk of any kind sold at the spring auction. Are you sure?"

"Charlotte bought it here. Was mad about it because she didn't want or need an ugly old trunk. The lock was welded shut and we had to saw it open."

Cleo straightened, her expression pinched. "You say she found a wedding dress inside?"

"Yeah, a pretty nice one. The auctioneer told her it was made in 1912." Tim perched on the upholstered chair across from Cleo. "She's since learned about two other women who wore the dress."

"Oh my . . . it can't be . . ." Up and in motion, Cleo tugged a set of keys from her slacks pocket, opened a narrow closet, disappeared inside, and came out with a picture frame in hand. "Is this the dress?"

Beneath the glass was an old newspaper print, grainy and faded, of Emily on the back of a horse, clinging to a dark-haired man. She laughed with her head back, mouth wide, joy spilling out of her. Tim nearly felt her emotion vibrating against his ribs.

She was wearing *the* dress. The vibration around his heart faded when a gut check warned him to keep quiet. He'd said enough. Maybe too much?

"Tim, tell me. Is this the dress?" Cleo tapped the picture. "It's satin and silk with pearls around the waist. The skirt is layered with swags. There's a V cut at the hem in front."

"I'm an architect, not a seamstress." Tim stood, backing up. "Thanks for your help, Cleo. I need to get going."

"Not so fast, buddy. Why are you asking about the Ludlows all of a sudden? Wondering about a trunk sold at the auction? You're hiding something." Cleo circled him, blocking the door. "Emily Canton was supposed to marry Phillip Saltonstall, of Saltonstall Industries."

"I know the Saltonstalls," Tim said.

"But on their wedding day, she changed her mind, and instead of marrying Phillip, she ran out of the church, hopped on a horse with Daniel Ludlow, and married him later that day. Unfortunately, all we have is this picture." She offered up the grainy newspaper image. "When she was alive, Emily claimed she didn't know what happened to this dress. Oddly enough, we don't have the dress she's wearing in that wedding picture either. But what estate wants a portrait of the matron's wedding wearing the wrong gown?" Cleo stared at Tim. "Know what I mean?"

"Yeah, that's too bad. And the heirs? To the Ludlow estate?" Tim inched toward the door.

"All gone. Colby was the last." Cleo cat-walked after him. "The foundation is the heir."

"He never married?"

"He did. Married a Woodward girl but they didn't have children. In the late nineties they divorced and she moved to Florence to be near her sister's family. Colby hired me to manage the estate after his grandmother died. Our mothers were friends," Cleo said. "When Colby died, a board of trustees took over but kept me on to oversee the day-to-day operations and administer the foundation."

"What if an heir showed up?" Tim landed his hand on the doorknob.

"Like fell out of the sky? Or emerged from the woodwork?" Cleo cradled the picture against her chest and snorted. "There is no heir, Tim. I don't know what you're up to with this inquiry, but we searched for an heir after Colby died. Even if one did pop up, the estate is in the hands of the trustees. Besides, Tim, the Ludlow history isn't of biblical proportions. There are people alive in this city who knew Daniel and Emily *and* Colby. Trust me, if there was an heir, we'd know about it. The Ludlow line has ended, sadly." Cleo marched to the closet, her footsteps confirming her assertion—*there is no heir*—and returned the framed newspaper image to the dark shelves.

"What happened to Colby?" Tim said. Maybe he was imagining it, but every time he looked at the picture with Phoebe and Professor Ludlow, he saw Charlotte. "He retired from UAB and what?"

"Played a lot of golf. He lived the life he wanted."

"Was he a good man?"

"As good as any man can be. He was generous, kind, decent," Cleo said. "You know, Tim, if Charlotte has the gown Emily was wearing on the back of the horse, it belongs to the Ludlow Foundation. It also belongs to the city and the civil rights museum. Emily wore the first wedding dress in the south made by a black designer. Got herself arrested for it too. We'll need it returned."

"Arrested over needle and thread and a few yards of fabric?"

"Hard for us to imagine, but yes, back then they took the separate but equal law seriously. So if you know where the gown is . . . you best do right by me and bring it back."

"Thanks again for your help, Cleo." Tim headed for the door, regretting his decision to come here. "I need to get to my meeting. I'll let myself out."

The last person he needed to do right by was Cleo Favorite. The first person Tim Rose needed to do right by was Charlotte Malone. And figure a way to prove Colby Ludlow was her father.

Chapter Twenty-Three

Charlotte

Charlotte rounded the corner from her office into the show-room, the Lifestyle section of the *News* in her hand. "Dix, we're at the tipping point. The article on Tawny's wedding is fantastic."

But instead of finding Dixie in the middle of the shop, she found the man in purple.

"Hello." Charlotte stopped. "You again."

"The dress is yours, you know," he said without so much as batting an eye.

Charlotte folded the paper and walked to the sales counter. "Why don't you just tell me who you are and your connection to the dress?"

"Have you tried it on?"

"No, and frankly I don't intend to try it on. I'm not getting married. But I'll find the right bride for it. Not that it's any of your business." The sales counter created the perfect barrier.

"But you are my business, you see." His gaze, the same intense polished blue, seemed to root around in her heart, turning over her foundation stones.

The ones that said *Charlotte Is All-Sufficient. Charlotte Doesn't Need Anyone. Charlotte Is Immune from a Broken Heart.*

She couldn't look at him. Not long anyway. She felt restless, like she was standing in the midst of holiness, and if she stood for one second longer, she'd implode.

Or worse, break down in tears.

Yet, in the midst of the swirl of heat and chills expanding in her chest, she was profoundly at peace.

"How can I be your business? You don't know me. I think you should leave."

"All right, I'll go." He backed toward the door. "Just remember, the dress is yours."

"I don't think anyone is going to sue me for it."

"The dress is yours."

The shop phone rang, a soft, muted melody. When Charlotte answered, a sharp voice hit her ear.

"This is Cleo Favorite from the Ludlow Foundation."

"Cleo, how are you?" Charlotte glanced back at the purple man. But the spot where he stood was empty. Now where did he go? How did he enter and exit without a sound?

"I want to see the dress."

"What dress?" Charlotte scanned the room and carried the portable phone with her as she moved up the stairs. He was gone.

"The dress you found in the trunk you purchased at our auction in April."

"How did you know I found—"

"Is it at your shop?"

"No, my loft. Cleo, how did you know I found a dress?"

"Does seven o'clock work for you?"

"Um . . . yeah, I think." Talk about being bulldozed. "No, wait, Cleo. Eight is better. What is this about? Who told you I found a dress in the trunk?"

"I'll tell you when I see you. What's your address? I'll Google the directions."

When Charlotte hung up, her emotions were taut and torqued. What was going on? First, the weird little purple man appears. *"The dress is yours.*" On the heels of him vanishing, literally, Cleo calls demanding to see the dress.

Charlotte came around the sales counter. "Sir? Little man?" She walked the shop. He wasn't in the fitting salon or the storeroom. Not in the kitchen or her office. "Sir? Man in purple . . ." He wasn't upstairs. He wasn't in the bathroom.

Out the front door, Charlotte stared down the sidewalk and across the street. Not a sign of him anywhere. The wind whistled down the lane and gooseflesh raised on her arms. Crossing the showroom, she stood where he'd stood and breathed the air he'd breathed. A soft, subtle but distinct spice hung in the air just above her nose.

"Char, I'm back." Dixie emerged from the kitchen, her thick heels clomping, her Dolce & Gabbana swinging from her elbow. She unwrapped a Tootsie Pop and shoved it in her mouth.

"That weird man was here. The one with the purple shirt and the Nikes." Charlotte raised a foot, motioning with her fingers.

"This is getting creepy. What'd he want?" Dixie disappeared into the storeroom and emerged wearing her Malone & Co. suit jacket. "Did you see the paper? The reporter did a great job on the story. The picture of Tawny is so good. You're a genius at dressing brides, Char." Dixie stopped behind the sales counter and picked up the newspaper Charlotte left there.

"He said the dress is mine."

"Who? The reporter?" Dixie popped open the paper, the lollipop jammed into the side of her mouth, her cheek puffed into a perfect round ball.

"No, Dix, stay with me." Charlotte popped her hands together. "The man, the weird one. Purple dude. He said the dress in the trunk was mine."

Dix made a face. "Of course it's yours. When was that a question?"

"I don't know, but he didn't say it like, 'Hey, the dress you found in the trunk is yours.' Of course it is. I bought the trunk. But he said it like, *it's yours*." Charlotte lowered and dragged out her voice. "Then about a minute after he said that, Cleo Favorite from the Ludlow Foundation called asking about the trunk and the dress." She held up the portable phone. "She wants to come over at eight o'clock tonight."

"How'd she find out there was a dress?"

"That, my friend, is a good question." Charlotte reached under the sales counter to place the phone on the receiver. "But the weird little man insisted on one thing. The dress is mine."

The last word of her sentence sent a hot tingle over her heart.

At five 'til eight, Charlotte let herself into her loft, fumbling to juggle her purse, iPad, a bag of groceries, and the key. The bag of groceries hit the floor, spilling bread, apples, oranges, and a bag of baked Goldfish over the tile.

"Need some help?" Tim slid past her, stooping to gather the fruit, tucking it into his arms, a folder jutted between his fingers. His chestnut-blond hair hung long and loose about his face. A light beard dusted his chiseled cheeks.

"What are you doing here?" What was with today—July 19— Charlotte woke up an ordinary girl in an ordinary day. Just the way she liked it. But ever since Purple Man appeared, she felt a shift in her spirit. Like the morning she went up to the mountain to pray.

"I was wondering if you'd care to grab a bite of dinner?" Tim dropped the apples and oranges one by one into Charlotte's fruit bowl on the counter. When he turned to her, he raked his hair away from his face.

"I can't." Charlotte averted her gaze. She loved Tim's hair and the fullness of his lips. If she looked at him too long, her heart would start to pound, and she'd get all breathless and girlie. "Someone's stopping by." Charlotte opened her pantry and set the torn bag on the shelf. Didn't even bother to take the items out. She shoved the door closed. "Where's your girlfriend?"

"Don't have a girlfriend." He hopped up on the counter, setting the folder beside him. It was his thing, sitting on her counter. He had a way of just making himself at home.

"Ah. Well, these things happen." When Charlotte looked at him, he flashed his pearly whites.

"How about dinner after your company?" He shrugged, holding up his hands. "Before your company?"

"Can't. Don't know how long *he'll* be here."

Tim's confidence faded a bit. "Do you have a date?" He slid off the counter.

"No, but it was worth faking it to see your face." Charlotte crossed the kitchen, heading for her room. "It doesn't feel good, does it?"

"I never went out on you, Charlotte." Tim reached for her as she walked by. "Hey, where are you going?"

"My room. To change. Do you mind?" Charlotte headed down the hall. When she closed the door, she fell against it, expelling the air from her lungs.

A smile pinged her lips. He *was* jealous, wasn't he? When he thought she had a date. So Mr. Cool and Confident wrestled with the green-eyed monster.

Charlotte changed into jeans and a pullover, then wriggled her toes into her favorite worn flip-flops.

As she went to her bathroom, a wave of gold light caught her attention. The dress. Still displayed in the corner. The silk skirt shimmered with light and the gold threads beamed. The waistband of pearls flowed around the gown like an incandescent river.

Charlotte sat on the edge of the bed. "Hey, magic dress. Cleo's coming to see you. What does she know that I don't? And who's

your friend, the man in purple?" Charlotte leaned to listen. "*Hmm* . . .
well, maybe you don't know either. After all, Hillary barricaded you
in the trunk for forty years. And oh, Tim's here. I *know*. What's that
about? You remember him, don't you? He helped redeem you from
the trunk." She slicked her fingers along the creamy folds of the skirt.
"Can you keep a secret?" Charlotte laughed low. "Of course you
can, look who, rather *what*, I'm talking to. I'm in love with Tim.
I shouldn't be, but I am." She flopped back on the bed. "With just
about every part of my being."

For a long moment, Charlotte stared at the ceiling. Then at the
dress. Why couldn't she be *over* Tim? And why did inanimate objects
have stories they can't tell?

She pulled her hair back, then flipped off her bedroom light and
went back to the kitchen and to Tim. It was after eight and Cleo
would be here any moment.

"So, what else is going on, bubba?" Charlotte clicked on the dining area lamp, then went for her iPad. *Friend, treat Tim as a friend.*
As a bubba. "How's the firm? You and David doing well?"

"The firm's fine." Tim slid down from the counter. "David is
fine. So, who's coming over here?"

"If you're here when she comes, I'll introduce you." Charlotte
flipped Tim a faux smile and set her iPad on the table. "Or maybe
you already know her."

"Cleo Favorite is coming here, isn't she?" Tim propped his hands
on his belt with an exhale.

"How did you know? Tim, what's going on?"

"She wants to see the dress. Man, she's a crafty one."

"Tim?" Charlotte regarded him, bells clanging, whistles blowing. "Did you tell her about the dress?"

"Sort of. I went up there today. Boy, she works fast." He smoothed
back his hair.

Charlotte walked around to the pencil jar by the phone and dug around until her fingers found a rubber hair tie.

"What were you doing up there?" She passed him the tie.

"Investigating." He twisted back his hair.

Charlotte sighed. With his hair away from his face, his eyes were blue quicksand. "Investigating what? Are they bidding for jobs? When I was there in April, the estate looked immaculate."

"I found a picture of Emily Ludlow while I was doing research for a project downtown." Tim angled back for the folder he'd carried in and removed a picture, offering it to Charlotte.

She glanced. The woman stood in the midst of other '20s women in big hats and baggy dresses. "What were they thinking with that drop-waist style? But after nearly a century of corsets, I suppose loose and baggy was the way to go."

"Emily's in the middle." Tim tapped the picture.

"I know what she looks like, Tim." Charlotte frowned. "Why are you showing me this?"

"Did you ever meet her?"

"Emily Ludlow? She was an old lady when I was born." Charlotte tugged open the fridge for a soda. She handed one to Tim, then took one for herself. "Where would I meet her? *Why* would I meet her?"

The doorbell rang. Charlotte returned her coke to the fridge. "There's Cleo."

"I'm staying." Tim locked his position in the dining area. "Okay?"

"Suit yourself." Charlotte cut him a glance, then opened the door. "Hey, Cleo, come on in."

"Sorry I'm late. My husband insisted on a bite to eat before I came here. I'm full as a tick." Dressed in a suit and heels, she looked composed and perfect, nothing like a full tick. A black attaché swung from her shoulder. "Hello, Tim. I didn't expect to see you here."

"Didn't expect to see you either."

"Must be a lucky day for both of you." Charlotte stood between them. "The dress is in the bedroom, Cleo. I'll go get it."

Just inside the bedroom door, Charlotte paused, listening. What was going on between them? But Tim and Cleo exchanged no words. Gently, she moved the gown and the dress form around her bed and out the door toward the living room.

Cleo gasped the moment Charlotte came into view. "That's the dress. Tim, you said you didn't know. My stars, it's so obvious." Cleo hovered around the gown as Charlotte set it by the sofa. "It's like time has never passed. It's . . . it's perfect."

"What are you talking about?" Charlotte looked at Tim. He shook his head slightly, eyes narrowed, as if trying to tell Charlotte something. "Do you know this dress, Cleo?"

"I most certainly do. It belonged to Emily Ludlow." She unsnapped her attaché and removed a picture frame. Beneath the glass was a yellow, faded, grainy newsprint photograph of Emily Ludlow, head back, laughing, her arm linked with a dark-suited elbow.

And she wore the gown.

"Where did you get this?"

"It's part of the Ludlow Foundation's history, Charlotte. This dress has been lost for decades. I asked her once where it was, but she was nearly ninety and she wasn't quite sure what I was talking about. Or so she pretended. Knowing her, she probably was faking." Cleo knelt, turning over the hem of the dress, running her finger along the seams. "My goodness, here it is."

Charlotte bent to confirm the seamstress's initials. "Do you know what TH stands for? Dixie and I couldn't figure it out."

"Taffy Hayes. She was a black seamstress in Birmingham. Born into slavery but freed when she was a baby. Emily wanted her wedding gown made by Taffy, but mercy, her parents and her groom resisted. Her mother had hired a well-known white seamstress, Mrs. Caroline Caruthers. She made the dress we have in the wedding portrait at the estate, but then about five years ago, I found this picture among some old things up in the attic. That's Daniel's arm she's holding on to. The caption says 'Emily Canton Leaves Church after Wedding.'"

"I've heard of Taffy Hayes," Charlotte said, studying the newsprint. Emily Canton wore the gown. She was the bride the purple man referenced. "She was well-known for her wedding dresses, but only in the black community."

"Emily was the first white woman to wear a wedding gown sewn by a black designer. There were black washerwomen and seamstresses, but Taffy was a *designer*. She made this dress especially for Emily. It was scandalous in 1912." Cleo walked around the gown, fascination rising in her eyes. "We've been looking for this gown for a long time."

"Then why'd you sell the trunk?" Charlotte kept her back to Tim and his shaking head, though his soap and cologne fragrance made his presence known.

"I didn't sell it, Charlotte. The trunk is not even listed in our inventory." Cleo tucked the picture back into her attaché. "Can you help me carry the dress down to my car, Tim? Charlotte, I'll compensate you for the purchase price."

"Whoa, whoa. Carry the dress down to your car?" Charlotte fanned out her arms and stood between the gown and Cleo. "This gown isn't going anywhere."

Now the purple man's visit made sense. *The dress belongs to you.*

"I'm afraid it is. That trunk, wherever it came from, was not to be sold at the auction."

Tim stood beside Charlotte. "Cleo, you didn't even have the

trunk listed in the auction inventory. If I hadn't come up there today, you'd have never known."

"But you did come up and now I know."

"Cleo, I bought the trunk, *and* its contents, fair and square. It didn't belong to you before and it doesn't belong to you now."

"You're right, the trunk never belonged to the estate. But this dress belongs to the Emily Ludlow Foundation and the Civil Rights Institute."

"It belongs to me." A royal purple wash splashed Charlotte's heart.

"City ordinance dictates that historical items found on-site belong to the estate. If they are not found on-site but are proven to belong to an historical estate, site, or registry, the item's ownership reverts to the estate or site." Cleo fussed with her attaché, producing a collection of papers. "And if none of those strike your fancy, Charlotte, the dress belongs to Birmingham's Civil Rights Institute for Emily's groundbreaking move to wear a wedding gown designed and sewn by an African American woman."

"Come on, Cleo. You're leaving something out," Tim said. "The ordinance dictates that historical items revert to the site *or* to an heir."

"There is no Ludlow heir, Tim." Cleo crossed her arms and tapped her foot. "What is your point?"

"Your researchers should've done a better job." Tim nodded, aiming his rakish smile on Charlotte. "There is a living Ludlow heir. And I'm looking right at her."

Tim

"What are you talking about?" Charlotte peered at him like he'd lost his mind. "I'm not related to anyone. Remember me? The one with one branch on her family tree? I'm especially not kin to the

Ludlows." She flipped her hands in the air without aim, her body swelling with big breaths. "I think you knocked the last bit of sense out of yourself when you crashed your bike."

"Crashing my bike is what gave me a moment to think about all of this." He went back to his folder and passed over the picture of Charlotte and her mom. "I called Monte Fillmore to see if he had anything of yours or your mom's among Gert's things."

"Why would you do that, Tim?" Charlotte stared at the picture. "I haven't seen this in twenty years. Where'd you get it?"

"Monte brought me a box of your mom's things. From her office. He meant to give it to you, but forgot and . . . anyway, Charlotte, this picture was in it. It was also filled with Ludlow newspaper clippings. Which I found odd until I saw this."

Tim passed over the FSU picture. Circumstantial evidence for sure, but it was all he had to make his case. To keep Cleo from walking out of here with the dress. He'd wanted to get to Charlotte before she did.

He'd brought the folder over, thinking he'd invite Charlotte to dinner, warm the waters of their relationship, then tell her Colby Ludlow was her father.

"That's Mama." Charlotte tapped the picture.

"Tim, come on, I can't stand by and let you fabricate a story to this poor girl." Cleo huffed and strutted in a circle. "You have no proof—"

"Stop." Charlotte pressed her palms against the air. Against Cleo's words. "Tim, what are you talking about?"

"Charlotte, I think Colby Ludlow is your father."

"What? How? He's . . . he's . . . old." Charlotte tapped the picture.

"He was forty-five in '81." Cleo blurted. The resident Ludlow encyclopedia.

"You're saying my mother had an affair with her professor?" She shook her head, handing Tim the picture. "She wasn't that kind of person, Tim."

"I'm not trying to impugn her character, Char, but Colby Ludlow taught at FSU one year when he took a sabbatical from UAB. And the picture is yours. Keep it."

Cleo folded her arms, "I told you so" on her lips. "I knew Colby and his wife, Noelia. She was a fine, classic woman of Birmingham society. Colby was his own man, but an adulterer? I hardly think so."

Tim sighed and angled his shoulder away from Cleo. She was wearing him thin. "Once I started piecing things together, I made a few calls of my own. Including one to Noelia Ludlow." Tim passed a slip of paper to Charlotte. On it he'd written Noelia's name, address, and number.

"You called her? Tim, what? Why? Why are you doing this?"

"When I asked her about Colby's year at FSU, she sighed. Know what she said?"

"What? What did she say, Tim?"

"She said, 'You want to know about Phoebe Malone?'"

Charlotte swatted at him. "You're lying. There's no way some seventy-year-old woman knows about my mother from 1981." She tore up the paper and tossed the pieces at Tim. "Just stop. What is wrong with you? What right do you have investigating in my life without my knowledge? Huh?" She slammed around him, clipping his shoulder with hers. But he remained steadfast and planted.

He exhaled and took it. Letting her steam.

"I'll just be going with the dress." Cleo dared reach for the back button. Charlotte's hand clamped down on her arm.

"Stand back. Get your hands off my dress. It's mine. And if you don't believe me, hunt down the little man in the purple shirt who sold it to me. He'll tell you."

"What little man in a purple shirt?"

"The one who sold me the trunk. At *your* auction."

"What do you care about this dress?" Cleo cackled. "You're not getting married. Even if you were—and boy, Tim, it looks like you escaped this briar patch—you own a bridal shop, Charlotte. Designers were probably begging you to wear one of their gowns. This old one means nothing to you."

Tim stepped forward and hooked his hand under Cleo's elbow. She needed to go. Upsetting Charlotte had never been his intention and he could see she was speeding for the edge.

"You'd better go, Cleo." He picked up her attaché as he swept her across the room to the door. "If you want the dress, you'll have to get a court order."

"You took the words right out of my mouth." She shook free of his grip. "You have no proof Colby Ludlow is Charlotte's father. None. A picture and the supposed testimony of his ex-wife? I've got more than that on my side."

The door slammed. Tim moved back into the living room. Charlotte sank down to the edge of the sofa, staring at the dress.

"All I wanted was to go to the mountain to think and pray. Look what happened."

"I'm sorry. I thought . . . I don't know." Tim brushed his hand over his hair. "When I saw all those Ludlow clippings in the box, it just struck me as odd."

"You should've talked to me first, Tim."

"Yeah, I get that now. I wanted to do something nice for you, Char." He perched on the sofa next to her. She smelled like summer. When she turned to him, there was a hint of forgiveness in her eyes.

"I was six or so when I first realized I didn't have one of those father-man-things in my house. I'd gone on my first sleepover at Gracie and Suzanna Rae's, and their dad was a firefighter. He took us for a short ride on the fire truck, then for ice cream. For dinner, her mother made fried chicken and biscuits with big tall glasses of the sweetest tea this side of heaven. We were halfway through dinner when Mr. Gunter got up for something and when he walked by Mrs. Gunter, he kissed her and said, 'Love you much.' She said, 'Love you more.' My little heart started pounding and I watched them with wide eyes the rest of the night." Charlotte crashed against the sofa cushion. "And I thought, 'What is this?'"

"Your mom never said a word about your dad? Not even a hint?"

"When I came home from Gracie and Suzie's, I asked Mom, 'Where is my firefighter daddy?' She said my father loved me but was unable to be my daddy. I don't know, I just accepted it. When I got older, I asked more questions."

Tim brushed the tears from her cheeks, sorry his gallant act had turned into this.

"Once Mom told me he'd died, then came into my room, apologizing, confessing her lie. She said one day, she'd tell me more. I was ten then and still rather innocent and happy with my life. Mom loved me, took really good care of me. We had so much fun, Tim. The first time I saw an episode of *Gilmore Girls*, I could've sworn the producers lifted the show from our lives."

"Then she died."

"I miss her." Charlotte tipped her head back, dropping her arm over her eyes. "And now I have so many questions only she can answer. Like, why, why, why did she not get along with my grandparents? Why did her mother leave her father? We moved to Birmingham from Tallahassee when I was three and never went back. Only saw my grandpa twice afterward." She peered out from under her arm. "What did you find out from her? Colby's wife?"

"All I asked for was her address and if she'd be willing to talk to you. This is where my journey ends and yours begins. But if I'm right, your mom was in love with Colby and she moved here to be near him. Maybe to get support or a chance for him to see you."

"Oh my gosh, Tim, all the times we picnicked up at the Ludlow estate." Charlotte sat up, fingers pressed to her temples. "There's a side service road."

"I know the one."

"We'd park, then hike just to the edge of the estate and spread a blanket, eat a bucket of chicken or McDonald's. Never once did she mention knowing the Ludlows or speak of them at all. Just, like, 'Isn't that an amazing house, Charlotte?' 'Wouldn't you like to live in a house like that, Charlotte?' When I was in junior high, we took a class trip up to the estate for a civics class. We learned"—she faced the dress—"that Emily Ludlow was the first southern woman to wear a wedding gown by a black designer. And, Tim, I grew up to deal in wedding dresses."

"Yeah, you did. What are you thinking?"

"I don't know, but . . . but, Tim, why did this dress come to me?"

He cleared his throat. Because she was supposed to get married. But he foiled the divine plan. Stupid. Stupid. Stupid.

"Because, Charlotte, Emily Ludlow is your great grandmother."

"My . . . great grandmother. But we don't really know. It's all speculation. I'm not sure I want to know, Tim. I've learned to live with the life I've been given."

"We all need to know where we come from, Charlotte. We can't live in a vacuum. You mean to tell me it's fine for you not knowing? No idea of your family heritage or who might have come before you? That's got to be an amazing feeling, to be related to Emily Ludlow."

"Tim, you seem to think I'm missing something I once had. I never had family. Just Mama. That was my world. Yours is brothers and cousins and friends from first grade, racing motorbikes and fortieth wedding anniversaries. I like my solitude. It's okay. It's what I know."

She stooped to pick up the torn pieces of Tim's note. "What was her name?"

"Noelia Ludlow. Do you have tape?" Tim eased off the couch, poised to follow her directions.

"In the kitchen."

Together, they stood at the counter and worked the tape.

"I didn't go looking for this, Charlotte."

"Then why did you call Monte?"

"Okay, maybe I did go looking for this, but Monte said he didn't know anything, so I let it alone. Then he brought over the box. I saw the Ludlow pictures. The clippings. The pieces seemed to align." Between them, on the counter, sat the taped note. Tim inched it toward Charlotte. "I don't think this was my idea, Char. I think it was God's."

She was silent for a moment, her chest rising and falling with her breath. "Why now?"

"How should I know? But, Charlotte, you're the one who redeemed your own inheritance."

"I bought a trunk."

"Charlotte, you bought your great grandmother's dress. Out of the blue. The idea boggles my mind. It's incredible." Tim walked to the door, pulling his keys from his pocket. She stood in the kitchen, watching him. "I was stupid to let you go." He twisted the knob and opened the door. "This is my way of saying I'm sorry."

"Some things aren't meant to be."

Tim paused in the open door. "But some things are. We just have to be smart enough to recognize them."

The next afternoon, Charlotte sat in Mary Grace and Thomas's warm apartment, fragrant with Bengay.

She wished the AC would kick on but didn't have high hopes. Thomas wore a thick sweater and Mary Grace, a robe and wooly slippers. Breakfast dishes sat on the tables next to their chairs. A church broadcast played on the TV.

Charlotte had been neck deep in a new shipment of dresses, not thinking about Tim, Cleo, Colby Ludlow, and his wife when Mary Grace called.

"I want to tell you the rest of my story."

When Dixie reported in, Charlotte escaped the shop and headed for Kirkwood by the River.

She welcomed the break, the step back into time, the inviting blue sparks emanating from Mary Grace's eyes as she talked.

"The dress came to me almost the same way it came to you and the other woman."

"Hillary," Charlotte said.

"Yes, Hillary. What a lovely name, don't you think so, Tommy? When you came the other day, I couldn't help but think about that dress over and over. It just took me back, reminding me of when I was young and vibrant, when I walked without a cane. Back when we traveled doing the Lord's work." Her voice softened. "Oh, how He loves us."

"How did you two meet?" Charlotte remained on the edge of the sofa seat, fanning herself with one of the residence social programs.

"We were kids in school together. Oh, Charlotte, you should've seen him." Mary Grace's vigor and energy wasn't absent in her tale. "So strong and handsome with this crazy mop of curls. He could outrun all the boys."

"Because there was some grown-up chasing us with a switch, I tell you." Thomas opened one eye and winked at Charlotte.

"Tommy, now, be serious."

"It's a good thing I was a fast runner, or I'd never've caught you, Gracie."

"Mercy, listen to you, I was standing flat-foot still, waiting." She gazed at Charlotte. "Fifteen years I waited, but he was worth it. I was twenty-one when he finally proposed."

"I'd done sowed all my wild oats. The feed bag and my heart were empty."

"Thomas's best friend drowned in the Black Warrior River, you see?"

"The day we graduated from the university, ole Cap, Fido, and I—we called him Fido 'cause he looked like a bulldog and was as tough as one too—we went up to the river, took to drinking as fraternity men often did, even in those days. The water was swollen over the banks from spring rains, but we thought we'd beat Mother Nature and take out Cap's daddy's fishing boat at midnight. Such foolish boys . . ."

"Cap fell overboard and was lost, Charlotte," Mary Grace said, low, like a whisper.

"It was my come-to-Jesus meeting right then and there."

"Thomas, that must have been so difficult." Charlotte noticed his dry lips and went to get him a glass of water, collecting dishes along the way.

"Thomas decided to go to seminary."

"But not alone. No sir, I was going to take the prettiest girl God ever created. I knew she could handle me and the ministry. She stood by me during the afterward of Cap's death. When the police investigated. When my daddy was so angry with my foolishness he couldn't speak to me for days. Mary Grace was the one whispering prayers over me. How could I go wrong with a woman like Gracie?"

Charlotte set the glass of water on Thomas's table.

"So he proposed. And I said yes." Mary Grace rocked in her chair, a serene, peaceful expression on her face. "My mother didn't want to waste money on a wedding dress. My father worked for the Coca-Cola company and we needed every penny of his paycheck to make ends meet. He was kindhearted, but gruff. Liked his whiskey, you know. So Mother insisted I get a nice practical suit for my wedding. There was a depression on, you know, and a nice suit would go a long way for a seminarian's wife."

Thomas reached for the water glass Charlotte had set beside him. His hand trembled as he slowly brought it to his lips. "But Mary Grace had been dreaming of her wedding for a long time."

"And I didn't want to get married in a dress that would suit a funeral either."

Charlotte smiled. Relaxed. Kicked off her shoes and curled her legs beneath her on her chair. She loved this story. So much better than the one Tim told her the other day about Colby Ludlow being her father.

"I worked as a shopgirl at Loveman's and had some money saved, but it was going to linens and household things. Mama was not letting me squander one red penny. But you know, one afternoon I was working and Mrs. Ludlow—"

"Emily Ludlow?" Charlotte said.

"One and the same. She came into the store and stopped at my counter. She was one of my best customers. Her husband had just taken over her father's financial business, and she was always seeking to do good in the Magic City. Such a good, good woman. She'd heard I was engaged and don't you know, she offered me her dress. Bold as you please, I said yes."

"But her mama's Irish pride just about ruined the whole thing. She'd have none of it," Thomas said. "None, I say."

Chapter Twenty-Four

Mary Grace

Birmingham, 1939

The moon rested on the crest of Red Mountain as Mary Grace snuck out to the front porch, away from the window of Mama and Daddy's bedroom, where they argued.

She curled up on the porch swing, pillowing her head against the chain links.

Mama's voice seeped through the thin windowpane. "I'll not kowtow to that woman. Emily Ludlow coming into Loveman's and filling Mary Grace's head with dreams of a wedding dress. Offering to give our daughter, *our* daughter, Clem, a wedding dress, her *used* wedding dress."

"I suspect Mary Grace already had dreams of her own about a wedding dress. And what's the harm of Mrs. Ludlow showing us some charity?"

"We are not charity. That's the harm. We work hard, we provide for our family, and we may not have all the Cantons and Ludlows have, but we have more than enough. Thank you and praise Jesus. Life isn't dreams and fairy tales. Mary Grace will do well to remember she's marrying a minister. She'll look lovely getting married in a nice, serviceable suit."

"You had a wedding dress, Vie."

"And Mary Grace could have worn it for her own wedding, but we all know that's not going to happen now, don't we?"

Mary Grace closed her eyes as the bedroom door slammed,

shaking the entire house, setting the swing in motion. The floorboard moaned and creaked under Daddy's heavy footsteps as he crossed the living room.

Daddy had sold Mama's dress. He'd lost it along with the china and silver, and his paycheck, betting on Jack Dempsey to knock out Gene Tunney in a heavyweight bout.

"Oh, Jesus, I don't need a wedding dress," Mary Grace whispered her prayer with the rhythm of the wind cutting under the tree limbs. "It's not practical. And it's way too extravagant." But the confession dropped to her lap, because in her heart, it contained no weight or truth. "But it sure would be nice."

She *wanted* a wedding dress. A beautiful white wedding dress like the ones she'd seen in magazines. Like the gown she'd seen at Loveman's. But it was seventy-five dollars. Practically a month's wages.

Mary Grace restarted her prayer but without faith, it was impossible to carry on.

The front door slammed and Daddy stood on the porch, staring out over the yard, tapping his cigarette pack against his hand. He pulled a cigarette out and lit it, leaning against the porch post. As he inhaled, the white paper burned with a red, ashy flame.

"Dempsey should've had him," Mary Grace said.

Daddy blew a stream of smoke out the side of his mouth. "He would've too, if they'd started the count when Tunney hit the canvas. Dempsey should've gone to the corner like the ref told him."

"It's okay about the dress, Daddy. Mama's right. I don't need something so fancy. I'm marrying a minister, and I'll need a good suit for weddings and funerals."

His hazel eyes snapped at her through the smoke circling up from his cigarette. "Then why'd you go asking for one?"

She shrugged. "I got excited when Mrs. Ludlow offered me her dress."

"Don't every girl want a wedding dress? Your grandmama wouldn't let us get married until she sewed your mama one. I was just home from the war and I would've married her in her housedress."

"A girl wants to be beautiful on her wedding day."

"You're pretty, Mary Grace, right where you are on the swing. I know Thomas would say so."

Mary Grace closed her eyes, seeing her kind, strapping Thomas with his "hey there" grin and his apple-green gaze, combing his golden hair back from his forehead because his thick locks refused to stay slicked in place. She mostly liked the way he talked to her, like her opinion mattered. And how he gazed into her eyes right before he kissed her.

Mary Grace shivered and sat up.

"You all right?"

"Fine, Daddy." A warm blush hit her cheeks. Studying the porch boards, she followed the long weathered cracks toward Daddy's work boots, grateful he couldn't read her thoughts.

"Mary Grace." He cleared his throat. "I ain't been the best father a girl could want. Been too gruff at times. Fought too much with your mother and busted too many paychecks chasing the bottle." He peered sideways at her. "I know you and your mother spend your Sundays praying the good Lord will set me free of my demons, but I ain't likely to change. I like my ways, but there's times like now, I have regrets. If I didn't owe so many people money, you could have your dress and fancy wedding."

"Don't, Daddy. It's okay."

"Here." He walked toward her in three long strides. "Take it before I spend it. I'm not sure what you can do with it, but—" Daddy smacked a folded bill against Mary Grace's palm and closed her fingers over it. The momentary glistening sheen in his eyes said more than a thousand words. Was worth more than the value of the bill he'd pressed into her palm.

"Thank you," she whispered, tears draining down the back of her throat.

"Clem." Mama stepped onto the porch. "What are you doing?"

"Talking to my daughter, do you mind, Vie?"

Mama softened. "I reckon not. I was going to fix supper. What do you want?"

"Whatever you serve is fine." Daddy walked toward the door, holding open the screen for Mama, listening as she suggested warmed-up beef stew. Just before he stepped into the house, Daddy glimpsed at Mary Grace through the screen.

When he was gone, she unfolded the bill with trembling fingers. Ten dollars. She sat back against the swing slats. Ten dollars. It would buy the cake and punch and the linen tablecloth she saw on sale in housewares at Loveman's.

But not a wedding dress.

She folded the money and slipped it into the top of her shoe, eyes tearing up. Oh, Daddy, he was nothing but tender mush under his crusty exterior.

Car tires crackled on the driveway gravel. Mary Grace walked to the porch post and leaned, watching Mrs. Ludlow exit her big, shiny Buick.

"Evening, Mary Grace."

"Evening, Mrs. Ludlow. What brings you all the way out to East Thomas?" Mary Grace glanced down at her faded, worn housedress and scuffed shoes.

"Are your parents home?"

Mary Grace didn't have to answer because Daddy and Mama stepped onto the porch.

"How can we help you?" Daddy said.

"I heard your daughter is getting married."

"She is." Daddy took a step toward the elegant Mrs. Ludlow, her light wool coat perfect for the spring evening.

Mama moved next to Daddy, pretty in her cotton housedress with the pleated skirt, worry lines etched into her freckled skin.

"We heard you offered Mary Grace your wedding dress, and while we appreciate your kindness, we won't be needing your charity."

Mary Grace rolled her back against the porch post and closed her eyes. *Don't embarrass us, Mama.*

"It's not charity, Mrs. Fox. It's a gift."

"A gift? We don't even know you. Mary Grace waits on you at Loveman's counter. Begging your pardon, but an extravagant gift such as a wedding dress to a girl you hardly know, who serves you, is charity."

"Vie," Daddy rumbled.

Mary Grace peeked around the post, expecting to see Mrs. Ludlow's back as she left. But she remained steadfast on the dirt path. She'd tucked Daddy's ten dollars into her sock and when she moved, it scraped against her ankle.

After what seemed like forever, she said, "Then I'll sell you the dress."

Mama's cheeks reddened. "We can't afford your kind of gown, Mrs. Ludlow. Tell me, did you intend to drive up here and humiliate us, or is this just spur of the moment?"

"Seems to me you're the one humiliating yourself, Mrs. Fox. I come bearing a gift, and you're refusing it. It's not good enough for you?"

"See here—"

"I offer to sell it and you tell me it's too expensive. You've not even heard the price."

"All right, tell us the price and don't say a dollar. That's more insulting than charity." Mama went down the steps to face off with Mrs. Ludlow.

Daddy just shook his head.

"Mama, please, can't we just accept—"

"Ten dollars." The amount burst into the air and hit Mary Grace's heart with a one-two punch. Mrs. Ludlow repeated the amount. "I'm asking ten dollars."

"Ten dollars?" Mama scoffed. "For a fancy, society wedding dress?"

"That's my price." Mrs. Ludlow raised her chin. "It seems like a fair price. I wore it once. Didn't get a spot on it. Had it special made by Taffy Hayes."

"The colored gal what sews for you?" Mama lowered her chin and tucked her hands into her pockets. "Naw, naw, no. Not even for ten dollars." She set her jaw, hard.

"I'll take it. I have ten dollars, Mrs. Ludlow." Mary Grace skidded toward her, taking the bill from her sock and unfolding it. She glanced back at Daddy. His eyes brimmed and glistened.

"Mary Grace, no . . . now, where did you get ten dollars?" Mama reached for the money but Mary Grace moved her hand away. "Did you hear who sewed that dress?"

"Yes, and I don't care. Daddy gave me the money." *Oh, Lord, thank you.*

"Taffy is the best dress designer in this city. Maybe in all of the south. You're lucky to have one of her dresses." Mrs. Ludlow took the money. "Now, a deal is a deal." She offered Mary Grace her hand. "Miss Fox, it's a pleasure doing business with you."

"Same to you, Mrs. Ludlow." She had a gown. Mrs. Ludlow's gown. Specially made. Mary Grace was smiling so wide she didn't dare look at Mama.

"Mr. Fox, do you mind?" Mrs. Ludlow held up her car keys. "The dress is in the back of my car."

Daddy stamped out his cigarette and took the keys as he passed the women.

"Mrs. Fox, your daughter is a special girl. It's my privilege to give her the dress I wore for my wedding. Daniel and I have been very happy. Take it with joy."

Mama sniffed, biting her lower lip. And said nothing.

"We are very much alike, Mrs. Fox," Mrs. Ludlow said. "Women who live and breathe in this town, who want good for our husbands and children and our community. I'm standing here now, woman to woman, wanting to bless your daughter. I have no daughters of my own, and for quite some time, I've admired Mary Grace. I suppose that's a compliment to you, Vie."

Daddy walked by with a trunk on his shoulders. "Sure this thing ain't empty? It's light as a feather. Vie, you got any iced tea in the kitchen? I'm parched."

"I assure you, the dress is inside." Mrs. Ludlow turned for her car. "Mary Grace, it's yours now. And here, Mr. Fox, thank you for helping me with my trunk." Mrs. Ludlow offered her hand. When Daddy took it, she smiled, pressing her fingers hard against his palm. "Now, Mary Grace, it's no ordinary dress. A very special dress to me and to the woman who made it for me. Wear it with love. I wish you the best."

As she drove away, Mama remained planted on the path, a thin skirting breeze yanking her hem and dusting dirt over her brown shoes.

"Mama?"

She didn't move, but stood there, trembling, fingers pressed to her lips, tears filling her eyes. Mary Grace slipped her arm around her waist and set her head on her shoulder.

"I won't wear it if you don't want me to."

"Goodness." Mama came alive. "You just paid the woman ten

dollars, Mary Grace. Do you think I'm going to let the dress rot in that trunk? And if it was good enough for Mrs. Ludlow to wear, sewn by a colored, then it's good enough for you, I guess." She wiped her face with her work-hardened hands. "Now, let's go see this work of art. I'll have to get sewing on it, fix it up. She's been married a good twenty-five years so no telling the shape it's in."

When they turned around, Daddy stood on the porch, the trunk open, the dress in his hands, dancing from his fingertips.

"She pressed this into my hand." He passed the ten dollars over to Mama. "Get whatever you need for fixing up the dress or whatever you ladies do with hand-me-downs."

"It's not a hand-me-down, Daddy." Mary Grace dropped to her knees. The white satiny silk shimmered and the orange glow of the sunlight set the band of pearls at the waist on fire. "Oh, Mama." She stood, taking the dress from Daddy. "It's perfect."

Daddy stepped back, clearing his throat, a goofy look on his face.

"All right, let's go inside and try it on. Clem, give me a few minutes for supper."

"Take your time, Vie. I'm all right." Daddy tapped Mary Grace on the shoulder. "You never give up your faith, Mary Grace. Never give up. Not for me or for any man." He stepped off the porch, cutting a new path across the yard down to the woods out back.

Charlotte

Charlotte eased the tension in her chest as Mary Grace's voice faded, the taut rope of her story letting go. "So the dress did belong to Emily Ludlow?"

"It sure did." There was a light of love in the elder bride's eyes. "She wore it to marry Daniel Ludlow. I tell you, that dress was a wonder. After that day, things were smoothed over with Mama and Daddy. Don't you know, Mama and Mrs. Ludlow became good friends, and Mama accepted quite a few gifts from her. But here's the best part." Mary Grace dotted the air as if to make sure Charlotte listened. "The dress fit as if it were especially made for me. Mrs. Ludlow was a slight woman. I've got my German granny's big bones and features. But don't you know, we didn't have to let out or add one stitch. Not one. Can you believe it?"

"Yes, Mary Grace, I believe it." The rush of gooseflesh down Charlotte's arm was becoming familiar. "I surely can."

Chapter Twenty-Five

Emily

$\mathcal{F}$ather sent Bernadette for the doctor. Poor maid of honor had turned into an errand girl. But her mother had collapsed on the fainting couch as Molly helped Emily out of Mrs. Caruthers's gown.

"I'm sorry, Father," Emily whispered as Molly loosened her corset strings. Being able to exhale almost made Mother's fainting worth it. The phantom weight of the first gown vanished as Molly buttoned up the feathery, silky gown.

"It's all right." He knelt beside Mother, patting her hand. "As long as you're sure?"

"I'm sure."

"Then I support you." He cleared his throat. "It's not going to be easy."

"Father, will it be too hard on your business?"

"I'll manage. Emily, forgive me for not telling you before now."

"I suppose I always knew, Father. But I thought we'd choose to love each other. I knew of Emmeline, but I didn't know his parents threatened his inheritance if he didn't marry me."

"I'm not sure Cam meant to confess that, but his brandy holds him rather than him holding it. He sounded quite pleased with the arrangement, as if I should be too."

Last night Father joined the "boys" at the club to celebrate, or mourn, Phillip's last night as a bachelor. He came home earlier than expected, solemn and disturbed, and retired to his room without a word to Emily. But she could hear his coarse whispers with Mother when she passed by their door. "All Cam wants is a good match for his son. They care little that Phillip's infidelities will be her problem."

The door burst open and Dr. Gelman rushed to Mother's side. "What happened?"

"She fainted." Father, pragmatic but tender, moved out of the doctor's way. "Must be the excitement." He winked at Emily.

It was the excitement all right. Father had brought the final truth about Phillip. He'd indeed signed out the warrant for her arrest. Father had overheard Phillip bragging at his bachelor party of how deftly he handled the situation.

Pride puffs up, Father always said. Pride can't be silent.

Dr. Gelman waved smelling salts under Mother's nose. She roused, coughing and gasping. Father helped her sit up straight but she fought him, straining to see Emily. When the doctor waved the salts under her nose again, Mother swatted at him.

"I'm revived. Emily, listen to me." Mother breathed deeply, coughing, gathering herself, struggling to her feet. "*They* had you arrested."

"Mother, I know. Father told me."

"How can you even think of wearing *that* gown?" She flipped her hand up and down, pointing. "You'll insult the Saltonstalls. Perhaps beyond repair."

"Maggie." Father cradled Mother to his chest. "This is our daughter's wedding. Let's not go on. What's done is done. We're late starting the ceremony." Father helped Mother to her feet, thanked the doctor, then paused at the door. "Emily, I'll return in five minutes."

When she was alone in the room, Emily tried to keep air in her lungs. When she opened the door and peered down the hall, she could hear the organ music coming from the sanctuary.

And she knew. She was not marrying Phillip Saltonstall today.

A giggle burst from her lips. Emily touched her finger to her mouth. Another giggle bubbled up.

She was free. Slipping out of the room, she scurried down the hall on her tiptoes, keeping her heels from clacking against the stone floor. Rounding the corridor to the foyer, she exhaled relief to see the sanctuary doors closed. Then she peered out the window.

He was here, waiting, just like Father said, sitting atop his glorious mustang, Two Tone. Father and his shouting out the window, "A holy night". Signaling to Daniel that he might have a chance.

But Emily lacked the courage until she slipped on Taffy's dress. It was as if all her prayers came together at once and awakened her heart.

Mrs. Potter, the reverend's secretary, came through the sanctuary doors. "Emily dear, there you are. The ceremony is starting. Phillip is at the altar."

"My dear, Mrs. Potter." Emily giggled, grasping the woman's hands. "I'm getting married."

"Of course you are, dear." She smiled and patted Emily's arm. "Let me locate your father."

"When you do, tell him I thought it through, made my decision, and followed my heart."

Without waiting, Emily pressed through the foyer doors and stepped into the cool, glorious air of a Birmingham New Year's Eve. Daniel stood beside Two Tone, resplendent in his tuxedo, his hair coiffed into place, his jaw firm and clean shaven. She loved the way his eyes shone.

Taking the steps down to him, Emily's dress flowed free and easy about her legs. "Father said he spoke to you."

"He did." Daniel bent to one knee, anchoring himself in the sidewalk around the church. "Will you marry me? Please?"

"Oh, Daniel—" Emily glimpsed back at the church's broad, oak doors. Father stood, watching, nodding.

Emily swallowed. She'd waited for this day. Dreamed of this day. But how could she leave Phillip at the altar? As cruel as he might have been, he was a man with a beating heart beneath his chest. She did not want to stoop to his level of play.

She'd given her word to Phillip. Friends and family, guests and colleagues waited inside for her to marry him. They'd sent gifts. They'd hosted teas and suppers, bridge games.

"Emily?" Daniel's confidence panicked a bit.

"Wait . . . please . . ." Emily turned, raising her elbow to Father. "Father, please escort me inside." As they ascended the steps, she glanced over her shoulder at Daniel. He remained, unmoving, beside Two Tone.

"Emily, is this what you want?" Father paused at the sanctuary doors. The organ music played over restless murmurings.

"I can't run out on Phillip. Not on his wedding day." She clung to his arm, shaking. Her veil and bouquet were in the bridal parlor but she did not go back for them.

"Then you are marrying him?" Father guided her toward the sanctuary doors.

"I'm not leaving him at the altar."

As Emily made her way down the aisle with Father, the guests rose to their feet, gasping and whispering.

Beautiful . . . gown . . .

Not Mrs. Caruthers . . .

Taffy Hayes . . . colored . . .

Before her, Phillip stood like a Greek statue, hands clasped, handsome as always in his tuxedo and his winged collar. His light brown hair shone and his smile challenged the brilliance of the flickering candles.

The foyer doors crashed open and the clattering of horse hooves drowned out the organ tones.

Shouts resounded. Screams billowed.

"Sir, you cannot go in there. Sir, I forbid you."

Emily whirled around to see Mrs. Porter chasing Two Tone down the broad aisle. She laughed. *Oh, Daniel.*

"Emily." Daniel sat straight and proud on Two Tone. "Marry me. Marry *me.*"

The sanctuary erupted with exclaims and shouts and protests. Phillip charged down the aisle, his best man heeling after him, slashing the air with his arm. "Get him out of here. This is my day, Ludlow."

Tiny rumbles of pandemonium shook the sanctuary. Two Tone reared, pawing the air, Daniel holding on to the reins.

A shrill whistle silenced through the confusion. All eyes fell on Father, who stood on the altar steps. "This is about no one but Emily. It's her decision. What do you want to do? Marry Ludlow or Saltonstall."

Oh, the kindness of her father's heart.

"Phillip." Emily tenderly gripped his arm. "You did have me arrested. And I know you still have a mistress. That your parents threatened to cut you off if you didn't marry me. So, dear Phillip, I cannot marry you. And *you* cannot marry me. You know it in your heart."

"What's the meaning of this?" Mr. Saltonstall interrupted, his chin flapping like a mad rooster. "Phillip, is this how I raised you? To be bested by this—"

"She's right. She cannot marry me. And I cannot marry her." Phillip's gaze lingered across the room toward the pale and willowy Emmeline.

"Oh, Phillip." Emily raised on her toes and kissed his cheek. "I wish you well." Then she turned to Daniel, reached for his offered arm, and with a small boost from . . . Mother! Emily lighted on the back of Two Tone.

Daniel gathered the reins and heeled the mustang's sides. "Yah!"

Two Tone launched down the aisle, hooves pounding, and dashed out the high foyer door, down the sanctuary steps, racing Emily to freedom.

A photographer from the *Age-Herald* jerked alive from his dozing stance against the street lamp. His big camera flashed with a poof and circled smoke in the cold morning air.

Emily tossed back her head to laugh. "Happy New Year." She crushed her cheek into Daniel's firm back. "I knew you'd come. I love you, Daniel Ludlow."

Two Tone galloped down the street, gentling around a trolley car, strutting as if he knew what kind of cargo he carried as the church bells began to peal. Then, at the corner of 5th Avenue and 19th Street, Emily saw *him*.

Mr. Oddfellow. The daring old man with the purple ascot. When their eyes met, he bowed, raising his hat, and cheered her on.

Chapter Twenty-Six

Charlotte

*D*riving back to Mountain Brook from the retirement center, Charlotte made a decision. The trunk, the dress . . . Tim had opened the door to the dark corridor of her life and she couldn't duck from the light any longer.

The taped piece of paper with Noelia's name rested on the car's console. Charlotte felt bold. Ready. But she didn't want to venture into the unknown alone.

She auto-dialed Hillary. "Hi, it's me. Want to go for a ride? Do some investigating?"

"Is it about the dress?" Hillary said, strong and clipped, like she was ready to charge!

"Yes, and me. It's about me."

"I'll be ready when you get here."

Thirty minutes later, Charlotte and Hillary were on 157-N to Florence, a contemplative silence in the car.

"I don't know why I'm doing this."

"Because you want to know."

"I've never wanted to know before." Charlotte squeezed her hands around the steering wheel.

"This is different. The situation came to you. You bought that trunk and your world, my world, changed."

"Should I give the dress to Cleo? Even if she can't get a court order?"

"I think you have a greater court on your side than the one Cleo is using to get her way."

Charlotte glanced over at Hillary. "What court would that be?"

"The court of heaven."

"Since when did you become a spiritual person?"

"I'm not." She shifted in her seat. Hid a smile. "Those are Thomas's words."

"Thomas?" Charlotte arched her brow, eyeing her friend.

"I've been visiting them. They may be old, but their hearts are young, full of life, and what I imagine might be God." She laughed low. "Every once in a while, Mary Grace fades away from the conversation and stares at the wall. At first, I thought she was just having a senile moment. She'll laugh, smile, and her eyes'll go wide. Then all of a sudden, she'll start singing 'Amazing Grace' or 'How Great Thou Art.' I've been in nursing long enough to know things happen when people get old, close to their time. But, Charlotte, I think she's seeing things."

"Gert used to say when the mind of a person starts to go, that's when their heart is really revealed."

"Then Mary Grace is all about Jesus. Nothing but Jesus. She'll mumble too. I thought it was craziness but now . . ." Charlotte hooked a glance at Hillary as the older woman looked at her, hesitating. "I think she's talking in tongues."

Charlotte laughed. "You sound like she's from outer space."

"Maybe she is." Hillary laughed. "Or maybe I am."

Around one, Charlotte pulled into Noelia's driveway. A Tudor home sat tucked back on a wooded acre.

"Finally." Charlotte stepped out of her little two-seater. She and Hillary had a terse exchange about which way to go off of County Road 24. Charlotte acquiesced to Hillary and ended up lost, back-tracking fifty miles.

"Don't start. We just got peace between us." Hillary smacked her car door shut.

"I'm not starting. I just said finally."

"Yeah, but it was your tone, young lady." Hillary squared her slacks and fixed her top. "This is a lovely place." The wind danced with her natural curls.

Charlotte smiled with a side glance at her friend. Her sister of the dress. Yes, *this* place was lovely.

Leading the way up the front walk, Charlotte slowed as the door opened and Noelia stepped out.

Noelia Ludlow could've been Mama's sister. Lean, with a short, narrow waist and long legs, scouting eyes set above a short nose and high cheeks. Graceful.

"Come on in, girls. Please." Noelia grasped Charlotte by the arms when she stepped onto the porch. "Well, we meet."

"Thank you for letting us come on short notice." Charlotte stepped inside the house and introduced Hillary.

Noelia bustled about, gathering her long, straight hair away from her face with a hair tie. When she sat in her chair, she exhaled. "I am so sorry for what Colby did to you and your mama."

"Please, I don't think it was your fault," Charlotte said. Sitting in the room with Noelia had a surreal, right feel.

"Yeah, baby, it was. It was my fault." Tears slipped from the corners of her eyes. "It was."

Everything she'd known about her life was paling in the light of all these new revelations. Two days ago she was just Charlotte Malone. Plain. Simple. Nothing fancy. Alone. Except for Dix and Dr. Hotstuff.

Now Charlotte was part of this network. Hillary, Mary Grace, and Thomas. Noelia.

She had a father with a name and reputation. Her great grand-mother broke laws for the sake of her convictions. Her great grandfather, Daniel, was a revered Birmingham banker and philanthropist.

Her family tree was revealing fine, thick branches.

When Noelia halted the conversation to serve iced teas, the pleas-antries took over. Weather. Summer vacations. News tidbits.

But when Noelia settled back in her chair, Hillary dove right into the meaning of their visit.

"Noelia, what happened?"

"Oh, so many things can happen in a marriage. Especially ones with cracks like mine and Colby's. We didn't have children so we were both more devoted to our careers than each other. When Colby had the chance to teach at FSU, we both agreed he should take it. I'd stay here and continue my work with the Alabama Fine Arts Institute. We'd visit on weekends and holidays. It was only for a year. We'd been married over twenty, so we believed we could endure. But then, all the cracks started spreading."

"Do you know why he took up with Mama?" Charlotte held her tea without sipping. She felt anchored to the cold glass in her hand.

"Sure. She was young, beautiful, intelligent. Called Colby out on his stuff and didn't let him run roughshod over her. Colby always did like a good challenge."

Charlotte smiled. "Sounds like Mama."

"From what I gather," Noelia said, "she fell pretty hard for Colby. He was fascinated with her, but coming out with a student affair would've ruined his career. Darn near ruined our marriage, but trust me, he cared more about his career than either Phoebe or me."

"Then why did he risk it all?"

"Midlife crisis? Wanted to feel young again? What would you do if you were a forty-five-year-old man and a beautiful twenty-one-year-old was willing to give herself to you? Colby had many strengths, but at that time, resisting temptation was not one of them."

"Did you ever meet Mama?"

"No, I didn't. While Colby and I weren't happily married, I loved him and didn't want to meet the woman who nearly stole him from me. Then I learned about you." Noelia eyed Charlotte while reaching for an envelope. "She sent Colby a registered letter." She passed the letter to Charlotte by way of Hillary. "She wanted support so she could buy a bigger house in a nicer neighborhood. She wanted Colby to recognize you. Admit you belonged to him."

Charlotte's hand trembled, fumbled, to read the letter. All the surreal rightness of this visit began to slip away. The cold sensation of the tea glass raced from her hand to her heart.

"But I didn't want her, or you, in our lives," Noelia said. "We'd patched a few of the cracks and were getting along. We had a life planned, trips to take, and frankly, at fifty, I didn't want half my weekends spent with a little girl consuming my husband's time. I tore up the picture she sent, but I couldn't bring myself to throw away the letter."

"You never showed it to Colby?" Hillary set her tea on the coaster and angled to read over Charlotte's shoulder.

"No, but, Charlotte, he did know about you. Unfortunately, out of sight, out of mind. We sort of arrived at this unspoken settlement that your mother surely had moved on, found a good man, married, birthed more children. It's what I wanted to believe. Since Colby never said otherwise, I assumed he did too. I heard Phoebe died about a year after the fact. A friend of Colby's brought word."

"So you knew she died? That I had no one? Yet you still kept my father from me." The woman who drew Charlotte in with her inviting, mama-like appearance left her trembling and angry.

"I'd convinced myself you were better off. That you didn't need to know Colby. Why interrupt everyone's life?"

"I was twelve. I had no life. And what little I did have was interrupted by someone crashing into my mother's car and killing her."

"I'm not proud, Charlotte." Noelia's voice trembled with watery emotion. "Just being honest. When Colby and I divorced, I realized how selfish we'd both been, but it wasn't my place to tell him to get in touch with you. Or my place to tell you about Colby."

"But it was your place to hide my mama's letter? To make sure he didn't get in touch with Mama or me?"

"When I was his wife, yes. I protected what was mine. But not a month went by I didn't think of you."

Charlotte walked around the coffee table. Sitting made her ache. But her legs were putty and her knees barely held her steady. "I'm not sure what to do with all of this . . . I . . ."

"I sent you some money last year."

Revelation dawned. Pieces fell into place. "The hundred grand," Charlotte whispered.

"Just something . . . just something . . ." Noelia brushed the first flash of tears from her cheeks, supple and slightly lined. She looked younger than her seventy-something years, but her shoulders rounded with the burden of her story. "After the divorce, I moved to Florence to be near my sister's children. I spent a lot of money on a house too big for me and spoiling my nieces and nephews. One day while looking for some bank papers, I found your mother's letter. I thought, mercy, where did the years go? So I looked you up on the Internet. I didn't expect to really find anything, but I discovered your shop. I felt proud for you. So I had my bank wire a hundred thousand dollars to you anonymously."

"Then I'll pay you back." Now that Charlotte knew where the money originated, the sheen was off the prize.

"You'll do no such thing."

"I don't want your guilt money."

"It's not guilt, Charlotte. I could hardly spend away my guilt, or even pretend to buy affection from a girl who didn't even know me. It was a gift. Hardly enough to compensate growing up without Colby." She smiled. "He'd have liked you."

Charlotte stared out the window, over a lush summer lawn, a heaviness rising in her chest. A hundred thousand dollars. A gift from her father's wife. She'd trade it all for a chance to have met the man face-to-face.

On the edge of the manicured grounds of the Ludlow Estate, Charlotte paused for a pure, deep breath. Blue sky, summer trees, sunlight bouncing off the sparkling windows.

Three months ago she'd driven up here to think, to feel closer to heaven. To Mama. Little did she know the ridge was burdened with secrets.

The mountain was quiet except for the wind. Charlotte made her way up the walk to the house and let herself in, standing in the expanse of the house her great grandparents built. The house where Emily had raised her grandfather.

The house where her father had played.

"Charlotte, what are you doing here? Did you bring my dress?" Cleo's walk hammered across the gleaming, spotless foyer hardwood.

"I'd like to see the library."

"All right." Cleo eyed her for a lingering moment before turning with a quick motion. "I'm working on the subpoena for the dress."

"What's the delay?"

"The judge wants more proof." She ruffled. "Seems just a picture isn't enough."

Charlotte pulled two photos from her purse as she broke into the bright, white library, the floor-to-ceiling windows framing a breath-taking view of the valley.

"I thought you'd like to see these." She offered the pictures of Mary Grace and Hillary in the gown. "Emily gave the gown to Mary Grace, who left it for Hillary. If a picture is proof of ownership, what are you going to do with these?" She pulled out Mama's letter to Colby. "And this certified letter from my mother to Colby asking for child support? His wife gave it to me."

"Oh mercy, what in the world . . ." Cleo walked to the window, reading the letter in the light. When she finished she turned to Charlotte. "So you're going to take this beautiful estate from the city? Claim your inheritance? It's probably too late. Besides, you can't manage this place, Charlotte. Once it becomes private, the public funds go away."

Charlotte laughed low. Poor Cleo. She had too much of her identity in her job. "I don't want this place, Cleo. All I want is the dress. The legend is that—"

"What legend?"

"The legend that the dress fits every bride who is supposed to wear it. It's never been altered." Charlotte walked along the wall of pictures, trying to grasp the faces and names that somehow belonged to her.

She paused in front of Colby. An image from his professor days. She could see something of herself in his eyes. "Do you think he's rolling over in his grave because his daughter didn't go to college?"

"Most likely . . . Charlotte, Noelia said you are Colby's daughter?"

"Yes, she did." Charlotte stopped in front of the picture of Emily in her wedding gown. "This is the one she was going to wear?"

"When she was to marry Phillip Saltonstall."

Charlotte turned to Cleo. "Did you know Hillary Saltonstall wore the dress in 1968? Phillip was her great-uncle."

Cleo buttoned her lip, her chest deflating. Her fight waning. Charlotte smiled. God had a way of weaving a lovely tapestry.

"Well then. What are you going to do with the dress, Charlotte? Sell it? You can't do that . . . it's . . . it's not right."

"Sell it? No, Cleo, no. I'm not going to sell it. I'm going to wear it."

Tim

Tim swept the last of the dust and grime from his garage. The hollow emptiness of the three-car space made him feel a bit empty. Out of sorts, maybe. But unbelievably free.

He leaned on the broom handle, peering toward the sunset that ribboned through the trees. With or without Charlotte, it was time to grow up. Maybe when and if he had kids, he could take up moto-cross again.

When he'd loaded his last bike into the truck bed of his final customer, the tightness in his chest released and he understood how long he'd been hanging on to something God had asked him to surrender.

He was free. He thought racing made him free, took the edge off, allowed him to burn off stress and energy, be adventurous. No. Racing kept him in bondage. He couldn't *not* race. Other factors in his life had gone cold, waiting on back burners, for him to get around to them.

Like taking up his guitar again. Giving more attention to his career. Settling down. Marriage. Time with his friend, Jesus.

A truck motor hummed in the driveway. Tim looked up as David cut the engine and stepped out.

"How's it feel?" he asked, making his way toward the garage.

"Like I lost fifteen hundred pounds."

"I can't believe you did it." David smacked Tim on the shoulder. "Good news. The downtown commission loved your designs for the remodel of the old Saltonstall offices and furnace, including the bronze memorial to convict labor."

Tim smiled, clapping his big brother a high five. Good. It was all good.

"And . . . ready for more good news? Brody Smart called on my way here. There's some new developments going on west of the city. He wants us to bid. Said unless we submit children's drawings, we have the job. They *want* to give it to us." David did a funny jig around the garage. "Finally, our ship is coming in."

Tim put the broom into action, unsure of the stream of emotion in his chest. One act of obedience and God opened up heaven. His garage was empty but his heart was full.

"Want to come to the house for dinner? Katherine is making sloppy joes and tater tots. Your favorite."

Tim shook his head. "She's going to have to get used to the idea that she's only married to you, Dave."

"Don't be like that, Tim. You're a brother to her. She wants the best for you."

"If she did, then she'd have loved Charlotte."

David stared toward the street, his hands on his belt. "Are you going after Charlotte again?"

"I don't know. Got to see if she's still talking to me after telling her Colby was her dad."

"I'm with you if you do, Tim. Whatever you need."

The brothers chatted a few more minutes, then David checked the time and said he had to get going.

Tim set his broom in the corner, flipped on the radio, and pulled a lawn chair to the center of the garage, facing the neighborhood.

Space. Glorious space. He was ready for whatever God raced his way next.

His neighbor zipped past on his motorcycle, beeping his horn, waving. Tim answered with an easy wave. He didn't envy the man at all. Not one tiny bit.

Chapter Twenty-Seven

Charlotte

*I*n the warm lamplight of her bedroom, Charlotte slipped the gown from the dress form. In ten seconds she'd know. Did the dress fit her? Was she the next bride?

"Charlotte, what's taking you so long?" Hillary banged on the door.

"Do you need help?" Dixie said.

"Hush up, give me a minute."

She'd showered. Donned clean undergarments. Then approached the dress. Slowly. Carefully. The dress held the hearts of three other women. The history of a hundred years.

It wasn't until Charlotte stepped into the skirt that she realized how much she wanted to be a part of their story, of the gown's history.

Please fit. Charlotte hesitated as she drew the skirt over her hips. "What if it doesn't fit?"

"Oh, merciful me, it'll fit, Charlotte." Hillary. Without doubt. "You think all this happened just so you could give it to someone else? It'll fit. Trust me."

"If it doesn't, you'll find the perfect bride, Char. It's what you do."

"Shush, Dix, what kind of thing is that to say? *She* is the perfect bride."

"Well, if she's not, she'll find one. Hillary, you're freaking her out."

Charlotte grinned at the banter on the other side of the door, slipping her arms gently into the sleeves, and settling the bodice on her shoulders. She loved Hillary like a sister, no, like a mother, already.

Gathering the dress in the back with her hands, Charlotte held her breath. Would it fit?

The waist of pearls pulled against her middle, hugging her ribs. Perfectly. It fit. The dress fit. *I won't cry, I won't cry.*

But her heart raced and when she tried to speak, tears weighted her words. "It fits, y'all. It fits. Come button me up." The bedroom door crashed open.

"I can't believe you doubted me." Hillary went right to the back buttons.

"Oh, Char." Dixie stood back, a wide smile on her face, a sheen in her eyes. "It's gorgeous. You are gorgeous."

"But how? Emily had to wear a corset. Mary Grace said she was thin. Oh, Hillary, the waist is going to be too tight."

"Charlotte, stop fretting and start thinking of what you're going to do when you see it does fit." Hillary hooked the rest of the buttons in silence. Only the sound of the women breathing.

Charlotte watched in the mirror as the dress formed to her figure, the bodice accenting her curves. The scoop neck nestled just under her collarbone. The pearls at her waist rested in a neat row, not strained or taut. The bell shoulders tapered to fitted sleeves and dropped just below her elbow.

"Here, put on these shoes." Dixie set down a pair of cream pumps from the shop. "The heel is about what Emily would've worn."

"All buttoned." Hillary angled around to see Charlotte's face, gently gripping her shoulders. "Exhale," she whispered.

When she did, her ribs rested against the sides of the dress and every fiber settled into place.

The mirror reflected more than a woman in a beautiful gown.

It reflected Charlotte's heart. And instantly she knew . . . she'd risk her heart again.

"I have to go." Charlotte yanked her purse off the bedroom floor. "Go where?"

"After love." Out of the loft and down to her car, it was all so clear to her heart and mind. She didn't belong to the dress. She belonged to Tim. That's what the dress had been trying to tell her all along, since that day up on the ridge.

Carefully settling in behind the wheel, she fired up her car and fifteen minutes later plus one close call with a cement truck, she whipped into Tim's driveway.

The garage door was open and he sat in the middle of an empty space, his hair flowing in long soft strands about his face, his bare feet sticking out from a pair of a creased jeans.

"Tim?" Charlotte tossed her keys into the driver's seat as she stepped out, holding the gown's hem off the ground.

"Charlotte." He jumped up, making his way to her. "You're wearing the dress?"

"Yes, it . . . it fit." She passed him for the garage. "Tim, where are your bikes?"

"Sold them. Finally listened to that still small voice in my soul." He fixed his gaze on her. "Why are you wearing your great-grandmother's wedding dress?"

She could tell he liked saying that—great-grandmother. "Because . . . I . . . ." She hadn't fully worked out what she'd say once she saw him. She was driven by her need to see him.

Tim pointed at her, skidding sideways toward the door to the house. "Don't move. I'll be . . . just . . ." He opened the door. "Wait." And disappeared inside. His footsteps thundered through the house and back again.

He burst through the door, his eyes sparkling, dancing, as he beelined for Charlotte. Without a word or hesitation, he bent to one knee and reached for her hand.

"Marry me, Charlotte. Please, marry me." He slid his grandmother's ring onto her finger.

"This is why I'm here, Tim. Wearing my great grandmother's wedding dress."

When Tim picked her up and whirled her around, Charlotte let out a laughing shout, tipping back her head and letting joy echo in the garage.

Tim buried his face against her neck, and for a moment, their heartbeats felt intertwined.

"The ring fits, the dress fits." He lowered her feet to the garage floor. "We fit, babe. We fit." He kissed her, his hands around her back, holding her to him. "Man, Charlotte, you smell good. You feel good."

"Hey, friend Tim?"

"Yeah?"

"Tell fiancé Tim I'm happy to have him back."

"Charlotte." He jerked his head up, holding her face in his hands. "What time is it?"

"Six thirty."

His breath on her face created tingles on her toes. "Marry me. Now. Tonight. You have a dress. A beautiful dress. I own a tux. Our license is still good."

"Tim, seriously? Now? Tonight?" Charlotte peered toward the August evening. The day still had a lot of light left. "Who will do the ceremony?"

She loved the glint in his eyes. "Leave it to me. What do you say?"

"Yes. Yes!" Her lips covered his, light and trembling at first, then with growing confidence and passion as he drew her into himself and poured his love into her.

It was the breeze that made her look up, a change in the texture of the unseen, a change in the texture of her heart.

She was ready. Charlotte moved with firm footing around a stand of beech trees and onto a moonbeam path. A pearly, full moon glowed over Red Mountain, burning back the curtains of night.

A midnight wedding.

Charlotte gripped her bouquet as a quintet began to play the "Hallelujah Chorus." Another round of joy swelled in her middle. Excitement tingled down her arms and legs. Her heart trembled with love. Her mind rested in peace.

"All right, Charlotte, are you ready?" Cleo popped out of the shadows, the pearls around her neck rivaling the moon's essence.

"Yes . . . I'm ready." Her escorts came from behind Cleo. Her sisters-of-the-dress, Hillary and Mary Grace.

The song on the strings intensified. The breeze ushered past and for a slight moment carried the fragrance of jasmine and cedarwood. Mama's scent. Charlotte closed her eyes and inhaled.

"I must say, Daniel, Emily and Colby would be proud." Cleo's typical bold voice wavered with emotion. "As am I."

"My mama would be proud too." Charlotte inhaled one last time, holding on to the fading scent.

"She sure would." On her left, Hillary slipped her arm through Charlotte's. "I know I am." She kept her gaze forward, her back straight. Charlotte pressed her cheek to Hillary's shoulder, seeing the slight tremble on the woman's lower lip.

"This might be the second-best day of my life," Mary Grace said. She stood on Charlotte's right and linked her arm tightly around the bride's.

"Mine too." Hillary straightened Charlotte's veil—*Emily's*

veil—and kissed her cheek, waving Cleo aside. "Let's get this girl married."

The music mounted. In the array of white string lights and candles, Charlotte saw Tim and David rise from the chairs and stand in front of the kneeling altar along with a proud, smiling Thomas.

Tim peered down the aisle at her. In the muted light, Charlotte could see the sheen in his eyes. On the waves of flickering flames, she felt his radiating heart.

He'd done this. All of it. Called Cleo. Rallied his family and friends. Within hours, a wedding and reception had been planned and executed.

When Tim called Hillary, she jumped into action, drove up to Kirkwood, and stirred Mary Grace and Thomas to attend. "Wouldn't miss it for the world," they'd said.

A midnight wedding.

Brother David contacted a Rose Firm client who played in the Birmingham Symphony. He in turn gathered a string quintet—two violinists, a violist, and two cellists—who were wholly inspired by a spontaneous, midnight nuptial.

Rosined bows drew "hallelujah, hallelujah" from the strings. Charlotte started down the aisle toward the circle of white chairs, toward Tim. Toward love.

The dress swished about her legs. The empire waist hugged her heart. Tears gathered in her eyes. Beside her, Hillary sniffed and cleared her throat while Mary Grace let her tears flow freely without shame.

"I never thought . . . oh, my dear, sweet Jesus, I never thought . . . at ninety-four years old, my, my . . ." she whispered.

"Me neither, Mary Grace," Hillary said, low and watery. "Me neither."

As for Charlotte, she never imagined feeling this happy, this satisfied with life. She'd settled for okay, getting by. But tonight she realized how much more God had ordained for her.

She strolled past Dad and Mom Rose, past Katherine and the kids. Past Tim's brothers. Past Hillary's husband, Greg. She nodded at Noelia, and Tawny, who came with her fiancé.

When she arrived at the end of the aisle, Dixie appeared from the end of the first row and took her place as Matron of Honor. Her face glistened with her own joy.

Tim watched Charlotte with a tender intensity, the misty sheen in his eyes evident now. Around them, the quintet's hovering notes dissipated, bonding with the moonlight.

Thomas raised his Bible, leaning on his cane. "Dearly beloved," his voice resonated clear and strong, "we're gathered here because of a destiny. Because of a wedding dress and the mighty power of love. A wedding is what Jesus Himself is waiting for. The Good Book tells us in Matthew 25 there will be a shout at midnight." Thomas punctured the air with his clear, youthful voice. "'The Bridegroom comes.' This wedding here is a foreshadow of that great day. It's no mistake we're gathered here with Charlotte and Tim at midnight. But they didn't haul me out of bed to preach." Thomas winked at Charlotte. "Let's get these two married. Mercy, what a great thing God has done. I'm just glad to be alive to see it."

Thomas asked Tim to take his bride's hand. Hillary and Mary Grace let go of her with sniffling kisses to Charlotte's cheeks and took seats on the first row.

Thomas talked about Jesus's first miracle being at a wedding. He told the story of a hundred-year-old gown and four special brides.

"Funny thing"—he sounded so clear and young—"the dress fit each gal like it was supposed to. It never was changed, not one stitch. It never wore out. Never faded. And if I do say so myself, looks as good and in style on Charlotte here as it did on my Mary

Grace seventy-four years ago. It's just like the good news of the gospel of Jesus. Always fits. It don't need no changing. The good news is always good. It never wears out and by gum, it's always in style. Don't we need Him now more than ever." The old preacher chuckled. "There I go again. Preaching. Let's get on with this wedding."

Charlotte faced Tim, handsome, strong with his hair swishing about his fine smile and framing the light in his eyes. He was tall and regal in his tailored black tux.

"You are beautiful," he whispered when Thomas told him to take Charlotte's hand.

"Hey, handsome, you ready for this?"

"Beyond ready."

"Tim, do you take this woman . . ."

At half past midnight on a cool, August morn, Charlotte Malone said "I do" to love and to the rest of her life, becoming what she was always meant to be.

Redeemed. And a Rose.

Reading Group Guide

1. Who was the man in purple? What does he signify to you? Is there a "man in purple" in your life? Charlotte is so close to her own situation, she can't see what's in front of her: the wedding dress. Are you aware of those thin-veil God moments where the supernatural impacts the natural? How can you be more aware of Jesus interacting with you?

2. Emily struggles with the rules of her society. She wants to be vocal; she wants to pursue her own desires. What might Emily have done to speak out against the convict leasing injustice? What can you do to speak against true injustice?

3. Charlotte and Tim had a whirlwind courtship. For a moment, it seemed like they wouldn't make it. But love triumphed. Is there a similar time in your life when love triumphed sorrow or injustice?

4. Hillary faced the most devastating heartbreak: losing her husband to war. What did you think of the way she responded? What would you have done different / the same? Do you know anyone who is struggling with this reality? How can you support her?

5. Mary Grace is a woman of faith. How did her quiet humility impact her father? Is there a time to be silent and just let the Spirit work in another person? How can you be successful at guarding your tongue?

6. In the midst of Hillary reliving her pain over losing Joel, Charlotte challenges her, "What if marrying Joel was not about you, but him?" We tend to believe everything we do in life pertains to us personally. Would you be willing to do something for someone if there was nothing in it for you? How can we live out this reality in every day life? Consider Jesus dying on the Cross as our highest example.

7. Charlotte learns she's not an orphan, but a descendent of a marvelous woman. What does this knowledge unlock in her heart? How would you have responded to such news?

8. In the wedding ceremony, Thomas talks about the dress being like the Gospel—it never fades, is always in style, never needs to be altered, and it fits everyone who tries it on. We see a lot of "tweaking" of the Gospel today to "fit our needs." Where have you allowed the truth of the Gospel to be altered to fit your own needs or desires? How can we remain faithful and true to the simplicity of Jesus' Gospel?

9. Tim sells his motocross bikes. What does this symbolize in his life? What change took place in his heart? Is there something you're hanging on to, good or bad, that you need to release to the Lord?

10. The affair Charlotte's birth father had with her mother nearly ruined his marriage. In order to heal his relationship with his wife, he gave up being Charlotte's father. We see in this how sin complicates the good things God gives us: marriage, children, love. What should Colby have done to show honor in this situation? Is there a situation you're facing where honor will cause healing—if not for yourself, for others?

11. Weddings are a joy! Discuss a happy memory from your wedding, or the wedding you hope to have one day.

Acknowledgments

*T*his book started on Twitter. In an exchange of 140 characters or less between tweet buddies.
Next time you're in town, call me, we'll get together.
Hey, I wanna come.
Me too.
Then let's do it.

Ten tweets and a couple of emails later, four friends put their talk into action and hightailed it to Tennessee for a girls' weekend.

Tami Heim, Kim Cash Tate, Jennifer Deshler and her adorable daughter Jordan, and I spent forty-eight hours talking, eating, and laughing. I spent an unprecedented sixteen hours in my pajamas. But I suppose that's too much information.

Tami's daughter had recently married so the conversation turned to weddings and wedding dresses. Something Tami said . . . something about her own wedding, something about finding her daughter's perfect gown, launched me into story world. I fell behind the conversation and started to dream.

What if there was one gown worn by four women . . . over . . . a hundred years?

Who were these women? What happened to them and the dress? How did they get the dress? Why would they wear it? When did they wear it? Does it fade or wear out? Does it fit everyone? I mulled the story over for the rest of the weekend.

My mom, brother, sister-in-law, and husband offered ideas and enthusiasm when I returned from the weekend and downloaded my idea on them.

I thought this would be a book for another time, but a week later, standing in the middle of Wal-Mart on a Friday afternoon, I called my editor and pitched her the idea. Thank you, Ami, for catching my heart and vision for this book.

I was blessed to spend a brainstorming weekend with amazing women of fiction, Debbie Macomber and Karen Young. Thank you so much, Debbie and Karen, for six hours of your time, brilliance, and storytelling savvy! Your support and ideas made writing this book so fun! Without your input, it would've taken me weeks to figure out how the dress moved from woman to woman, decade to decade.

Susan May Warren, for being more than moral support, as well as a gifted story crafter who daily, hourly, lent me your talent. I thank God for you always. You are a jewel in my heart!

Ami McConnell, for your insights and input to make Emily and Charlotte stronger characters. Thank you for your partnership on this book.

Rachelle Gardner, for being in the copyedit trenches with me. Your insight, encouragement, and comments blessed me!

Beth Vogt, for unending enthusiasm for a book you've not even read yet. Thank you, friend.

Tish Patton, my "big sister" from Ohio State and now a Birmingham transplant. Thank you for the glorious details of your city. Love you.

My sister and brothers, for showing up in these pages as characters. Love you all.

Mom and Grandma, for listening to my ideas and stories, for being my biggest fans. You too, Aunt Betty!

My husband, who could pen a humorous best seller about life

with an author. He'd have writer-husbands bobbing their heads all over America. I love you for reminding me I do this for Jesus, not for myself. And to "have fun, babe."

My agent, Chip MacGregor, for helping me to see it, believe it, and achieve it. ☺

Allen Arnold, Natalie Hanemann, Becky Monds, Eric Mullett Katie Bond, and the team at Nelson for being such an amazing, supportive, encouraging team. You make ordinary writers feel like rock stars!

To the Scrivener guy who made such an incredible writing program!

Author Note

As I prayed over this book, I began to see the wedding dress as a symbol for the Gospel of Jesus Christ. It never wears out. It fits everyone who tries it on. It doesn't need to be altered. And it's always in style.

The truth and love of Jesus is alive today. It is for everyone. Whether you've been hindered through culture or family like Emily, or gifted with the Gospel like Mary Grace, or wounded like Hillary, or lost and looking for redemption like Charlotte, Jesus provides the healing and answer we are all looking for. He is the way, the truth, and the life. Not for a select few. But for each one of us.

For you.

Love is in the South Carolina air . . .

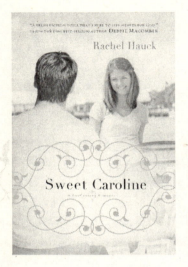

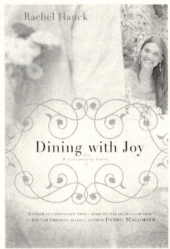

CPSIA information can be obtained at www.ICGtesting.com
Printed in the USA
LVOW042202150413

329208LV00001B/5/P